The events in this book are real.

Names and places have been changed
to protect the loric,
who remain in hiding.

Other civilizations do exist.

Some of them seek to destroy you.

United as One

PITTACUS LORE

MICHAEL JOSEPH
an imprint of
PENGUIN BOOKS

MICHAEL JOSEPH

UK | USA | Canada | Ireland | Australia
India | New Zealand | South Africa

Michael Joseph is part of the Penguin Random House group of companies
whose addresses can be found at global.penguinrandomhouse.com.

First published in the USA by HarperCollins Publishers 2016
First published in Great Britain by Michael Joseph 2016
001

Copyright © Pittacus Lore, 2016

The moral right of the author has been asserted

Set in 11.75/16 pt Eurostile and 11.75/16 pt ITC American Typewriter
Typeset by Jouve (UK), Milton Keynes
Printed in Great Britain by Clays Ltd, St Ives plc

A CIP catalogue record for this book is available from the British Library

HARDBACK ISBN: 978-0-718-18488-9
OM PAPERBACK ISBN: 978-0-718-18490-2

The girl stands on a rocky precipice, her toes curled over the edge. A dark chasm opens up in front of her, and a few pebbles dislodge beneath her feet and fall away, disappearing deep, deep down, into the shadows. Something used to be there, a tower or maybe a temple – the girl can't remember exactly what. She stares down into the bottomless hole before her, and, somehow, she knows this place was once important. A safe place.

A sanctuary.

She wants to step back from the steep drop-off. It is danger-ous, teetering here on the edge of nothingness. Yet she finds herself unable to move. Her feet are rooted to the spot. She feels the rocky ground shifting and crumbling beneath her feet. The pit before her is spreading. Soon, the edge she balances on will break and she'll fall, swallowed up by the darkness.

Would that be so bad?

The girl's head hurts. It's a distant pain, almost like it's happen-ing to someone else. It's a dull throb that starts at her forehead, wraps around her temples and down her jawline. She imagines her head like an egg that's begun to crack, the breaks in the shell fanning out across the entire surface. She rubs her hands over her face and tries to focus.

She vaguely remembers being thrown down on the craggy ground. Over and over again, swung by her ankle with a force too powerful to resist, her head smashing and rattling on the unfor-giving rocks. It's like it happened to someone else, though. The memory, just like the pain, seems so far away.

In the darkness, there's peace. She won't have to remember

the beating or the ensuing pain or what was lost when this bottomless pit was blasted into the earth. She'll be able to let go, once and for all, if she just slides the rest of the way over the edge and falls.

Something pulls her back. A knowledge, deep inside herself, that she shouldn't run from the pain. She should charge back towards it. She needs to keep fighting.

There's a flicker of cobalt blue in the darkness below her, a solitary ember of light. Her heart flutters at the sight. It reminds her of what she fought to protect and why she's so hurt. The light begins as just a pinprick, like she's looking down at the night sky and its solitary star. Soon it expands and zooms upwards, a comet coming right for her. She wavers on the edge of the chasm.

And then he's floating in front of her, aglow just like the last time she saw him. His curly black hair a perfect mess, his emerald-green eyes fixed on her – he is exactly how she remembers him. He smiles at her, that devil-may-care smile, and holds out a hand.

'It's okay, Marina,' he says. 'You don't have to fight anymore.'

Her muscles relax at the sound of his voice. The darkness stretching out below her doesn't seem so ominous anymore. She lets one of her feet dangle over the abyss. The pain inside her head seems even more diminished now. Further away.

'That's right,' he says. 'Come home with me.'

She nearly takes his hand. Something isn't right, though. She looks away from his eyes, his smile, and sees the scar. A thick band of upraised purple tissue that wraps all the way around his neck. She jerks her hand back and nearly stumbles over the edge.

'This isn't real!' she yells, finding her voice. She gets both her feet planted firmly on the rocky ground and pushes away from the darkness.

She watches as the curly-haired boy's smile falters, turns into something cruel and mean, an expression she never saw on his actual face.

'If it isn't real, why can't you wake up?' he asks.

She doesn't know. She's stuck here, on the edge, in this place in-between with the dark-haired boy – she loved him once, but that's not really him. It's the man who put her here, who beat her so badly and then destroyed this place that she loved. And now he's desecrating her memories. She locks eyes with him.

'Oh, I'm going to wake up, you bastard. And then I will come for you.'

His eyes flash, and he tries to put on an amused expression; but she can tell that he's angry. His perverse trick didn't work.

'It would've been peaceful, you little fool. You could've just slipped down into the darkness. I was offering you mercy.' He begins to recede into the chasm, leaving her alone in this place. His words float back to her. 'Now all that awaits you is more pain.'

'So be it,' she says.

The one-eyed boy sits on his backside in his prison of pillows. He hugs himself – not by choice; his arms are secured inside a straitjacket. His one eye stares dully at the white walls, everything padded and soft. The door has no handle, no discernible way to escape. His nose itches, and he buries his face in his shoulder to scratch it.

When he looks up, there's a shadow on the wall. Someone is standing behind him. The one-eyed boy flinches as two powerful hands set down on his shoulders and squeeze them gently. The deep voice is right in his ear.

'I could forgive you,' says the visitor. 'Your failures, your insubordination. It was, in a way, my fault. I should not have sent you to these people to begin with. Asked you to infiltrate them. It's only natural that you would develop certain . . . sympathies.'

3

'Beloved Leader,' says the one-eyed boy in a mocking singsong. He strains against the straitjacket. 'You've come to save me.'

'That's right,' the man says with a voice like a proud father, ignoring the boy's sarcastic tone. 'It could be like it was before. Like I always promised you. We could rule together. Look at what they've done to you, how they treat you. Someone with your power, and you let them lock you away like some kind of animal . . .'

'I fell asleep, didn't I?' asks the one-eyed boy flatly. 'This is a dream.'

'Yes. But our reconciliation, that will be very real, my boy.' The strong hands fall away from his shoulders and begin to unbuckle the straitjacket. 'It is a small thing I want in exchange. A demonstration of your loyalty. Simply tell me where I can find them. Where I can find *you*. My people – *our* people – will be there before you even wake up. They will set you free and restore your honor.'

The one-eyed boy doesn't really listen to the man's proposal. He feels the straitjacket begin to loosen as the buckles are unsnapped. He concentrates and remembers that this is a dream.

'You tossed me away like garbage,' he says. 'Why me? Why now?'

'I've come to realize that was an error,' the man says through his teeth. It's the first time the one-eyed boy has ever heard the man apologize. 'You are my right hand. You are strong.'

The one-eyed boy snorts. He knows this is a lie. The man came because he thinks the boy is weak. He manipulates. Probes for weaknesses.

But this is just a dream. The one-eyed boy's dream. That means his rules.

'What do you say?' the man asks, his breath hot against the one-eyed boy's ear. 'Where did they take you?'

'I don't know,' the boy answers honestly. He doesn't know where this padded cell is actually located. The others made sure he couldn't see. 'As for . . . what did you call it? Reconciliation? I have a counter-offer, old man.'

He imagines his favorite weapon, the needle-shaped blade that attaches to the inside of his wrist, and just like that it exists. He pops it, the deadly point punching through the fabric of the straitjacket, and swivels around to stab the blade right at the man's heart.

But the man is already gone. The one-eyed boy grunts bitterly, disappointed at the lack of satisfaction. He takes a moment to stretch his arms. When he wakes up, he'll be in this very same place, except his arms will be bound again. He doesn't mind the padded cell. He's comfortable, and there's no one around to bother him. He could stay here for a little while, at least. Do some thinking. Pull himself together.

When he's ready, though, the one-eyed boy will go ahead and let himself out.

The boy walks across a football field at the beginning of winter. The grass, brittle and brown, crunches beneath his feet. To his left and right, the metal bleachers are completely empty. The air smells like fire, and a gust of wind blows ash against the boy's cheeks.

He looks at the scoreboard up ahead. The orange bulbs flicker and pop, like the electricity is coming and going.

Beyond the scoreboard, the boy can see the high school, or at least what's left. The roof has collapsed, blown in by a missile. All the windows are shattered. There are a couple of mangled school desks on the field in front of him, all hurled this way by whatever force destroyed the school, their glossy plastic tops wedged into the ground like tombstones.

He can see it, on the horizon, hovering over the town. The

warship. Like a muscular scarab made of cold gray metal, it prowls the skyline.

The boy feels nothing but resignation. He made some good memories in this place, at this school, in this town. He was happy here for a while, before everything went to hell. It doesn't matter what happens to this place now.

He looks down and realizes that he's holding a torn scrap from a yearbook in his hand. Her picture. Straight blond hair, perfect cheekbones, those blue eyes. A smile that's like she's inviting you in on some private joke. His stomach clenches at the sight of her, at the memory of what happened.

'It doesn't have to be this way.'

The boy whips around at the sound of the voice — melodic and calming, totally out of place in this burned-out setting. A man walks across the football field towards him. He's dressed unassumingly, a brown blazer over a sweater, some khaki pants and loafers. He could be a math teacher, except there's something regal about his posture.

'Who are you?' the boy asks, alarmed.

The man stops a few yards away. He holds up his hands like he doesn't want any trouble. 'That's my ship back there,' the man says calmly.

The boy clenches his fist. The man doesn't look like the monster he caught a glimpse of in Mexico, but here, in the dream, he knows that it's true.

So he charges forward. How many times has he run down this field, an opposing player in his sights? The thrill of sprinting across the dead grass lifts the boy's spirits. He punches the man, hard, right in the jaw, and rams him with a shoulder tackle on the follow-through.

The man falls to the ground and lies there on his back. The boy looms over him, one fist still balled, the other clutching her picture.

He doesn't know what to do now. He expected more of a fight.

'I deserved that,' the man says, staring up at the boy with watery eyes. 'I know what happened to your friend, and I . . . I am so sorry.'

The boy takes a step back. 'You . . . you killed her,' he says. 'And you're *sorry*?'

'That was never my intention!' the man says pleadingly. 'It wasn't me who put her in harm's way. But all the same, I'm sorry she was hurt.'

'Killed,' the boy whispers. 'Not hurt. *Killed*.'

'What you consider dead and what I consider dead . . . those are two very different things.'

Now the boy is listening. 'What does that mean?'

'All this ugliness and pain, that's only if we keep fighting. It's not my way. It's not what I want.' The man continues. 'Did you ever stop to consider what I might want? That it might not be that bad?'

The man hasn't tried to get up. The boy feels in control. He likes that. And that's when he notices how the grass is changing. It's coming back to life, emerald green spreading out from the man. In fact, it seems to the boy that even the sun is starting to shine a little brighter.

'I want our lives — all our lives — to get better; I want us to grow beyond these petty misunderstandings,' the man says. 'I'm a scholar, first and foremost. I've spent my life studying the miracles of the universe. Surely, they've told you about me. Lies, mostly, but it is true that I have lived for centuries. What is death to a man like me? Merely a temporary inconvenience.'

Without realizing it, the boy has begun to nervously rub the scrap of paper he's holding between his fingers. His thumb brushes across the girl's jawline. The man smiles and nods at the torn piece of yearbook.

'Why . . . why would I trust you?' the grieving boy manages to ask.

'If we just stop fighting, if you listen for a while, you'll see.' He sounds so sincere. 'We'll have peace. And you'll have her back.'

'Have her back?' the boy asks, stunned, a surge of hope rising in his chest.

'I can restore her,' the man says. 'The same power that brought your friend Ella back to life, it is now mine. I don't want to fight anymore, my young friend. Let me bring her back. Let me show them all how I've changed.'

The boy glances down at the picture in his hand and finds that it has changed. It's moving. The blond girl pounds her fists against the inside of the photograph like it's a glass wall and she's trapped behind it. The boy can read her lips. She's pleading for his help.

The man holds out his hand. He wants the boy to help him up.

'What do you say? Shall we end this together?'

I

This room reminds me of the kind of places that Henri and I used to stay in during the early days. Old roadside motels that the owners hadn't updated since the seventies. The walls are wood paneled, and the carpet is an olive-green shag, the bed underneath me stiff and musty. A bureau rests against one wall, the drawers filled with a mixture of clothing, different sizes and different genders, all of it generic and dated. The room doesn't have a TV, but it does have a radio with a clock that uses those old-school paper numbers that flip around, every minute punctuated by a dry slap.

4:33 A.M.

4:34 A.M.

4:35 A.M.

I sit here in the Patience Creek Bed & Breakfast and listen to the time pass by.

On the wall across from my bed, there's a painting that looks like a window. There aren't any actual windows, on account of the room being located deep underground, so I suppose the designers did the best they could. The scene in my fake window is bright and sunny, with tall, green grass blowing in the wind and the indistinct shape of a woman in the distance clutching a hat to her head.

I don't know why they made the room look like this. Maybe it was meant to convey a sense of normalcy. If that's the case, it isn't working. Instead, the room seems to magnify every poisonous emotion you'd expect staying in a scuzzy motel by yourself — loneliness, desperation, failure.

I've got plenty of those emotions on my own.

Here's what this room has that some dump off the interstate doesn't. The painting on the wall? It slides aside, and behind it is a bank of monitors that broadcast security feeds from all around the Patience Creek Bed & Breakfast. There's a camera pointed at the front door of the quaint cabin that sits above this sprawling underground facility, another pointed at the serendipitously flat meadow with its hard-packed soil and perfectly maintained grass that just happens to be the exact dimensions necessary to land a medium-sized aircraft, and dozens of other feeds surveilling the property and what lies beneath. This place was built by some very paranoid people who were planning for a potential invasion, a doomsday scenario.

They were expecting Russians, not Mogadorians. But even so, I guess their paranoia paid off.

Beneath the unassuming bed-and-breakfast located twenty-five miles south of Detroit, close to the shore of Lake Erie, are four subterranean levels so top secret they have been virtually forgotten. The Patience Creek facility was originally built by the CIA during the Cold War as a place for them to ride out a nuclear winter. It fell into disrepair over the last twenty-five years, and, according to our hosts in the US government, everyone who knew about it is either dead or retired, which means that no one leaked its existence to MogPro. Lucky for us a general named Clarence Lawson came out of retirement when the warships appeared and remembered that this place was down here.

The president of the United States and what's left of the Joint Chiefs of Staff aren't here; they're being kept someplace secure, probably someplace mobile, the location of which they aren't divulging even to us allied aliens. One of his handlers must have decided it wouldn't be safe for the president to be around us, so we're here with General Lawson, who reports only to him. In our conversation, the president told me he wanted to work together, that we had his full support against Setrákus Ra.

He said a lot of things, actually. The details are fuzzy in my memory. I was in shock when we spoke and not really listening. He seemed nice. Whatever.

I just want to finish this.

I've been awake since — well, I'm not exactly sure when. I know I should try to sleep, but every time I close my eyes I see Sarah's face. I see her face back on that first day at Paradise High School, half hidden behind a camera and then smiling as she finishes snapping my photo. And then my imagination takes over, and I see that same beautiful face pale and bloodied, lifeless, the way she must look now. I can't shake it. I open my eyes and there's a twisting pain in my gut, and I feel like I've got to curl up around the hurt.

Instead, I stay awake. This is what it's been like for the last few hours, alone in this strange place, trying to wear myself out to the point where I'll be able to sleep like, well . . . like the dead.

Practice. It's the only hope I have.

I sit on the bed and look at myself in the mirror that hangs over the bureau. My hair is getting a little long, and there are dark circles around my eyes. These things don't matter now. I stare at myself . . .

And then I disappear.

Reappear. Take a deep breath.

I go invisible again. This time I hold it for longer. For as long as I can. I stare at the empty space in the mirror where my body should be and listen to the paper numbers on the clock tick by.

With Ximic, I should be able to copy any Legacy that I've encountered. It's just a matter of teaching myself how to use it, which is never easy, even when the Legacy comes naturally. Marina's healing, Six's invisibility, Daniela's stone gaze — these are the abilities I've picked up so far. I'm going to learn more, as many as I can. I'm going to train these new Legacies until they come as naturally to me as my Lumen. And then I'm going to repeat the process.

All this power, and only one thing to look forward to.

The destruction of every Mogadorian on Earth. Including and especially Setrákus Ra, if he's even still alive. Six thinks she might have killed him in Mexico, but I won't believe that until the Mogs surrender or I see a body. A part of me almost hopes he's still out there so that I can be the one to end the bastard.

A happy ending? That's out the window. I was stupid to ever believe in it.

Pittacus Lore, the last one, the one whose body we found hidden in Malcolm Goode's bunker, he had Ximic, too, but he didn't do enough. He couldn't stop the Mogadorian invasion of Lorien. When he had the chance to kill Setrákus Ra all those centuries ago, he couldn't do that either.

History will not repeat itself.

I hear footsteps in the hallway that stop right outside my door.

Even though they speak softly and even though I'm listening through a reinforced steel door, with my enhanced senses, I can still hear every word Daniela and Sam say.

'Maybe we should just let him rest,' Daniela says. I'm not used to hearing her speak in such a gentle tone. Usually, Daniela's a mix of abrasive and gung ho. In just a couple of days, she's completely left behind her old life and joined our war. Although she didn't have much choice considering the Mogs burned her old life to the ground.

Another human swept up in our war.

'You don't know him. There's no way he's sleeping in there,' Sam replies, his voice hoarse.

Sitting in this stale room, reflecting on the past and the damage I've caused, I started to wonder: How would Sam's life be different if Henri and I had chosen Cleveland or Akron or somewhere else instead of Paradise? Would he still have gotten Legacies? I'd be worse off, maybe dead, without him. That's for sure.

Sarah would still be alive, though, if we'd never met.

'Uh, okay, I'm not really talking about him getting a good night's sleep. Dude's a superhero alien; for all I know he sleeps three hours a night hanging from the ceiling,' Daniela replies to Sam.

'He sleeps same as we do.'

'Whatever. Point is, maybe he needs some space, you know? To work his shit out? And he'll come to us when he's ready. When he's . . .'

'No. He'd want to know,' Sam says, and then knocks softly on my door.

I'm off the bed in a flash to open the door. Sam's right about me, of course. Whatever's happening, I want to know. I want to be distracted. I want forward momentum.

Sam blinks when the door opens and stares right through me. 'John?'

It takes me a second to realize that I'm still invisible. When I appear from thin air in front of them, Daniela stumbles back a step. 'Goddamn.'

Sam barely arches an eyebrow. His eyes are red rimmed. He seems too worn-out to be surprised.

'Sorry,' I say. 'Working on my invisibility.'

'The others are about ten minutes out,' Sam tells me. 'I knew you would want to be there when they land.'

I nod and close my door behind me.

The illusion of a motel disappears as soon as I'm outside my room. The hallway beyond, more like a tunnel really, is all austere white walls and cold halogen lights. It reminds me of the facility underneath Ashwood Estates, except this place was built by humans.

'I got a VCR in my room,' Daniela says, trying to make conversation as the three of us walk down one of the identical hallways in this mazelike complex. When neither Sam nor me immediately responds, she presses on. 'You guys got VCRs? Shit's crazy, right? I haven't seen a VCR in years.'

Sam looks at me before answering. 'I found a Game Boy wedged under my mattress.'

'Damn! Want to trade?'

'It's got no batteries.'

'Never mind.'

I can hear the distant hum of generators, the buzz of tools and the grunts of men working. The one drawback of Patience Creek being so under the radar is that a lot of its systems aren't what you'd call updated. For security reasons General Lawson had decided they should run a stripped-down operation here. With everything going on, there's not exactly time to call in civilian contractors. Still, there's got to be almost a hundred army engineers working around the clock to bring the place up to date. When we arrived late last night, I saw that Sam's dad, Malcolm, was already here, helping a crew of electricians install some of the Mogadorian tech recovered from Ashwood Estates. As far as the army is concerned, Malcolm's basically an expert on the extraterrestrial.

Sam and Daniela's conversation has trailed off, and I quickly realize that it's because of me. I'm silent, eyes straight ahead, and I'm pretty sure my expression is stuck in neutral. They don't know how to talk to me anymore.

'John, I –' Sam puts a hand on my shoulder, and I can tell he's going to say something about Sarah. I know what happened to her hurt him bad, too. They grew up together. But I don't want to have that conversation right now. I don't want to give in to grieving until this is over.

I force a halfhearted smile. 'Did they give you any tapes for that VCR?' I ask Daniela, clumsily changing the subject.

'*WrestleMania* III,' she says, and makes a face.

'Hell yeah, I'll be by to pick that up later, Danny,' Nine says, emerging from one of the many hallways with a grin.

Out of all of us, Nine looks the most rested. It's only been about a day since he and Five brawled all over New York City. I healed the big goon back in New York, and his own superhuman stamina has apparently done the rest. He pats Sam and me hard on the back and joins our procession down the hallway. Of course, Nine acts like there's nothing wrong at all, and, honestly, I prefer it that way.

As we pass by, I glance down the hallway Nine came from. There are four heavily armed soldiers there, standing guard.

'Everything squared away?' I ask Nine.

'Yeah, Johnny,' Nine replies. 'They got some pretty whacked-out prison cells in this place, including one that's straight up padded walls. With Chubby tethered to some cushions and strapped into a straitjacket, he ain't going anywhere.'

'Good,' Sam says.

I nod in agreement. Five is a complete psychopath and deserves to be locked up. But if I'm being brutally practical about winning this war, I'm not sure how long we can afford to keep him in a cage.

We round a corner, and the elevator bank comes into view. Overhead, the halogen lights buzz loudly, and I notice Sam pinching the bridge of his nose.

'Man, do I miss your penthouse, Nine,' Sam says. 'Was the only hideout we ever had with mellow lighting.'

'Yeah, I miss it too,' Nine replies, a note of nostalgia creeping into his voice.

'This place is already giving me a serious migraine. Should've gotten some dimmer switches to go with those VCRs.'

There's a crackle of electricity over our heads, and one of the bulbs flickers out. The hallway lighting is suddenly a whole lot more tolerable. Everyone except for me pauses to look up.

'Well, that was weirdly timed,' says Daniela.

'Better, though, isn't it?' Sam says with a sigh.

I hit the button to call the elevator. The others gather around behind me.

'So, they're, uh . . . they're bringing her back here?' Nine asks, his voice lowered, being about as tactful as he can manage.

'Yeah,' I say, thinking about the Loric ship right now descending towards Patience Creek, filled with our friends and allies, and the lost love of my life.

'That's good,' Nine says, then coughs into his hand. 'I mean, not good. But we can, you know, say good-bye.'

'We get it, Nine,' Sam says gently. 'He knows what you mean.'

I nod, not prepared to say anything else. The elevator doors open in front of us, and when they do, the words come spilling out.

'This is the last time,' I say, not turning around to face the others. The words feel like ice in my mouth. 'I'm done saying good-bye to people we love. I'm done with sentiment. Done with grieving. Starting today, we kill until we win.'

2

Twisted metal shrieks by overhead. Clumps of dirt and ash batter my face, the wind whips at what feels like one hundred miles per hour, and I throw everything I have into it. Blaster fire sears across my legs. I ignore it. A jagged strut from an exploded Mogadorian Skimmer crashes into the dirt next to me. Only a few feet closer and I would have been impaled.

I ignore that too. I'll die here, if that's what it takes.

Across an empty pit where the Sanctuary used to stand, Setrákus Ra staggers up the ramp of his warship. I can't let him make it back on board the *Anubis*. I shove out with my telekinesis, and I don't care about the consequences. I hurl every goddamn thing at him, and he pushes back. I feel his power strain against mine like two invisible tidal waves crashing together, sending up a spray of metal parts and dirt and stone.

'Die, die, die . . .'

Sarah Hart is next to me. She screams something into my ear that I can't hear over the roar of the battle. She grabs my shoulder and starts to shake me.

'Die, die, die . . .'

'Six!'

I gasp and wake up. It isn't Sarah shaking my shoulder. It's Lexa, our pilot, seated behind the controls. Through the windshield, I can barely make out the peaceful countryside zipping by underneath us. In the glow of the control panel, I can see a look of concern on Lexa's face.

'What is it?' I ask, still groggy as I gently push her hand away.

'You were talking in your sleep,' Lexa replies, and goes back to looking straight ahead, our flight path mapped out on the screen before her.

My feet are up on the dashboard, my knees tucked in close to my chest. My toes are all pins and needles. I set my feet down on the floor and sit up straight, then strain my eyes into the darkness outside. Just as I do, the countryside drops away and is replaced by the blue-black water of Lake Erie.

'How close are we to the coordinates Malcolm sent us?' I ask Lexa.

'Close,' she replies. 'About ten minutes out.'

'And you're sure we lost them?'

'I'm sure, Six. I ditched the last of the Skimmers over Texas. The *Anubis* broke off before that. Seemed like the warship didn't want to keep up the chase.'

I rub my hands across my face and through my sticky tangle of hair. The *Anubis* stopped chasing us. Why? Because they had to rush Setrákus Ra somewhere? Because he was dying? Or maybe already dead?

I know I hurt him. I saw that metal bar pierce that bastard's chest. Not many could survive that injury. But this is Setrákus Ra. There's no telling how fast he heals or what technology he's got at his disposal to nurse him back to health. It went straight into his heart, though. I saw it. I know I got him.

'He has to be dead,' I say quietly. 'He has to be.'

I unstrap from the copilot's seat and stand up. Lexa grabs hold of my forearm before I can leave the cockpit.

'Six, you did what you had to do,' she says firmly. 'What you thought was best. No matter what happens, if Setrákus Ra is dead or alive . . .'

'If he's alive, then Sarah died for nothing,' I reply.

'Not for nothing,' Lexa says. 'She pulled you out of there. She saved you.'

'She should've saved herself.'

'She didn't think so. She — look, I hardly knew the girl. But it seemed to me that she knew what was at stake. She knew that we're fighting a war. And in war there are sacrifices. Casualties.'

'Easy for us to say. We're alive.' I bite my lip and pull my arm away from Lexa. 'You think — shit, Lexa. You think any of that cold-ass pragmatic talk is going to make it easier for the others? For John?'

'Has anything ever been easy for any of you?' Lexa asks, looking up at me. 'Why would it start now? This is the end, Six. One way or the other, we're closing in on the end. You do what has to be done, and you feel bad about it later.'

I exit the cockpit with Lexa's words ringing in my ears. I want to feel anger. Who is she to tell me how to act? The Mogs weren't hunting her. She hid for years without ever trying to contact us. She only showed up now because she realized how desperate our situation had become, that it was all hands on deck. Telling me what to feel.

Thing is, she's right. She's right, because the truth is, I wouldn't change what I did. I'd take my shot at

Setrákus Ra, even knowing what would happen to Sarah. Potentially billions of lives are on the line.

I had to do it.

In the main cabin, someone has used the touch-screen walls to command cots to emerge from the floor. Those are the same cots we slept on all those years ago when we first came to Earth. I carved my number into one of them.

Sarah's body rests on that one, because the universe has a sick sense of humor.

Mark sits next to Sarah's cot, chin against his chest, asleep. His face is puffy, and he's covered in dried blood, like pretty much all of us. He hasn't left Sarah's side since it all went down. Frankly, I'm glad he's finally asleep. I couldn't handle many more of the accusatory looks the guy has been throwing around. I know he's angry and hurting, but I can't wait to get off this cramped ship and away from him.

Bernie Kosar lies on the floor next to Mark. He watches me emerge from the cockpit and quietly stands. The beagle comes over and nuzzles against my leg, whining quietly. I reach down to scratch absently behind his ears.

'Thanks, boy,' I whisper, and BK whines again, softly.

I move farther back. Ella is curled up on one of the cots, her face turned towards the wall. My gaze lingers on her for a second, just long enough to make sure that she's still breathing. Ella was the first person I watched die yesterday, except she somehow managed to come back to life. When she tossed herself into that pillar of Loric energy at the Sanctuary, she broke the charm that Setrákus Ra had placed on her. Apparently, there are side effects to bathing in a bunch of Loric energy and briefly dying. Ella's returned to us as . . . well, I'm not entirely sure.

At the very back of the ship, I find Adam sitting on the edge of another cot. Looking at the dark circles around his eyes and his increasingly pale skin, I know for sure that Adam hasn't slept. Instead, he's been keeping his eye on Marina. She's strapped down on the same cot Adam sits on, her eyes closed, her face horribly bruised, blood still crusted around her nostrils. Setrákus Ra smashed her into the ground over and over, and she hasn't regained consciousness since. She's holding on, though, and hopefully John will be able to heal whatever's wrong with her.

Adam manages a weak smile as I sit down across from him. Another one of our wounded friends is bundled in his arms. Dust was nearly killed back at the Sanctuary. Although he's still twitchy and weak, Dust has regained some of his movement and has at least managed to change his shape into that of a wolf cub. Not exactly ferocious, but a step in the right direction.

'Hey, doc,' I say to Adam, keeping my voice quiet.

He snorts. 'You'd be surprised how little practical medical training we Mogadorians receive. It's not a priority when most of your soldiers are disposable.' Adam turns his head to regard Marina. 'Her pulse is strong, though. Even I can tell that.'

I nod. That's exactly what I wanted to hear. I reach across the gap between us and scratch Dust on his nose. One of his back legs starts to pump in response, though I'm not sure if it's from enjoyment or the lingering effects of his electroshock.

'He's looking a little better,' I say to Adam.

'Yeah, he'll be howling at the moon in no time,' Adam replies, looking me over as he does. 'What about you? How are you feeling?'

'Like shit.'

'I'm sorry I couldn't do more,' Adam says. When the battle at the Sanctuary came to an end, it was Adam and Mark who got Marina on to Lexa's ship before Setrákus Ra could finish her off. That's how it came to be me and Sarah facing Setrákus Ra, alone.

'You did enough. You saved Marina. Got her back here. I . . .'

My gaze involuntarily drifts towards Sarah. Adam clears his throat to get my attention back. His eyes lock on to mine, wide and steady.

'That wasn't your fault,' he says firmly.

'Hearing that doesn't make it easier.'

'It still needed saying.' Now it's Adam's turn to break eye contact. He looks over at Ella's huddled body and frowns. 'I hope you killed him, Six. The thing is, knowing you, if you'd have known the consequences, you would have stopped.'

I don't interrupt Adam, even though what he's saying about me might not be true. It's weird to feel hope that I killed Setrákus Ra at the same time as the guilt for what happened to Sarah, all of it worsened by an undercurrent of dread that I accomplished nothing at all. I'm a mess.

'I respect that about you guys,' Adam continues. 'Most of you Garde, it's like they built strength and compassion into you. It's the opposite for my people. I . . . I would've pressed on no matter what happened.'

Back at the Sanctuary, Adam had a moment when he'd got the drop on Setrákus Ra. This was back before Ella broke the charm that bound her life to her evil great-grandfather's. Even knowing that it would kill Ella, Adam went right for Setrákus Ra's jugular.

'Your people,' Adam continues after a moment, 'you consider the costs, you mourn your losses, you try to do what's right. I envy that. The ability to know what's right without – without having to fight against your nature.'

'You're more like us than you realize,' I tell him.

'I'd like to think that,' Adam replies. 'But sometimes I don't know.'

'We all regret things,' I say. 'It's not a matter of nature. It's a matter of moving on and being better.'

Adam opens his mouth to respond, but no words come out. He's looking past me. A soft blue glow emanates from over my shoulder.

I turn around to see Ella has sat up on her cot. She still crackles with Loric energy, her brown eyes completely replaced by roiling orbs of cobalt blue. When she speaks, her voice has that odd echoing quality, like it did when Legacy was speaking through her.

'You don't have to feel guilty,' she tells Adam. 'I knew what you were going to do as soon as I got off the *Anubis*. I was rooting for you.'

Adam stares at Ella. 'I didn't – I didn't even know what I was going to do when you got off the *Anubis*.'

'Oh, you did.'

Adam looks away, clearly uncomfortable under Ella's stare. If he's relieved that Ella let him off the hook for what happened at the Sanctuary, it doesn't show.

'And Six.' She turns to me now. 'As she left this world, Sarah thought about many things. Mostly about John and her family. But also she thought about you, and how she was glad you would be here to take care of John and the rest of us.'

'You were in her head when she died?' I ask Ella, still trying to get a grip on her new and expanded Legacies.

She pinches the bridge of her nose and shuts her eyes, which causes the room to get a little darker. 'I'm still getting used to what I can do. It is hard sometimes to . . . tune out.'

'Is that all she was thinking about?'

The question comes from Mark. I'm not sure how long he's been awake and listening to our conversation. He looks at Ella with desperate hope, and I notice that his lower lip shakes. Ella looks back at him coolly, and I wonder if some emotional wiring got fried during her encounter with Legacy.

'What do you really want to ask me, Mark?' Ella says calmly.

'I . . . nothing. It's not important,' Mark replies, looking back down at the floor.

'You crossed her mind, too, Mark,' Ella says.

Mark swallows hard when he hears this and nods, trying not to show any emotion. Studying Ella, I'm not sure if she's telling the truth or just trying to make Mark feel better. Her electric eyes are unreadable.

'We're here,' Lexa announces over the intercom. 'I'm bringing us down.'

Lexa lands the ship in a wide-open field next to a small log cabin. Looking out the window at the place, it's hard to believe that this is where the government is planning its counterattack against the Mogadorians. I guess that's sort of the point. With the sun just beginning to rise over Lake Erie, pink flares of light bend across the surface of the water. It's a tranquil scene and would look totally like some hippie yoga retreat if not for the presence of the armed soldiers and their Humvees camouflaged in the tree line.

There are two groups waiting for us outside the cabin and, even in my rattled state, it's easy to read the situation based on the distance between the factions. The first group is our people – John, Sam, Nine, Malcolm, and a girl who I recognize from Ella's telepathic summit but whose name I don't know. Behind them, separated by about thirty yards, is a contingent of military personnel who watch our ship with keen interest. It seems to me that even though the military is working together with the Garde, they're still very much keeping an eye on us. Together, but apart.

In that group of soldiers, I recognize Agent Walker. As I watch, she nervously stubs out a cigarette and turns to answer a question posed by the older man standing next to her. He's clearly in charge. The guy sports a silver buzz cut and a leathery tan, like they just pulled him away from the golf course. He looks like one of those senior citizens who's still out there running marathons, all rigid posture and stringy muscles. He wears formal military attire covered with a stupid amount of medals. He's surrounded by a half dozen soldiers with assault rifles – for our protection, I'm sure. Two guys in his retinue stand out; they're twins if I'm not mistaken, and look to be about my age, too young to really be enlisted soldiers, although they wear the starched light-blue uniforms of cadets.

I observe all this during the few seconds it takes Lexa to extend the exit ramp and power down the ship. Surveying our surroundings is a good distraction, a way to avoid looking at John. His face is a mask, his gaze icy, and I still haven't figured out what the hell I'm going to say to him.

Our battle-ravaged group slowly walks down the ramp. I hear mutterings from our military observers and can't help noticing the cringing looks on our friends' faces. We're covered in blood and dirt, beat up, exhausted. Plus, Ella is giving off that faint glow of Loric energy. We look like hell.

Malcolm's got a gurney, and he pushes it across the grass to meet Adam, who is carrying Marina in his arms. It takes me a second to notice that Mark hasn't gotten off the ship; he's staying with Sarah's body.

Before I can stop him, Sam has me wrapped in a hug. Only when his arms are around me do I realize how badly I'm shaking.

'You're all right now,' he whispers into my tangled mop of hair.

I steel myself, trying not to break down even though I very badly want to, and wiggle out of Sam's arms. I look towards John, but he's already standing over Marina, his hands glowing softly as he holds her head. There's a look of deep concentration on his face as he heals her, and it takes so long that I start to hold my breath, worried that the damage Setrákus Ra inflicted is too great. After a long moment where everyone watches in total silence, John steps back with a drained sigh. Marina shifts a bit on her gurney but doesn't wake up.

'Is she . . . ?' Adam starts to ask.

'It was bad, but she'll be okay,' John replies, his voice completely neutral. 'She just needs some rest.'

With that, John steps away from the group and walks up the ramp of the ship.

'John, hold on,' I hear myself say, even though I've got no idea what my follow-up is going to be.

He pauses and looks over his shoulder at me, although he doesn't meet my eyes.

'I'm sorry that we couldn't – that I couldn't protect her,' I tell him, my voice getting shaky and, even though I'm mortified to hear it, a little desperate. 'I swear I killed him, John. I put one right in his goddamn heart.'

John nods, and I can see a vein in his neck twitching, like he's trying to control himself.

'We aren't to blame for the actions of our enemies,' John replies to me, and the line sounds canned, practised, like he knew this conversation was coming. Without another word, he climbs the ramp and disappears into Lexa's ship.

A somber silence follows. The military personnel return to the cabin, which must have some pretty major underground levels to accommodate them all, and Nine starts to lead our group inside after them. I gaze after John, Sam lingering at my side.

'I'm sorry, Six, but you didn't.'

It's Ella. She stands next to me, looking up at me with those eyes empty of everything but swirling Loric energy. I must look shaky again, because Sam puts his arm around me, holding me up.

'Didn't what?'

'Kill him,' Ella replies. 'You hurt him bad, but . . . I can still feel him out there. Setrákus Ra is alive.'

3

As soon as I'm on board the ship, Bernie Kosar steps in front of me. His tail droops between his legs, and he stretches his front paws out, arching his spine low, his head down. It's like he's bowing to me, or expecting me to swat him with a rolled-up newspaper. From deep in his belly, he lets out a low, mournful howl.

It takes me a second to realize why he's doing this. Back in Chicago, the last time I saw Sarah, I'd sent BK with her. I'd told BK to keep her safe.

Oh God, BK, *it's not your fault*, I say to him telepathically. I kneel down, put my arm around his furry neck and hug him close. BK slobbers wetly against my cheek and whines. Tears sting the corners of my eyes, the first ones that have come since I heard Sarah's fading voice piped over my satellite phone.

The tears aren't for me. First Six, now BK — the guilt they're feeling, it wrecks me. Sarah was their friend, too. They're feeling this loss just like I am, and it's compounded by the fact that they both think they let me down, that I'm going to blame them. I should've spoken to Six, should've said something more, but I just couldn't find the right words. I should've told her that there are only two people I hold responsible for what happened to Sarah.

Setrákus Ra.

And myself.

I've never been good at expressing those kinds of feelings, talking about myself, my fears and weaknesses. Really, there's only one person I've ever felt truly comfortable opening up to about that stuff.

Sarah.

I stand up, walk farther into the ship and see her. In the ship's dim lighting, stretched out on a cot, a sheet pulled up to her chin — she could be sleeping. Her blond hair is fanned out on the pillow beneath her. Her skin is pale, so pale, the color drained from her lips. I walk forward feeling like I'm in a dream.

Mark James is here, too, sitting next to Sarah's bed. He stands up when I walk forward, and I'm vaguely aware of a murderous look on his face. For a second, I think he might get in my way. Looking at me he must think better of it, because he steps aside in a hurry. The anger in his eyes is replaced by curiosity, like I'm some strange animal.

Or like I'm an alien, capable of things he can't possibly understand.

He doesn't say anything when I kneel down next to Sarah. I pull the sheet back from her body, and it sticks to her side where the blood from her wounds has dried. She's all torn up.

I feel like I should cry. Or scream. But all I feel is empty.

And then my hands reach forward, unthinking, acting on some combination of instinct and desperation. I press down on her wounds, her skin cold beneath my fingertips, and let my healing energy flow into her.

When Sarah and Ella were riddled with blaster fire at Dulce Base, I managed to heal them. They were close to death, and I pulled them back. Maybe . . . maybe there is still hope now.

My hands heat up. They glow. Sarah's pale skin is suddenly tinged pink, and my heart skips a beat.

It's a trick of the light. My Legacy isn't working. There's no spark in Sarah left to rekindle.

I let the power seep away. Now that I've seen Sarah's wounds firsthand, the horrific visions that haunted me during the hours I'd waited are gone. It's become reality. With shaking hands, I cover Sarah's body with the sheet.

The morbid details aren't what I find myself focusing on. They aren't what will stick with me. It's her face – tinted blue in the muted light. She doesn't look like she's in any pain; there are no lines creasing the skin and her eyes are closed. Sarah's lips are forever pursed into an almost-curious smile. I lean down and gently kiss that smile, not surprised by how cold her lips are. Then I put my head down, rest it on her chest. It probably looks like I'm listening for a heartbeat, but I'm just saying good-bye.

I don't cry. She wouldn't want me to do that. But the insomnia I was feeling before, it's gone now. I feel like I could finally rest, right here, with Sarah.

'Is that it?'

Mark. I'd completely forgotten he was in the room with me.

I lift my head and turn around slowly, without standing up. Mark's head is cocked; he stares at me, his fists clenching and unclenching.

'What?' I ask, surprised by how tired I sound.

'I said, is that it?' he repeats, the words harsher now. 'Is that all you're going to do?'

'There's nothing else I can do, Mark,' I reply with a sigh. 'She's gone.'

'You can't bring back the dead?'

'No. I'm not a god.'

Mark shakes his head like he expected that answer and is disappointed all the same. 'Shit,' he says to himself, then looks me right in the eye. 'What the hell are you good for?'

I'm not going to do this with him. Not here. Not ever. I stand up slowly, take one last look at Sarah and walk wordlessly towards the ship's exit ramp.

Mark gets in my way.

'I asked you a question,' he says.

For a moment, his tone brings me back to Paradise High. I know this isn't the same jock who tormented me and Sam – now he's got a wild and haunted look in his eyes, unkempt hair and filthy clothes that would've embarrassed the hell out of the old Mark James. But he's still a master of that alpha-male voice. It makes him seem bigger than he is in reality.

'Mark,' I say warningly.

'You don't get to just walk away from this,' he replies.

'Get out of my way.'

He shoves me. The contact actually surprises me and causes me to stumble back a few steps. I stare at him.

'You're angry; you're hurting . . .' I say to Mark, keeping my voice measured even though I want to scream at him. Like I'm not feeling the same way. Like I don't want to punch through a wall. 'But this — us? Fighting for no reason? That's not happening.'

'Oh, spare me your bigger-man routine, John,' Mark says. 'I was there when she died. *Me.* Not you. She spent her final moments on the goddamn phone with you, giving you a pep talk. *You.* The guy who got her killed.'

It stings to hear Mark say what I'd already been thinking.

'We were in love,' I tell him.

Mark rolls his eyes at me. 'Maybe. Maybe you really were. But — come on. Mysterious new kid rolls into the small town, and oh, he's got superpowers. And oh, he's trying to save the world. What girl wouldn't fall for that shit, huh? Hell, look at me, standing here. Look at dumb-ass Sam Goode. We all got sucked into your vortex of suffering.'

'She didn't fall for anything. I didn't trick her.' My words are sharper now. He's starting to get under my skin. 'We were in love before — before she even knew about me and what I am.'

'But you knew!' Mark yells, taking a step towards me. 'You always knew what it meant to be around you and you — you went for her anyway! In all those towns you traveled to before Paradise, how many — how many other girls were there?'

I shake my head, losing the thread of what Mark's trying to prove. 'There weren't –'

'Exactly! You kept it in your pants because you knew that being around you is a death sentence. Until Sarah. You just couldn't leave her alone. You got selfish, or lonely, or whatever, and you – you got her killed. She'd be alive and happy if you had just gone to another town, John. Yeah, this whole invasion would still be happening, but I got a feeling the Mogadorian warships are a long way from Paradise. Without you, without your needy bull-shit, she at least would've had a chance.'

I don't know how to respond. Part of what Mark's saying is true, but it ignores so much of what Sarah and I shared. Maybe it was selfish of me to involve her, except that every time I pushed her away she would come back. She made her own decisions. She was strong and made me stronger. And she was the first person on Earth who made it feel like I actually had a chance at a normal life, like there was something more than just endless running and fighting. Sarah gave me hope. But I don't have the words to explain that to Mark, and I don't even want to. I don't need to defend myself.

'You're right,' I say coldly, hoping that's enough to end this.

'I'm – I'm right?' Mark asks incredulously, eyes widening. 'You think *that's* what I want to hear?'

I sigh. 'Mark, the truth is, I don't care what you want. I never have.'

He hits me then. I see the punch coming a mile away, but I don't bother defending myself. It's a short uppercut that catches me right in the stomach and causes me to suck in a sharp breath. It's not the first time that Mark has punched me, and he hits hard – maybe a little harder than I remember. But I've taken a lot of shots over the last few months, ones harder than Mark could begin to imagine, and this one I barely feel.

When I don't react to the first punch, Mark tries another. His heart isn't in it, though. He throws a haymaker at my head but seems to change his mind at the last moment, and his fist simply glances off the corner of my jaw. The force of his own punch carries Mark to the side, where he stumbles over one of the empty cots, landing in an awkward sitting position.

He stays there, staring at the floor, and takes deep, heaving breaths. I can tell he's trying not to cry.

'Do you feel better?' I ask, rubbing the middle of my chest.

'No,' he replies. 'No, I don't.'

'What about when we end this war and destroy every Mog that stands in our way? Will you feel better then?'

Mark looks up at me, and what I see on his face surprises me. It's pity. I realize what I just said wasn't really a question for him. It's a question for me. I'm a little afraid to find out the answer.

'That won't bring her back,' he says.

I don't respond. I take one last look at Sarah and walk back towards the ship's exit. In the doorway, I pause and half turn.

'Will you do something for me?' I ask him, my voice low, all the feeling sapped out.

Mark works his thumb across his raw knuckles. 'What?'

'I'm going to get our military friends to loan us a vehicle. We're only a few hours away from Paradise. Would you . . . ?' My voice catches, and I brace one hand on the cool metal of the doorway. 'Would you bring her home?'

Mark snorts. When he speaks, that bitterness is back in his voice. 'Sure, John. I know you're busy, so I'll do the hard part for you. Should I tell her mom you say hi?'

I close my eyes, take a deep breath and let it go.

'Thank you, Mark,' I say without feeling, and then I'm leaving him and Sarah's body behind. I stride down the ship's ramp and across the lawn, heading back to the unimposing cabin that currently hides humanity's best hope for survival. The sun is coming up, a bright orange slash on the horizon, heating the cool blue of the lake. I think of Sarah's pale face, her icy lips, and then I remember how the sun would filter through her blond hair and she would've turned to me during a moment like this and squeezed my hand in that way of hers, and we would've shared it together.

I put the memories away. Bury them down somewhere deep. I head inside the cabin with one purpose and one purpose only.

I used to think there could be more for me than running and fighting.

Now all that's left is killing.

4

When I wake up, it takes me a moment to realize where the hell I am. Some bad motel art stares down at me from the wood-paneled walls. I'm all tangled up in a scratchy sheet. Must have been tossing and turning like crazy. It feels like I've only slept for a few hours.

The Patience Creek Bed & Breakfast. An old spy hangout from the Cold War era. Sam filled me in on the details while he half carried me through the halls. I was so spent and delirious, I'm a little amazed that I retained any of what he'd told me.

Sam.

He's next to me. On the other side of the bed. Already awake and sitting up, his feet on the floor, back to me. He hasn't noticed that I'm stirring yet. Sam scratches his neck and yawns. He took off his shirt to sleep, and I watch him reach out towards the worn gray T-shirt where it hangs over the back of a chair, concentrate and float the shirt towards him with telekinesis.

I smile drowsily. It's hard to believe this is the same kid who bumbled around the halls of Paradise High School nearly getting himself killed the night we first met. That wasn't so long ago, but so much has changed. Sam's still skinny and a little on the gangly side, yet there's a scrappy layer of muscle on him now. And then there are the scars, fresh pink and upraised on his wrists and forearms, the results of Sam's time getting tortured by Setrákus Ra.

I put my hand on Sam's back and trace down the bumps of his spine. He jumps, loses his concentration, and his T-shirt flops out of the air.

'Good morning,' I say quietly. 'It is morning, right?'

'Almost noon,' Sam replies as he turns around to look at me with a smile. His eyes linger on me for a moment but then he catches himself, flushes and shyly looks away.

It occurs to me then that I'm not wearing any clothes.

Now I remember what happened. After Ella broke the news to me that I didn't kill Setrákus Ra, I about broke down. Once Sam got me to his room, he strongly encouraged that I take a shower, and I did, washing off the gray-green dust of what used to be the Sanctuary along with Sarah's dried blood. I remember very clearly the way that the grime pooled around my toes and circled down the drain. I inhaled steam and pressed my forehead against the cool tiles, let my skin wrinkle and turn bright red from the heat.

And then, at some point, I crawled into bed. Sam had tried to stay awake, I think, but he couldn't pull it off. He hadn't left me anything clean to wear, so . . .

'I put some clothes on the desk,' Sam says cautiously.

'Oh, I guess you did,' I say out loud. A loose-fitting flower-print tunic and some jeans that looked dangerously close to bell-bottoms wait for me across the room. I guess we're picking from whatever leftover garments are floating around the hideout. At least they're clean.

'I, uh, well, you just kinda fell asleep in here . . .' Sam proceeds awkwardly. 'I didn't want to wake you up. Sorry if it's – Uh, anyway, we can get you your own room . . .'

'It's okay, Sam. Relax,' I reply as I sit up, not feeling very modest. I sidle over to him, drape one arm over his shoulder and hook the other around his waist, hugging him close. His skin is warm against mine.

'After what happened, I thought you would . . . I don't know. Push me away again,' Sam says quietly, half-distracted, probably on account of me kissing the back of his neck.

'Nope,' I reply.

'Good,' he mumbles.

Okay, so maybe this isn't the most appropriate time. I've still got a lot on my mind and on my conscience, but if I learned anything from John and Sarah, it's that you have to embrace these moments, not run from them. You never know when it might be your last chance.

Of course, we're interrupted about two minutes later by a knock on the door. Sam leaps off the bed like he's going to get in trouble, pulls on his shirt and goes to the door. He looks back at me, and I smirk, pulling the sheet up to my chin.

Sam opens the door a crack. I'm surprised to see the young buzz-cut twins who I noticed when we arrived, the ones who were with that General Lawson dude who Sam told me is in charge.

One of them just stares at Sam, completely deadpan.

The other, a little friendlier but still economical with his words, announces, 'There's a meeting.'

'All right,' Sam replies. 'We'll be out in a minute.'

The twins raise an eyebrow in unison at Sam's use of 'we.' He shuts the door in their faces.

'Guess we're on,' he says to me.

'Back to the war,' I reply with a bittersweet smile.

As I begin to get dressed, I nod my head in the direction of the door. There's a lot about our situation that I still don't know. Better to get my questions out of the way before we head off to this meeting with the military.

'What's with the twins?'

'Caleb and Christian.' Sam tells me their names and shrugs. 'They're a couple of military school kids. They're LANEs.'

'Yeah, they seemed like lames.'

Sam laughs. 'No, not "lame". "LANE". L-A-N-E. Not sure why I'd expect you to know brand-new acronyms that the government just invented. It means Legacy-Afflicted Native Earthling.'

'Afflicted?' I pause while pulling on my shirt. 'They make it sound like a bad thing.'

'Yeah, they use "augmented" instead of "afflicted" when you Garde are around, but my dad saw one of the internal emails.' Sam shrugs apologetically, like he's the ambassador for all humanity. 'I guess the people in charge aren't entirely sure yet if Legacies are a good thing for a bunch of human teenagers to develop. They're concerned there could be drawbacks or side effects.'

'Yeah, one of the side effects is that it makes it a lot harder for the Mogs to shoot you in the face.'

'Come on, I know that,' Sam replies. 'For your average human, though? This is a lot to take in. I mean, we've got two brand-new types of intelligent life to wrap our heads around, and that's before we even get to how you Loric mutated us.'

I raise an eyebrow.

'Mutated in a good way,' Sam adds.

'So what do those twins do?' I ask, circling back.

He shrugs. 'Only telekinesis, as far as I know.'

I'm fully clothed, but I've still got more questions. I stand in front of the doorway with my hands on my hips.

'So that Lawson guy. What's his deal?'

'He was the chairman of the Joint Chiefs back in the nineties, I guess. Retired.'

I give Sam a blank look.

'Chairman of the Joint Chiefs is, like, the highest military posting in America. Reports directly to the president, yadda yadda yadda.' Sam rubs the back of his neck. 'I didn't know what it was either, and I was actually born on this planet.'

'Okay, so what happened to the current chairman?'

'He was MogPro. They brought Lawson back because he'd been retired so long, no one bothered corrupting him. He's like the human version of this place.'

'Speaking of MogPro, I saw Agent Walker hanging around last night, too,' I say, a little edge to my voice. 'You trust her? You trust this Lawson guy?'

'Walker's all right. She fought alongside us in New York. As for Lawson . . .'

Sam frowns. 'I don't know. Hard for me to trust

any kind of organization after MogPro, but they'd have to be crazy to turn on us now –'

While Sam speaks, an old TV set perched on a stand against the far wall suddenly comes to life with a burst of static. We both turn in that direction.

'What the hell?' I ask.

Sam rubs his temples. 'This old place is wired weird or something. That TV's probably filled with spiders.'

'Or hidden cameras.'

Sam smirks at me. 'I hope not. Anyway, I don't think they're organized enough to be spying on us yet.'

Sam wanders over to the TV and hits the button to turn it off. Nothing happens.

'See? Broken,' he says, before smacking the side of the TV. 'Come on!'

When Sam speaks, all the electronics in the room – the TV, the nightstand lamp, the ancient rotary phone – they all flare to life for a second. A burst of static from the TV, a flicker of light from the lamp, a shrill ring from the phone. Sam doesn't notice. He's too busy unplugging the TV from the wall, which finally turns it off.

'See? Crazy. Whole place is nuts.'

I stare at him. 'Sam, it's not the wiring. It's *you*.'

'What's me?'

'You did that just now with the electronics,' I tell him. 'I think you're developing a new Legacy.'

Sam's eyebrows shoot up, and he looks down at his hands. 'What? Already?'

'Yeah, they come on quick once the telekinesis

manifests,' I reply. 'You saw that kid in Ella's dream-share thing. The German.'

'Bertrand the Beekeeper,' Sam says, reminding me of his name. 'Daniela got one, too. I guess I didn't think it would happen so soon for me. I'm still getting used to being telekinetic.'

I don't know who Daniela is, but I nod along anyway. 'The Entity knew the world needs protecting in a hurry.'

'Huh,' Sam says, mulling this over. 'So, it's something to do with electronics.'

He turns back to the TV and thrusts his palms at it. He succeeds in emitting a telekinetic burst that knocks the TV off its stand and to the floor with a loud crash.

'Oops.'

'Well, you've got the telekinesis down at least.'

Sam turns to me. 'If you're right, how do I get it to work?'

Before I can tell Sam that I have no idea, we're interrupted by another knock on the door. A second later, one of the twins' muffled voice reaches us.

'Uh, whatever you guys are doing in there, could it wait? General Lawson told us if we didn't round everyone up by oh-nine-hundred, it'd be our asses.'

I exchange a look with Sam. 'We'll talk about this later,' I say.

He nods, and we open the door to join the two sullen military cadets. As we head down the hallway, Sam stares at every overhead light like an enemy that needs to be conquered.

5

Not much for conversation, the twins lead us through the twisting corridors of the subbasement. Soon we're outside the conference room. Malcolm arrives at the same time from a different hallway and waves to us. The twins dart inside, probably worried about being late, while the Goode men and I linger outside.

Malcolm puts a gentle hand on my shoulder. 'How you holding up, Six?'

I manage a smile. 'I'm hanging in there.' I glance at Sam, and the smile doesn't seem so forced anymore. 'Your son's helping me keep it together.'

Sam blushes and turns away from his dad a bit. Malcolm pats him on the back.

'Good, good,' he says. 'In times like these, we need to lean on each other.'

'How's Marina?' I ask Malcolm. The last I saw of her, he was wheeling her into the cabin on a gurney.

'The medics say her vitals are strong, and she woke up a little while ago to take some food,' Malcolm replies. 'John healed her, yes, but when the damage is that severe, you don't want to rush anything. She's resting.'

'Six was asking about Lawson,' Sam says to his dad, lowering his voice. He looks at me. 'My dad was with Walker's people at Ashwood until they all had to evacuate. Then you were . . . where was it?'

'Liberty Base. I met the president,' Malcolm says with an amused smile. 'He told me he was a big fan of my papers on intergalactic communication. Quite the skilled bullshitter.'

'The president, is he here now?' I ask.

'No, I left Liberty Base in a hurry to reconnect with you guys, but the last I heard they were going to keep Jackson moving. Safer that way.'

'On the run,' I say. 'Yeah. Been there.'

'One interesting fact I picked up . . .' Malcolm lowers his voice, even though we're alone out here. 'The president's daughter, Melanie, she's one of you.'

My eyebrows shoot up. 'Get out. When does she report for duty?'

Malcolm's smile tightens. 'I don't think that's going to happen. But at least it means we've got the president on our side.'

'And Lawson reports directly to him . . .' Sam brings his dad back to what we were originally talking about.

'Ah, right. Well, he's a difficult man to read,' Malcolm says thoughtfully. 'Seems like a straight shooter, although the ruthlessly pragmatic type. A bit old-school, as they say. At the very least, we all want the same thing.'

'Yeah, dead Mogs,' I reply, and nod towards the conference room. 'Let's see what he has to say.'

By the time we walk in, most of our group is already seated around a long, oval table. John sits at one end, slouching a little. Lexa sits next to him, the two deep in a hushed conversation. Lexa holds something out for John to inspect, and I recognize it as one of the cloaking devices we recovered in

Mexico. That's our key to getting through the shields that surround every Mog warship.

John's gaze flicks in my direction when I enter, and I practically freeze. He nods to me, though, and once I nod back, immediately returns to his conversation with Lexa. I guess we're staying focused on the task at hand and grieving later.

Good.

Nine sits on John's other side, and next to him is Ella. Her eyes haven't stopped glowing, which is drawing a lot of stares from the military personnel clustered in the room. As we take seats by them, Nine leans over to Ella.

'So, Lite-Brite, is this like a permanent thing now or can you turn it off?'

I study Ella for a reaction. I'm happy to see a small and embarrassed smile cross her face. The girl used to have such a crush on Nine, and his complaining about her perpetual light show seems to get through. So there's still a little bit of the old Ella in there. Before responding to Nine, Ella concentrates, and the cobalt energy sparking around her chills out a little.

'Better?' she asks him.

'Just remind me to keep sunglasses handy when you're around,' Nine replies.

Ella smiles, this time more easily, and leans in Nine's direction.

'Six.' Sam nudges me. 'This is Daniela. We met her in New York.'

Across the table from me sits the lean girl with braided hair who I noticed first in Ella's dream meeting and then again last night. She waves awkwardly, looking more than a little uncomfortable to be sitting in this room.

'Good to meet you,' I say. 'Sam said you've already developed a Legacy besides telekinesis.'

'I shoot rays out of my eyes that turn things to stone, apparently,' Daniela says warily. She tosses her head, her braids bouncing. 'Would've changed my hair up at least if I'd known you people were gonna stick me with such a stupid superpower.'

'I got it,' Nine says, pointing at her. 'Because Medusa.'

'Yeah, dummy,' Daniela says, rolling her eyes. 'You got it.'

'I like her,' I say to Sam.

Although no one forced us to choose seats at opposite ends of the table, there's a very clear line between us and the military personnel that outnumber us almost three to one. They're all arranged at the far end where Lawson sits at the head. The closest one to our part of the table is Walker, a human buffer zone, seats empty on either side of her. She stares down at the notes in front of her, none of the other government types making any effort to chat with her.

The twins take seats a little behind and on either side of Lawson. They look like bodyguards. Hell, it occurs to me that most of the people in this room are armed and would protect a guy like Lawson before us. Besides the official types sitting at the table, there's a bunch of straight-up soldiers hanging around against the walls, their rifles pointed down but still very much loaded and ready. I'm pretty sure we could take this whole bunch, guns and all, but that doesn't mean I'm not a little concerned at being in close quarters with all this firepower.

On the wall behind Lawson there's a huge touch-screen display with a map of the entire world. There are zones highlighted with ominous red heat signatures: New York City, Los Angeles, London and about twenty more. Those must be where Setrákus Ra's warships are posted. Then, in the United States only, there are a bunch of green dots, much smaller than the warships but numerous. As I look closer, I realize that those dots all form loose circles around the Mogadorian hot spots. These must be the cells that Caleb was talking about, small but organized and ready to strike back.

When I look down from the display, I catch Lawson studying me. He's been watching me take stock of his map. He gives me a little nod before turning his attention to the rest of the room.

'I think we're about ready to get started,' Lawson announces, his voice casual but carrying, with a soft Southern accent. All the side conversations immediately cut off.

I glance around. Mark and Adam still haven't showed up. I open my mouth to say something, but Lawson's speech is already under way.

'For those of you who don't already know me, my name is General Clarence Lawson.' The general clearly intends this for our group, since there's no doubt in my mind all the military and government flunkies know him well. 'Full authority has been granted to me by the president to coordinate the country's response to the Mogadorian invasion.'

Lawson pauses and waits for a response. None of us say anything. Personally, I'm not sure what he expects from us. Our own introduction? I glance down the table and see John staring straight at the general, waiting for him to continue.

Lawson crosses his arms and clears his throat. 'You let me know if I move too fast for you,' he says with a dry smile. 'I'm not a man who wastes his words, and I don't often find myself addressing matters of strategy to civilian teenagers, be they extraterrestrials or otherwise.'

'You won't go too fast for us,' John says, his gaze unwavering.

Lawson nods once, then looks at the nonpowered humans in the room. 'As for the rest of you, keep in mind that these young people have likely killed more hostile aliens than all the branches of our armed service combined. Respect that and respect their presence.'

I don't know what to make of this guy. One minute he's ragging on us for being young and the next he's singing our praises at the expense of his people. Maybe he's just one of those dudes who tries to keep everyone on their toes through constant negativity.

Lawson picks up a tablet device and hits a button. A countdown clock appears on the screen behind him, highlighted in red and in the negative.

'We are approximately ten hours beyond Setrákus Ra's deadline for unconditional surrender, which included a demand to turn over all so-called "renegade" Garde as well as LANEs. To our knowledge, only Moscow has complied with this ultimatum. The Russian government began arresting dozens of youths last night. Our agents report that many of them haven't even manifested Legacies and are likely antigovernment agitators whom the administration

saw as an opportunity to get rid of while simultaneously placating the hostiles.'

'Something will need to be done about that,' John
interjects. His voice is cool and authoritative.

'Agreed. Although humanitarian abuses by other
governments will have to be back-burnered,' Lawson
replies. 'Frankly, we should consider ourselves lucky
that only the Russians have kowtowed to the hostiles. We've been able to communicate with most of
our international allies and are encouraging them to
evacuate the cities threatened by warships while
covertly organizing counterstrike forces in the event
we can crack the Mogadorian shields. However, if
Setrákus Ra executes his promised attacks – and
they're on the level of New York or Beijing – I'm not
sure if these other countries will have the ability to
stay the course. I think we can all agree that we're
up against a ticking clock. It's not *if* Setrákus Ra
makes good on his threats, but *when*.'

At the mention of New York, Daniela loudly clears
her throat. John glances at her, then looks back at
Lawson.

'What's the situation in New York?' he asks.

'Same,' Lawson replies. 'Mogadorian ground troops
hold Manhattan, with our forces working triage and
evacuation in the outer boroughs. Also not a priority
at the moment, unless the warship returns.'

Daniela doesn't react much to the news. At Lawson's assessment, her lips bend in a tight frown, and
she drums her fingers on the table in front of her,
like she needs to get some aggression out. I wonder
if she lost family back in the city. I wonder if they're
still trapped there.

'Are you tracking the *Anubis*?' John asks.

'We are. After attacking your people in Mexico, the Mogadorian flagship did not return to New York. Our recon shows it holding in West Virginia over a mountain in Hawks Nest State Park. Some MogPro agents who we've interrogated indicate this place is –'

'Yeah, yeah,' interrupts Nine, clearly bored. 'Most of us have had the shit luck to be stuck in the place once or twice. It's their big base.'

When Nine is done speaking, Lawson lets the ensuing silence linger. Behind him, the twins bristle at this breach of decorum. Lawson stares at Nine like he might an out-of-line cadet, but Nine doesn't even notice. He's right back to doodling explosions on a piece of US Army stationery.

'We're aware of the base,' John says diplomatically. Or maybe just without any emotion. 'We infiltrated it once before, but we've never had the resources to properly attack it until now.'

Lawson nods at that and seems about to respond. Before he can, I lean forward to look at Ella. Maybe she knows why he's parked himself in West Virginia and hasn't made good on any of his threats.

'Ella, why has Setrákus Ra stopped the *Anubis* there? What is . . . what is he waiting for?'

All eyes turn to Ella, although a lot of the military people look uncomfortable to be gathering intelligence from a preteen girl sparking with otherworldly energy. Ella looks equally uncomfortable with all the attention, and she emits a harmless flare of Loric energy when she opens her mouth to respond.

'Do you want . . . ?' She hesitates. 'Do you want me to make contact with him?'

'Whoa, hold on –' I say.

'Can you do it without him knowing?' John asks Ella. 'Without putting yourself in danger?'

'I think so. If I'm quick,' Ella says, and then before anyone can protest, she closes her eyes. The glow emanating from her skin intensifies once again.

Everyone in the room goes silent, watching Ella warily. It's a little bit like being at a séance.

'She's a telepath,' Sam explains lamely, looking around at the baffled faces.

With a gasp, Ella opens her eyes. A whole lot of people jump, myself included. I can't help it. Ella's a little creepy.

'You okay?' John asks her.

She nods, taking a deep breath. 'He almost sensed me,' she says, a note of pride in her voice. 'His mind is busy. He was hurt badly.' Here Ella glances at me, and my stomach tightens. 'His trueborn aides placed him in the vats to accelerate the healing process.'

'They use the vats to grow their soldiers –' John begins to explain to Lawson.

'We already know about the vats,' he says, waving this off. 'Do you have any idea when he'll be done with . . . whatever he's doing? When the attacks will resume?'

Ella shakes her head. 'His wounds were almost fatal,' she says. 'They would've killed someone without his augmentations.'

I feel a brief swelling of pride at that. Pride and a massive ache of missed opportunity. If I'd only hit him a little harder.

'We talking hours? Days? A week?' Lawson persists.

'I can't be sure. More than hours, I'd guess, but probably not days . . .' Ella cocks her head, remembering another detail that clearly troubles her. 'There are also *others* down there with him.'

'In the vats?' John asks.

'Yes,' Ella replies.

Nine makes a face. 'Like, floating in goop together? Damn, that's nasty.'

'The vats work differently than before, now that they're powered with what . . . what he stole from us,' Ella continues. 'While he heals, Setrákus Ra is also working. He is – I don't know exactly. These others with him, he is making them into something new.'

I don't like the sound of that. Judging by the faces around the table, no one does. I remember back to that vision of Setrákus Ra's past that we all shared – how hell-bent he was to grant people Legacies. That's got to be what he's doing down there.

Before I can say anything, Lawson butts in, his head cocked. 'What did Setrákus Ra steal from you?'

Ella first looks at me, then at John, like she's asking for permission to tell Lawson that Setrákus Ra mined a bunch of Loric energy from the ground in Mexico. I don't know how honest we're supposed to be with these people; my instinct is, not very. I'm sure everyone on our side of the table has figured out what that scumbag is up to, but it doesn't seem wise to share that information with the military. No need to freak them out any more than we need to. Or give them any ideas about what's possible when you hideously exploit a resource.

I'm relieved when John subtly shakes his head in response to Ella.

Ella turns back to Lawson. 'Something precious to our people,' she says.

Lawson seems to know there's more to the story, but he doesn't press the matter. Instead, he motions to one of the officers standing by the door. The guy immediately exits, off to fetch something for his boss. I get a sinking feeling. Mysterious hand signals are always a bad sign.

'All right, then. If we're ready to discuss counter-strike opportunities –' Lawson begins.

'About time,' mutters Nine.

'– we should have all our intelligence assets available,' Lawson finishes.

At that moment, the officer who Lawson sent scurrying into the hall a second ago returns. He leads in two guards, both of them armed with assault rifles and in full combat gear. They don't take their eyes off the prisoner who stands between them, shackled hand and foot, and looking close to exhaustion.

It's Adam.

6

For a few minutes there, I actually thought this meeting might go off without a hitch and I could quickly get back to my own plans to take down Setrákus Ra. Guess I underestimated the depths of the government's stupidity.

Six is the first one to her feet when they bring Adam into the room, his chains clanking together. She's up so fast that her chair topples over. Some of the armed soldiers at the room's edges anxiously lift their weapons just a fraction. When she stands up, so do Sam and Nine.

'What is this bullshit?' Six yells at Lawson while pointing at Adam.

'It's all right, Six,' Adam says tiredly, his eyes on the armed guards. 'I'm fine.'

Nine turns around to look at the guards with a grin. He nods to one guy whose finger is hovering just over his assault rifle's trigger.

'He's with us, old man,' Six growls at Lawson, ignoring Adam's attempt to defuse the situation. 'He's our *friend*.'

Lawson hasn't even moved from his seat. In fact, he looks amused by the whole situation. I wonder if this is him trying to get a rise out of us on purpose, trying to see just how far he can push us, wondering what kind of allies we'll be.

'Your friend,' Lawson responds calmly, 'is a member of a hostile alien race that is bent on the subjugation of this planet. You brought him here — to the doorstep of humanity's best hope for resistance — and expected, what? That we let him roam around freely?'

'Pretty much,' Nine says.

When she first came into the room, I noticed the way Six sized up the military firepower. I recognized that look. She was figuring out our odds of taking them in a fight. Though I didn't expect things to go south, I have to admit that I made my own similar calculation. It's a survival instinct we'll probably never shake.

Judging by the apprehensive looks on a lot of the soldiers' faces, they've also done the math. They don't know Six or some of the others, but I'm sure they've seen footage or heard rumors about what I did in New York City.

They know they can't win.

I think of Sarah. I know she'd tell me to stay calm, and she'd be right. I don't want to hurt anyone. We need to work with these people if we're going to save the planet. I know that. But they also need to know just what we're capable of, especially General Lawson. He needs to know that we aren't *his* asset in the war against Setrákus Ra.

He's *ours*.

I stand up very slowly so that no one gets more jumpy. As I do, I look around and use my telekinesis to eject the cartridge from every firearm in the room. The soldiers' eyes widen when their ammo spills across the carpet.

Everyone is watching me now. Good. I step around the table and approach the two guards holding on to Adam's arms.

'Step back,' I tell them.

They do.

Adam catches my eye, and I see him subtly shake his head, like he doesn't want me to make a bigger scene. But I've got to get my point across.

I ignite my Lumen, my hand white-hot in a matter of seconds. I reach out and carefully melt through Adam's chains so that his hands are free.

With that done, I turn around and look at the others. The

government types all wear the same expression, caught somewhere between anger and fear. Some of our people – like Daniela and Sam – look nervous. Others, like Nine and Six, look at me with devilish encouragement. Agent Walker, surprisingly, hides an amused smile behind her hand.

I focus on Lawson. His expression remains completely controlled and neutral.

'You could've just asked for the keys,' he tells me.

'We don't answer to you,' I reply, putting my now-cool hand on Adam's shoulder. 'You don't get to make decisions about us. Do you understand, *sir*?'

'I understand, and it won't happen again,' Lawson replies without even an ounce of bad feeling. His mellowness is almost worrying. 'You need to understand, we had to make sure your . . . your friend here was on the level.'

'And you need to understand that we're going after Setrákus Ra as soon as my people are well enough,' I say.

And as soon as I'm strong enough, I almost add. As soon as I've added as many Legacies to my arsenal as possible.

'We're going to kill him and bury him inside that mountain of his,' I continue. 'How does that align with your plans for a counterattack?'

'Sounds pretty darn great,' Lawson says, and motions for me to retake my seat. I nudge Adam and let him take my chair at the head of the table instead.

With the situation relatively defused, Six and the others sit back down. The soldiers around us don't make a move to pick up their ejected magazines. While everyone's getting settled again, Six leans across the table to Adam.

'You all right?'

He nods quickly, brushing the whole thing off, even though there are still handcuff bracelets around his wrist. 'All they did was ask me questions, Six. No big deal.'

I fold my arms and look down at Lawson. 'So what else is there to discuss?'

Lawson clears his throat, still unperturbed. 'While we support your assassination of the Mogadorian leader wholeheartedly, we do have some timing issues that need to be ironed out. As well as some other questions and concerns.'

'Timing issues,' I repeat dully. 'Questions and concerns.'

'For instance,' Lawson continues. 'I'm aware that you recently used a sort of extrasensory perception to communicate with what's believed to be hundreds of LANEs around the world.'

I blink at that. He's talking about the telepathic summit that Ella dragged us into. For a second, I'm off balance, not sure how Lawson could possibly be aware of that. Then I glance over his shoulder at the two stone-faced twins – Christian and Caleb – who have been hovering around Lawson constantly since we got here. They've got Legacies, so of course they were in the room when I met all the newly powered-up humans. They must have reported the details to Lawson. If not them, then maybe it was the president's daughter.

'What about it?' I ask him.

'Well, John, these are hundreds of minors who you're recruiting from all over the world. There are concerns for the safety of these children.'

I shoot a meaningful look at the twins flanking Lawson before responding, hoping that he appreciates the irony.

'There's going to be nowhere safe on this planet soon,' I tell Lawson. 'They need training that only we can give them.'

'I get that,' Lawson responds. 'But you understand why it might make some people nervous, don't you? You building an army from our young people?'

I shake my head in disbelief and hope my expression conveys just how ridiculous I find this bureaucratic nonsense. It almost makes me look back fondly on my days on the run.

'We aren't building anything,' I say, then look at the twins. 'You two. Did I demand that you come here? Did I force the others?'

The twins look taken aback to be spoken to directly. They exchange a glance, then look to Lawson for permission.

'Speak freely,' he says.

'No. You didn't do anything like that,' Caleb replies immediately, his brother sitting there stone-faced. Caleb points at Nine. 'That one did call us all wimps, though.'

Nine shrugs at that. I look at Lawson.

'Satisfied?'

'For now,' he replies. 'At least give us a heads-up if you're going to do anything like that again.'

I sigh. 'You said something about timing concerns?'

Lawson motions to the map behind him, the one depicting the positions of two dozen Mogadorian warships.

'Like I said, we're all for you trying to chop the head off this snake. Hell, I'll send as much backup with you to West Virginia as we can afford to spare,' Lawson begins. 'But right now the enemy thinks we're belly-up. When we strike, what happens to all these cities? Everyone's in evacuation mode right now, but it isn't easy moving millions of people. One attack on Setrákus Ra could open up battles on every front.'

Lexa speaks up. 'As the only survivor of our planet's Mogadorian invasion old enough to really remember how it went down, let me tell you, their tactics have changed. They laid waste to our planet in hours . . .'

'Heartening,' Lawson responds.

'They want to occupy Earth, not blast it to inhabitability,' Lexa continues. 'Doesn't knowing that give us some advantage?'

'Could Setrákus Ra be bluffing?' Lawson asks.

'It's true that my people want to occupy,' Adam says with a thoughtful frown. 'In all likelihood, the fleet isn't capable of another intergalactic trip. They need to stay here. But if you think that somehow limits their willingness to destroy even dozens of cities, you underestimate them.'

'So we're back to a doomsday countdown,' Lawson replies. 'Once you attack Ra, we have to assume that countdown stops and the destruction begins.'

'What happens when he recovers and realizes his deadline passed while he was licking his wounds?' Six interjects. 'He'll attack then anyway.'

'Exactly.' Lawson nods. 'The attacks are an inevitability either way. That doesn't mean we want to hurry them up. We want to be as ready as we can be. Get as many civilians to safety as possible. Use every minute of this delay you've given us.'

'You want us to wait,' I say, gritting my teeth. Although I still need more time to collect Legacies, I'm eager for a fight. Right now, it's what I'm living for. Sitting through this meeting has been difficult enough. 'How long?'

'It isn't easy coordinating a series of international strikes against a technologically superior opponent,' Lawson says. 'We've received the cloaking devices your team recovered from Mexico, and our science guys are attempting to reverse engineer them.'

Lawson's people have probably spent more time with those cloaking devices than I have. Lexa – who I only met in person this morning – brought the Mogadorian technology to me first thing. They don't look all that impressive. Solid black boxes with a few inputs and wires, about the size of a paperback book, but they're the key to the human armies having a chance. We turned most of them over to Lawson a couple of hours before this meeting. We kept the one already installed in Lexa's ship, and I set one aside for myself.

'I can help with that,' Adam says to Lawson. 'I know the tech fairly well.'

'I appreciate that, Mr Mog,' Lawson replies. 'Even if we do

crack the devices and put them into production, we've still got to get this tech into the hands of our allies around the world. Now that we know what they look like, other countries, particularly India, have had some success knocking down the Skimmers during skirmishes and stripping out the cloaking devices themselves. Assuming we get beyond the shields, we're still assessing whether we'll be better served attempting to board these warships or rely on ballistic missiles.'

'Neither approach will be easy,' Adam replies.

'Can't you just nuke them?' Nine asks.

Lawson's eyes narrow. 'We're evacuating our imperiled cities, young man, but there are still people down there. Nuclear warfare is off the table here in America. I can't say the same for other countries . . .'

'Bad enough to blow up those giant ships over the cities,' Daniela mutters.

Lawson holds up a hand. 'One problem at a time. Regardless of what approach we take, the cloaking devices remain our biggest hurdle. We're working with an incredibly small stockpile when we need one per ship or one per missile. And then there's the small matter of getting them into the hands of our allies.' Lawson pauses for breath. 'How long will it take to have enough on hand to mount an attack on the warships?'

'All of them?' I ask. 'At once?'

'That's how this operation plays out, John. We hit them all at once to maximize our only advantage . . . the element of surprise. If we let them know we can break their shields too early, the parameters change. They might step up their attacks. Right now, they've got a boot on our necks; they think we're pinned, out of the fight. They don't know we've still got a knife up our sleeve. But we need that tech. And we're up against a ticking clock. Unless you know how long Setrákus Ra will be in this vat of his?' he asks, looking at Ella.

Ella shakes her head.

'Then you understand how precarious our situation is,' Lawson concludes. 'We'll likely get one shot at this, and it needs to be soon.'

I take all this in, a little on my heels. Lawson doesn't paint a very rosy picture. Maybe I'm not in the right mind-set to help coordinate an international counter-attack. Luckily, I've got backup.

Six peers down the table at Ella. 'There are new Loralite stones growing across the Earth, right?'

'Yes,' Ella says. 'I can sense them.'

Six snaps her fingers. 'There you go. We use those to deliver the cloaking devices around the world.'

Lawson looks at me. 'These are the stones you mentioned to the LANEs in your . . . ah . . . psychic briefing, yes?'

I nod.

'Hmm.' Lawson glances at the map over his shoulder. 'Once we caught wind of those, we encouraged our international partners to lock down as many of them as they could find.'

I cock my head. 'You did?'

'Yes, John, of course we did. That said, some leaders have outright laughed at me when I asked them to divert resources to guarding some magical rocks. Not to mention, we only know the location of a fraction of these Loralite growths.'

'How many human Garde have been intercepted?' I ask, my voice cold.

'A few,' Lawson replies cagily. 'For their own protection. Most of them are still overseas. Assuming we survive the next few days, maybe we can discuss how you'll train them. With proper supervision, of course.'

I don't like this. It feels like we're giving away too much too easily, turning over the Loralite locations to Lawson, not to mention the fledgling human Garde he's so interested in. Still, what choice do we have? Practically speaking, using the Loralite stones is our only way to get a counterattack ready fast.

'We'll help you locate the rest of the Loralite,' I tell Lawson. 'Once we're ready to move the cloaking devices.'

Lawson smiles at my reluctant concession but moves on quickly. 'That's transport squared away. It still doesn't solve the problem of quantity.'

'If we can't make them quickly enough, we'll just have to get you more,' I say, the beginning of a plan starting to take shape in my head.

Nine flashes me a wolfish grin. 'Maybe we should go somewhere that we know will have a lot of them.'

'And where is that?' Lawson asks.

'One of the warships,' I reply.

'Didn't I just explain −?' Lawson snaps, frustration breaking through his patient granddad routine for a moment. He gets hold of himself quickly. 'If we attack them − any attack − we risk them laying waste to another one of our cities.'

'What if we could get in and out of one of their warships without them even noticing?' I pose this to Lawson, but it's Six who I'm looking at. She smiles at me. I smile back. 'What if we could get you a battalion's worth of cloaking devices before the Mogs even notice they're missing?'

'That . . .' Lawson rubs a hand across his jaw, considering. 'That I could live with.'

7

Here's the to-do list.

Sneak aboard a Mogadorian warship.

Steal every cloaking device they've got without tipping off the Mogs.

Arm the governments of the world for one big counterstrike.

Meanwhile, learn every Legacy I can wrap my mind around.

Kill Setrákus Ra.

Not necessarily in that order. Especially not the 'learn every Legacy' one. Because if I'm going to sneak aboard a Mog warship the way I'm planning, there's one Legacy in particular I'm going to need first.

I have to learn how to fly.

The meeting breaks up after I promise General Lawson we'll have a plan in place to covertly attack a Mogadorian warship by the end of the day. Hopefully, Ella was right and Setrákus Ra will be out of action for at least that long. It's barely even noon yet, and I feel like we've already burned too much of the day.

As everyone hurries through the hallways of Patience Creek to go about their tasks, I pull Adam aside. He looks pale as usual, with the addition of some dark circles around his eyes. Everyone at that meeting had a little bit of similar wear on them. Invasion fatigue is setting in.

'You all right?' I ask him. 'What did they do to you?'

Adam stares at me, shaking his head. 'I'm fine, John. It was nothing. I should be asking how *you're* doing.'

I figured that was coming. Everyone who knew Sarah — from Sam to Walker — all of them keep looking at me like I might fall apart at any second. I hate that. I don't want to be coddled. I want to fight. I was at least hoping that when it came to Adam, I'd get a pass on the sympathy. Never thought I'd be yearning for some cold Mogadorian logic.

'I'm dealing,' I tell him, and am surprised by how much edge is in my voice.

'All right,' Adam replies, obviously getting the hint. He holds up his hands to show me his wrists where the handcuffs are still attached to them. 'You mind getting these the rest of the way off?'

'Yeah, sure. Forgot about those.'

'It was more about delivering a message to that Lawson guy than getting me out of chains,' Adam says. 'I get it.'

'Well,' I reply with a small smile. 'You did look uncomfortable.'

'So did all those soldiers.' Adam laughs. 'It was a good move. You showed strength.'

I light up my Lumen again, this time focusing it so that it's limited just to the tip of my index finger. Careful not to burn Adam, I melt through the lock mechanisms on the cuffs until they fall open.

'What kind of questions were they asking you?' I ask while Adam rubs some feeling back into his wrists.

'Like I said, it wasn't so bad. They wanted to know weapon and ship schematics. They wanted to know about the structure of the Mogadorian government and military, which is easy because they're basically the same thing. They wanted to know what will happen to Mog society if Setrákus Ra is killed.' Adam shrugs. 'I would've told them all these things even if they hadn't put me on lockdown and kept me up all night.'

'Huh,' I say, thinking for a moment. There was actually a question in there that I'd never thought to ask myself. 'What *will* happen when we kill Setrákus Ra?'

Adam smiles at me, appreciating the certainty in my voice. Then he runs a hand through his stringy black hair, looking thoughtful.

'Well, I don't remember a time when there wasn't a . . . "Beloved Leader". I've got no concept of what our world was like before. Hell, I doubt my parents would even remember. Setrákus Ra rewrote our history books, so, according to them, we weren't much more than animals before he came along and "raised us up".'

'I guess it's too much to ask that they'd just give up and go away,' I reply.

'Without strip-mining Earth like they did Lorien, the fleet doesn't have enough fuel to go anywhere.' Adam pauses thoughtfully. 'Over a long enough timeline, though, they might go away . . .'

'What do you mean?'

'For all his bluster in that so-called Great Book of his, Setrákus Ra never actually fixed the fertility problems we trueborn experience. He can grow an endless number of vatborn soldiers. Doesn't change the fact that the trueborn birth rate is totally stagnant.'

'So the trueborn will slowly die off,' I say, trying to keep my voice suitably grim considering the company, but really feeling nothing for the slow extinction of Mogadorians. 'And the vatborn?'

'As far as I know, the secret to creating them would die with Setrákus Ra.' Adam sees my smile and holds up a cautioning hand. 'You need to realize a few things about my people, John. First, the vast majority completely buy in to Setrákus Ra's twisted idea of Mogadorian Progress, and all of them believe that Setrákus Ra is unkillable. That's the only thing that's kept them in line all these centuries. When you kill him, you'll cut off the vatborn and maybe get a few of the Mogs like me to lay down their weapons –'

'You think there could be others like you?' I ask, interrupting. I always thought of Adam as unique and considered his seeing the light a side effect of his brush with Number One.

He looks away. 'I . . . don't know. I've met others who I thought . . . maybe . . . I'm not even sure they're alive at this point.' Adam waves this off. 'The point is, even without Setrákus Ra, you'll still have a heavily armed race of zealots who believe might makes right. How I imagine it going down? First, the trueborn decide who's strongest by blowing each other up with Earth as their battlefield. Then whoever survives tries to pick up where Setrákus Ra left off. There are a lot of generals, like my father, who would think they're next in line.'

'They won't succeed,' I say absently. In truth, I'm thinking about the idea of Mogs blowing themselves up. If only we could speed that part of the process along.

'In the long term, no. That's still years of conflict, John. Here on Earth.'

'Humanity would be collateral damage,' I say, considering the effects of a Mogadorian civil war. The loss of life would be like New York City all over again. Unless the Mogs did their fighting over cities that were already evacuated . . .

'Anyway, first we've got to actually kill Setrákus Ra, right?' Adam says, patting me on the back. 'Let's not get ahead of ourselves.'

'I'm going to throw everything I've got at him,' I say. 'And then some.'

'We'll help, too, you know. You've got friends in this.'

I nod. 'Yeah. Of course. I know that.'

Adam starts walking towards the elevator and motions for me to follow. 'You got another few minutes? There's something else I want to show you.'

I raise my eyebrows and follow after him. The military types coming and going down the brightly lit halls give the two of us a wide berth. I wonder which one of us they're more afraid of.

I did a cursory exploration of the Patience Creek facility when I first arrived, familiarizing myself with the important areas – the officer sleeping quarters where we're staying, the barracks, the holding cells, the gym, the garage – and glossing over the areas where the military are doing their thing. I'm not sure what Adam could've discovered in the brief time he was being held prisoner that I haven't already seen. Then again, a place built as a hide-away for spies would have a lot of secrets.

'After they interrogated me, they took me down here,' Adam explains as we ride the elevator down two levels. 'I guess they didn't have much hope of this project paying off, so they stuck it out of the way.'

The level that we exit on to is mostly storage. I passed it over pretty quickly during my walk through. Half the lightbulbs in the hallway need changing. Adam brings me by a few rooms completely filled with dusty crates of dry rations and boxes of Tang, plus a storage space cluttered with seventies-style beach chairs and a moth-eaten volleyball net. Finally, we turn a corner, and Adam opens a door into a room cluttered with stacks of books. A library. At a glance, I realize that most of these yellowed hardbacks are dedicated to topics a spy might find useful in a post-apocalyptic pinch: volumes on gardening, electronics repair and medical treatment.

I flinch. The small room is filled with the harsh and guttural sounds of Mogadorians barking at each other.

On a desk in the middle of the room, there's a wide piece of electronic equipment that looks vaguely familiar. The Mog voices emanate from that. It's about the size of a car dashboard and covered with strange knobs and gauges. The thing looks like someone recently set fire to it and then dropped it off the side of a building. It's hooked up to a tangled mess of wires and batteries, apparently drawing a lot of power.

Then it hits me. What I'm looking at is the control console of a Mogadorian Skimmer, ripped out from the rest of the ship. The console is powered on, thanks to some complex wiring, and that means the communicator is active.

Seated in front of the dissected console is an olive-skinned guy who I'd put in his early thirties. His dark hair is cut short, and his cheeks are losing ground to a few days' worth of stubble. I think I've seen him before, although I can't quite place where and when.

'Adam, you're back,' the man says, nodding tiredly. 'Been pretty quict.'

I turn to Adam and raise an eyebrow.

'This is Agent Noto,' Adam tells me. 'Formerly of MogPro.'

That's where I know him from. He was part of the group that Walker brought to Ashwood Estates after they turned on the Mogs.

'I was worried you wouldn't be coming back when the soldiers hauled you off earlier,' Noto says. 'Got pretty Orwellian for a minute there.'

Adam smiles at me. 'See? I told you my detainment wasn't all bad. I made a friend. I've been helping Noto with his Mogadorian language skills.'

'You speak their language?' I ask, taking a fresh look at the man.

'I was liaison to the Mogs during my MogPro days,' Noto explains. 'Picked up a few phrases here and there. I can understand so long as they talk slow and at a kindergartner's level.'

I step farther into the room, peering at the open notebooks fanned out on the desk. They're filled with symbols I recognize as Mogadorian letters, each of those represented by a phonetic translation.

'We're monitoring the communication between the Mogadorian warships,' Adam says. 'I've encrypted this module so they won't have any idea we're listening in.'

'With the security you downloaded on to here, we could broadcast back to them, and they still wouldn't be able to find us,' Noto says admiringly.

Now I realize why Adam looks so utterly exhausted. It wasn't just the interrogation keeping him up all night. He's been sitting here listening to these Mog transmissions, knowing he's the only one who can translate them.

'How long does it take to teach basic Mogadorian?' I ask him with a glance at Noto.

Noto rattles off a series of harsh noises. 'It's not so tough.'

Adam laughs. 'Your accent is getting better, but you just said you'd like a stomach filled with leeches.'

Noto makes a face. 'I thought I was asking for some coffee.'

'I helped Noto make a list of key words to listen for,' Adam tells me. '"Beloved Leader", warship call signs, "Garde" – any time he hears those words, he makes sure to flag the transmission.'

'I'm recording everything in case I need to listen again,' Noto says. 'Which I usually do.'

'This is good. It'll be really helpful to know what the Mogs are saying to each other,' I tell them, putting a hand on Adam's shoulder. 'Don't burn yourself out, though. We're going to need you.'

Adam nods. 'I know. I won't.'

I say good-bye to Agent Noto, then lead Adam into the hallway where we can talk privately.

'So, from what you've listened in on so far, what are the Mogs saying?' I ask him.

'They're freaking out about Setrákus Ra,' he replies. 'Well, freaking out as much as Mog trueborns can freak out. There's a lot of concern about why he hasn't ordered the attack or made any announcements to the fleet, but they won't outright question him because to do so is pretty much treason. Mostly, they're like . . . "This is warship *Delta*, awaiting orders, requesting guidance from Beloved Leader."'

'That alone tells you they're freaking out?'

'Mogs don't go around *asking* for orders, John. They do what they're told. They speak when spoken to. They don't passive-aggressively prod their Leader.'

'And there's been no response from the *Anubis* or the West Virginia base?'

'Nothing,' Adam confirms. 'Radio silence.'

'Hmm.'

The plan I've been formulating is a little crazy, a lot dangerous, and, you know, that doesn't bother me nearly as much as it probably should. I mull over everything that Adam has told me about Mogadorian culture, in particular the likelihood of them descending into civil war once Setrákus Ra is dead. If they took out each other, that'd make it a whole lot easier on the rest of us. What if there was something we could do to speed that process up? To get the Mogs at each other's throats before Setrákus Ra is even turned to ash? A little bit of psychological warfare.

Before I can give that any more thought, Noto pokes his head out of the library and waves Adam over. 'There's a lot of chatter all of a sudden,' he says.

Adam and I jog back into the room. I cock my head to listen to the transmission coming through, but it all sounds like angry barking to me. The Mogadorian who's broadcasting sure is excited, though.

Watching Adam's eyes slowly narrow, I can tell this isn't good news. After a few seconds, he turns to me.

'John, we should get the others,' he says. 'Someone's made a terrible mistake.'

8

Never post anything on the Internet. It's like Rule #1.

Granted, all of us have broken Rule #1 at some point and ended up hunted by Mogs as a result. Because sometimes desperation outweighs your desire not to be stupid. It happens. No judgment.

But man, it's dumb to post things on the Internet.

The video, obviously shot on a cell phone, begins with a thunderous rush of water. A massive waterfall that I instantly recognize as Niagara Falls appears on screen. Whoever's filming this is standing on a grassy outcropping level with the waterfall's drop-off.

'Oy, it's bloody loud —'

The camera gets jostled as whoever's holding the phone jogs away from the waterfall. In those few seconds of bouncing around, I'm able to pick out a few details: a blond girl who looks like she should be yodeling on a six-pack of imported beer stands near the edge of the cliff right next to a jagged protrusion of otherworldly blue stone.

Loralite. A new growth, just like Ella said there would be.

Before I can examine the stone too closely, the camera steadies and is turned around so we can look straight into the pockmarked face of a grubby teenage boy. He's gaunt, with a Mohawk that's bleached nearly white and patches of peach-fuzz stubble. He wears a torn-up denim vest covered in patches, a ratty tank top, and while I can't see his feet, I can almost guarantee he's rocking combat boots. Of course, I recognize him from the telepathic summit Ella held for us. He's one of the kids who seemed most eager to heed John's call to action.

Even though he moved away from the edge, the kid still has to yell to be heard over the waterfall.

'Hello, John Smith and super-friends! You out there? Nigel Rally here. We met at . . . uh. The thing. Found your bloody stones, and, y'know, it's been a real laugh popping round the world and all, but at what point are you lot gonna come pick us up?'

It doesn't surprise me at all that these international Garde are lost and confused. John told them to come help us, and Ella explained that they could use the Loralite stones to teleport around the globe simply by picturing a location. But Setrákus Ra crashed our meeting before we could give them any concrete idea how to find us, which isn't exactly an easy task considering we're in hiding.

'I ran into a couple of others while taking the tour, eh?' Nigel continues, and turns the camera to pan around his surroundings. 'Wave to John Smith, protector of the world and absent Big Brother who has apparently forgotten to fetch us.'

Behind Nigel, the blond girl I caught a glimpse of before waves. Next to her, there's a stocky boy with a shock of brown hair who waves awkwardly. I recognize him immediately as the German from the meeting, Bertrand, the beekeeper who can control bugs. Also, standing a little off from the others is a frail-looking Asian girl who stares blankly into the camera before tossing up a halfhearted peace sign.

'That's Fleur and Bertrand,' Nigel narrates, 'and over there . . . well, I think she calls herself Ran. Doesn't speak any English that one, not since your mega-psychic bird with the glowing eyes stopped with the translating anyway.'

Nigel flips the camera back around to himself.

'So look, we're at Niagara Falls, if you haven't figured that out yet. I memorized as many spots on that map you showed us for five bloody seconds as I could, but I've never been to the States, so I had to bop around Europe for a bit until I met ol' Bertrand. Picked up some other tagalongs on the way . . .' Nigel blows out a sigh. 'Lotta weird places on your map, John Smith. New Mexico? What the hell does that look like, eh? Stupid, I bet. Bertrand was here once for a family vacation, so . . .' Nigel lowers his voice. 'If you read me, Major John, we're waiting for a pickup. If not, well, I guess we'll just start walking towards the nearest alien battleship and hope for the bloody best, eh? Cheers.'

And with that, the YouTube clip ends. It's attached to the comment thread on the video Sarah made introducing John to the world, and it's already got a ton of likes and views. Nigel posted his video about three hours ago. Me, John, Adam, Nine, Ella, Sam and Daniela are all huddled around a cell phone that Daniela swiped from one of the soldiers.

We're all crowded into John's room. Before we started the video, I couldn't help but make note of some of the grim details of John's room. The bed hasn't been slept in, and there are scorch marks on the kitschy wallpaper, like he punched the wall with his Lumen on. Nobody remarks on this, although Sam does raise an eyebrow when he catches me looking.

'Dibs on Fleur,' Nine says as soon as the video is over.

I elbow him in the ribs, and Daniela makes a face. 'You're nasty.'

'I'm lonely,' Nine replies.

'This video was posted three hours ago,' Adam explains, ignoring Nine 'I've been monitoring Mogadorian transmissions, and it seems like they've just picked up on it. The closest warships to Niagara Falls are in Toronto and Chicago. They'll be sending in Skimmers.'

'Posting on the web,' Nine says, clicking his tongue. 'Rookie mistake.'

'We've all been there,' I say. 'So, the Mogs have a head start on us. Let's get some jets and get out there.'

'We want to keep this quiet, which is why we're hiding out in here,' John replies. 'Better if we do this ourselves without Lawson's people knowing.'

I give John a questioning look.

'I'm not sure what his intentions are with the human Garde,' John elaborates. 'Until we decide he's on the level, I want our people to be the ones bringing them in. I don't want to leave it up to Lawson to decide who's ready to fight and who need his "protection".'

'Whoa, hey, what kind of intentions you worried about?' Daniela asks.

'I don't know,' John says with a sigh. 'Compelled enlistment into a secret military organization? Who knows?'

'You learn not to be so trusting of people in power when you've been through what we have,' I tell Daniela.

She nods. 'Sounds totally sketch.'

'I've already reached out to Lexa telepathically,' Ella says, her eyes still sparking with Loric energy. 'She's getting our ship ready.'

'Nice,' Nine says, and claps his hands. 'Let's go save some newbies.'

'I need you to stay here with me,' John says to Nine, and immediately Nine's face falls.

'Aw, come on,' Nine replies. 'What the hell for?'

'You think I wouldn't rather be out there fighting?' John asks, his tone resigned. 'We've got preparations to make if we're going to sneak our way on to a warship. I need your help with that. Six can handle Niagara Falls.'

'You know it.' I grin at John, feeling as eager as Nine to get back out there and fight. I look around at the others. 'The rest of you in?'

'I should stay back and monitor the Mog communications. They don't know we're listening, so I'll be able to tell you what their status is,' Adam says. 'I'm also supposed to meet with Malcolm and some of the engineers about replicating the cloaking devices.'

'I'm with you,' Sam says to me.

'Me too, if that's cool,' Daniela replies.

'And me,' says Ella.

That makes everyone pause. I watched Ella die just yesterday. I'm not wholly sure that she's ready for combat yet. She must pick up on that vibe – probably because she can read our minds. Ella puts her hands on her hips.

75

'If the Mogs get there first and these other Garde have to go on the run, I can track them telepathically,' she says, a note of defiance in her voice, which is still all resonant and Legacy-like. 'I'll be *fine*.'

'Good enough for me,' I say.

'Me too,' John adds. 'Take the Chimærae with you.'

'We'll take a couple,' I say. 'Not going to leave you guys without backup here in case something else goes down.'

John nods. 'Just make sure you're packing enough firepower to knock out whatever the Mogs send.'

'Oh, don't worry,' I tell him. 'We're gonna do more than knock them out.'

Fifteen minutes later we're in Patience Creek's underground garage. Like the rest of this dusty hideout, the garage isn't as sophisticated as other militarized places we've seen, particularly the ones augmented by Mogadorian tech like Dulce and Ashwood. Still, the garage is big and high ceilinged, with enough space to store a convoy of armored Humvees and a couple of tanks. I expect the domed ceiling itself to open up and a ramp to extend for an exit, but the old-school spies who built this place didn't roll that way. Instead, there's a huge tunnel dug into one wall, barely lit and nothing fancy, just thick sections of lumber holding back the hard-packed dirt. The tunnel's wide enough to bring a tank through, and it leads to an innocent-looking cave a few miles away from Patience Creek. If the little bed-and-breakfast that hides all this is in the middle of nowhere, then the cave exit is to the east of nowhere. Basically, you'd never catch us coming or going.

Lexa flew our ship through the tunnel last night. She managed it, even though it was a bit of a squeeze. She's already got the ramp extended and the nose pointed towards the exit when we enter the garage.

On our way here, we picked up two of the Chimærae from Malcolm Goode's small laboratory. To hear them talk about him, most of the military guys think Malcolm is some kind of eccentric genius. Maybe he is, in a way. The bunch of random animals he keeps as pets haven't done anything to dissuade folks from that notion. Even though Walker and her team know about Chimærae from our run-in back at Ashwood Estates, we've still tried to keep their existence quiet. You never know what some of these overzealous government types might get up to if given the opportunity to experiment on an alien life-form.

We take Regal, whose preferred form is a hawk, and Bandit, who sulks around as a raccoon. The other Chimærae stay back with Sam's dad, watching as he runs an unending series of tests on the Mogadorian cloaking device, trying to figure out a way to copy its frequency. Adam's with him, making suggestions on what Earth-made technology might be able to match the signal. So far they've had no luck, and neither has the team of military engineers working next door to them.

In the garage, Lexa comes down the ramp to meet us.

'Good to go?' I ask her.

'Just finished the diagnostic,' Lexa replies. 'We pushed her pretty hard getting out of Mexico, and she took some shots from the *Anubis*. Old girl's ready to fly, though.'

Daniela shakes her head and stares at the ship. 'I'm about to ride on a UFO,' she says.

'Yeah, you are,' Sam replies. He flashes me a gentle smile, then leads Daniela and the Chimærae on board.

Like me, Ella doesn't follow them right away. She takes a deep, shuddering breath, glances at me with her flickering eyes and then trudges up the ramp. I hesitate until Lexa touches me on the elbow.

'It's all right,' she says quietly. 'I . . . I cleaned everything up.'

I nod at her. 'So many bad memories on this ship.'

'I know,' Lexa says. 'When the war is over, you can help me destroy it.'

I smile at the thought, both of wrecking this ship and of the war being over. I climb up the ramp, following a few steps behind Lexa.

At the top of it, I pause to look around the rest of the garage. There are a handful of soldiers milling around down here, making sure the vehicles are all in working order. I know they've seen us. Some of them are even outright watching us. However, none of them show any sign of trying to stop us.

Back at the elevator, I notice Caleb and Christian. They weren't here when we first entered. Someone must have reported our presence, and those two came down to observe. They both stare at me, their expressions blank. I smile and wave, even though they kind of give me the creeps. They don't acknowledge me at all.

So Lawson knows something is up and that we're leaving the base. Oh well. That's John's problem to deal with.

Inside the ship, the passenger area is spotless.

Using the touch-screen controls that cover the walls, Lexa extends some bucket seats from the floor, and everyone straps themselves in. Under the floor, the cots are hidden away – including the one where Sarah Hart breathed her last. My mouth suddenly feels dry. I hate being back here.

I take the copilot seat next to Lexa while she powers on the ship. Sam comes up behind me and leans down, his hand on the back of my chair.

'You okay?' he asks quietly.

'I'm fine,' I say quickly.

Sam looks over his shoulder as if trying to imagine the grisly scene that took place here just yesterday. He shakes his head.

'I still can't believe it,' he says. 'I keep expecting her to just, I don't know, pop up somewhere. Alive . . .'

When Sam trails off, I turn to Lexa.

'The Mogs have a head start on us,' I tell her. 'We need to get to Niagara Falls in a hurry.'

'Oh, don't worry,' she replies as she slowly amps up the power to the engines. 'We'll go fast.' Lexa glances back at Sam. 'You better get strapped in.'

I put my hand on top of Sam's. 'Let's focus on the people we can still save, okay?'

Sam takes one last look at me before he retreats to the passenger area and puts on his seat belt. As soon as she hears his belt click into place, Lexa thrusts forward the lever for acceleration.

'Here we go!'

The ship zips forward into the tunnel. Aside from a whoosh of air, the takeoff is completely silent, the engines purring calmly even as we rapidly speed up. There can't be more than a couple of feet of clearance between us and the walls rushing by. There are a few times where I swear I hear the ship scrape the tunnel. Lexa focuses straight ahead, handling the curves like she's done this a hundred times.

'Oh shit, oh shit, oh shit –' I hear Daniela muttering behind me.

We round a gentle curve, and there's the sky, a white dot at first that gets bigger and bigger as we scream forward. And then, with a release that feels almost physical, we're out in the open air, gaining altitude, soaring first over a dirt road and then Lake Erie. I can't help but let out a relieved sigh as we leave the claustrophobic tunnel behind us.

'Fast enough for you?' Lexa asks with a grin.

'Yes!' Daniela shouts from the back.

'You could've waited until we got out here to really open it up,' I say, although I can't help grinning back at Lexa.

'Where would be the challenge in that?' she replies.

Even with Lexa flying us at top speed, we're still about an hour away from Niagara Falls. Once it's clear that the course is set and we're on our way, I unbuckle and pop into the back to check on the others.

Much like the ride back from Mexico, Ella is curled up with her arms around her knees and her eyes closed. Interestingly, the Chimærae seem drawn to her, both of them huddled at her sides. I wonder if that's because of the Loric energy flowing through her or because she just seems like she needs a bit of comforting.

Across the aisle, Daniela watches Ella like she's trying to make sense of her. She looks up at me as I walk over and nods in the younger girl's direction.

'What's with her?' she asks cautiously.

'She –'

Ella opens one eye and interrupts. 'I died yesterday. For a little while.'

'Oh,' Daniela replies.

'And then I bonded with a godlike entity that is still kind of inhabiting me.'

'Okay, that's normal.'

'It's taking some getting used to,' Ella admits, then closes her eyes again.

Daniela gives me a wide-eyed look as if to ask if all that was for real. I shrug, and Daniela lets out a breath, slouching low in her seat.

'Man, I should've stayed in New York. We had aliens, yeah. But they weren't zombie aliens.'

'Not a zombie,' Ella says without opening her eyes.

Next to Daniela, Sam has produced an ancient-looking handheld video game from one of his pockets.

'Turn on,' he whispers insistently to the video game. 'Turn on.'

He looks up when he senses both Daniela and me watching him.

'What?' he says.

I cock my head to the side. 'Why do you have that?

'That thing's from the eighties; you can't talk to it, dude,' adds Daniela.

I point at the game. 'There's a power button on the side.'

'Thought you said you didn't have any batteries anyway.'

Sam looks briefly flustered as we pepper him with questions and comments. He takes a deep breath. 'I found some,' Sam replies distractedly to Daniela, looking at me. 'And I didn't bring it to, like, pass the time before we save some people. I brought it to try re-creating what happened before. In our room?'

Daniela raises her eyebrows. 'Oh, what happened in your room?'

'Sam made the lights flicker,' I reply.

'Did he now?' Daniela says, grinning at Sam until he blushes a little.

'Literally,' he says. 'I think – well, Six thinks – that I might be getting another Legacy. Like maybe I can control electronics or something.'

Daniela crosses her arms. 'Man, that's way better than stone eyes.'

I take a seat next to Sam so he's between me and Daniela, then lean forward to look at the other girl.

'How did you know when you were getting a Legacy?' I ask, wondering if it feels different for the humans.

'It felt like my head was gonna explode if I didn't . . . I don't know. Let it out?' responds Daniela. 'My adrenaline was pumping. It all happened fast.'

'That makes sense,' I say. 'Happens like that a lot. They tend to kick in when you really need them. Your instincts take over. After that, you learn how to fine-tune them.'

Daniela listens to me, then leans back and starts massaging her temples. She stares intently at the wall across from us. 'Yeah, I can feel it in me now. I could do it again if I wanted to without so much pain.'

'Please don't turn the ship to stone while we're flying in it,' Sam says, then faces me. 'My telekinesis came when John was about to get mauled by a piken.

It'd be nice if I could get this new Legacy down without the whole death-defying-situation thing. I mean, if the Legacies manifest when we really need them, I'd say right now, considering the situation the whole planet's in, we really need them.'

'So keep trying,' I say, motioning for Sam to look at his retro Game Boy. 'Maybe imagine something horrible is about to happen.'

He frowns. 'Shouldn't be hard.'

Sam goes back to speaking insistently to his video game. Nothing happens. Every few minutes, he closes his eyes and grits his teeth, like he's trying to get himself into the right mind-set of panic and terror. Sweat beads on his forehead. Still, he can't get the video game to turn on. I lean my head back, close my eyes, and listen to his mantra. 'Turn on, turn on, turn on . . .'

'We're about ten minutes out,' Lexa calls from the cockpit a short time later.

I open my eyes and glance towards the cockpit. The copilot seat is now occupied by Regal, the hawk perched on the back of the chair, his eyes straight ahead as we zip through the clouds. Ella is still resting her eyes or meditating, I'm not sure which. Meanwhile, Bandit paces back and forth across the aisle in front of us, anxiously waiting for us to land. Daniela watches the raccoon pace, looking a little nervous herself as we approach what might be a battle. It occurs to me that this is all still extraordinarily new to her. She's hasn't even had her Legacies for a week yet and now she's got to get used to charging into dangerous situations alongside shape-shifting alien animals.

'Don't worry. We can handle this.' I lean across Sam to tell her, even though I've got no idea what we'll be facing once we arrive at Niagara Falls.

'I'm good,' Daniela reassures me.

I turn to Sam to say something but cut myself off when I notice the look of deep concentration on his face. His eyebrows are scrunched up, and he's staring down at that inert Game Boy as if it's his worst enemy.

'Turn *on*,' he says through gritted teeth.

I actually jump when the handheld game chimes to life. Sam nearly fumbles the thing as he turns to grin at me.

'Did you see that?' he exclaims.

'Nuh-uh,' Daniela replies, leaning over. 'Your finger was on the button.'

'It was not!'

'You did it, Sam!' I say, squeezing his leg. I'm thrilled for him, my own grin almost the same size as his.

Ella opens her eyes to watch the scene, a small smile on her face. 'Congratulations, Sam.'

'Did it feel different?' I ask. 'Do you remember how you did it?'

'It's hard to explain,' Sam says, looking down at the video game almost like he still doesn't believe what just happened. 'I tried to picture the circuitry. At first it was just, like, a made-up picture in my head. I don't know what the inside of a Game Boy looks like or how it works. But then, I don't know, the visual started to get clearer and clearer. Like a blueprint was forming in my mind. At first it was all made-up nonsense, but gradually it changed into something . . . I don't know. Something logical? Like I was learning the machine. Or the machine was telling me how it works. Does that make sense?'

'No,' Daniela replies immediately.

'It sounds kinda similar to how I use my telepathy,' Ella says.

I shrug at Sam. 'Whatever works. Do you think you could do it again?'

'I think so,' Sam says, and once again concentrates on the video game. This time he raises his voice like he's scolding a badly behaving pet. *'Turn off.'*

The Game Boy blinks off.

'Nice,' Daniela says. 'You really are doing it.'

Instead of congratulating Sam, I tilt my head to the side. Something isn't quite right. The wind outside the ship is suddenly much louder. It takes me a moment to realize the reason why.

'We're falling,' Ella observes.

The ship's engines have stopped humming.

'Guys!' Lexa's voice comes from the cockpit, a slight note of panic there. 'I've got some kind of malfunction up here! My systems just went dead!'

From the cockpit, I hear Lexa slamming levers and slapping buttons, cursing when they don't do anything to turn her systems back on. Sensing trouble, Bandit scurries beneath a seat and puts his paws over his head. We're gliding now, and a quick glance out the window shows me that we're losing altitude fast. A golf course zooms by beneath us, a small town, a river.

Daniela and I stare at Sam in unison. His eyes are wide. He swallows hard.

'Oops.'

9

'You're sure we should be doing this?' Nine asks me.

'We don't have a choice.'

The two of us walk down one of Patience Creek's many non-descript hallways. While the military presence has most of these hallways humming with activity as they get their operation running, this part of the facility has been left pretty much alone. We're in the small section that was built to hold prisoners, and, at the moment, we've only got one of those.

'All these new Garde popping up around the world, you'd think one of them would have the flying Legacy,' Nine says.

'Maybe one of them does,' I reply. 'But we don't have the time to find them.'

'All right, all right,' Nine finally concedes, shaking his head. 'Just let it be known, for the record, I'm against this.'

'Yeah, I get that. You put a signpost through his chest just a couple of days ago.'

'Ah, that's a nice memory.'

'Your reservations are clear.'

'I'll kill him if he tries anything.'

I glance at Nine. 'I know. Why do you think I made you come along?'

Nine and I stop talking when we reach the padded room where we're holding Five. The reinforced steel door only has a small porthole for a window and opens with a heavy-duty wheel like you might find in a bank vault or on a submarine. There are two guards posted in front, grim-looking marines clutching automatic assault rifles that wouldn't do them a bit of good if Five managed to break out. They both look surprised to see us.

'I need him,' I say to the guards, nodding towards the locked door.

They exchange a look. 'He's a prisoner,' one of them says.

'I know. He's *our* prisoner,' I reply.

'We are definitely not planning to let him loose,' Nine adds.

One of the guards steps aside and mutters something into a walkie-talkie. I let this all play out. Might as well make it look like I respect Lawson's authority here.

The guard returns, shrugs his shoulders and produces a key ring.

'The general would like you to come see him on . . . another matter,' the guard tells me as he unlocks a mechanism that holds a three-prong wheel in place.

'Oooh, you're in trouble,' Nine says.

'You can tell him I'll catch up with him as soon as we're done here,' I reply to the marine.

I figure word has reached Lawson that Six and the others left the base without notifying him. I've got no intention of wasting my time explaining our moves to the general; if he wants an update, he can come find me. I've got things to do. Of course, I don't say any of that to the guard.

The wheel creaks when the soldier turns it, the door swings open and both guards step aside in a hurry.

'Wondered when you would visit.'

Five sits cross-legged on the floor of his padded cell and smiles at me and Nine. His arms are secured in a straitjacket, his legs in a pair of loose-fitting pyjama pants and he's barefoot. The floor underneath him is like one big cushion. There's nothing in this room for Five to touch that would allow him to activate his Externa. Worst-case scenario, he turns his skin to cotton.

87

I didn't supervise Five's imprisonment. I wasn't really in an emotional state to worry about him, so Nine and Sam arranged this setup. Looking at the padded room, you'd think it was specifically designed to hold Five. Lucky for us the spies who'd originally built this place were prepared for every possibility, including one of their number losing their mind in a post-apocalyptic scenario.

Five's face is still bruised and swollen from where Nine decked him right after our battle on Liberty Island. In securing him down here, Sam and Nine even took away the grubby patch of gauze he'd been keeping over his eye. The empty socket stares at me.

'I need your help,' I say. The words leave a bitter taste in my mouth.

Five cocks his head to the side so that his good eye is focused on me. 'You saved my life, John. I know you'll never trust me. Not after everything that's happened. But I'm at your service.'

Next to me, Nine groans. 'I want to barf.'

Five turns to Nine. 'You know, I accept responsibility for my actions, Nine. I know that what I did was . . . *misguided*. But when will you accept your part?'

'My part?'

'Always running your goddamn mouth,' Five growls. 'If you only shut up once in a while . . .'

'So my jokes turned you into a psychotic traitor,' responds Nine. I notice his fists are clenched. He looks at me. 'This is a stupid idea, John.'

I shake my head. 'Look, when all this is over, if you two want to lock yourselves in a steel cage and work your shit out once and for all, that'll be fine with me. But right now, we can't waste any more time.'

Nine frowns and falls silent. Five keeps on staring at me like he can see right through me. After a second, he clicks his tongue.

'What a difference a day makes,' Five says. Then he addresses Nine like I'm not even in the room. 'Yesterday he was doing everything he could to keep us from killing each other, remember? The Boy Scout. Now it's all changed.' He fixes me with a smile that looks almost proud. 'I see that look in your eyes, John. You weren't ready before, but now you are.'

'Ready for what?' I ask, inwardly kicking myself for how easily I took the bait.

'For war,' Five replies. 'Ready to do whatever's necessary to win. Maybe ready to do more than what's necessary, hmm?' He looks at Nine again. 'You see it, too, don't you? He's like us now. Bloodthirsty.'

Nine doesn't immediately respond. He's got an uncertain look on his face; and, I realize, despite his hatred for Five, what's just been said about me has struck a chord. How could I not be changed after what's happened? If I'm bloodthirsty, if I'm willing to do whatever it takes to end Setrákus Ra, well, I'm not ashamed of that.

I ignore the entire exchange and look Five in his one eye. 'I need you to teach me to fly,' I say.

Five concentrates for a moment and then he floats up from the cushioned floor. Cross-legged and with his shaved head, hovering four feet off the ground, he looks like a twisted version of a monk.

'This what you want?' he asks.

I study the way he floats. 'It isn't enough.'

He frowns at me. 'You've got the copycat Legacy like Pittacus Lore, right? I saw what you did in New York with the new girl and her stone eyes. You just had to observe her Legacy. So, observe.'

It wasn't as simple as Five seems to think. First of all, I was desperate. That always seems to help when it comes to mastering Legacies. I could also feel the power building when I tried to heal Daniela's headache. My Ximic tapped directly into her budding Legacy, and I could actually sense how it worked. I think that's why I was able to copy Marina's healing Legacy without even knowing what I was doing and why I was able to re-create Six's invisibility without too many problems. I've actually felt those Legacies before, had them used on me, touched the power. Watching Five float around like a sociopathic Buddha isn't nearly hands-on enough.

'With Daniela, it was heat of the moment. Plus, I could sense how the Legacy worked,' I explain to Five. 'Staring at you isn't going to do me any good.'

'I've flown you around before,' Five reminds me. 'Back on the first day we met. Don't you remember what it felt like?'

'Probably like being carried around by a chubby ass hat,' Nine offers unhelpfully.

Ignoring Nine, I close my eyes and try to recall what it was like flying with Five. The feeling of weightlessness, my legs dangling, the idea that he might drop me at any second . . .

I look down at my feet, unsurprised to find them still on the floor.

'I remember what it was like to be carried,' I say. 'That's a lot different than actually propelling myself up in the air.'

Five gets a thoughtful look. It's almost nostalgic. Not something I've ever seen before on his usually rage-filled face.

'Flying is a lot like telekinesis,' Five says after a moment. 'Like how you visualize an object you want to move floating through the air. How you imagine making that happen and it happens. You guys did that crap a million times just like me, right?'

Nine and I both murmur agreement.

'Well, imagine you're doing that to your own body,' Five continues. He jerks against his straitjacket suddenly and frowns. He was trying to spread his arms and forgot that they were strapped tight across his chest. 'Hold out your arms and imagine strings underneath them, pulling you up.'

'Like a puppet,' Nine says.

'Like an actor in a show,' Five answers, glowering. 'Rising up above the stage. Graceful.'

'Even lamer,' Nine says.

'Try it, John,' Five says gently. 'Hold out your arms. Imagine you're safely attached to the wires. Imagine your telekinesis can manipulate those wires and then stop imagining and *do it*.'

Even though I'm not entirely comfortable taking coaching from Five, I still extend my arms from my sides. I concentrate and try to imagine strings looped around me, connecting me to the ceiling, just like Five said. I pull at those strings with my telekinesis. I picture my feet leaving the ground, my body weightless on the air.

And then it happens. Something clicks, and I feel my sneakers lose contact with the floor. It's only a few inches at most but still — it's happening.

'Easy now,' Five says, his voice a whisper. 'That's good. Focus on keeping your body straight. Keep pulling yourself up on your strings.'

Even as Five says this, I can't help but glance down at the floor to check on my progress. There's a foot of empty space beneath where my feet dangle, and seeing that is somehow completely disorienting. My instinct is to wave my arms like I'm losing my balance. Suddenly, I'm pitched forward, still floating, but horizontal now, facing the floor.

'Focus!' Five snaps. 'Remember the strings!'

The yelling doesn't help. I do remember my imaginary strings, but instead of gently pulling on them to straighten back up, I give them a frustrated mental tug. I rocket upwards, feel my spine smack hard against the ceiling and then fall on to my face. Lucky for me the floor of Five's room is padded.

Behind me, I hear Nine trying to stifle laughter. I push myself on to my hands and knees and glare at him.

'You could've caught me.'

Nine grins and mimes waving his arms in the air for balance. 'Oh man, it was too good. I wasn't thinking.'

I stand back up. Five still effortlessly floats in front of me. At least he doesn't think my failure is hilarious like Nine does.

'It's a start,' he says, and shrugs through his straitjacket. 'I don't recommend practising where there's a ceiling, by the way. I learned mostly over water, so the falls don't hurt so much.'

'How long?' I ask. 'How long did it take you to master?'

Five snorts. 'It's not like shooting fireballs, John. It's more like learning to walk again. It took me months.'

I shake my head. 'I don't have months. I need to fly up to one of the warships as soon as possible.'

Five raises an eyebrow. 'Well now, that sounds interesting.'

'You aren't invited,' Nine says quickly.

Five sighs. 'If you're determined to do it yourself, there's another training technique we could try.'

'What is it?'

I've barely gotten the question out when Five hits me in the stomach with his shoulder. The air goes out of me immediately. He's like a cannonball. He doesn't have arms to grasp me, so it's all force that keeps my midsection pressed firmly to Five's shoulder. We careen straight out the door of his cell, right past Nine, who doesn't react quickly enough. The marines outside scream in surprise.

We let our guard down for one second and this is what happens. How stupid could we be?

Five slams me up against the wall opposite his cell, high up, so the top of my head actually brushes the ceiling. I hear shouts from the soldiers, hear their weapons cock.

'Don't!' Nine shouts. 'You'll hit John!'

Five flies away from me, and I start to slide down the wall. But he isn't letting me go; he's just getting a better position. As I fall, his legs wrap around my chest. One of my arms is pinned against my side in his leg-lock. The other I manage to squeeze free.

I fire up my Lumen on my free hand and grasp at Five's leg, trying to pry myself loose. I burn through the front of his pyjama pants, hear the skin on his leg crackle and pop and then –

Whoosh!

All of Five's skin becomes fire, his Legacy kicking in. Even though I'm immune to being burned, I still jerk backwards, surprised. The straitjacket burns clean off him, fiery shreds falling to the hallway floor beneath us. Now he doesn't need his legs to grasp me. He reaches down and wraps his flame-covered hands around my throat.

'Thanks for the fire, John, you predictable, arrogant prick!'

He flies us up, hard, and slams me against the ceiling. Then, immediately, back down, dashing me against the floor. Nine leaps at us, and Five swings me around like a human shield. I hear Nine grunt as my legs hit him across the side of the head. Then I'm rising up again, Five flying me down the hall at great speed.

'That first time I took you flying? God, how bad I wanted to drop you! You don't even know. Time to make up for that!'

It's dizzying. We go slamming through doors, into empty cells, into new hallways where panicked shouts greet us. Five takes every opportunity to throttle me against a wall or a ceiling or the floor. It's hard to tell sometimes just which surface my ribs are cracking against, it's so disorienting. I catch a glimpse of Nine sprinting along behind us and realize that he's running on the walls, using his antigravity Legacy to keep from having to plow through any bystanders. Five must see him, too, because he doubles back, and we streak towards Nine like a meteor. Nine has to dive out of the way to avoid getting crushed or burned, and, before he can recover, Five has zipped us around another corner.

I'm on my own here.

Thanks to being fireproof, I'm not concerned with Five's literally flaming skin. It's the way his hands are crushing my windpipe that I really have to worry about. Every time Five dashes me against a new surface, his grip slackens a bit, and it gives me a chance to breathe. With the way he's buffeting me around, it's a constant struggle to keep getting oxygen.

'Beloved Leader came to me in a dream!' Five shouts right into my face. The socket of his missing eye is completely filled with fire. 'He said he'd forgive me if I told him how to find you. I told him I'd do cvcn bottor and kill you myself!'

A snarl of rage builds in my aching throat. Enough!

I pound both of my fists down on Five's forearms in an effort to break his grip. He grunts but doesn't let go of my neck. We go careening into a wall, then the ceiling, always with me cushioning the hit for Five.

I lean my head back, make sure my eyes are aimed directly at Five, and let loose Daniela's stone-vision.

He's too fast. As soon as the beam leaves my eyes, Five gets one of his hands up to block me from blasting him full in the face. That's one less hand around my neck, though. Five lets out a creepy little laugh as his hand turns to stone, then mashes that newly leaden appendage right into my face. He keeps the pressure on, covering my eyes so that I can't get off another shot with the stone-vision.

Still, it's an opening. I can breathe now with only one of Five's hands holding my throat. Not only that, but I've managed to gain some leverage. I grab him around the neck and twist, spinning us so that he takes the brunt of the next fall. We crash into something — it must be the floor, I still can't see — and I immediately make sure that I keep Five pinned. In control now, all my weight thrown against Five, I throttle him against the floor over and over.

His stone hand drops away from my eyes, and I can see the

look of pain cross his face. The flames covering his body blink out, leaving behind fragile, normal skin. I don't stop. I keep slamming him. Now it's Five gasping for breath.

'John – John – look down!' he manages to wheeze out.

Another trick, probably. But there's something about the way Five says it, all that malice gone from his voice.

I glance down and see the floor, fifteen feet below us. I'm not slamming Five against the ground at all; I'm pressing him against the ceiling.

I'm flying. In complete control.

'You said – you said heat of the moment,' Five croaks. 'I thought some motivation might – might help you learn. Do it – do it by instinct.'

I don't know what to say. I let a deep-breath whistle through my teeth and my fury dissipates, while still holding Five against the ceiling. Slowly – in control now – I float us down to the ground. I glance around. We're in a hallway in the infirmary section of the base. It's all but deserted over here. Distantly, I hear footsteps racing down a nearby hall. Probably Nine and the soldiers trying to catch up.

'There were better ways to do that,' I say, turning to Five. I ignore the fact that he's completely naked, all his clothing having burned off when he turned his skin into fire.

'Can't argue with results,' Five replies, hunched over. He holds up the hand I turned to stone in front of his face. I can tell by the way his arm muscles flex that he's trying to move his fingers but isn't able. 'This feels weird.'

Five turns his entire body to stone to match his hand. When he turns back to normal, the stone hand stays the same. He frowns.

'Shit. Is this permanent?'

'I don't know,' I tell him. 'I could try healing it.'

'Please do,' he says, and holds out his hand.

I take Five's arm and let my healing Legacy pour into it. It takes a little more effort than normal; my Legacy has to work through the cold stone and find some live tissue to rebuild. Eventually, the stone starts to crumble away, revealing smooth skin underneath.

'Maybe just leave my pinkie,' Five says suddenly, like an idea just occurred to him. 'I don't need my pinkie.'

I make a face. He wants me to leave his finger so he'll always be able to turn his body to stone. I shake my head.

'Not going to happen.'

'Come on, John,' he says, and grins at me. There's blood on his teeth. 'Don't you trust me?'

In answer, I heal his hand the rest of the way. I don't let go of his arm just yet.

'When we were fighting, you said Setrákus Ra came to you in a dream. Was that just you trying to fire me up?'

'No, that happened,' Five states. 'I didn't accept his offer, though. I'm done believing what that old bastard says.'

Before I can press Five further, Nine barrels around the corner in a full sprint. With my enhanced hearing, I can make out another dozen sets of running feet a few seconds behind him. I can also hear the telltale clicks of automatic weapons. I immediately hold up my hands in Nine's direction and put myself between him and Five. After Five's stunt, I don't want this situation to get any more out of hand.

'I'm all right!' I shout. 'It was just a misunderstanding!'

Nine skids to a stop, his fists balled. He puffs out his cheeks with exertion, then raises one eyebrow, looking past me.

Behind me, Five grunts in surprise.

'Uh, John —' Five manages.

I turn around to find Five standing as still as a statue. He's barely even breathing. An icicle hovers in the air right in front of his face. The point glints in the brightly lit hallway, sharp as a dagger. The frozen shard is a hair away from Five's remaining eye.

Marina stands a few feet behind Five, far enough back that he wouldn't be able to reach out and grab her. Her dark hair is a tangled mess matted to one side of her face. She looks like she just woke up, except for the eyes – those are wide and glaring, focused on Five.

'Marina, easy –' I start to say. She doesn't even hear me.

'What did I tell you, Five?' Marina asks, her voice cold. 'What did I say would happen if I ever saw you again?'

'We're supposed to be saving the world from evil aliens and instead we're going to die in a plane crash!' Daniela moans, her face pressed to the nearest window. 'So messed up!'

'We are not going to die,' Lexa snaps from the cockpit. 'I can land this thing without power. It just won't be pleasant.'

Unpleasant seems like it might be an understatement. A glance out the window shows me that we're still awfully high up, the tops of trees pointy green spears down below. Lexa has us gliding in lazy circles, trying to slow our descent as much as possible. Without power, the ship rocks back and forth with every gust of wind, and I can feel Lexa jerk the controls every time that happens, to keep the ship's nose from going down. So far, she's been able to keep us relatively steady. Once we hit those trees, though, we're going to be bounced about like crazy.

Sam stands in the middle of the aisle. He looks panicked. I can't blame him, since this abrupt descent is pretty much his fault.

'This ship is fucking cursed,' I mutter to myself.

'Turn on!' Sam yells for like the twentieth time. 'Ship! I command you to turn back on!'

'It's not working. Systems are still off, and I'm totally locked out,' Lexa calls back from the cockpit. 'Maybe try asking nicer.'

Sam clears his throat, and his voice goes up an octave, like he's talking to a baby. 'Ship? Please turn back on?'

Nothing happens.

'Goddamn it, turn on!'

I grab Sam by the shoulders and make him look at me.

'You're just yelling right now; you get that, right? You need to focus. Stop freaking out and use your Legacy.'

'I don't know how, Six. Yelling is seriously all that's worked for me so far.'

'You did it before with the game player. Just – I don't know. Visualize?'

'I'm going to get us all killed,' Sam groans.

'I have seen very few futures where that occurs, Sam,' Ella interjects. She's still calmly seated in her chair. Sam stares at her.

'See? Very few,' I say to Sam.

Sam swallows hard. 'Not helpful.'

The ship suddenly lurches to the right. Lexa curses and bangs against the steering column, trying to correct course. We definitely just picked up some downward velocity.

'Six, maybe you could help me out with the wind situation?' Lexa calls over her shoulder.

'Good idea,' I reply. I start to step away from Sam. His eyes widen immediately, like I'm abandoning him. I grab his shoulders and squeeze. 'Relax. You can fix this. I'm just gonna slow us down a bit so you have more time.'

I go to the nearest window and concentrate on the weather outside. It's a clear-blue sky out there. I focus on the wind – it's blowing hard at this altitude, but not so strong that I can't control it. Instead of buffeting against the side of our ship, I command the wind to change directions, pushing it across the ship's underbelly, cushioning us. Combined with Lexa's careful navigation, soon we're circling gently, like a leaf caught up on a breeze.

I've slowed us down. This ship still probably weighs half a ton. I won't be able to keep us gliding around forever, not without some help from the engines. It's only a matter of time.

I'm sure Sam knows this. He keeps at it, trying different tones of voice, commanding the engines to start back up. The ship's not listening, though.

In my peripheral vision, I notice Ella gets out of her seat. Little flecks of blue energy spit from the corners of her eyes. She holds Bandit under one arm; the raccoon was losing his mind as we started to crash. As soon as Ella picked him up, he calmed right down. I don't know what he's so worried about anyway – unlike the rest of us, he can sprout wings.

Ella studies Sam for a moment. She nods once, like she's come to a conclusion.

'Before, you said you pictured the inner workings of the video game player and that helped, right?' she asks.

'I said they popped into my head eventually,' Sam replies. He runs both of his hands across his scalp. 'I don't know how it happened.'

'Okay,' Ella replies. 'Give me a second.'

Sam blinks at her, trying to work some moisture into his mouth. He watches as Ella strolls casually towards the cockpit. I half turn to watch, too, still giving most of my attention to padding the wind.

'This thing's gotta have parachutes, right?' Daniela asks me.

'Don't worry,' I reply, watching Ella. 'I think we've got this.'

Daniela looks at me like I'm crazy. She's not used to this whole close-calls thing.

'You know how this ship works, right?' Ella asks Lexa, standing right at the pilot's elbow. 'You could, say, picture the engine?'

'What? Yeah, I guess,' Lexa answers, although she's more focused on navigating us towards a patch of flat land newly visible on the horizon. It won't be enough space to land us clean, but at least we won't be getting thrown between trees.

'Could you do it right now?' Ella asks patiently. 'Just – visualize the engine or the power system or . . . I dunno. Whatever you think Sam screwed up.'

'I'm kind of busy with . . .' Lexa responds sharply, then thinks better of it. She makes sure the controls are pointed in the right direction before leaning back for a second and closing her eyes. 'Okay, I'm pictu –'

Lexa breaks off suddenly with a shudder, like a chill just went up her spine.

'Thanks, got it,' Ella says.

Lexa reopens her eyes. She squeezes the bridge of her nose for a moment before wordlessly refocusing on her controls. 'That was weird,' she mutters.

'Sam, I'm going to send this image over to you,' Ella says, peering back at Sam from the cockpit.

'Send it to me how?' he replies, though the answer

should be obvious. Telepathically. Sam's head jerks back, and his eyebrows shoot up. 'Oh. There it is.'

'Try your Legacy now,' Ella suggests. She leans against the cockpit entrance and gently strokes Bandit's fur. She's so confident, I let my grip on the supporting winds slip a little. Our ship dips suddenly to the left. Daniela's the only one who notices – she lets out a quiet moan of despair; everyone else is focused on Sam.

His eyes are glazed over, and he stares into the distance, like there's something floating out there that only he can see. His lips move wordlessly, rapidly, as if he's whispering a quick count to one thousand.

'Ship, turn on and stabilize, return control to pilot,' he says confidently.

Immediately, there's a whir of activity under our feet. The ship's engines turn back on, and there's a satisfying chorus of buzzes and beeps from the cockpit. We level off and begin to gain altitude.

'All good!' Lexa yells. 'Crisis averted.'

I lunge away from the window and squeeze Sam. 'You did it!'

Sam smiles dazedly at me, like he's not sure what he even did. 'I did it,' he repeats.

'You didn't kill us, hooray,' Daniela adds sarcastically.

'I felt like I was supercharged or something,' Sam says, his gaze drifting towards Ella. 'Like I was connected to the machine. I could make out all its workings . . .'

Ella shrugs. 'I only plucked out what was in Lexa's mind and gave it to you. That's all.'

'So it seems like you have to understand the

machine before you can control it,' I say, thinking out loud.

'But with the Game Boy, I just sat with it, thought about it, and eventually the wiring came to me,' Sam counters. 'And shutting down the ship, that was a total accident. Like an overreach.'

'You also talked funny this last time,' Daniela says. 'Like a robot.'

'Did I?' Sam asks, and raises an eyebrow at me.

'You did,' I reply. 'Seems like we've still got some work to do figuring out this Legacy.'

'Man, I need a Cêpan,' Sam says, rubbing the back of his neck.

Lexa clears her throat. 'Look alive, everybody. We're closing in on Niagara Falls, and I've already got visual on two – no, make it three – Skimmers.'

Everyone in the back immediately falls silent and gets serious. The thundering majesty of Niagara Falls becomes visible down below as Lexa makes a quick pass overhead. Unsurprisingly, the falls are completely devoid of tourists. With the world at war, no one has time for sightseeing.

I make out a shimmer of cobalt blue on the grassy mountainside adjacent to the falls. That's the newly grown Loralite stone, the one our new Garde tele-ported in with.

And parked around it? The three Skimmers that Lexa spotted.

'You see 'em?' Lexa asks.

'Yeah,' I reply. 'Not seeing any movement, though.'

'Hold on; let me enhance the image.'

I hear Lexa tap out a few commands on her console. A moment later, the view from the window blurs and then expands. Now we're zoomed in on the Loralite stone and the ships surrounding it. The camera, which must be mounted on the underside of our ship, effortlessly tracks the stone as we glide through the air above.

'Whoa,' Daniela says. 'Cool.'

Now I can make out more details of the three Skimmers. Only one of them actually looks intact, with its ramp extended and cockpit doors open. The second Skimmer has a ribbon of black smoke curling away from its engine, like something recently exploded there. And the third Skimmer is overturned on its side, half in the rushing river that leads to the falls. The ship shudders even now; any minute the current will take it over the edge.

It looks like the Mogadorians got more than they bargained for. Even so, I don't see any signs of life below. That makes me nervous.

'How do you want to play it?' Lexa asks.

I think her question over for a second. 'Bring us down in the open. Our approach wasn't exactly subtle. Anyone with eyes probably spotted us already.'

'You'd think the Mogs would be shooting at us by now,' Sam says, frowning at the scene on screen as Lexa brings us around for a landing.

'Could be an ambush,' I say.

'Or they could've had more ships. Maybe we're too late. They could've already nabbed these kids and jetted back to their warship,' Daniela suggests grimly.

'Let's hope not,' I reply.

Lexa sets us down as close to the Loralite stone as possible, near the undamaged Skimmer. Now that we're on the ground, she returns the windows to normal. Ella stares out at the glowing stone, seemingly mesmerized.

'We need to help the government secure the rest of these places,' she says after a moment. 'If the Mogs find them first, the new Garde could end up teleporting right into their hands.'

'Could you make contact with them again?' I ask. 'If they're coming to fight, maybe we could tell them all to teleport here.'

Ella shakes her head. 'My range isn't that strong anymore,' she says.

'We could post it on YouTube,' Sam says dryly.

'No YouTube, ever,' I reply. 'We'll just have to trust Lawson and his people will do right by them.'

'Glad I'm with you guys and not detained,' Daniela says.

Lexa puts us on an angle so that our exit ramp will open towards the falls. That means no threats will be able to come from behind us, and we'll be able to use the ship for cover if this is an ambush. Any Mogs looking to attack us will be coming from the small patch of evergreen forest to the north. That little forest is half-flooded by the river as it rages its way towards the falls, so we should have an advantage if we keep to the solid ground.

'Ready?' Lexa asks.

I nod, and she deploys the ramp. No one starts shooting. I'm not sure I'd hear blaster fire over the cacophony of the waterfall anyway.

'Adam should be on the comm,' I say to Lexa. 'Call in, tell him we've arrived and see if he's picked up any Mog chatter. Otherwise, keep the ship ready to haul ass in case we need to leave in a hurry.'

'You got it,' Lexa replies.

I extend my arm, and Regal immediately lands on my forearm, his talons careful not to clutch too tightly.

'Scout it out,' I tell the Chimæra, and he swoops away, through the exit and into the blue sky. I start towards the ramp after him, motioning to Daniela. 'Come on, get up front with me. Anything that seems hostile, go ahead and turn it to stone.'

Daniela smirks, but I can tell that she's nervous. 'Let's do this.'

With Daniela and me leading the way, we edge our way down the ramp. I glance to the side quickly, sensing motion, but it's just Sam picking up a jagged rock from the river with his telekinesis.

He shrugs at me. 'In case I need to clobber some-one,' he says quietly.

Daniela's gaze darts about as we make our way around the front of our ship and approach the burned-up Skimmer. Bandit trundles alongside us as we move slowly north. The raccoon has gotten bigger since we landed, puffed up, his claws now a vicious length. He scratches at the dirt, ready to charge at the first sight of danger. His claws kick up a chalky gray substance that I immediately recognize.

Mogadorian ash. Pretty fresh, considering it hasn't all blown away yet. And there, next to the ash, the left-behind weapons of some killed vatborn. There was definitely a fight here, and the Mogs took casualties.

'The newbies did some damage,' I say.

'No kidding,' Sam replies, eyeing the smoking Skimmer. On closer examination, it looks like a grenade went off right in the ship's cockpit. Something exploded, that's for sure. I'm just not sure what.

I glance behind us and see Ella drifting away from our tight little group. She's headed towards the Loralite stone, which would put her right out in the open.

'Ella,' I hiss. 'Stay close.'

She waves at me without looking away from the stone. 'I'll be fine, Six.'

Sam and I exchange a look.

'I guess you got pretty daring when you can see the future,' Sam says.

'Or when you've already died once,' I reply.

Trusting that Ella can take care of herself, I lead the others cautiously towards the woods. We pass by the Skimmer that landed safely, then edge closer to the river and the Skimmer that's been flipped into the depths. Daniela puts a hand on my arm.

'You hear that?'

At first, I don't hear anything except the water. But then I make out a droning buzz, high-pitched and incessant. I squint at the Skimmer in the river. It looks blurry, strange somehow . . .

Bugs. Even half-submerged in water, the Mogadorian ship is covered by a swarm of bugs. There have to be thousands of them, bees and gnats and flies and who knows what else, darting in and out of the engine vents, crawling over the armored hull. They only break away when the river water laps at them.

'The beekeeper at work,' Sam says.

'Has to be,' I agree, then motion us forward. I'm feeling a lot more confident about this mission. In fact, it doesn't seem to be a rescue at all.

From above, ringing out over the pounding waves and the buzzing bugs, comes a piercing shriek. A falcon's cry. Regal sending up a warning.

'The hell is that?' Daniela yelps, pointing into the sky.

From the tree line, a glowing object was just lobbed directly towards us. It floats through the air on an impossible arc – there's telekinesis guiding it, for sure. If I had to guess, I'd say someone just tossed a pinecone at us. Except I've never seen one pulsing red waves of crimson energy like this one.

A vision of the blown-up Skimmer we just walked by suddenly comes to mind.

'Shoot that,' I say to Daniela.

I didn't have to bother; she's already on it. A silver-tinged current of energy bursts forth from Daniela's eyes – the force of it actually looks painful, and Daniela gasps when it happens. Her aim is true, though, and the glowing pinecone is soon just a hunk of stone flying through the sky.

Not wanting to take any chances, I swat the rock down with my telekinesis. It lands about twenty yards in front of us and immediately explodes, the red energy from the charged pinecone shredding Daniela's stone carapace. We get hit with a few pebbles, but it's otherwise harmless. I'm not sure what the blast would've been like if Daniela hadn't muffled it.

'There!' Sam yells, pointing at the edge of the woods.

I see her too. The frail-looking Japanese girl from the video. She stands where the trees thin out, close to the river, shin-deep in water. She must've been hiding before and popped out of cover as we approached.

There's a cut above her eyebrow, and blood trickles down the side of her face. She's scuffed up, and, on her arms, I can see the telltale burns from Mogadorian blasters. She stares at us, uncertain.

Then she quickly bends down and grabs a handful of rocks from the river. In her hands, these all start to glow.

'Don't do that!' I shout as the girl jerks her arms back like she's going to throw.

'Easy, Ran! Easy!' shouts a second voice. It's the punk looking British kid who filmed the video that brought us here. Nigel, I think his name was. He darts out of the trees, splashes through the shallow water, and grabs Ran around the waist.

Ran breaks from her attack trance when Nigel grabs her and lifts her up. The stones slip free from her hands and splash into the water. A few heartbeats later, a half dozen geysers of water explode upwards where the stones detonated.

'She makes grenades,' Sam says. 'That should be useful.'

'That's badass. Why couldn't I get that one?' Daniela complains, rubbing her head.

Holding Ran with one arm now, Nigel waves at us. The other two – Bertrand and Fleur – cautiously emerge from the trees. They both hold Mogadorian blasters. I get a weird feeling of nostalgia looking at this ragtag group. Is this what we used to look like after surviving those early skirmishes?

'Good afternoon, alien allies!' Nigel yells cheerily, advancing towards us ahead of the others. 'Bloody took you long enough.'

11

'Marina, I need you to calm down.'

Probably a bad choice of words. I realize that immediately.

'Don't tell me to calm down, John,' she replies hotly. 'I wake up. I don't know where I am. And this – this bastard is the first thing I see?'

The lethally sharpened icicle still hovers an inch from Five's good eye. I could try to use my powers to bat it down, but it's fifty-fifty that I could either disarm her or accidentally shove the ice right through Five's face during the struggle. Five must know this too. He doesn't move at all, as frozen as Marina's weapon, his hands splayed at his sides to show he's unarmed. Unarmed and totally naked, actually.

'You're safe,' I tell Marina.

'Forgive me, but it does not seem that way,' Marina replies.

I glance over my shoulder. Behind me, farther down the hall, there's a dozen heavily armed soldiers. Their guns aren't raised. I don't think they know what to make of this scene, but they're still not a very welcoming sight. Nine stands a few feet ahead of them, his arms crossed, his mouth closed. I shouldn't expect him to stick up for Five. In fact, it's probably a show of restraint on Nine's part that he isn't cheering Marina on.

'We're in a secret military base outside of Detroit,' I explain to Marina, keeping my tone neutral. 'You were hurt in the battle with Setrákus Ra. I healed you, and you've been resting.'

'Then Setrákus Ra is still alive.'

'Yes,' I reply. 'Six hurt him badly, though. He hasn't made good on those attacks yet. We've got time, not much, but enough to plan our next move . . .'

'And what about this one?' The icicle bobs in front of Five's face for emphasis. Five flinches, the icicle dips dangerously close in response and he goes rigid once again.

'We captured Five in New York. He's our prisoner.'

'He doesn't look like a prisoner.'

'He was helping me with something. He's going back to his cell now. Right, Five?'

Five's eye flicks briefly in my direction. He swallows hard and cautiously leans his head back so that he can nod. 'Yes,' he says quietly.

Marina sneers when he speaks. She turns to look at me, and I can see that, mixed with the rage and confusion that came on when seeing Five, she wants to trust me.

'Please, Marina,' I say. 'I know what I'm doing.'

Slowly, she starts to lower the icicle. As soon as it's away from his face, Five darts around it and puts me between himself and Marina. He looks at her, a mixture of fear and shame on his face, then hustles down the hallway towards Nine and the soldiers.

'Of all the horrors of war I've seen, this is the worst one,' Nine observes as naked Five approaches him. Some of the soldiers chuckle. I shake my head – that's exactly the kind of comment that could set Five off.

To my relief, Five squares his shoulders and doesn't respond. The crowd of soldiers part for him, staring and murmuring. Five ignores them all. For now, he seems content simply to return to his cell of his own volition. That's a good thing. Maybe he's learning to pick his battles.

'Show's over, people!' Nine yells, waving the crowd away. He follows Five around the corner, his voice carrying as he yells at a soldier, 'Do your patriotic duty and find this boy some pants!'

It's just me and Marina now. She floats the icicle over to herself and plucks it out of the air, breaks off the sharpened tip and presses what's left over against her forehead. She looks up at me with a shaky smile.

'I'm sorry if I reacted . . . poorly. Waking up here and seeing him, I just – I am trying not to be so . . . so vengeful.'

'You reacted like I would've,' I tell Marina. I nod to the chunk of ice against her head. 'How are you feeling? Head still bothering you?'

'Just a little headache,' she replies. 'I remember Setrákus Ra smashing me against the ground and then . . .'

'You were in rough shape,' I say. 'I healed you as best I could.'

'You saved my life,' Marina says, touching my arm, 'I was close to death. On the precipice. I know this for a fact.'

I raise an eyebrow at that. Marina's right; she was barely hanging on when Lexa's ship arrived here. The way she talks about it, though, I can tell there's something more.

'While I was out, I dreamed about Setrákus Ra. Or, he invaded my dream. He pretended . . .' A look of deep revulsion crosses Marina's face. She shudders. The ice chunk in her hand cracks and expands, a fresh burst of frost coating her fingers. 'He took on Eight's appearance. Tried to coax me into . . . into letting go.'

I glance over my shoulder in the direction that Five went. He mentioned a dream about Setrákus Ra as well. I guess just because he needs to recover physically doesn't mean he can't keep screwing with us telepathically.

'He showed up in Five's dream too,' I tell Marina. 'Asked him to give us up.'

Marina arches an eyebrow. 'And did he?'

'He claims he didn't,' I reply. I believed Five when he said he didn't betray us, but I know that's a stretch for Marina. 'Anyway, we brought him here blindfolded. He couldn't give us away if he wanted to.'

'Setrákus Ra must have come to me because I was vulnerable and to Five because . . . well, their history . . .' Marina pauses, thinking out loud. 'Did anyone else . . . ?'

'No, I saw everyone this morning; they would've said something,' I tell Marina, although something nags at the back of my mind.

'So Five and I are the easy targets,' Marina says, frowning. 'That is disheartening.'

'He's desperate,' I say, although I'm not sure I entirely believe that. 'He doesn't know where we are, but we know he's hurt, and we know where to find him. As soon as we sort some things out for the military, we're going to West Virginia, and we're going to finish this.'

Marina stares blankly at my mention of the military. It occurs to me how much she's missed in the short time that she's been unconscious. I walk her back into the medical room. There's not a lot inside except for some cots partitioned by curtains and monitoring equipment, the place completely empty since Marina was the only patient. Now that we're alone, I bring her up to speed. I tell her about the battle in New York, the call from the president, the origin of Patience Creek and the appointment of General Lawson as special commander. I know what I sound like — all business, like a commander bringing a soldier up to speed — but I can't stop myself.

Marina listens patiently, but I notice her eyes begin to narrow as she studies me closely.

'John,' she interrupts when I pause for breath. 'Where are the others? Is everyone all right?'

I look down at the floor. It occurs to me then why I've been giving her such a detailed account. Obviously, Marina should know what's going on with our war, but it's more than that.

She doesn't know.

I'm avoiding telling her about Sarah.

I haven't had to do that yet. Haven't had to break the news. Haven't even actually said the words.

Marina watches me expectantly. She knows that something isn't right.

'Sarah, she . . .' I rub my hands over my face. I can't look at Marina when I say it, have to stare at the floor. 'She didn't make it.'

Marina covers her mouth with her hand. 'No.'

'She was trying to help Six, and Setrákus Ra . . .' I shake my head, not wanting to picture it. 'She saved Six, even wounded, but she lost so much blood . . .'

Marina grabs hold of me. Her one arm goes around my shoulders, her other hand goes behind my head and she squeezes me tightly. It's only when I feel her arms around me that I realize how tense I've been, so rigid that I can barely relax into the hug. This doesn't stop Marina, though. I let out a deep breath and am surprised to hear myself shudder. It's been so chaotic – I didn't realize how badly I needed something like this. For a moment, I rest my forehead against her shoulder, and I feel something inside me break. My vision gets blurry, and I squeeze Marina back, probably harder than I should, although she doesn't say anything.

I realize my cheeks are wet. Hurriedly, I let go of Marina and wipe off my face.

'God, John, I am so sorry. I am so . . .' Marina pauses and looks down at her hands. 'If I hadn't been . . . I could've done something. I could've saved her.'

'Don't,' I reply. 'Don't even think like that. It isn't true, and it doesn't lead anywhere good.'

Both of us fall silent, sitting next to each other on one of the infirmary's stiff cots. Marina leans against me and holds my hand. Both of us stare down at the speckled-tile floor.

After a little while, Marina begins to speak softly. 'After Eight was killed, I was so angry. It wasn't just the way it happened. It wasn't just that I was falling in love with him. It was . . . we've all lost people before, you know? But with Eight, he was – he was the first person I imagined a future with. Does that make sense? Growing up in the monastery, with Adelina avoiding my training, denying the war — it was like knowing a disaster was coming and taking no precautions. Like doom was always right around the corner, just a few more scars to go before they'd come for me. I prayed with the sisters, heard them talk about heaven like the humans believe, but I never dared imagine myself in that world. I never imagined an after . . . an after *anything*. Not until I met Eight. I could imagine what might happen next when I was with him. And the present, that got better, too. When Five killed him, all that got taken away. I felt . . . I still feel . . . *cheated*, I guess. Robbed.'

I nod along with Marina's words. 'I met Sarah right after the third scar, when I was next. Marked for death. It should've been the worst time of my life, but somehow, meeting her, she made it all better. My Cêpan, Henri, he thought I was nuts. I think he understood eventually, though. She gave me something to fight for. Kinda like what you said, it felt like there was finally something beyond just surviving for the sake of more surviving. And now . . .'

'And now,' Marina repeats, her voice sad and thoughtful. 'Now what do we do?'

'Nothing left to do but finish this,' I say, feeling my muscles tighten at the words. Marina doesn't loosen her grip on my hand.

'At the Sanctuary, before Setrákus Ra destroyed it, the Loric Entity let me speak with Eight,' Marina says. I give her a stunned look. I didn't know something like that was even possible. She smiles sadly in response. 'It was so brief, just a few seconds. But it was really him, John. It gave me faith that there could be something more. It isn't all darkness and death.'

I turn away from her. I know she's trying to give me hope. I'm just not ready for that yet. The only thing I want is revenge.

'Afterwards, I felt such a sense of peace. My anger was gone.' Marina chuckles harshly, as if remembering what happened a few minutes ago, how she nearly took Five's remaining eye out.

'Obviously, it didn't last. I've tried — I've always tried — to live honorably, righteously, the way the Elders would want. In the face of everything that's happened, I've tried to hold on to myself. Yet all it takes is seeing Five in the hallway to bring out the worst in me, to make the rage come back.'

'Maybe that's not your worst self,' I tell Marina. 'Maybe that's just who we need to be right now.'

'And who will we be after, John?'

'After doesn't matter anymore,' I tell her. 'We've already lost so much. If we don't win, if we don't stop Setrákus Ra, then what was it all for?'

I realize that Marina's hand has begun to emanate a painful cold. Instead of jerking my hand away, I let my Lumen turn on. I push heat back at her.

'Without Sarah, I don't care about what happens to me,' I continue. 'I just want to destroy them, destroy Setrákus Ra, once and for all. That's all that matters anymore.'

Marina nods. She doesn't judge me for these words. I think she understands. She knows what it's like to want to throw yourself forwards, maintain momentum to keep from breaking down.

'I only hope there's something left of the people we were, something left of us to rebuild, when it's all over,' Marina says quietly.

'I hope so too,' I admit.

'Good,' she replies. 'Now, let's get started.'

Lexa keeps the flight back from Niagara Falls low and cautious. We don't want to ping on any Mogadorian radar if they're sending more ships into the area. I stand beside her in the cockpit, the waterfall battleground receding behind us.

Adam's voice comes in clear and excited over the comm.

'I've got a lot of chatter from the warship in Chicago. They're missing some Skimmers they sent to Niagara Falls. And that other ship from Toronto is on its way there; you're getting out just ahead of it,' Adam reports. 'The trueborn in command is worried that his Skimmers haven't checked in. I assume that's you guys' doing, right?'

I chuckle. 'Not us. The newbies.'

'Oh, good for them,' Adam replies, his surprise audible.

'Crushing a crew of Mogs is like initiation,' I say casually. Lexa glances up at this, a tight frown on her face. I look away from her.

'Probably helped that the vatborn had orders to take them alive,' Adam adds.

'Really?'

'Yeah. I guess the commander wanted to make a gift of them to Setrákus Ra.'

I roll my eyes. 'Well, he screwed up.'

'Anyway,' Adam continues, 'this commander, now

he's requesting permission to divert from his position in Chicago, especially since the bombardment orders haven't come in like promised. He wants to lock down the Loralite stone at Niagara Falls in case more Garde teleport through.'

I grimace. That's exactly what Ella was worried about.

'They won't find anything,' I tell Adam. 'We took care of the stone.'

Back at Niagara Falls, while Sam and Daniela helped the four new Garde on to the ship, I walked over to where Ella was having a weird little commune with the outcropping of cobalt-blue rock. She had her arms wrapped around the smooth stone, her cheek pressed against its side. It throbbed with Loric energy, and for a moment I was worried that she might be about to teleport away. Or do something even weirder.

'Ella, you ready to go . . . ?' I asked softly, not wanting to disturb her.

She didn't respond right away. The Loralite stone flickered brightly for a moment, suddenly transparent, veins of electric energy visible inside. Then, a moment later, the stone faded, the cobalt blue seeped away and it looked dull, like any number of rocks jutting out around the falls. Ella turned around, frowned and dusted off her hands.

'Ready,' she said to me.

I didn't move. Instead, I pointed at the stone. 'What did you just do?'

'I turned it off,' she replied. 'Don't want anybody teleporting here if the Mogadorians know about it.'

I looked from the stone to Ella. 'You can do that? Control them?'

'Didn't know until I tried,' Ella replied, her eyes literally aglow. 'Since the Sanctuary, since I . . . fell into the energy, I've felt connected.'

'Connected to what? Lorien?'

'That, yes. And Earth. *Everything*. It's fading, though. Whatever Legacy did to me, I don't think the effects are going to last.' Ella started walking towards the ship. 'Come on. I need to go have a very unpleasant conversation with John.'

I nodded like I understood what Ella was talking about. I decided it was in all our best interests just to let Ella do her thing. She'd been through a lot, seen more than I could imagine. Let her handle the mystical. I'd handle the dirty work.

'Six, you there?'

Adam's impatient voice comes over the radio. I'd spaced out, thinking about Ella and her effect on the Loralite. From her seat behind the controls, Loxa peers up at me with a raised eyebrow.

'Yeah, sorry, I'm here,' I reply. 'What's the response been from the Mogs? They going to move that warship?'

'They don't know what the hell they're doing. With Setrákus Ra out of commission, they're all just yelling at each other. Some think Setrákus Ra would appreciate the commander's decision to pursue Garde; others think he's mad to question Beloved Leader's orders to stay put. You really messed up their whole operation, Six.'

I'd be lying to myself if I didn't feel a bit of pride

at Adam's words. Still, a nagging voice in the back of my mind knows that it wasn't good enough. Eventually, Setrákus Ra will rise, and this temporary advantage will be gone.

'Their entire chain of command is starting to unravel,' Adam continues, energized. 'I mean, there's no page in the Great Book that tells the Mogs what to do if their immortal Leader suddenly vanishes. John and I think we should seriously be exploiting this before Setrákus Ra wakes up and reasserts control.'

'You have ideas?'

'I think so.' Adam pauses. 'They might be a little dangerous, though.'

'What *isn't* dangerous?' I reply.

When Adam's off the comm, Lexa catches my eye. I can tell that she's got something to say, so I linger in the cockpit.

'Those kids we picked up . . .' she says quietly.

'Yeah?'

'They seem ready to you?'

'Were the nine of us ready when we boarded this ship?' I reply.

Lexa gives me a look. I stare back, and she eventually turns to the front window, letting the matter drop. I leave her side and open the door to the passenger area, lean against the frame and observe our new arrivals.

There's Fleur, her blond hair pulled back and damp with sweat and river water. I get why Nine was panting like a cartoon dog when he saw her in the video. She's beautiful. Except now there are blaster burns up and down her arms, on her shoulders, the side of her neck – charred skin, blisters, bubbles of flesh. She shivers as Daniela carefully presses a cold compress to her wounds.

'You're gonna be just fine,' Daniela says to her. 'John can heal these burns right up. Good as new.'

Fleur nods, though the motion seems pretty uncomfortable. She has to grit her teeth to respond to Daniela in accented English. 'You've – this has happened to you before, yes?'

Daniela blows one of her braids out of her face. 'Actually, I've been pretty good about not getting shot so far. Only been doing this whole defend-the-planet shit since the invasion started, though. So I got time.'

'Oh,' Fleur replies, seeming almost disappointed. 'I thought you were one of them. Or at least had, ah, been doing this for a while.'

Daniela beams at that but shakes her head. It's crazy to me that Daniela is being seen as a veteran Garde. She survived New York City; that's no small accomplishment. Doesn't mean she isn't green. Us original Garde had years to train for a battle like this. These new kids don't have that luxury. They're getting thrown right into the mix.

Daniela notices me watching her. She leaves Fleur with the cold compress and walks over to join me in the door of the cockpit.

'All good?' I ask her.

'They'll live,' she replies. 'The bug kid, he won't let me look at him.'

She's talking about Bertrand. Through the open door, I can see him lying on his side in the medical bay. He looks like a freaking teddy bear. He's got blaster burns, same as Fleur, but most of them are on his back and butt.

'Why not?' I ask Daniela.

'Either he doesn't want me to see his ass, or he's embarrassed that he ran from the Mogs,' she replies.

'He only ran after he used his bugs to clog the engines on one of those Skimmers and crash it,' I say. 'He's got nothing to be ashamed of. Shit, you know how many times I ran away or turned invisible to hide in my younger days? You can't always fight.'

Daniela laughs. 'Younger days,' she repeats. 'You're what . . . two years older than them? Yeah, you're a real old lady, Six.'

'Feels that way,' I reply, flashing her a smile. Daniela's right. These four, they're only a year or two younger than me, at most. Yet they strike me as just kids. Hell, Ella seems older than this bunch. Although maybe I'm confusing hardness with age.

My gaze drifts to Nigel. He was the essence of confidence in that YouTube video, the clear leader of this ragtag group. He's still trying to exude that now, his arms stretched across the backs of two seats, wanting to look supercasual about his first-ever ride in an alien spacecraft. The whole punk-rocker costume, now splattered with blood and mud, looks like a kid playing dress-up. As I watch, he reaches one of his slender hands inside his vest and pulls out a crushed pack of cigarettes. He manages to find a cigarette that's mostly whole and sticks it between his lips. When it comes to lighting up, Nigel can't manage it. His hands are shaking too bad.

'You can't smoke that in here,' I tell him. That's

not really true. There aren't any rules about smoking in this cursed ship, and if there were, I wouldn't care about breaking them. I just want to give Nigel an excuse to stop struggling with his lighter.

Nigel puts away the cigarettes and flashes me a crooked grin. 'Hoped you aliens would have a more enlightened perspective on lung cancer, what with your healing powers and all,' Nigel says, anxiously cracking his knuckles. 'So, ah, we off to the next fight now or . . . ?'

'You can relax,' I tell him. 'We're going someplace safe. Hopefully, no more fighting today.'

They shouldn't be fighting at all.

A voice in my head. In the last row of the passenger area, Ella peeks over the back of a seat. Her vivid electric eyes meet mine.

What do you mean? I ask telepathically, remembering Lexa's comment about this group's readiness.

They're being brave, but there is so much fear, Ella says. *We were born into war, Six. Even I had years to prepare myself for this possibility. They've had hours. We should be protecting them, not marching them into battle.*

As if on cue, Fleur begins to cry quietly. Daniela goes to her and gently rubs her back.

What other choice do we have? I ask Ella. *It's now or never. Win or die.*

When all was lost on Lorien, the Elders sent us here to fight another day, Ella responds. *Setrákus Ra doesn't want to destroy Earth; he wants to colonize it. If we fail to stop him, these new Garde could form the backbone of the resistance to come.*

That's a bleak outlook, I say.

When you can see the future, you start to plan for all eventualities.

Looking around the cabin, I have to admit that Ella might be right. Some of these kids would be liabilities if we brought them to the assault on Setrákus Ra's base. We'd have to spend half our time making sure they didn't get killed.

Well, Ella adds, reading my mind. *There's one exception.*

We both look at Ran, sitting rigid in her seat with her hands on her knees, palms up, almost like she's meditating. Of the four, she's the only one who doesn't look at all shaken. She was ready to blast us when we landed at the falls and probably would've if Nigel hadn't stopped her. She's got the look of a survivor.

Ran senses me watching her and looks in my direction. According to Nigel, she hardly speaks any English. She holds my gaze for a moment, nods once and then goes back to her staring contest with the wall.

What's her deal? I ask Ella.

She's already endured great loss and much pain, Ella replies cryptically. *She's a fighter.* Ella pauses. *I'm sorry, Six; I shouldn't be prying through their minds, and I shouldn't be telling you all this.*

I cross my arms and think about these new four, about the human Garde popping up all over the world, knowing that Ella's still listening in.

Did the Entity put any thought into which humans it granted Legacies? Was it dumb luck? Were they selected for their potential? Did the Entity put them in places where it knew we'd need them?

124

You could ask the same questions about us, she replies.

That's not an answer.

Isn't it?

I give Ella a dirty look, but her eyes are closed now. She's out of my head.

Maybe it's better not to know how much of our lives is luck and how much is destiny. Better just to keep plowing forwards. If we can keep them alive long enough, maybe these kids will one day get to ponder the same existential questions on their way to doing something heroic. Hopefully, I'm alive and retired to an island by then.

An island with Sam. If there's anyone on this planet who earned his Legacies, it's him. No way is it just a coincidence. Everything he and his family have done to help the Garde, the Entity must have recognized that. He's the one piece of this whole cosmic Legacy bullshit that makes sense to me.

I watch Sam from the cockpit doorway as he stares out the window, chewing on his lip, lost in thoughts of his own. I've seen that look before, just like I've seen the one that follows – his eyebrows shoot up, and he flinches like he just got splashed with cold water. That's how Sam looks when he gets an idea.

He's out of his seat quickly and headed in my direction, blushing a bit when he realizes that I've been watching him this whole time.

'Hey, can I check out something in the cockpit?' he asks.

I raise an eyebrow. 'You're not going to almost crash the ship again, are you?'

'Not planning on it, no.'

With a lingering glance at Ella, I walk with Sam into the cockpit and close the door behind us. Lexa looks up as we crowd in.

'You've still got one of those Mog cloaking devices hooked up in here, don't you?' Sam asks.

Lexa nods and points to a spot underneath the dashboard, where a bunch of wires have been yanked out of the console and hooked up to a plain-looking black box. 'Right there.'

Sam bends down to have a look, then picks up the box in his hands. He studies it.

'What's he doing?' Lexa asks me. 'Should I be worried?'

'Sam's assured me he's not going to crash us.'

'Oh good,' Lexa replies.

With Sam engrossed with the cloaking device, I sit down on the arm of Lexa's chair.

'Hey, I'm sorry if I blew you off before,' I say. 'I think you're right. Some of those kids probably aren't ready. They did good today, maybe got a little lucky, but other than Ran and Daniela . . .' I shake my head.

'You see what I mean,' Lexa says. 'Granted, I'm no Cêpan, but they need training before they do anything.'

'We can't expect all of them to fight. Not yet,' I agree. 'It seems almost cruel to run up against Setrákus Ra at this point.'

'I always thought that about you Garde,' Lexa replies. 'And you had years of training to prepare you, thanks to the protective charm. There's nothing shielding these humans.'

Sam looks up from messing with the cloaking

device. 'I don't know about the other leveled-up humans, but when we go against Setrákus Ra, there's no way I'm sitting out.'

I decide maybe it's a good time to change the subject. 'What're you doing down there anyway?'

He holds up the cloaking device. 'I thought, with my Legacy, I don't know – maybe I could *talk* to this thing. My dad and those scientists have been trying to duplicate the frequency. Maybe I can help somehow.'

If Sam's right and he can use his Legacy to crack the Mogadorian cloaking frequency, then he's got exactly the Legacy we need. That can't just be dumb luck, right? It's destiny.

I grin at Sam. 'If you can figure that out, Sam, when this is over, I'll make sure they build you a statue.'

Sam smiles back at me and then returns to fiddling with the cloaking device. I glance over my shoulder, back into the cabin, and again consider the humans we picked up.

Sam, Daniela, these others . . .

To me, it feels like we're heading towards a final battle. But it doesn't have to be that way for them. We could throw everything we've got at Setrákus Ra and still not be assured of victory. Or we could protect some of them, leave them ready to pick up the pieces if we fail.

I sigh. I wonder if this is how the Elders felt before they sent us here.

It's not an easy thing, deciding how much to sacrifice.

13

I'm on the way down to meet the group returning from Niagara Falls when I bump into Agent Walker. It isn't so much that I'm surprised to see her trudging from one of the retro kitchenettes to one of the subterranean conference rooms; it's that I'm surprised to see what she's carrying.

A tray of Styrofoam cups filled with freshly made coffee.

When she spots me, Walker looks away, even though the hallway is empty and we're bound to cross paths. It's the first time I've ever seen Karen Walker embarrassed.

'This is what they've got you doing?' I ask, trying to keep any trace of mockery out of my voice. Old habits are hard to break.

Walker grimaces. 'How the mighty have fallen, huh? This is what happens when Lawson and his people want to discuss something sensitive. I get sent on an errand.'

'I don't understand. Why would they want to exclude you?'

She snorts at that. 'I was MogPro, John.'

'You *were* MogPro. You're basically the only reason we were able to stop those people.'

'Once a traitor, always a traitor, is Lawson's thinking,' Walker explains. 'I don't blame him for being cautious. Hell, I'd be in a jail cell, or worse, if I hadn't helped track you down in New York. They don't fully trust me, probably never will.'

'I trust you,' I say, though the words ring pretty hollow. 'More than the rest of them anyway.'

'Yeah, thanks,' she says, waving this off. 'Only reason I'm still around is because Lawson thinks I might be able to handle you. How little does he know . . .'

I chuckle at that, and Walker finally allows herself a thin smile.

A few minutes later, in the hangar, I recognize the truth of what Walker said when I see the scraggly group Six leads off the ship. Four new Garde, two of them hurt, all of them staring around at the heavy-duty military presence like wide-eyed kids on a nightmarish field trip. They all look like they'd fall over from exhaustion if they weren't so overwhelmed and terrified.

Marina and Nine stand next to me to greet the new arrivals. Six and Ella both look relieved and happy to see Marina up and about. Marina flashes them both a quick smile before rushing forwards, immediately pulling aside Fleur and Bertrand and tending to their injuries. If anyone could put these kids at ease, it would be Marina.

Nine opens his mouth to say something. I'm expecting one of his typical boisterous comments aimed at the skittish new kids. He reins himself in, though, and instead turns to me.

'This what you were expecting when you put out the call for fighters?' Nine asks me quietly.

I shake my head, not sure exactly what I was thinking when I suggested a bunch of untrained humans stand up and defend their planet from a vicious enemy with a track record of destroying entire worlds.

Nine puts his hand on my shoulder. 'On our own as ever, bro. Forget the army; forget these kids. We do it ourselves. Like always.'

'They need our protection,' I say to Nine. 'And more training than we can give them in twenty-four hours.'

Nine puffs out his chest a bit. 'You let me think about their training, Johnny. I'm good at that kinda shit.'

'Come on,' Sam says to the humans, now that Marina is done healing them. 'We'll take you inside and show you around. Sorry to say, it's as weird and Big Brother-y as it looks. But it's safe.'

Nine and I watch as Sam and Daniela lead the four across the underground hangar towards the elevator. That's good. They'll probably find it easier talking to other humans than they would talking to me; Sam and Daniela can be like camp counselors in this bizarre new world they've landed in. I see the four of them stealing looks at me, especially the British kid, Nigel, and I force what I hope is a welcoming smile. He looks away. I wish I had another speech to give, but I don't. I'm just about out of words.

Six walks over to Nine and me, her hands thrust into her pockets.

'How'd it go?' I ask her.

'Well, they took down three Skimmers' worth of Mogs before we got there,' she says. 'That's no joke.'

'I'm sensing a "but". . .' Nine says.

'They don't seem up for it,' Six concludes. 'I mean, maybe if we had a couple of months or even a few weeks to train them. Right now, it's all raw power.'

'What's your problem with raw power?' Nine asks.

'I'm not saying they wouldn't be useful, if you want to look at it that way,' Six says. 'It's just that . . . I don't know. I can tell some of them wouldn't make it. I know the Elders were cool with losing a few of us to protect the majority. Not sure I am.'

'Soldiers die; that's how it goes,' Nine says, glancing over to the elevator. The new kids are just now piling on, and we all get a look at Bertrand's butt, exposed from where he got sprayed with blaster fire. Nine sighs. 'But those sure as hell aren't soldiers.'

'I called them all to fight,' I say quietly, looking down at the floor. 'I should've told them to focus on surviving. Like we did the first years. Now, instead, I've drawn them into a battle they might not make it back from.'

'I mean, only the ones dumb enough to listen to you in the first place,' Nine adds with a shrug.

'Their best chance of surviving long-term is still finding us and getting training,' Six counters. 'What we need to do is make sure those Loralite stones you sent them to are safe and secure.'

At that moment, Ella wanders over to us. She'd been standing at the exit ramp of the ship, staring up at the domed hangar ceiling. 'I can help with that,' she says.

'Ella knows where all the stones are,' Six reminds me.

Ella looks up at me. 'Can we talk alone, John?'

I'd been planning to corner Ella when she got back anyway. I need her to teach me how to mimic her telepathy – being able to communicate with the others will be integral to everything we've got planned. Yet, for some reason, I get a real sense of foreboding when she asks to speak with me.

'Sure, Ella. Right now?'

'In a little while. I need to prepare something,' she says, then wanders off to the elevator. Mechanics working on the vehicles in the hangar stop what they're doing to stare at the trail of Loric energy that sparks out from her eyes, how it floats through the air like a comet's tail and then dissipates to nothing.

'What was that about?' Nine asks quietly.

I shoot Six a questioning look.

'Your guess is as good as mine, John,' she says. 'I think the girl's got a lot on her mind.'

I should've asked Ella exactly where she wanted us to meet. I spend more time than I should wandering the subterranean halls of Patience Creek looking for her. At one point, I pass by the laboratory where Sam and Malcolm are hard at work on reverse engineering the Mogadorian cloaking device. From the hallway, I can hear Sam repeatedly saying, 'Broadcast at that frequency,' almost like it's a mantra. Six mentioned that he's developing a Legacy that lets him communicate with machines. So far, it doesn't sound like the cloaking device is willing to listen.

As I walk by, Bernie Kosar trots out from the Goodes' laboratory, where he's been hanging out with the other Chimærae. I pause to reach down and scratch behind his ears.

Want to help me track down Ella? I ask him, using my animal telepathy.

BK wags his tail and begins leading me down the hallway, back the way I came. He seems excited to have something to do, his little beagle legs pumping, tail straight out behind him. We end up at the elevator, and, once inside, BK hops up on his back legs so he can push the button for the top floor with his snout.

What would I do without you, BK?

The elevator doors open, and right in front of me is a wooden wall. I push against it with two hands, and it easily slides forward, its hinges well-oiled. I step into a retro-looking bedroom, now on the top level of Patience Creek, the above-ground level, the part of the complex that looks exactly like an abandoned bed-and-breakfast because, for all intents and purposes, it really is one. The room I'm in smells musty, the double bed looks like it hasn't been slept in for years and dust motes hang in the air. Through the window — a real window with actual sunlight, not like the simulated ones in the subterranean rooms — I can hear birds chirping away the late afternoon. I push the hinged bookcase back into place so the elevator is concealed.

With all the action and facilities underground, and considering the vehicle entrance is about two miles away via tunnel, no one spends much time up here. I know Lawson's got a few guards posted on the grounds, just in case, but Patience Creek has survived this long because no one's interested in an abandoned cabin in the middle of nowhere. Especially not invading aliens.

BK leads me onwards, out of the bedroom and down a wood-paneled hallway, leaving a trail of paw prints on the floorboards. I could find Ella myself now; she left her own trail in the accumu-lated dust, but I don't mind having BK along.

We find Ella in what was once a lounge area adjacent to Patience Creek's unmanned front desk. I glance to the space over the desk where there's a mounted moose's head. There's a hidden camera in there. I remember that from scanning the security feeds last night. I wonder if anyone is watching me now. I imagine Lawson's got eyes on me and the others near constantly. It's what I would do if the roles were reversed. At least he hasn't been pushy or tried to interfere with anything I'm doing.

The walls in the lounge are lined with bookcases filled with either yellowed volumes from the seventies or smooshed board game boxes. All the furniture is under tarps except for the central dining table, which Ella has uncovered. She's taken a heavy-duty atlas down from one of the bookshelves and is in the process of marking it up with a blue pen when I enter.

'Almost finished,' she says, without looking up at me. She flips to a page dedicated to the western coast of Africa and begins scratching a thick blue dot on to the southern edge of the continent.

BK sits down next to me, his tail thumping the floor. I tilt my head, trying to get a look at Ella's project.

'You know, we have computers downstairs,' I tell her, feeling a need to break the silence.

'I didn't want to risk putting this information into the system before you had a chance to look at it,' Ella replies matter-of-factly. 'And I had to get it down before it fades from my memory.' She flips to the front of the atlas, where a world map is already covered in her little blue dots, then pushes the volume across the table in my direction, her glowing eyes fixed on me. 'Done.'

'What is this?'

'A map.'

'I see that.' I stare down at the fifty-odd locations scratched into the world map, then page through to find the same dots reproduced on more-detailed maps right down to the longitude and latitude.

'Six probably told you, I tapped into the Loralite stone at Niagara Falls. I could see them all. The stones, the new growths. It was beautiful, John. Like roots growing through the entire world. I can do that because of my melding with Legacy. It isn't going to last, though. I'm beginning to feel my connection slipping away, my brain going back to normal. I'll miss it but I won't, you know? It makes me feel connected to the world but distant from people. Anyway, I'm rambling. Sorry.'

I shake my head at Ella's burst of conversation, still paging through the atlas. 'These are all active? A Garde could use any of these to teleport?'

'Yeah. You should give this to Mr Government. He needs to get these sites secured. New Garde could be teleporting them-selves into danger.' Ella pauses, still studying me. 'Unless you've got a better idea.'

I frown at the idea of turning this information over to Lawson. Still, what other choice do I have? I can't keep all the Garde safe on my own. I need to come to terms with that. I need to accept help, even if it's coming from people I don't really trust.

I close the atlas and put my hand on the front cover. *World Atlas 1986*. I trace my fingers over the embossed drawing of the earth.

'We really changed this place, didn't we?'

'That's our legacy,' Ella replies. 'It won't be a bad thing, if we can save it.'

'Is that a prophecy?' I ask. 'Did you see the future?'

Ella looks away from me. 'No. I'm making it a point to stop doing that.'

My immediate reaction is to think about all the strategic value we'd lose if Ella was to ignore her visions of the future. I lean for-ward, putting both my hands on the table in between us.

'Why would you do that?' I ask, keeping my voice neutral.

'Sometimes I don't have a choice; a vision just comes to me,' Ella explains, choosing her words carefully. 'Those are hard enough to deal with. But when I go looking for something, with all the variables, all the possible futures . . . it just complicates matters. Knowing a thing will happen, it inevitably changes the way we act, which changes the possibilities, which changes the future, which means there was no point looking ahead in the first place. Or, even worse, sometimes you know what's coming and are still powerless to make a change. Never know which of those scenarios you're stuck in until it's too late.'

I think back to a conversation Ella and I had in her mind space. I asked her if she'd seen a version of the future where we come out victorious against the Mogs. She told me that she had, but that I wouldn't like the cost. I assumed that she meant I would die in the battle – I wasn't entirely comfortable with that idea at the time, but I've been warming up to it these last few hours.

Now, I'm not so sure that's what she meant at all.

'Ella, did you know what would happen in Mexico? Did you know what would happen to Sarah?'

'Yes,' she replies.

My mouth gets dry.

'You –'

I stop myself. I don't know what to say. My fists clench and unclench. Heat rises through my fingers, and I realize I'm close to firing up my Lumen. I take a deep and shaky breath, glaring at Ella.

The rational side of me knows there's nothing to be done now. That cold part of me, the part that's been in charge since Sarah died, wants to stay on mission. But another part of me wants to scream with incoherent rage at the unfairness of it all.

She could've warned me! I think. *She could've told me, and I could've done something! Better yet, she could've warned Sarah!*

I told them to run. Ella's voice rings out clear in my head. She must be reading my thoughts. *Even though I knew they wouldn't, I tried to convince them. And, John, would you have wanted that decision hanging over you? Would you have wanted to choose between Sarah and winning this war?*

I would've found another way, I reply, grinding my teeth.

Of course you would have. Her voice sounds cutting, even in my mind. *There are infinite ways! Maybe you'd have saved Sarah at the cost of someone else. Or maybe you'd just kick her death down the road, like what happened with Eight and his prophecy. That's my point, John. That's why looking at the future is no good. You know, I thought I had to die for our friends to survive the battle at the Sanctuary. I threw myself into the Loric energy thinking that would be it, but . . . I hadn't seen all the possibilities. It'll drive you insane trying to sort through all those possibilities, all that second-guessing.*

Our eyes are locked. The room is totally silent. If anyone's watching us on the security camera, they must think we're engaged in one epic staring contest.

Why did you tell me this?

Because I felt guilty, John. I thought you should know. Because I knew you'd ask to try copying my power, the clairvoyance, and I don't think you should.

'Okay, Ella; please, just get out of my head.'

Ella narrows her eyes at me.

'*You* were in *my* head,' she says, both of us back to using our voices. 'You initiated that.'

'I did?'

Ella nods and walks over to the window. She hugs herself and gazes out at the tranquil lake.

'I'm not surprised you'd pick up the telepathy,' she says. 'I've used it on you enough times. Plus, if you can speak to a Chimæra telepathically, it's not such a dramatic leap to a person.'

I clear my throat and try to put aside the conversation we just had. 'Any tips?'

'Aim your thoughts,' she says with a shrug, not looking at me. 'Direct them and they'll find their target.'

'What about when I can't see the person or we're separated by a long distance? How do you do that?'

'Did you ever . . .' Ella pauses, struggling to put her thoughts into words. 'Say you're in a house and you know someone's in another room. You kind of know, instinctually, how loud you need to yell to make them hear you, right?'

'I guess.'

'Think of it like that,' Ella says. 'The better you know the person, the more familiar their mind is to you, the longer your range with them will grow. You'll figure it out with practice. Sometimes it feels more natural than regular talking. At least to me.'

I'm not sure what else to say. I got what I wanted and more than I bargained for. I pick the atlas up from the table and tuck it under my arm.

'Thank you, Ella,' I say, hoping it doesn't sound too cold, not sure if I could muster anything warmer.

'You're welcome.'

I glance out the window. The sun is starting to get low in the sky, the light turning a muted gray.

What Legacies do I still need?

Five's Externa and Adam's seismic Legacy would be good; Eight's teleportation would be incredible. If I had the time, maybe I could meditate on when I used the Loralite stones before, try to remember that feeling and figure out a way to reproduce it using my Ximic.

If I had the time. It's already getting late.

I head back towards the elevator. Back down into the depths of Patience Creek.

Invisibility. Flight. Telepathy.

These are the tools I've got.

They're enough.

Enough to take on a warship.

14

The waiting has to be the worst part.

The sun has set, not that you'd be able to tell down here in our latest subterranean hideout. Patience Creek still buzzes with activity; soldiers working on logistics and training against observed Mog tactics, researchers along with Sam and Malcolm trying to puzzle out the cloaking device, officers coordinating a worldwide war effort. Adam's offered all the input he can and is now downstairs, helping to monitor the Mog communications.

Right now none of that involves me.

'Nine's penthouse, that was really the best,' I say, pulling my hair back while I stare at an off-white wall. 'I don't think I really appreciated how great those windows were.'

Marina laughs softly. She sits across the table from me in one of Patience Creek's small lounges. There's a half-eaten microwave burrito, now cold, between us. The food selection here is really lacking, and neither of us has much of an appetite.

Marina smiles at me. 'You remember that dinner we had before we went off to Florida? All of us together?'

'Yeah. Right before everything went to hell.'

'That was a good night,' Marina says with a quiet laugh. 'We should've, I don't know, taken pictures or something. Like normal people would've done.'

Marina's smile slowly fades. I can tell that she's thinking about Eight. I try to lighten the mood. 'God, I remember being grossed out by that penthouse because it was Nine's and he used to strut around with his shirt off like he was some hot-shit playboy. In retrospect, Nine overcompensating sure beats out an abandoned Mog Stepford community and this grungy basement.'

Marina laughs again. She reaches across the table and puts her hand on top of mine. I cross my eyes at her. I feel tired and wrung out – maybe that's why I'm getting a little punchy and reminiscing.

'Six,' Marina says softly. 'Can I just tell you ... I never made many friends before, while I was staying in the monastery. It was lonely.'

'Okay?'

'And then you came along. You ...' I make a face as Marina's eyes get watery. 'You've been there for me in the worst times, Six. You always made me laugh or propped me up. Sometimes you literally carried me. I just wanted to tell you that you're pretty much my best friend.'

I blow a stray curl of hair out of my face. 'Oh, goddamn, Marina, don't start talking like that. It's bad luck.'

Marina chuckles. 'It needed to be said.'

'Yeah, no it didn't,' I reply, squeezing her hand. 'But back at you anyway.'

Someone clears their throat, and both of us turn towards the doorway. John stands there, a heavy, leather-bound atlas with yellowed pages tucked under his arm. There are dark circles under his eyes, and his shoulders are slumped. I don't really know how else to expect him to look after what's gone down recently.

'Hey,' he says.

'Hey yourself,' I reply. 'Where you been?'

John looks longingly at a free chair by our table. Something in him won't let him relax, not even for a few minutes.

'Working some stuff out,' he says. 'I'm going to see Lawson. Wouldn't mind some backup.'

I exchange a look with Marina, and we both stand up. 'Sure,' I say. 'You just going to socialize or . . . ?'

'We've wasted enough time here,' John answers quickly. 'We need to start making moves.'

I nod in agreement, and the three of us exit the lounge and start navigating the endless hallways.

'Should we gather up the others?' Marina asks.

'I don't want to disturb Sam and Malcolm while they're working,' John replies. 'Nine isn't the most diplomatic, and Adam probably wouldn't be welcome in this context.'

'What about Ella?'

John's mouth tightens. 'She doesn't need to be here for this.'

There's an edge in John's tone. 'You guys have your talk?' I ask.

'Yeah.'

'And?'

'Can we just leave it alone, Six?'

I shoot Marina a look. She subtly shakes her head, as if to tell me that I should drop the matter. I take her advice, and we walk on in silence.

Lawson has set up his office in a part of the complex referred to as the nerve center. We pass by rooms filled with communications officers coordinating with other governments around the world. It's noisy; there are about a dozen languages being spoken. Around the world, the Mog warships still haven't attacked. They haven't even moved, except for the *Anubis* taking Setrákus Ra to West Virginia and the ship we lured to Niagara Falls. From the urgency down here, it's clear the humans are utilizing every second of this lull to prepare.

The twins, Caleb and Christian, stand guard before a closed door at the end of the hall. Marina hasn't had a chance to meet these two weirdos yet. As we arrive, she puts on her gentlest smile and extends her hand to the blank-faced one that I think is Christian.

'Hi, I'm Marina,' she says. 'I've heard you received Legacies. Quite amazing for it to happen to both of you. If you'd like to talk about it –'

Christian just stares at her and makes no move to take her hand, like he doesn't even understand what she's saying. Caleb quickly interjects himself. He shakes Marina's hand loosely, like it's covered in germs.

'Uh, we're good, thanks,' he says brusquely, then looks at John. 'General Lawson sent for you hours ago.'

'I haven't had a lot of free time,' John replies. 'Is he in or what?'

Caleb steps aside with a grunt, and a moment later Christian does, too, maintaining his cold stare the entire time. As we follow John into Lawson's office, Marina gives me a look.

'What's with them?' she whispers.

'No idea,' I reply. 'I guess not everyone who got Legacies is as charming as Sam.'

Marina smirks at me. We fall silent as we look around Lawson's office. It's a pretty ordinary setup, a beat-up desk where Lawson sits in a lumbar-support chair, a few folding chairs positioned in front of that, a little table against one wall with a drip machine currently brewing a fresh pot from freeze-dried, army-issued coffee crystals.

What really catches my attention, the reason why I'm sure Lawson moved down here, is the bank of monitors that cover the wall behind his desk. The screens feature all kinds of things; some show grainy footage of warships that must come direct from cameras in the occupied cities, others are tuned to the few news networks still able to broadcast and some are set to security footage of Patience Creek itself.

Lawson turns away from this array of information as soon as we enter. He stands up, brushes a hand down the front of his uniform and smiles congenially.

'Ah, hello there,' he says, taking in the three of us. All our looks are varying degrees of confrontational, so he first addresses Marina. 'I'm glad to see you up and around, young lady.'

'Thank you,' she replies.

'I've heard nothing but good things about you,' Lawson continues.

'What . . . what have you heard?' Marina raises an eyebrow.

'I heard you're a healer, which, if you ask me, is about the most blessed power you folks can develop.'

He lowers his voice conspiratorially. 'I also heard from some of my boys that you're a real badass with an icicle.'

Marina reddens at this reference to her confrontation with Five. Before anything else is said, John jumps in.

'You wanted to see me.'

Lawson nods and retakes his seat, motioning for us to sit in the folding chairs arranged in front of his desk. We all remain standing.

'Yes, I did want to speak with you,' Lawson says to John, then points at me. 'I wanted to know why Six here and some of your other associates were leaving the base. Now that she's back and brought some LANEs with her, I don't feel all that concerned.'

'You never needed to be concerned,' I say.

'Yes, well, I worry,' Lawson says to me, playing up that folksy-grandfather vibe. He turns his attention back to John. 'Maybe we got off on the wrong foot earlier. I realize your group isn't used to working with others. And you should realize that it's a strange experience for my people as well. I don't want you to feel that I'm threatening your autonomy – I doubt I could do that even if I wanted. But we are fighting towards a common goal here. It would be ideal if we knew what each other was doing.'

'I agree,' John says, though it sounds like he mostly wants the old man to stop talking.

Lawson runs a hand over his silver hair, his attention back on me. 'For instance, your operation in Niagara Falls caused the warship that was located in Toronto to move down there. It's the first movement we've seen out of the hostiles since Setrákus

Ra went quiet. Caused quite a stir that could've been avoided if you'd been open with me.'

'Nobody fired off any nukes, though, right?' I ask. 'No harm done.'

'Not this time, no,' Lawson replies through his teeth. 'The Canadians had units stationed around that warship that'll need to be repositioned in Niagara Falls, which is a pain in the ass. On the other hand, a major population center that hadn't been fully evacuated is out of the crosshairs, at least for now. If that happened somewhere else in the world, though? Where our allies weren't so disciplined? Could've created some difficulties.'

'It won't happen again,' John says, with his agreement undercut by his dismissive tone. He sets the atlas he's been carrying down on top of Lawson's desk. 'I've marked locations of the Loralite stones in here.'

Lawson smiles and puts a hand on top of the atlas. 'Ah, low-tech. I like it.'

'We really need these sites secured before the Mogs can sniff them out,' John continues. 'Especially if you want to use them to transport the cloaking devices.'

'I'll make sure that happens.' Lawson pats the atlas. 'And I'll keep it on a need-to-know basis. No leaks.'

'You might get some more human Garde teleporting in, too,' I add. 'Make sure nobody screws with them. Mog *or* human.'

Lawson strokes his chin, clean shaven, even at a time like this. 'You think we plan to hurt these gifted young people?' he asks, sounding mildly affronted.

We all speak at once.

'Perhaps not hurt . . .' Marina begins diplomatically.

'Enlist them,' John says.

'Exploit them,' I throw in.

'We just don't want anyone forced to do anything they aren't prepared for,' Marina concludes.

Lawson stares at us for a moment. He glances at the door, making sure that it's shut, probably so the twins outside won't overhear what he's about to say.

'Look, I'll be straight with you,' he says. 'There are going to be elements in our government, hell, in nations all around the world, who are going to see these young people you've gifted as . . . assets. You saw what happened with MogPro. Dangle a little extraterrestrial power in front of these folks and they'll sell their souls, invasion be damned.'

'And you're not one of those people?' John asks.

'No, son, I am not,' Lawson replies. 'I'm an old man who was happy playing golf a few weeks ago. I'm not interested in profit or power. I'm interested in keeping this world safe. I believe you folks can be a force for good. I've seen all the footage: the healing, the self-sacrifice. I've also met that one-eyed fellow you've got down in the basement. We don't want any more of those, do we?'

I glance in Marina's direction. 'No, we definitely do not.'

'I'm all about keeping the world safe. Training your people, putting them in positions where they can use their gifts for the greater good.' John's about to say something, but Lawson holds up a hand. 'These are all just words if we don't win this war, and considering your past experiences with government organizations, I'd think you were fools if you didn't distrust me. But when all this is over, I want you to be involved. I want *you* to tell *me* what's best for these young people, for our planet. And I'll want your help making that happen.'

The three of us exchange looks. If Lawson's playing us, he's doing a real good job of it. But judging by John's distant expression, I'm not sure all his concerns have been put to rest. Or maybe, like me, he's realizing how pointless it is to argue about the future in the face of certain death.

I clear my throat and change the subject. 'So, about those cloaking devices.'

'Still no progress from my R&D on engineering our own version,' Lawson replies, relieved to be back on mission.

'That's all right,' John says. 'We're ready to steal you some. That warship that the human Garde lured to Niagara Falls is a perfect target. Isolated, distracted, overextended.'

'YouTube stupidity occasionally pays off,' I add.

'I'm going to take a small team and slip on board, steal the devices,' John continues. 'Ready to go with that as soon as possible.'

Lawson nods. 'Excellent. I'll want to have a team of my own in place nearby, just in case things go haywire and you need extraction.'

'I don't have a problem with that, so long as they aren't spotted,' John replies.

Marina's been quiet for a while. She stares at one of the news channels, watching footage from London. Thousands of people are marching through the streets, evacuating with only the possessions they can carry, while a warship looms in the background.

'What's being done to protect the people in the cities with warships?' she asks. 'The Mogadorians will inevitably press their attack. . .'

'All but a few cities have an evacuation in progress,' Lawson replies. 'Last I checked, most of them were at about eighty per cent relocation. This extra day really bought us some ti–'

Lawson is interrupted by a hurried knock on the door. Before he can answer, an FBI agent with a thick five-o'clock shadow enters, even though the twins try to block him. I recognize him as Noto, the guy Adam is teaching how to speak Mogadorian way down in the sub-sub-basement.

'Excuse me, sir,' he says to Lawson before he turns his attention to John. 'You should probably come down to our monitoring station. Something's happening.'

That can't be good.

The three of us, plus Lawson, the twins and Noto, hustle down to where Adam is monitoring the Mogadorian transmissions. On the way, Noto brings us up to speed as best he can.

'The Mog warship captains were going back and forth like they've been all day, especially since the one disobeyed orders and moved his ship to Niagara Falls,' Noto explains hurriedly. 'Just now, a new voice came on –'

'Setrákus Ra?' I ask.

'No, a woman,' Noto replies. 'She's been giving a speech, putting everybody in their place by the sounds of it. Adam looks . . .'

He looks pissed, that much is obvious as soon as we

enter the room. Adam sits on the edge of his chair, hands clasped tightly in front of him, his dark eyes glaring at the Skimmer console. Of course I recognize the voice that's got Adam looking so murderous.

'Phiri Dun-Ra,' I say.

'Who?' John asks, turning to me as we all crowd around Adam.

'A most unpleasant person, even in terms of Mogadorians,' Marina says.

'She's the bitch who was in charge of breaking into the Sanctuary,' I tell John. 'We had some run-ins.'

'She almost killed me and Dust,' Adam says quietly, not taking his eyes off the console, listening to Phiri's every harsh-sounding word.

'Last I saw her, she was dragging Setrákus Ra on to the *Anubis*,' I say.

General Lawson clears his throat. 'Son, what's she saying?'

Adam takes a deep breath and lets it hiss through his teeth. 'She's putting the fear into the trueborn captains, taking them to task for doubting their Leader. She says the delay in the attack is inconsequential, as humanity is weak and a Mogadorian victory is all but assured.'

Lawson stiffens at that.

'Did she mention that I impaled their Beloved Leader?' I ask.

'Of course not,' Adam grumbles. 'She claims Setrákus Ra has been busy finishing his life's work of elevating the Mogadorian race. She says that what he's accomplished is nothing short of a miracle and that the faithful will be rewarded. The doubters? She says there's nothing in store for them but pain beyond belief.'

'Lead with the carrot or the stick,' Lawson mutters.

'What kind of miracle could that monster work?' Marina asks.

'We know what his life's work is,' I say. 'We saw it in that vision.'

'The energy he stole from the Sanctuary,' John says quietly. 'The process we saw in Ella's vision, turning it into that black ooze of his. He must be back to that.'

'I don't know what the hell all that means,' Lawson interrupts. 'But it sounds like our time is running out.'

Adam holds up a hand as Phiri Dun-Ra's speech reaches a crescendo. His mouth hangs open, like he can't believe what he's hearing.

'She claims . . . she claims that, thanks to the wisdom of Beloved Leader, she's been granted Legacies,' Adam says, the sound of Phiri Dun-Ra's happy laughter almost drowning him out.

'Bullshit,' I say. 'Even assuming that's true, whatever they've got *are not* Legacies.'

'We saw him do it,' Marina says, a low note of dread in her voice. 'The people working with him on that machine, he'd given them telekinesis.'

'Those people looked sick. Monstrous.' That observation comes from Caleb, the first words he's said since we came down here. I look over at him, and he's staring down at the backs of his hands as if looking to see if there's anything running through the veins there. His brother, Christian, meanwhile, remains completely still and silent.

'He's had hundreds of years to perfect his experiment,' John says. 'He only needed access to more of the raw materials.'

'And we unlocked it for him,' I say, shaking my head.

A new voice comes over the broadcast. Not a voice at all, actually – a scream. An anguished cry from what sounds like a boy being tortured. Everyone in the room falls silent as Phiri Dun-Ra resumes speaking over the screaming, her tone upbeat and chipper.

'What in the hell is that?' Lawson asks.

Adam swallows hard. 'She says it's a Garde they captured in Mexico City. A human. They're extracting his Legacies. Killing him.'

'Turn it off,' Marina says, looking like she's going to be sick.

Adam turns first to me, then to John. Both of us nod. This kind of thing can't go unanswered.

'Do it,' John says.

Adam reaches forward but doesn't turn off the broadcast. Instead, he picks up a microphone and opens up a channel.

Lawson starts forward to stop Adam, and the twins follow suit; but John puts a hand on the older man's chest, stopping him.

'Can they track our signal?' Lawson whispers with wide eyes.

'No,' John whispers back. 'He already took care of that. We're a ghost.'

Lawson doesn't seem entirely convinced. He shoots a look in Noto's direction. The agent nods curtly, affirming what John said.

Anyway, it's too late. Adam's already started talking.

'Phiri Dun-Ra is a liar,' Adam announces in English, though he amps up the harshness in his voice, utilizing that guttural Mogadorian accent. He must be using English for our benefit – so that Lawson knows he's not giving away any secrets. 'What she's telling you is only meant to advance her own power.'

The screaming cuts off. A few confused voices answer in Mogadorian. Phiri Dun-Ra's voice carries over them all.

'Is that you, Adamus?' she asks, laughing. 'How did you get on this channel, little boy?'

Adam ignores her, presses on. 'My name is Adamus Sutekh, son of General Andrakkus Sutekh. I faced my father in single combat and defeated him. I pried his blade out of his dead hand, and I put it to its intended use. I used it to kill a Loric. A Loric who called himself Setrákus Ra.'

Now there's shouting. Outraged cries in Mogadorian from a dozen different voices. I can't help but smirk at the chaos and panic created by just a few words.

Phiri Dun-Ra screeches to be heard over the others. 'These are the fabrications of a disgraced trueborn! A traitor to our race!'

'Then let Beloved Leader answer me!' Adam shouts back. 'Perhaps he can speak through the hole I put in his chest! Phiri Dun-Ra knows the truth, brothers and sisters, and she now seeks to rule us through the same lies that Setrákus Ra used for centuries. Do not let it happen!'

'These are blasphemies –!' shrieks Phiri.

'Let him answer, then!' Adam yells again. 'Let the immortal Setrákus Ra answer, if he still draws breath.'

For a moment, all lines go quiet, waiting for something to happen.

Only silence from Phiri Dun-Ra.

'You will pay,' she says finally, her voice filled with hate. 'You will pay for your lack of faith.'

There's a sharp beep, the sound of her cutting off communication. Immediately, the dozens of warship captains who have been listening to this entire exchange begin to shout at each other.

Adam turns off his mic and swivels around to face us.

'Now,' he says. 'We let them kill each other.'

15

Sydney gets it the worst.

The warship captain there begins a full-scale bombardment of the city a few hours after Adam interrupted Phiri Dun-Ra's speech. This captain claims the destruction is in honor of Beloved Leader, a fiery sacrifice for Setrákus Ra's death. Adam explains that he's showing off; the captain wants to look good in case Setrákus Ra is alive, and position himself for leadership if he's not.

Images of the opera house in flames, the bridge behind it collapsing, are broadcast on the world's few remaining news channels. It's hard to watch, knowing that our lie about Setrákus Ra caused this. Adam looks like he's going to be sick. Lawson shakes his head, his lined face grim.

'Psychological warfare has costs,' he says matter-of-factly. I get the feeling he'd have a different outlook if this was an American city burning. 'If it's any consolation, my sources tell me that Sydney was mostly evacuated.'

'Mostly,' Adam repeats.

'Yes, mostly,' Lawson replies. 'Collateral damage can't always be avoided. It's horrible, but you learn to live with it.' He pauses thoughtfully. 'Wouldn't have expected so much empathy from one of your kind.'

Adam eyes the general. 'Right.'

I don't say anything. I just make a mental note of the Mogadorian's name. Rezza El-Doth. I add him to the list of Mogs that I'm going to kill.

It's the middle of the night. The three of us — myself, Adam, Lawson — are the only ones still down in the monitoring room hours after Adam's surprise broadcast. The others went to get some rest, something that I should probably be doing but don't feel at all capable of. Instead, I slouch in a chair and listen as Adam robotically describes the various transmissions going out over the Mog comms. Next to me, Lawson keeps an eye on a tablet computer, monitoring reports from around the world.

'I admire the moxie it took for a stunt like that,' Lawson continues. 'You had to know there'd be consequences. You did the math and calculated that the benefits outweighed the costs. Of course, if it hadn't played out in our favor, we'd be having a different conversation, wouldn't we?'

I glance at Lawson. He stares at me, appraising. Again I stay silent. He's right, though. As soon as Adam told me about the dissension among the Mogs in Setrákus Ra's absence, I knew we had to exploit it. Adam agreed. Like Lawson said, I knew there might be dangers.

I didn't care.

Sydney went bad, but in other locations, Adam's announcement had better effects.

In Beijing, where the Chinese army has been resisting the Mogadorians heavily and pursuing some pretty reckless counterattacks, the Mogs actually pulled their Skimmers back to the warship. The captain declared he wanted to hear from Setrákus Ra before he wasted any more of his vatborn on securing the city. No response has come from West Virginia, which means a reprieve for the Chinese.

Meanwhile, the warship captain in Moscow declared himself the new Beloved Leader. I guess he got himself a big head after seeing how quickly the Russians complied with his occupation effort. This declaration didn't sit well with the captain of the warship stationed in Berlin; he diverted his ship to attempt to assassinate the usurper.

The two warships met over Kazakhstan and started blowing

each other apart. Luckily, this happened over the Kazakh Steppe, which is hardly populated. Because of the lack of eyes on the scene, reports out of the area are sketchy. We aren't sure if they destroyed each other, fought to a stalemate, or if one of them came out victorious. There's no bad result for us, though.

And, maybe best of all, the warship positioned over São Paulo simply left. It floated up, out of the atmosphere, and is apparently orbiting the moon. The ship has gone completely radio silent. No idea what's going on with that guy.

The rest of the Mog fleet ignored Adam, choosing to believe Phiri Dun-Ra. Still, the cracks were beginning to show. They weren't an unstoppable force. Three warships out of the fray, and we never left Patience Creek. Still twenty to go, but we're making progress.

Yet something about this victory feels hollow to me. It isn't satisfying. My hands are too clean.

With both Adam and me lost in thoughtful silence, Lawson continues to reflect on our success. 'A strategic risk,' he says thoughtfully. 'You boys would make fine generals one day.'

'I intend to do the rest of my fighting on the front lines,' I say, finally breaking my silence.

'Well, that's a young man's prerogative,' Lawson replies. He stands up and cracks his back. In the hours since we hijacked the Mogadorian discussion, things have calmed down. No new developments have come in for some time, just the usual status reports. I think our ploy has produced all the results it's going to.

Lawson looks down at me. 'It's late. Or rather, it is now very early. I'm going to get some shut-eye before we mount this operation. You should do the same, John.'

I give the general a lazy salute, and he replies with a thin smile. The old man nods curtly to Adam and exits, leaving the two of us alone. Adam sits slumped in front of the console, his eyes bleary.

'You planning to sleep at all?' I ask him.

'Are you?' he counters.

We settle in.

I cross my arms and let my chin rest against my chest. I get an occasional jolt from a snarling Mogadorian's voice coming over the comm, but Adam doesn't bother translating any of it, which means it can't be important. We're going to board one of those warships in just a few hours. It's going to be the first combat I've faced since I started collecting Legacies, my first chance to test out these new powers.

My first chance for some revenge.

I really should sleep. It's irresponsible of me to keep avoiding it. But the last time I tried, all that I could see was her face. . .

I can't keep doing this to myself.

I stand up and stretch my arms over my head. They feel heavy. Everything does. The air feels thick, almost like I'm swimming through it. Finally, that feeling of exhaustion I've been chasing after since we got here is beginning to set in.

'You'll come get me if anything major happens, right?' I ask Adam.

He doesn't reply. He keeps his face turned away, intently staring at the console. The Mogadorian communications have gone eerily silent. For some reason, instead of asking Adam what the hell is up, I say nothing and just step out of the room.

And into a cavern.

This isn't Patience Creek.

I've been here before.

I'm in a long, dimly lit corridor. The walls are rust-colored stone augmented with steel beams. The air is hot and musty and stinks like something rotten and alive. I do a quick 360 and try to orient myself. If I go down the hall in the direction where it gently slopes down, I know I'll reach the breeding area where piken, krauls, and any number of other twisted beasts are created. If I go uphill, towards where the lights are brighter, I'll eventually reach a row of cells.

This is West Virginia, under the mountain. The headquarters of the Mogadorians.

I feel pulled towards the cells, so I begin to walk slowly in that direction. Muffled screams reach me from up ahead. Even so, I keep my walking pace casual and relaxed.

I'm not stupid. This is a dream. And I'm happy to play along.

I know who's waiting for me up ahead, and I'm glad. I want to look him in the eyes.

I reach the area where an alcove in the cave has been filled with claustrophobic cells. Each reinforced door is equipped with a bulletproof glass porthole to spy on the dank conditions inside. The first few cells I pass are empty. Then I come across one where a dark-haired girl presses her face against the glass. Her eyes and mouth have been stitched permanently closed with wire.

It's Six.

I stare at her. I make a point to let my eyes linger, to let the terror and revulsion wash over me.

It isn't real. He's trying to mess with me, and it isn't going to work.

Another horrific vision greets me in the next cell. Nine, back when I first met him, except now there's a bedsheet tied around his neck, and he dangles from a rafter. I don't spend so much time staring at that one, mostly because I don't buy it for a second.

'Why don't you cut the shit and show yourself?' I say out loud, knowing he can hear me. 'This is getting boring.'

Up ahead, the screaming grows louder. I approach a room that I remember the Mogs set aside for interrogation. There's a window to watch through. In the middle of the chamber, a set of thick chains hangs from the ceiling.

Sam is wrapped in the chains. Those are his screams. A viscous black acid trickles down the metal links and burns fresh scars into his wrists.

Setrákus Ra stands in front of Sam, but not the way I'm used to seeing him. His head isn't pale and bulbous and black veined, he's not eight feet tall and he doesn't have that thick purple scar around his neck. This Setrákus Ra is a young man, like the guy I saw in the vision of Lorien's history. His dark hair is slicked back from a widow's peak, his features are sharp and stern and he looks distinctly Loric.

He's one of my people. The thought is still mind-boggling.

He acts like he hasn't noticed me, although I know that isn't true. After all, he brought me here. I stand outside the interrogation room and watch him. Setrákus Ra paces back and forth, and every time he crosses in front of the chains, momentarily blocking them from view, the person tangled up in his torture device changes.

Sam becomes Six, her screams filling the room.

Then Adam.

Marina.

Nine.

Sarah.

I punch through the glass that separates the hallway from the interrogation room. It shatters easily and doesn't hurt at all. I float over the waist-high wall and land a few strides away from Setrákus Ra. He turns to face me, smiling like we just bumped into each other on the street.

'Hello, John.'

I try to keep my gaze from drifting towards the vision of Sarah, tortured, unconscious, that hangs behind him.

She isn't real. She's not here. She's at peace.

I make a show of looking around the room and whistle through my teeth.

'You know, back in the day, these dreams used to spook me.'

'Did they?'

'Now I know it's just you casting about in desperation.'

Setrákus Ra smiles indulgently and crosses his arms. 'You remind me so much of him,' he says. 'My old friend Pittacus Lore.'

'I'm not like him.'

'No?'

'He showed you mercy. I'm going to kill you.'

Setrákus Ra circles around, putting Sarah's body between the two of us. He gives her a gentle shove, and she begins to swing back and forth.

'How is my great-granddaughter?' he asks, making small talk.

My eyes track Sarah, then flick back to Setrákus Ra.

'Much better than when she was stuck with you.'

'She'll come around,' he replies with a smile. 'When I'm done with the rest of you, she'll come back to me.'

'Will your army come back to you too?' I ask, tilting my head. 'While you lick your wounds and hide out in my dreams, they're abandoning you.'

His expression darkens, and I feel glad that I've struck a blow to his ego. He steps away from Sarah and towards me.

'The Mogadorians were always just a means to an end for me, John. A neutered species of beasts that made their own home world unlivable with their thick-headed love of war and pollution.' He spits on the floor. 'The humans will make for much better subjects once they're brought to heel. The others will be ashes on the wind.'

'Is this why you brought me here?' I ask, staring at this younger version of my most hated enemy. 'To drive home how evil you are? Because I get it.'

Setrákus Ra smiles, comes closer, studying me. His eyes aren't the pure inky black that I've seen before. They're dark but normal, not changed through years of experimentation. The sick mind behind them is still the same.

'I am old, John,' he intones. 'Those visions my great-granddaughter put us through, to see my youth again. . . I felt something like nostalgia. Once Pittacus Lore was my friend. If he had only listened to me, if we had worked together, we could have spared the universe so much death. We could have uplifted all life.'

'Aww — do you need a friend? Is that what this is? The part where you offer me a chance to join forces?'

Setrákus Ra sighs. We're only separated by a few feet now. I have to remind myself that it isn't real. That there's no point in reaching out and trying to rip him apart.

Even though I so badly want to.

'No, John. When I allowed you to live in New York, I promised that I would let you watch this world burn. I intend to keep my word.'

'Then what?'

'Like I said, you remind me of Pittacus,' Setrákus Ra responds. He drifts back towards Sarah, strokes a hand up her bluish arm and grabs hold of the chain supporting her body. 'I tried to show him, just like I will now show you. I wanted you to know what you're missing out on.'

Setrákus Ra yanks down hard on the chain. Impossibly, with a logic available only in nightmares, the entire ceiling collapses. The room is flooded with that viscous black ooze.

'I wanted you to feel my power.'

It's like a dam breaking. Within seconds, the interrogation room is completely lost to me, and I'm awash in the inky liquid. It's ice-cold and slimy against my skin. I try to swim against it, but it's quickly over my head, stinging my eyes, creeping into my lungs.

I panic and thrash. For a moment, I forget that this is only a dream.

There's a heaviness inside me now, like my guts are filled with thick sludge. My skin prickles. It feels like thousands of tiny mouths are trying to gnaw on me.

But I can breathe. I'm alive. The realization helps me to calm down.

I can see, even though there's nothing around me except for solid, impenetrable darkness. As I float through the oily slime, I look down at my hands and light up my Lumen. It works — light shines in a halo around me.

The effect only lasts for a moment. In my glowing hands I can see veins of cobalt-blue Loric energy running beneath the skin. The sludge painfully burrows into my fingertips, drawn to that energy, and begins to eat away at it.

'Doesn't it feel good?'

I look up. Setrákus Ra floats in the darkness above me. He's dropped the whole young-Setrákus thing and now looks like I expect: hideous. He's shirtless — maybe entirely naked, the ooze thankfully obscures his lower body — his skin startlingly pale in the darkness, the purple scar around his neck thick. His eyes, hollow and empty like a skull, bore into me.

There's an open wound on Setrákus Ra's chest. The gash is just to the left of his heart. That must be where Six hit him. She really was so damn close. Tendrils of the ooze lap at the broken skin, worm their way inside his body. The substance isn't healing the wound; it's filling it in, replacing the ghastly hole with a chunk of pure obsidian.

Another body floats in front of Setrákus Ra. It's a Mogadorian woman with dark hair drawn back in thick cornrows. I notice that she has burn scars all across her hands. She seems to be unconscious. Setrákus Ra waves his hands over her, and the slimy substance surrounding us all moves at his command, bur-rowing under her skin, reshaping her.

I open my mouth, and although the slime rushes down my throat, I find that I'm still able to speak.

'This is where you are, isn't it?' I say. 'This is real. Your great idea of progress, it's . . . this sewage bath.'

Setrákus Ra smiles at me. 'You resist. But here, John, here I control the fate of all our species. Here, I make Legacies. I take the mundane and shape it, augment it to my will.'

He holds up his hand, two fingers extend towards me, and my

arm raises in response completely out of my control. My Lumen glows, the ooze tendrils coalescing around my hand. It feels as if my skin's being peeled away.

A ball of Loric energy is ripped out of my hand. My Lumen grows dim as the energy floats through the sludge. It's slowly eaten away, transformed, until Setrákus guides it into the Mogadorian woman. Her body convulses for a moment, sending waves through the slime.

But then fire surrounds her. She turns her head and grins at me, her teeth bared like a wild animal.

'I am the creator now, John,' Setrákus Ra says. 'Come. See for yourself.'

My hands shake. My Lumen won't work. The darkness surrounds me. . .

'John! John!'

My eyes snap open. Adam's got me by the shoulders, shaking me. I'm back in the sub-sub-basement of Patience Creek, not drowning in black muck, not having my Legacies stolen by a Mogadorian.

'You fell asleep,' Adam says, eyes wide. 'And then, well . . .'

I glance down. My hands, which were resting on the arms of my chair, left blackened imprints in the fabric. My Lumen must have triggered while I was in that nightmare. The smell of burned fabric fills the room.

'Sorry . . .' I say, shakily standing up.

Adam hesitates, waiting for an explanation. 'You okay?' he finally asks.

'Yeah, I'm fine,' I say, slowly walking out of the room.

There'll be no more sleep for me. Not until this is over.

16

'I just need a little more time with it,' Sam says. 'I swear I can get it to work. I mean, it could already *be* working. I've got no way to test it. . .'

It's dawn. Sam paces in front of our bed, talking fast. I notice a pile of crushed soda cans on the desk behind him, all their logos very out-of-date. I guess stale soda still has a bunch of caffeine. I watch him patiently, a small smile on my lips.

'My dad tried to give me a crash course in electro-magnetism,' Sam continues. 'Frequencies, ultraviolet, uh, the ionosphere. Do you know what the iono-sphere is?'

I shake my head.

'Okay, me neither. I mean, I didn't know until my dad explained it, and now I only sort of know. The ionosphere is part of the atmosphere. It's like nature's force field. Radio waves bounce off it. If you want to understand how a force field would work outside of science fiction, you'd start there. Or at least you would've until aliens came to Earth and changed our understanding of, well, all kinds of shit. . .'

'You're getting off topic, Sam.'

I was already in bed last night when Sam came into the room. I'd listened drowsily as he com-plained about how Malcolm had made him go to bed – like he was a kid again and not trying to save the world. He tossed and turned next to me for a while. Eventually, he went over to work at the room's small desk. By work I mean insistently whisper a bunch of nonsense phrases to an assortment of handheld devices – the now-infamous Game Boy, an array of cell phones, tablets, an e-reader. Sam's quiet voice lulled me back to sleep.

'Sorry. So, some of the engineers working on the cloaking device tried to go into more detail about force fields – did you know the military already had a working prototype? It keeps stuff out, but you can't see through it, so you'd be shielded but blind. Anyway, I think they eventually started to feel like explaining all that was a waste of time since I'm technically a high school dropout.'

'They underestimate you at their peril,' I say with a sleepy smile.

Sam holds the Mogadorian cloaking device he uninstalled from our ship in one hand and an old flip phone in the other, hoisting them up and down like he's a scale.

'Are you making fun of me?'

'No. Keep going.'

'So, my dad and the science team, they've already figured out the basics of how this thing works,' Sam says, holding up the black box that allows Skimmers to pass unharmed through warship force fields. 'It emits an ultrasonic frequency that, according to the dudes downstairs, we'd be able to replicate no problem. What's slowing them up is that the sound wave is, uh, thickened somehow, I think they said, so that it can carry through a data packet to the warship. That data packet identifies the Skimmer as friendly.

Problem is, it's written in code that we don't under-stand, that we can't even create yet, in a programming language that none of our machines are coded to work with –'

'Sam,' I say, interrupting as soon as he takes a breath. 'I'm sure this is all very interesting but . . .'

'Ha, no it isn't,' Sam replies with a sheepish grin. He sets aside the cloaking device so he can rub the back of his neck. 'All right, cutting to the chase –'

'Please do.'

'All those guys downstairs, they're trying to copy this data packet thingy. But that's hard, because a. they don't have Mog technology to work with, and b. they'd still need to learn how to use that even if they did. So I was thinking – why not let the machines do the work for us?'

'Okay . . .' I say, waving my hand to speed him up.

Sam holds up the flip phone. 'I've been talking to this guy here.'

'Talking *to* it?'

'Well, *at* it – it doesn't talk back. Not like you do anyway.' He opens and closes the phone like a mouth. 'I've been telling it just to copy the cloaking device signal. The whole thing. Sound and data. I mean, we don't need to understand *how* this works, Six; we just need to rip it off.'

I take a closer look at the cell phone. 'Why'd you pick such a shitty phone?'

'The older stuff is easier for me to work with because it's less complex,' he says with a shrug. 'They're better listeners.'

'And you think it worked? That it listened to you?'

'I don't know,' Sam says. 'I can tell that it's emitting the frequency, but I can't tell if it copied the data packet, too. Not unless . . .'

'Unless you use it to pass through a force field.'

'Bingo,' Sam says, and tosses me the phone.

I catch it and turn it over in my hands. The plastic is hot to the touch, and it's only got about 83 per cent battery life.

'The battery drains fast when it's emitting the frequency, and it's doing that constantly once I give it the command,' Sam says. 'And when it shuts down, the phone forgets what I told it. Even with those limitations, I think it could make a difference.'

I nod my head, remembering how Lawson plans to coordinate a worldwide assault on the warships. Assuming all goes smoothly this morning and we manage to steal the cloaking devices from aboard the Niagara Falls warship, that's what? A few hundred cloaking devices? That means a few hundred missiles for the world's armies to bombard those huge warships with. How many hits would it take to bring down one of those colossal ships? Seems to me like they'd want as many shots as possible and then some.

I look behind Sam. He's got all his devices plugged into a few overloaded power strips. He's also got a fire extinguisher parked nearby, just in case.

Seeing where I'm looking, he says, 'If it's working, I've already taught those dozen things to speak cloaking device. I'm getting pretty good at it – I think. It feels like it's getting easier anyway. Although, I could be doing nothing and having, like, a Legacy placebo effect.' Sam sighs tiredly and waves this thought away. 'I'm going to use my Legacy on every mobile thing I can get my hands on until it's verified one way or the other.' He sighs. 'Or maybe I just wasted one of the last days of my life talking to a bunch of cell phones like a crazy person. No big deal.'

I leap off the bed and kiss Sam. 'No way. This is going to work.'

Sam returns my smile, holding my hand. 'Just be careful today, all right?'

'When am I not careful?'

Down in the hangar, a large space has been cleared, the military Humvees parallel parked impossibly close to the walls. They're arranged neatly, one right next to the other, so they can speed on out at a moment's notice, convoy-style. I can tell by the precision of the parking arrangement that it was either done by some really anal-retentive drivers or with telekinesis.

The new Garde – Nigel, Fleur, Bertrand, Ran and Daniela – are all lined up in this open space. They look sleepy, nervous, excited. Daniela gives me a little wave when she sees me watching. I smile at her.

Caleb and Christian stand apart from the others, closer to the handful of marines spectating than to their fellow Garde. As usual, Christian looks completely stone-faced. Caleb, on the other hand, appears more attentive than his brother.

'So, first lesson. You've all got telekinesis, right?'

Nine strolls across the line of new recruits, awaiting their answers. I cringe when I see what he's got in his hand. A semiautomatic pistol, likely borrowed, or maybe stolen, from one of the soldiers on the sideline. Nine twirls it around his index finger like he's a cowboy in an old Western movie.

The new recruits all nod in response. Except for Daniela, they look universally intimidated by Nine in drill sergeant mode. They've got reason to be since, as soon as they answer, Nine points his gun at them.

'Cool. So who wants to try stopping a bullet?'

'*Psh*, I will turn your ass to stone, you point that thing at me again,' Daniela says.

Nine smirks and makes sure to aim away from Daniela. If I really thought he was going to shoot at one of the new kids, I'd step in. He's not that stupid, though. I don't think.

Nigel glances down the line of his fellow Garde. When it's clear no one else is going to volunteer, Nigel steels himself and steps forward.

'All right, mate,' he says, tentatively holding out a hand in a 'stop' motion as Nine points the gun at him. 'I'll give it a whirl.'

Nine grins. 'That's brave of you, John Lennon –'

'John Lennon was a wanker.'

'Whatever that is,' Nine continues. 'I bet he had more common sense than your scrawny ass. Stopping bullets is some advanced-class shit that you're definitely not up for yet. And anyway, if you're fighting Mogadorians, which you can expect to be, those bastards use energy weapons. Can't turn energy away with telekinesis. So what's the smarter, safer, easier thing to do?'

'Disarm the enemy,' Caleb calls from the sideline.

Nine points at him with his gun-free hand. 'Very

good, weirdo twin number one.' He looks back at Nigel. 'Give it a try. Pull the gun out of my hand.'

Nigel scowls like he's annoyed at being lectured. All the same, he makes a grasping and jerking motion. Nine stumbles forward like his arm was tugged, but he maintains his grip on the gun.

'That's decent power,' Nine says. 'But you're pulling my whole arm. Focus on the weapon itself. Be precise. Someone else want to try?' Nine glances down the line. He squints at Ran, the small Japanese girl staring blankly at him. 'She understanding anything I'm saying?'

'She doesn't say much,' Fleur responds. 'But we think she understands.'

'Huh,' Nine says. He points the gun at Ran. The second he does, she whips her hand up, and the barrel of the gun crumples like paper, the trigger mechanism pinching closed on Nine's finger. He drops the weapon with a cry.

'Hell yeah,' I say.

Nine flashes me a pissed-off look, but I can tell it's all show. He's as impressed as I am. He looks back at the group and nods. 'That's another way to do it.'

There's a small commotion at the elevator as John, Marina and Adam enter. Ella and Lexa follow a few steps behind them, along with a bounding Bernie Kosar. Last comes Dust, back in wolf form, looking much healthier than when I last saw him. Everyone comes to stand by me except for Lexa, who goes off to get the ship fired up.

It's time to go.

Catching a look from John, Nine walks down the

line of human Garde, handing out unloaded weapons. 'Practise on each other,' he says. 'I'll be back later, and I expect your badass quotient increased by, like, tenfold.'

Daniela raises an eyebrow, looking past Nine to John and me. 'What're you guys doing? Leaving us here?'

John waves us over towards Lexa's ship, and the whole group of us – humans and Loric and reformed Mogadorian – gather at the base of the ramp. Even Caleb and Christian join the impromptu huddle.

'We're going to make a covert assault on one of the Mogadorian warships,' John says, his voice gravelly. He looks like he hasn't slept at all. 'Only myself, Six and Adam will actually be boarding the ship. The others coming along will be strictly backup in case things go bad.' He looks at the humans. 'You guys should stay here, hone your powers. We don't need you on this one. It's an unnecessary risk.'

Fleur and Bertrand look relieved. Daniela shakes her head and jabs a finger into John's chest.

'I saved your ass in New York,' she says, pointing her thumb at the other humans. 'And now what? I'm demoted to rookie with these losers?'

'You promised us action,' Nigel complains next.

John sighs. 'Look, we've been doing this a lot longer than you. It was stupid of me to ask you to throw yourselves into the fray without proper training. Right now, the best thing you can do to help the earth is get stronger, get better. Your time will come.'

Nigel glances down at Bernie Kosar. 'You're bringing a beagle along.'

'They also have a wolf,' Bertrand points out. 'May I ask why you have a wolf?'

'That little dog would have you shitting your knickers,' Nine says to Nigel.

'LANEs aren't authorized to go on this op anyway,' Caleb puts in.

'Oh, piss off, Captain America,' Nigel replies. 'I'm ready to fight.'

'Aw, kid,' Nine says. 'You aren't.'

'Look, here's what John's really saying,' I say, crossing my arms. 'In the event that we all get killed, which isn't totally out of the realm of possibility, it's going to be up to you guys to save the world. So, better if you're not there.'

'Nice, Six,' Marina murmurs, shaking her head.

Nine claps his hands. 'Let's do this.'

We leave the human Garde behind and board Lexa's ship. Minutes later, we're strapped in and rocketing out of the tunnel, taking the exact same course as yesterday.

Once we're in the air, John stands up.

'There's one thing I didn't bring up back there,' John says. 'I didn't want the military getting wind of it.'

Everyone stares curiously at John. 'What're you talking about?' I ask.

'We aren't just going to steal the cloaking devices,' John says. 'We're stealing the warship too.'

17

There's a platoon of canadian special Ops camped in a patch of woods three miles south of Niagara Falls. They're about fifty strong, built to move fast but also equipped with some serious firepower, including surface-to-air missiles. The warship we've come here to commandeer isn't visible from where they're stationed. They've made it a point to stay out of sight, for obvious reasons. However, they've got a few scouts skulking around Niagara Falls, broadcasting back grainy footage of the warship hovering, Skimmers combing the nearby wilderness, vatborn troops on the ground inspecting the dormant Loralite stone.

They feed us all this intel as soon as we land and otherwise don't interfere. I could get used to Canadian hospitality.

If things go bad on the warship, this small team of Special Ops will cover our retreat. Our survival, according to their commanding officer, is their only priority. They've been apprised of our 'strategic value'.

All this is thanks to General Lawson. I guess sometimes it isn't so bad to have the government in your corner.

In Lexa's ship, parked now alongside the Special Ops Humvees, I buckle an improvised vest across my chest. A cloaking device is hooked up to the front, plugged into a battery pack hastily stitched at the small of my back. This is what's going to get me on board that warship.

'You sure I can't come?' Nine asks me for the twentieth time.

'I can only carry two,' I reply. 'Six needs to come in case I screw up our invisibility, and Adam is obviously crucial to —'

'Flying your stolen warship,' Adam interjects with a shake of his head. I glance at him, catch him running a hand through his black hair. He looks skeptical. In fact, most of my friends have looked skeptical since I unveiled my plan to commandeer the warship. Adam continues on. 'You know, I've only flown a warship in a simulator. It's also not a one-person job. Not if you want weapons on line.'

'I have faith in you,' I reply. 'Worst-case scenario, we crash the thing into the falls. One less of them to worry about.'

'How many Mogadorians will be on that warship?' Marina asks, directing her question to Adam.

He gives me an uncertain look before answering. 'Probably thousands,' he says. 'To get control of the ship, we'll need to make it to the bridge.'

'And the bridge is where?' I ask Adam.

'Assuming we get in through the docking bay, it'll be at the opposite end of the ship.'

'Thousands,' Marina repeats.

'At least we're lucky that some are patrolling the surrounding area. Spreads them a little thinner,' Adam adds, although he sounds apprehensive.

'It's an *army*,' Marina says. She shakes her head. 'That's crazy, John. Stealing the cloaking devices from under their noses was one thing, but taking on this many alone . . .'

'We won't be alone.'

With the vest strapped securely to my chest, I open up a zippered pocket on the front. Immediately, Bernie Kosar shrinks down to the size of a mouse. With a glance at his fellow Chimæra, Dust does the same. We left the rest of the Chimærae at Patience Creek with instructions to watch over the human Garde. I crouch down and pick up both Chimærae, depositing them safely in my vest pocket. Marina raises an eyebrow at me.

'So you've gone from thousands-against-three to thousands-against-five,' Marina replies. She clears her throat. 'John, I know what you're feeling —'

173

I cut her off with a wave of my hand and meet her eyes. I know that the odds seem bad. I know that I've seemed cold the last couple of days and maybe a little crazy, and I'm sure the vibe I'm giving off hasn't gotten any better since the dark dream I shared with Setrákus Ra last night. I can tell from the way they're all looking at me that I'm coming off a little unhinged. But even if that's true, I know I can accomplish this. I can feel the power coursing through me.

One warship isn't enough to stop me.

'You have to believe in me,' I tell Marina, keeping my tone measured, hoping that she can feel my certainty, see it in my eyes. 'I know what I'm doing. I've got it under control.'

'Look,' Six says before Marina or Nine can register any more protests. 'Adam and I will focus on getting the cloaking devices off the Skimmers without being noticed. Like the plan was originally. And John will concentrate on holding off the Mogs. If he happens to kill a couple of thousand of them in the process, all the better. If not, we bail.'

Marina breathes out through her nose. 'How will we know if you're in trouble?'

Ella raises her hand. She hasn't said much since yesterday, and I'm glad for that. The last time we talked, it was a bit too much to take in. The glowing spark in her eyes is a little dimmer than it was yesterday.

'I'll check on them telepathically,' Ella says.

'And if we're in trouble, you'll hear me calling,' I add.

'Oh,' Marina says, her head tilted. 'You can do that now.'

Lexa leans against the cockpit door, listening to everything we've said without comment. 'I've got a second cloaking device installed on our ship,' she says. 'We'll bypass the force field no problem, but you'll need to leave a door open for us.'

'It won't be necessary,' I tell her.

Six snorts. 'We'll leave you an opening, Lexa.' She flashes me a meaningful look. 'Better safe than stupid.'

'And bring some of the Canadians along,' Adam adds. He glances at me. 'You know, if we do hit a snag.'

I double-check that everything is secured to my vest and that the cloaking device is active, then take one last look at the others. 'We good?'

When no one replies immediately, I head down the metal ramp, off Lexa's ship and into the misty morning air. There's a squad of soldiers standing nearby, waiting to see if we'll need them for anything, the rest of their unit forming a loose and stealthy perimeter in the trees. It's still strange to me, being constantly surrounded by armed men and women who are expecting me to command them. Or save them. I take a deep breath and tilt my head back, looking up at the gray sky and the pointy tops of the pine trees.

'You sure you know what you're doing?'

That's Six, next to me, her voice pitched low so the others won't hear. Adam trails a few yards behind her, still on the ramp.

'I have to do this,' I tell her, my voice quiet as well. 'I need to know what I'm capable of.'

'You know it sounds a little suicidal, right?'

'I'm far from suicidal,' I reply grimly.

'Just remember, you aren't doing this by yourself,' Six replies, and pats me on the shoulder. 'I know the feeling of wanting to throw yourself at the enemy until they break or you break but –'

As she speaks, a memory flashes to the surface of Six's mind with a force that's impossible for me to ignore. I'm still trying to master this whole telepathy thing. The most difficult part about it is letting the thoughts of others stay private. They just come rushing into my mind, unwanted, like this vision of Six standing in front of a gaping hole in the ground, wind swirling all around her, metal and rock debris tearing through the air. Across the gap from her is Setrákus Ra, fleeing and on his heels, pushing against her with his own telekinesis. And next to her . . .

Next to her is Sarah. She pulls at Six's arm, tries to get her to retreat from the whirlwind of shrapnel around them.

Mexico.

I flinch at the memory – all this floods into my brain in less than a second – and Six stops talking to look at me funny.

'You okay?'

'I'm fine,' I reply, and brace myself telepathically, close off my mind. I need more practice with a lot of these powers, but there's no time for that.

Six frowns at me but doesn't press. She reaches into her pocket and produces an old-looking flip phone that she pops open to check the display. 'What's that?' I ask, wanting to change the subject.

'Sam's attempt to mimic the cloaking device,' Six replies, holding up the phone. 'He wants me to try it out before the battery dies.'

I didn't realize Sam had made progress with that. The phone doesn't look like much, but Sam's never let me down before. I touch the Mogadorian cloaking device hooked to my vest. 'Should we use that instead of this?'

'Uh, let's not experiment while we're flying through the air,' Adam says, joining us. 'If all goes well, we'll have plenty of opportunities to test Sam's device.'

Six nods in agreement and puts the phone away. I look between the two of them. 'Ready?'

'Ready,' Adam replies.

Six eyes us. 'How exactly are we doing this?'

It takes a little work to get us arranged. Six gets on my back in a piggyback position, her legs hooked around my waist. I hug Adam from behind, my hands locked across his chest. From there, Six is able to reach past me and put a hand on Adam's shoulder, in case she needs to take over and make us invisible. I feel BK and Dust squirming around in my chest pocket trying to get comfortable. We must look pretty ridiculous; I can see some faint smiles and raised eyebrows on the faces of the nearby Special Ops, and I'm pretty sure I hear Nine catcall us from Lexa's ship.

The embarrassment is only temporary because we quickly turn invisible.

'Are you doing that or am I?' Six asks.

'Better that we both do it,' I tell her. 'I've only had the Legacy for a few days I could make a mistake.'

'Oh, that's heartening,' Adam says.

'Don't worry,' I tell him. 'It's really only flying that I'm still a little shaky with.'

'But we're about to —'

Before Adam can finish that thought, I launch us up in the air. It's not the most graceful takeoff. It's a lot more forceful than necessary; but it does the trick; and soon we're soaring above the treetops at high velocity. I remember what Five taught me — basically not to think too hard about what I'm doing and trust my instincts. That means going fast and forward. Adam's hands grab my forearms hard, and I can hear Six laughing against my ear as the wind whips across our faces.

'This is so weird,' she says. 'I feel like a ghost.'

'Let's hope not literally,' Adam yells back.

It's definitely strange: being invisible, flying through the sky, like we're the breeze itself. I wish I had more time, or maybe the capacity, to appreciate this. All I can think about is what's ahead, and soon that comes into view.

The steel-gray bulk of the scarab-shaped warship looms over Niagara Falls, casting a dark shadow on the rushing water. This warship isn't as big as the *Anubis*. But it is still a frightening sight to behold.

'There's the Loralite stone,' Six says. 'That, uh, nondescript gray one down there.'

I glance to a patch of wilderness level with the start of the falls. I can't pick out the stone from this height, but I can easily make out the crowd of Mogadorians securing the area. I can also see the three downed Skimmers that were taken out by the human Garde. More of the little ships zip through the air around the warship, patrolling the nearby woods in slow circles. I fly us closer to the warship while looking down.

'John,' Adam says as I survey the Mog patrols. 'John!'

I look up just as I first hear the vibrating hum of a Skimmer's engine. It's practically right on top of us, the scout ship headed back to the warship. The pilot can't see us, but he's flying dangerously close all the same. I bank us hard to the right and narrowly avoid getting clipped by one of the Skimmer's slender wings.

'Shit!' Six yells. Her nails scratch my neck as she almost loses her grip.

We do a barrel roll. The spinning disorients me, and for a moment we're plummeting towards the rapids below. My fingers loosen, and Adam slips a few inches away from me. I grasp him hard under the armpits.

Gritting my teeth, I stabilize us and get myself flying straight again. Everyone's holding on a little tighter now.

'Sorry,' I say.

'I take back any misgivings I had with your plan,' Adam says breathlessly. 'If it means never flying with you again, I'll steal a dozen warships.'

The Skimmer that shook us up leisurely flies into the docking bay of the warship, the doors left open behind it. Despite the scare, that's perfect timing. I pick up speed, intending to get us through those doors.

As we near the warship, the force field finally becomes visible. You can't really see it until you're rushing right towards it. Once you're within a hundred yards or so, the air around the warship seems to bend like heat lines rising from pavement on a hot day. I can make out a faint gridwork of energy, like a net surrounding the warship, which gives off a faint red hue. It reminds me of the aura that surrounded the mountain base in West Virginia, the one that made me sick for days after I ran headlong into it.

'We're sure this cloaking device is going to work, right?' I ask, too late, as there's no way I've got the flying skill to put the brakes on now.

'Ninety-nine per cent sure,' Adam replies.

We hit the force field.

And pass through it.

There's a faint buzzing in my ears and an electric vibration in my teeth as we go through the field, but otherwise we're fine. I glide us forward, slowing my speed so I don't crash when we enter the Mogadorian docking bay; and seconds later we're inside the warship, right as the Skimmer we followed touches down for a landing.

I keep us hovering for a moment so I can get the run of things. Even though Ella walked me through the *Anubis*, I've never actually been inside one of these ships. The docking bay is a huge, high-ceilinged area, with dozens of Skimmers arranged in neat rows. It seems they've only got a quarter of their fleet out searching Niagara Falls, and that's a good thing for us since we need those ships stationary if we're going to dismantle them. Besides the Skimmers, there's not much going on here, just a lot of repair machinery, a few blaster racks and some fuel tanks.

And about fifty Mogadorians, hard at work at various tasks, including the small crew of the Skimmer we followed in here. They get out of their ship and begin refueling.

Slowly, I set us down on the deck. Adam's sneakers squeak when they touch the metal floor, and he nearly loses his balance.

None of the Mogs notice.

Six, do you have Adam? I ask telepathically.

I feel Six's arm tense on my shoulders as I speak in her mind. She shifts position, presumably so she can get a better grip on the Mogadorian, which isn't exactly easy since none of us can see each other.

Got him, she thinks back after a moment.

I let go of both of them, now maintaining only my own invisibility.

I'm going to clear the room.

Do you need he–? Six thinks back, but I close off the telepathy before any more thoughts get through.

I don't need help.

Carefully, I roll up the sleeve of my shirt. There was something I didn't want the others to see me using, afraid of the bad feelings it might bring up. In truth, I'm kind of glad I don't have to see it myself, still invisible as I am. It might make me wonder what I've become.

Shink.

I deploy Five's forearm blade. We took it off him in New York, and I claimed it from Nine's things this morning. It's the perfect lethal tool for a job like this. Needle sharp and quiet.

I float across the hangar so that I don't make any noise. There's a panel on one side of the room with an intercom and some video screens. Communications. There are two Mogs sitting there as I approach, watching live feeds sent in from the Skimmers patrolling the falls.

I drive Five's blade into the base of their skulls, one after the other, so quick that neither of them even notices the other's been dusted.

I turn around. None of the Mogadorian mechanics or pilots have noticed.

I won't let any of them get by me. I won't let any of them call for help.

Methodically, I start to work my way through the hangar. I pick off the stragglers first, the ones who are isolated. I can float right up to them, right in front of their hideous faces, and the blade goes in easy. None of them even get a scream out. At a certain point, maybe after the tenth or the twentieth, my mind goes on autopilot. It starts to feel like I'm not even the one doing this. It's just happening in front of me.

I'm a ghost. A vengeful ghost.

It's quick the way I kill. Merciful. A better death than these bastards gave the people of New York or any of the millions of others they've murdered.

Sarah.

After a few minutes, one of the Mogs shouts out a warning. It was bound to happen eventually with all the dust floating through the air, with their numbers being thinned by half. They start to search around frantically. One of them screams something in Mogadorian and falls to his knees, looking hysterical. A couple of others follow suit. I'm not sure what to make of that. Most of them make a run for the racks of blasters or for the unmanned communications array.

Blaster fire sizzles through the air from the direction of the comm panel. Blaster fire from blasters that I can't even see. Looks like Six and Adam helped themselves, then doubled back to make sure the Mogs were cut off. Smart.

Guess I did need a little help.

It doesn't take long for the hangar to be cleared. Unprepared and fighting against invisible opponents where they thought they'd be safe, the Mogs don't have a chance.

When the last Mog is just a grainy film on the windshield of one of the Skimmers, I turn visible. Six and Adam quickly follow suit, both of them now holding blasters. Adam stares at me, eyes wide, maybe a little overwhelmed by the slaughter.

'Shit, John,' Six says, raising an eyebrow at my choice of

weaponry. 'That was pretty intense.' Six jogs over to the double doors that separate the hangar from the rest of the ship and checks to see if there are re-inforcements waiting. We cut off the Mogs before they could raise an alarm, but someone passing by could've heard the blasters. She flashes me a thumbs-up. 'All good.' I catch Adam's eye and point to the spot where the Mog fell on to his knees. 'The one who panicked. What was he saying?'

Adam swallows hard. 'He said that Setrákus Ra has truly abandoned them. That their lives are ending now that Beloved Leader is dead.'

'So some of them actually believed that,' Six says.

'Oh yeah,' Adam replies. 'Especially once John started going all wrath-of-god.'

'They haven't seen anything yet,' I reply.

I open the pocket on my vest and finally let Bernie Kosar and Dust loose. They transform into their beagle and wolf forms and seem glad to be out of captivity. Dust starts to sniff around the floor, eventually making his way to the exit with Six. BK sits down next to me and licks my fingertips. If a dog could look concerned, he does. I ignore him.

'Okay, how long before they notice we just took out their whole grease monkey division?' Six asks, walking closer now that Dust is watching the doors.

Adam shrugs. 'Depends when the next patrol's supposed to go out.'

'Don't worry,' I say, striding towards the double doors. 'You focus on getting those cloaking devices detached. I'll see to the rest of the ship.'

'Be careful,' Six says.

And then I'm through the doors, BK and Dust on my heels. The short hallway outside the hangar is empty, so I take a moment to crouch down and speak to the Chimærae.

Watch my back, I tell them. *I can do this as long as none of them get behind me, take me by surprise. And we don't want any of them getting through to Adam and Six.*

As I speak, both Chimærae transform into more imposing creatures. They're both still doglike, but they're thickly muscled and razor clawed, with durable, leathery skin and wicked fangs. The only way I can tell them apart is from the streak of gray fur that runs down Dust's spine.

'Good look, boys,' I say, and stand up and start deeper into the warship.

There's an airlock on the next door that requires some strength to turn. Through that, the hallway opens up, red lit and austere, with doors branching off on either side of me. There's a pair of Mogadorians walking right towards me, the two of them studying a digital map of Niagara Falls.

I fly forward, stab the first one through the eye and grab the other one around the throat.

'Which way is the bridge?' I ask him.

He points straight ahead. I snap his neck.

I don't want any of these bastards getting behind me, so I take each room one by one. I'll save the bridge for last.

The first area I step into looks like a barracks. The walls are honeycombed, with narrow pill-shaped beds. The vatborn basic- ally sleep right on top of each other. There are hundreds of Mogs here now, at rest, many of them hooked into intravenous lines of that black ooze Setrákus Ra loves so much, augmenting them- selves while they doze. I suppose they sleep in shifts, resting up for the next assault.

Today, their alarm clock is a fireball.

I hold out both my hands and let as much fire rush out from my fingertips as I can manage. I let loose until my clothes actu- ally begin to smoke. Soon, there's a wall of fire crackling out from me, roaring into the room. I smell burned plastic and a rotten roasting smell that I know is that black ooze boiling.

The fire begins to spread beyond my control. It occurs to me that I don't want to do any irreparable damage to the ship. As soon as that thought crosses my mind, the sensation in my hands changes. I go from pouring fire into the room to spraying the charred space with crystals of ice and frost.

One of Marina's Legacies. Hadn't even realized I picked that one up. It works so similarly to my Lumen, it's just like throwing a car into reverse.

What Mogs managed to escape their bunks and avoid getting torched are soon picked off by a volley of icicles.

Rampaging through the barracks gets their attention. As I exit, a small squad of warriors rushes down the hall towards me. BK and Dust dispatch them quickly, pouncing out from adjacent rooms just as the Mogs draw near.

The Mogs aren't prepared for this, I realize. They're not prepared at all.

Now they know how it feels.

I turn invisible before stepping through the next set of doors. Immediately, I'm greeted by a robotic voice alternating between English and Mogadorian. 'Surrender or die,' says the voice. 'Put down your weapons.' 'Beloved Leader.'

It's a language course, I realize. The Mogs are drilling their English skills. And that's not all. . .

Deeper into this room, I spot a firing range. People-shaped targets scream and run against an ever-changing backdrop of famous Earth cities: New York, Paris, London. There's a digital readout for the shooter's score, which currently sits at zero on account of the program being abandoned.

The Mogs training here – they heard me coming. They've quit their tasks and formed two groups on either side of the doorway, blasters at the ready. If I had walked in here, they'd have lit me up.

Too bad. I'm a different kind of target.

I quietly step into the middle of the room and turn visible. The Mogs yell — surprised — and open fire. Quickly, I turn invisible again and fly up, over their blaster fire. They end up shredding each other in the crossfire.

The survivors I finish off while floating over them. Stabbing down with Five's blade, blasting them with fire and ice at close range, turning others to stone with a glance.

A few of them try to book it out of the room. BK and Dust wait outside, greeting them with claws and gnashing teeth.

At some point while I'm clearing out the training room, a shrieking alarm begins to go off. It echoes through the entire ship and is accompanied by a rhythmic flashing of the dull red lighting that runs across the walls and ceilings.

No more element of surprise. Now they know I'm coming.

When I start making my way towards the bridge, the passageway is conspicuously empty of enemies. Prowling a few steps behind me, both BK and Dust let out growls of warning. The Mogs have almost surely fallen back into a defensive position, a choke point, where they can throw all their firepower at me.

Well, let's see what they've got.

Two high double doors stand in front of me. Beyond them is the bridge. The alarm continues to blare; the lights continue to flash.

When I get within twenty feet of them, the doors open with a hydraulic whoosh.

Through the doors is a wide staircase that leads up. Above the staircase, I can just barely glimpse the domed windows of the bridge's navigation area, the blue sky of Canada visible. The ship is controlled from here. Surely, the trueborn commander is up there somewhere.

On the stairs, between me and my goal, are about two hundred Mogadorians. The first row on their stomachs, the next row on one knee, the next row standing, the row behind them on the first step, and on and on, filling the entire staircase. Each of them holds a blaster pointed in my direction.

Once upon a time, this would have terrified me.

'Come on!' I scream at them.

The hallway crackles with energy as hundreds of blasters are fired off at once.

18

'You think he's all right?' Adam asks.

I take my eyes off the door leading out of the hangar for a moment to shoot Adam a look. He doesn't notice on account of his face being buried in a tangle of wires and cords. He's lying on his back beneath the ripped-open dashboard of a Skimmer. His hands work quickly to disconnect the cloaking device.

'John's still alive, if that's what you mean,' I reply. So far, a new scar hasn't burned its way across my ankle.

Adam sits up. I stand nearby, hunkered low, the cockpit of this latest Skimmer popped open. I'm carrying a Mog blaster and have my aim leveled on the door, just in case any Mogs should manage to get by John and interrupt what we're doing. So far, it's been quiet.

'That's not what I mean, and you know it,' Adam replies.

'You mean psychologically,' I say.

'Yeah.'

We climb out of this Skimmer and move on to the next one. I place the detached cloaking device inside a toolbox that we emptied out, stacked next to the others that we've filled.

'I think he's doing about as well as any of us,' I say. 'I mean, what do you expect?'

'I don't know,' Adam admits. 'But he scares me a little bit.'

I don't respond to that. I'd be lying if I said the changes that have been taking place in John lately weren't a little frightening. He's still the same guy I've known, relied on, loved – just, with an edge. With power. And a hunger for revenge.

Maybe that's exactly what we need right now.

An alarm begins to whine, and the lights in the docking bay flash off and on. Adam snaps free another cloaking device before looking up at me with raised eyebrows.

'I take it that's a bad sign,' I say.

Adam shrugs. 'It's the high alert. For intruders or attacks.'

'So they know we're here.'

'They were always going to find out eventually, right? If John's going at the same rate he did down here, that alarm's about twenty minutes too late to do any good.'

We move on to the next Skimmer, my grip now a little tighter on the blaster handle. Before we climb aboard, something catches my attention. A buzzing from the docking bay's communications array. I touch Adam on the shoulder.

'What is that?'

He cocks his head to listen but can't hear over the alarm. We jog over to the control panel in time to hear a brusque voice barking in Mogadorian. Adam immediately looks towards the wide-open entrance of the docking bay, the one we came through, blue sky and crisp air out there.

'The Skimmers on patrol detected the alarm; they're asking for confirmation.'

As Adam says this, a couple of the small scout ships come into view, gliding towards the landing zone.

'Great,' I say. 'Get ready for a fight.'

'Not necessarily,' Adam replies. His fingers hover, poised over a red button on the control panel.

The two ships zoom closer. I put my hand on the back of Adam's neck, ready to make us invisible at a moment's notice. But just as the Skimmers are about to reach the docking bay, Adam hits the button. Two heavy blast doors snap closed like steel jaws right in front of the Skimmers, sealing off the landing zone. The Skimmers never have a chance to change course. There's a jolt as both ships slam into the side of the much larger warship. Adam and I rock back and forth from the force. I can hear the ships explode on impact, and a thin tongue of fire manages to slip in between the thick blast doors.

'That should keep them out for a while,' Adam says. He throws a few more switches on the control panel to lock the blast doors in place.

'Nicely done,' I say. 'Now we only have to worry about the couple of thousand Mogs we're trapped in here with.'

As if on cue, the ship-side door to the docking bay swings open. I immediately turn my blaster in that direction, finger half depressing the trigger.

'Easy, it's just me,' John says.

John strides into the room, BK and Dust right on his heels looking monstrous. The two Chimærae stand guard at the door, teeth bared, ready in case any Mogs followed John through the ship. John's breathing pretty heavily, and he's literally smoking. His shirt has caught on fire in places, and there are blaster burns on his shoulders, arms, chest and legs. He doesn't even seem to notice. Adam and I exchange a look.

'John, are you –?' I shake my head, feeling like it's moronic to ask if he's okay. 'You're hurt.'

John pauses in front of the rack of Mogadorian weaponry. He looks down at himself, like he hadn't even noticed.

'Oh yeah,' he says. He starts running his hands over the wounds he can see on his arms, using his healing Legacy to mend them, then pauses. He squints for a moment, and the injuries across his body all simultaneously begin to close.

'Whoa, that's new,' I say.

'Yeah,' John replies, looking a little surprised himself. There's a distance in his eyes, like he's still coming down from the adrenaline of the battle. 'Everything seems . . . easier since I began really using my Ximic.'

Adam creeps over to the door to check the hallway. He makes a point of scratching behind Dust's ears when he does, which makes a sandpaper noise thanks to Dust's bestial form. Dust's massive tail thumps on the metal floor.

'Easier,' Adam repeats, noting John's condition. 'Did you . . . did you already kill them all?'

John crouches down in front of the weapons rack. He shoves aside blasters and battery packs, searching for something.

'No. There are a lot of them,' he says simply. 'I'm regrouping. So are they. They won't survive another round.'

'What're you looking for?' I ask.

'Grenades or anything explosive,' he says. 'Something I can throw at them.'

'There's some fuel cans there,' I point out.

John looks over at the tanks used to refill the Skimmers. He hoists one with his telekinesis. 'That's perfect. I think.' He glances at Adam. 'The ship can sustain one of these exploding, right?'

Adam purses his lips. 'Probably. I wouldn't want to fly it into outer space afterwards, but it should handle Earth's atmosphere fine.'

'Great,' John replies. He looks over at the box filled with cloaking devices. 'You guys doing good?'

'Almost finished,' I say.

Just then Dust lets out a low growl, and Adam ducks out of the doorway. BK arches his back and gets low, ready to pounce. From where I'm standing, I can hear the airlock door just outside the docking bay open.

'Got some coming in,' Adam whispers.

"They think I'm hurt,' John says, and rolls his eyes. 'Figured they'd send a few to get the drop on me.'

John strides right into the doorway and, a second later when it opens, unleashes a beam of rippling silver energy from his eyes. I run to his side in time to see a dozen or so Mogs with blasters, all of them now turned to stone, crowding the hallway outside the door. John raises his hand, and the air gets cold. A barrage of railroad-spike-sized icicles fly from his palm, disintegrating the stone Mogadorians.

'You learned that one too, huh?'

'Some Legacies are clicking into place easier than others.'

With the Mogs dispatched, John turns to me. It's like he just swatted a fly.

'I'm about to take the bridge,' he says. 'I could use your help.'

Moments later, we're following John through the segmented halls of the warship. It looks like a war zone in here. I have to cover my mouth and nose with the crook of my arm on account of how much Mogadorian ash is in the air, not to mention the acrid black smoke that pours from one section where it looks like an inferno erupted.

'You did all this?' I ask.

John nods. He brought one of the fuel tanks with him, carrying it along with his telekinesis.

'What do you need that for?' I ask, nodding to the tank. 'Seems like your Lumen was working pretty well.'

He flexes his hands in answer. I notice that his skin is bright pink, like he just soaked his hands in hot water. Apparently, that didn't heal with the rest of his wounds.

'Might have overdone it with the fire,' John says thoughtfully. 'Fried some nerve endings or something.'

'So I guess you still have some limits.'

'Apparently.' John frowns at the thought. 'Anyway, there's a bunch of them barricaded in front of the bridge. It's a bottleneck. I went toe-to-toe with them for as long as I could. Decided I needed to get creative.'

'Kill smarter, not harder,' I say dryly.

It's just a short walk through more debris and carnage to the hallway that leads to the bridge. John stops us short with a raised hand, not letting us go around the corner.

'Figure they're shooting anything that moves at this point,' John says.

'Logical strategy,' Adam replies.

John turns his gaze towards the fuel tank, and the air in the passageway gets cold. Slowly, a shell of ice begins to form around the metallic keg until the canister isn't even visible anymore. When the frozen wrecking ball is complete, John forms sharp icicles across its surface. Some of these crack and break off, and John has to redo the work.

'I haven't exactly mastered this,' he says while Adam and I look on.

'You're doing fine,' I reply. 'Shit. Better than fine.'

After a few minutes' work, John has a spiked boulder of ice with a fuel core.

'You're going to chuck that at them,' I observe.

John nods. 'You want to help me out? Could use the extra telekinetic force.' When I nod, John turns towards Adam and the Chimærae. 'This probably won't get them all, but it should shake them up. When you hear the explosion, come in hot.'

'You got it,' Adam responds, arming a blaster he picked up in the docking bay.

John takes my hand, then floats the ice-covered fuel tank in front of us so we can both rest a hand on it. We turn invisible, disappearing the tank along with us, and edge around the corner. My hand starts to get numb, but the temperature doesn't seem to bother John.

There are blaster burns all over the walls from John's earlier skirmish with this entrenched bunch of Mogs. At the end of the hallway, over a hundred vat-born are crowded up and down a short staircase shoulder to shoulder. The air in between us and them is hazy with particles. Their blasters are leveled, ready to fire, but all they see is empty hallway.

That changes when John and I send the ice ball speeding towards them. It turns visible as soon as it leaves our touch and must look like a boulder appearing from thin air. We shoved it into the Mogs, crushing the first of them. Then we swipe it from side to side, impaling a bunch more on the spikes.

The Mogs recover from the surprise quickly and begin firing at our icy weapon. They blow off the spikes and begin chipping away at it. Some of them start to look confident.

But then one of them shoots into the center and detonates the fuel tank.

The resulting explosion knocks me off my feet. John falls to the side, banging his shoulder against the wall, but keeps his balance. My ears ring. The hallway is filled with choking black smoke, at least until I conjure up some wind to blow that bad air towards the Mogadorian bridge. As Adam helps me to my feet, I see BK and Dust charge down the hall, pouncing on the few stragglers that survived the explosion.

'That worked better than expected,' Adam says.

'*Ow*. No shit,' I reply.

From the bridge, we can hear shouts in Mogadorian. These aren't battle cries. These are screams of desperation, and they're being responded to by a cold female voice that I'd recognize anywhere.

194

Phiri Dun-Ra. Someone, probably the ship's captain, has Phiri Dun-Ra on the communicator.

'What're they saying?' John asks Adam as we gather ourselves and march towards the bridge.

Adam strains to listen. Small fires, piles of ash and chunks of rapidly melting ice litter the staircase. We ascend cautiously.

'The commander, he's reporting that his ship is under attack. He's begging for reinforcements. He wants to speak with Beloved Leader,' Adam translates.

'Are reinforcements coming?' John asks.

Adam shakes his head. 'She's blaming the commander. Telling him he shouldn't have left his posting in Chicago. Says this is punishment for his lack of faith, that he's not worthy of command.'

I snort. 'Give us a little credit, Phiri. Come on.'

We stride on to the bridge like we own this warship because, frankly, we do. There's a domed-glass ceiling that sweeps down to the floor, so we can see a wide vista of Niagara Falls. There are a dozen little stations with attached chairs, each of these occupied by a Mogadorian tasked with flying the warship rather than fighting. The commander, dressed in a severe black-and-red uniform that's covered in more ornaments than anyone else, stands in front of a holographic display that's currently broadcasting an image of Phiri Dun-Ra's ugly face. She actually sees us enter the room before any of the other Mogs and, without another word to the commander, cuts off her signal.

'Guess she didn't want to chat,' I say.

Most of the Mogs immediately leap away from their stations and bring blasters to bear on us. I rip the guns out of their hands with my telekinesis, and John impales each of them with a javelin of ice. These are trueborn Mogs, not the endless vatborn, and so they don't disintegrate quite so quickly as the others. In fact, some of them only melt away partially, leaving behind half-formed corpses.

The commander, wild-eyed, in a gesture that he must know is futile, draws a sword like the one Adam's father used to carry around and screams at us.

'You'll never take my ship –'

Before he can even finish his sentence, a burst of Mogadorian blaster fire takes the commander's head off. We all spin towards a young Mog holding a blaster, his face a mixture of relief and resignation. John raises his hand to dispatch this last-surviving trueborn with an icicle.

'No!' Adam shouts, and stomps on the floor.

A seismic wave causes the entire warship to lurch, and the floor where Adam slammed his foot down crumples like tinfoil. John is actually knocked off his feet, but only for a moment. He uses his flight Legacy to float upright, looking bewildered as he stares at Adam.

'Don't – don't kill him,' Adam says.

The Mog in question, probably about our age and well built, his dark hair cut short, tosses aside his blaster and falls to his knees in front of us.

'My name is Rexicus Saturnus,' the Mog says, although I've got a feeling Adam already knows this. 'And I am at your mercy.'

19

The guy goes by Rex for short.

It turns out this is the second time Adam saved his life. The first was after an explosion at Dulce Base. Adam nursed Rex back to health after that, and the two traveled together for a while. Rex eventually helped Adam gain access to the Mogs' Plum Island facility, which is where they were experimenting on our Chimærae. He even helped Adam escape once the Chimærae were freed. Rex justified this as paying his debt to Adam rather than betraying his fellow Mogs, even though it was both.

'Do you think we can trust him?' Nine asks me.

'Adam does,' I reply. 'They spent weeks together. Adam nursed him back to health.'

'Yeah, but . . .' Nine lowers his voice. 'Like it or not, he's one of them.'

We stand on the bridge of the warship, cleared now of everyone but our people. We're flying the warship slowly up the Niagara River, looking for a safe place to land so that we can pick up the squadron of Canadian Special Ops. Lexa flew Nine and the others up here once the sky was cleared of straggling Skimmers and the Mogadorian ground troops were eliminated.

The warship took care of them all without even unloading the full power of its energy cannons. Adam and Rex handled the weapons, working together.

'He killed his commanding officer,' I tell Nine. 'He helped us finish off the Mogs outside the warship.'

'Desperation,' Nine responds. 'Dude would've done anything to save his own ass. You know those trueborn ones don't give a shit about the vatborn. He'd probably blow up a million of them if it meant he could keep breathing.'

'Maybe.'

Nine and I stand on the commander's perch overlooking the various stations down below. From here, we can watch Adam and Rex pilot the ship and talk between them without being overheard. Six and Marina are down below with the two Mogs, looking over the controls and talking with Adam.

'You don't think they're capable of change?' I ask Nine. 'Adam changed.'

'Yeah, but I always thought that was because he banged Number One or something.'

I give him a tired look.

'What?' he replies.

I shake my head. 'Anyway, Rex is only one Mog. Even if he wanted to betray us, what do you think he could really do?'

What I leave unspoken is that I've just killed an entire ship's worth of Mogadorians. One left alive isn't going to stop what I've got planned. As for my question about Mogadorians learning to change, I'm not sure I want to know the answer to that myself. It's easier if I imagine them as vicious enemies that would never listen to reason, that are incapable of knowing justice or mercy. But the more I get to know Adam and now Rex, the more I see of Mogadorians like that one who died thinking his 'god' Setrákus Ra had abandoned him, the more I wonder if they haven't just been completely brainwashed as a people. Given time, could they change? I'm not going to stop fighting and ask the invaders if they'd like to be rehabilitated. It's too late for that. But I wonder what will happen once I cut off the head of their twisted society – once I kill Setrákus Ra.

I intend to find out soon.

'He doesn't have any bad intentions.'

Nine visibly jumps, and my shoulders tighten as Ella creeps up behind us. She smiles a bit, and for a moment I wonder if she's having some fun with how spooky she's been lately. Her eyes spark with Loric energy as she scans the two of us.

'Goddamn, Ella,' Nine says, catching his breath. 'Did you read his mind or something?'

'Yes,' she responds. 'He has harbored doubts about the morality of his people ever since he first encountered Adam. He's been too frightened to act on them until you gave him an opportunity, John.'

'Well, that'd make me sleep easier if I planned to sleep anywhere on this gross-ass ship,' Nine says, already losing interest. 'Maybe we should just have Adam talk all nice to the rest of the Mogs, huh? Go all social worker on 'em.'

Ignoring Nine, I turn to Ella. 'The Loralite stone near the falls that you turned off. Can you reactivate it?'

'Yes,' she replies.

'Then let's go.'

'Okay, bye,' Nine says, frowning as we exit.

I lead Ella through the empty halls of the warship. The traces of my battle with the ship's crew are everywhere: burns, debris, damaged panels. The two of us don't say anything until we're almost at the docking bay. Ella finally breaks the silence.

'You're mad at me.'

I run a hand through my hair, find it sticky and matted with sweat. 'I . . . no. Yes. I don't know.'

'You wish I had warned Sarah. Or warned you.'

I shake my head. 'It doesn't matter now, does it?' I slow my walk down and turn towards her. 'In your visions —'

'I told you; I'm not looking at the future anymore.'

'When you were, then. Did you see me like this? Did you see what I'd become?'

'What have you become, John?' Ella asks, tilting her head.

I bite the inside of my cheek before answering. I remember

the looks I was getting from Six and Adam during our attack on the warship.

'Something my friends are afraid of.'

Tentatively, Ella reaches out and brushes her fingertips against mine. 'They aren't afraid of you, John. They're afraid *for* you.'

I shake my head. Whatever that means. I've already wasted too much time here. There's still so much to be done.

Of course, even though I'm doing my best not to show it, I'm feeling tired in a way that I've never felt before. It's beyond exhaustion. It's like my every atom is splitting apart, like I've exploded, except my body doesn't know it yet. Pushing so much power through me, using so many different Legacies, it takes a toll. I was running on adrenaline by the end of the battle.

But I'm still standing. That means I'm still fighting.

We enter the docking bay. Lexa stands next to her ship, the Loric vessel sticking out like a sore thumb among all these Mog-adorian Skimmers.

'Need a ride back down?' Lexa asks, seeming eager to get off the warship.

'That's okay. I've got it.'

I pick up Ella around the waist, and we fly through the re-opened docking bay blast doors, into the blue sky. My body aches from the exertion, but I'm not wasting even the seconds it would take for Lexa to power up the ship.

It's a short journey back towards the falls and dormant Loralite stone. Down below, I catch glimpses of Skimmer wreckage, the result of our turning the Mogs' own guns against them. I can also see the bulk of our Canadian friends, now securing a perimeter around the Loralite stone.

'You're getting good at this,' Ella says as I set us down.

'Yeah, thanks.'

The nearby soldiers gape at us. Still not used to seeing people flying around, I guess. As we walk towards the Loralite stone, Ella turns to me.

'You're going to go after Setrákus Ra soon, right?'

I nod.

'You'll need my Dreynen,' she says.

'I know.'

'Honestly, I'm surprised you haven't tried learning it already.'

I look up at the warship hovering above us. 'I needed the other Legacies first. Needed to make sure I had the power to push through Setrákus Ra's guards and get to him. Dreynen's only got one use.' Like all the Legacies I've observed, I think I can feel the Dreynen lurking inside me. A negativity, a vacuum, a cold absence. In truth, I haven't wanted to try it out. It feels wrong.

As if reading my mind, Ella gives me a grim look. 'When I was prisoner on the *Anubis*, Setrákus Ra made me practise on Five. It wasn't fun.'

'Practising on Five. I should've thought of that,' I say, only half joking.

'Setrákus Ra can take away Legacies with a thought. I haven't gotten to that level yet. I'm still stuck charging objects. Maybe you'll learn it faster than me . . .'

'That's a stretch,' I say. 'I haven't even tried yet.'

Ella purses her lips. 'Actually, that might be for the best. Make a Dreynen-charged weapon, like Pittacus Lore had. That way, even if he stops your Legacies first, you'll still have that to fall back on.'

'Good idea,' I reply, subconsciously touching Five's blade, which is sheathed and concealed on my forearm. 'Thanks.'

From our left, one of the higher-ranking soldiers timidly approaches holding a satellite phone. I pause to acknowledge him, and Ella wanders on, heading for the Loralite stone.

'Your CO is on the line,' the soldier says, holding out the phone.

'I don't have a CO,' I reply. The soldier only shrugs, like he's just the messenger.

I take the phone from him, knowing that it's going to be Lawson expecting a progress report. Before speaking with him, I watch Ella wrap her arms around the Loralite stone. It goes from dull, ordinary gray to a glowing azure in a matter of seconds. Some of the soldiers watching *ooh* and *ahh*. Ella rests her cheek against the stone, letting its restored energy pulse over her.

'This is John,' I say into the phone.

'What's this I hear about you taking over a Mogadorian warship?' Lawson barks into the phone.

'I figured since I was already up there . . .' I reply.

Lawson sighs into my ear. 'Well, I suppose that's one less of the big bastards we have to take down. On the other hand, probably only pissed off Setrákus Ra even more. Feel like this cease-fire won't last much longer, you keep taking his ships.'

'It won't have to,' I say. 'We got what you wanted. You get coordinating with the other armies. Tell them to go to the Loralite locations I showed you, and I'll have my people deliver the cloaking devices.'

'I hope it's enough,' Lawson grumbles tentatively. 'Eggheads here haven't made much progress. Then again, if all we need is you to bring down these warships . . . Hell, you know we've got ones hovering over Washington and Los Angeles still, right? Not to mention the big bitch herself in West Virginia.'

I peer up at the sky while Lawson speaks. Could I do it again? Take on another warship the way I'm feeling? I flex my hands, feeling the burning sensation in my fingers that I haven't been able to shake. I asked Marina to use her healing Legacy on them, but she said she couldn't sense anything wrong. The only explanation is that I pushed my powers too far, and this is my body showing it. Just like we can't heal exhaustion, we can't heal Legacy burnout.

How much more fighting can I do before I need a serious rest? A rest. That's funny. As if there's time for that with warships still hovering over twenty-odd cities, simply waiting for Setrákus Ra to finish his sick experiments, finish getting stronger, before finally attacking. There's no time to rest. So the question becomes, how far can I push myself — how much damage can I do — before I finally collapse?

Guess I'll find out.

'I'll see what I can do. In the meantime, make sure your people are ready to launch the attack as soon as possible.'

Before Lawson can respond, I hang up.

Finished with the Loralite stone, Ella walks back over to me. I toss her the satellite phone, and she catches it with two hands.

'Tell the others they should coordinate with Lawson on delivering the cloaking devices,' I say. 'We'll meet in West Virginia. Bring the warship. We'll take down the *Anubis* and finish off Setrákus Ra.'

'Um, okay,' Ella says, and raises an eyebrow. 'What are you going to do?'

I gaze in the direction of our stolen warship, still visible on the horizon.

'I'm going for a repeat performance.'

Ella's eyes widen. 'Another warship?'

'I'm just getting warmed up.'

'Wait, John —'

Before Ella can try to talk me out of it, I'm back in the air, streaking away from Niagara Falls. This is how it has to be. I need to keep going. No matter how tired I feel, I need to keep fighting.

The sun is already getting low in the sky. It took the better part of the day to get up here, to take that warship, to organize everyone. Too slow. Pushing myself to fly faster, an odd sensation that's a bit like diving upwards into a pool, I decide that I'll head for DC. I'm not a GPS, I don't know exactly where I'm going but I figure that if I head southeast I'll start to see landmarks and cities that I recognize and, eventually, my target.

I tell myself that I'll be faster this way, more efficient, and that it's ultimately safer for the others. Even so, I think, I should've at least brought Bernie Kosar along. He and Dust watching my back was invaluable, and he would've fitted right into the pocket of my vest until I needed him.

Oh, damn it. My vest.

I look down at myself and cringe. I'm an idiot. I took some major volleys of blaster fire during my assault on that warship. The cloaking device I had strapped to my chest along with the battery pack that provided its juice are both completely fried. I'm flying around with two useless pieces of plastic strapped to my body.

With a disgusted shake of my head, I unclip the vest and let it fall to the ground below.

I can't go back to Niagara Falls. Ella will have definitely told the others by now, and they'll try to talk me out of going off on my own. Part of me knows this is a crazy idea that wouldn't stand up to Six and Marina getting in my face. No, can't go back there.

I'll have to make a stop at Patience Creek. I've got a better chance of not facing any lectures there.

Luckily, I'm not too far from Lake Erie, and once I get close it's not all that hard for me to retrace the flight path that Lexa took earlier today. After only a few swoops in wrong directions – and one stretch where I found myself stuck in a bank of clouds unable to navigate – I see the faux bed-and-breakfast on the lakeshore. Even with the wrong turns, the trip was still quicker than in our ship. And I've only just begun pushing this flight Legacy.

My plan is to fly in through the cavern a few miles south of the complex, shoot through the tunnel and enter directly into the underground garage, where I know the cloaking devices are kept. In and out. Except when I glide by the main cottage, something doesn't look quite right.

The sun is just beginning to set, causing the trees to cast long shadows across the grounds. I know for a fact that Lawson had a few soldiers hidden out here, acting as sentries. Maybe the weird lighting is messing with my vision, but I swear I don't see them.

I fly lower and notice something else. There's a black government SUV parked in the gravel driveway right in front of the house. That's unusual. This place has been kept such a secret because everyone uses the cavern entrance. None of Lawson's people would be dumb enough to park a blatant government vehicle right in front of this top secret location.

But then I remember, I loaned one of those cars to someone else. For a personal matter.

Mark James.

I come in for a landing a few yards from Patience Creek's porch. To my left, the tire swing attached to an old maple tree sways gently back and forth. Everything seems quiet and normal, but I'm getting a weird sense that I'm being watched.

I see Mark right away. He stands in the doorway to Patience Creek, his back to me. Last time I saw him, he was a mess and punched me in the face. Now he's stiff, his head cocked in a strange way.

'Mark,' I say cautiously. 'You're back.'

He turns to me, his motions all herky-jerky. I see it immediately — how pale his skin is, the dark-black veins that make a spiderweb across his cheek. Mark's eyes are wide. He's crying, but other than that his face is completely devoid of emotion. I note that his fingers are clenched into claws, like he's paralyzed.

'I'm — I'm sorry, John,' he manages to stammer out.

'Mark —'

'They muh— muh— made me.'

205

I almost manage to spin around in time. Three tendrils of black ooze lance towards me, the tip of each one sharpened like a drill bit. One pierces the back of my shoulder, the other shoots through my hip and the third penetrates my armpit as I raise my hand to defend myself. It's like being stabbed by something living, something that burrows. I feel the tendrils digging deeper into me. My healing Legacy kicks in, tries to fight them off. When it does, an acidic burning washes over my every nerve ending. I scream and fall to my knees.

'We did make him,' says a cheery female voice. 'But we didn't have to try very hard.'

I recognize her from the Mog communicator and from the others' stories. The trueborn standing over me is Phiri Dun-Ra.

I twist around in the grass to get a look at her. Phiri Dun-Ra's entire left arm is missing, replaced by a writhing mass of Setrákus Ra's black ooze, thick and oily, shaped like a dead tree. The three tendrils spearing me, they emanate right from her. I try to pry them out of my body with my bare hands, but the ooze hardens at my touch, becomes razor sharp, and I only succeed in cutting my palms.

I try to shove her away with my telekinesis. It doesn't work.

Nothing works.

As I struggle, I see sparks of Loric energy pulsing out of me, traveling up my connection to Phiri Dun-Ra and guttering out inside her arm. Her eyes roll back in her head for a moment. Then she holds out her normal arm, palm up.

Phiri Dun-Ra's hand glows. A ball of fire rises up from her palm, the flames tinged with purple.

'Oh, this is nice, John Smith,' she says. 'I could get used to it.'

More Mogs begin to emerge from the trees around Patience Creek. I don't know how I missed them, there's so many. But then I see one step out of a shadow – literally step out from where there was nothing before – and I realize that they're teleporting in somehow.

Setrákus Ra has succeeded. Some of these Mogs, like Phiri Dun-Ra, have Legacies. No — I won't call them that. They're sick.

What word did Setrákus Ra use? 'Augmentations.' That's what these twisted powers are.

An older trueborn, bald and impossibly thin, comes to stand next to Phiri Dun-Ra. His eyes are completely glazed black. He ignores me, staring instead at Mark. The Thin Mog curls a finger in Mark's direction, and I'm vaguely aware of a sound like locusts moving through leaves.

The ooze under Mark's skin moves, and he's forced into motion. He stumbles down the steps of Patience Creek, his hands pulling out something from inside his coat, each movement looking painfully forced.

'We heard stories about these Inheritances you Loric received from your dead parents or whoever,' Phiri Dun-Ra says conversationally, smiling. 'Little keepsakes from your dead planet. Here's a secret, John . . . Beloved Leader kept some things too. Mementos. Trophies to help him remember his first great conquest.'

Mark holds in his hands something that looks like a rope, except it's deep purple in color and glistening. Something not found on this world.

I recognize it. Of course I recognize it. From a vision of the past.

It's the noose Pittacus Lore once tied around Setrákus Ra's neck. The one that gave him his scar. I remember from Ella's vision that the material is called Voron, that it only grew on Lorien and that my Legacy won't heal its wounds.

Mark kneels down and loops the noose over my head.

Phiri Dun-Ra grins at me. 'Beloved Leader thought you would enjoy the irony.'

20

'He did *what*?' Marina exclaims.

Ella shrugs her shoulders and looks down at her feet. 'He . . .'

'She heard you,' I tell Ella, my lips pursed. 'She just can't believe John would do something so completely stupid.'

Next to me, Nine winds up and kicks a big tuft of dirt out of the ground. 'What the hell, Six? Are we like sidekicks now or something? This is bullshit.'

The four of us stand in a clearing about a mile upriver from Niagara Falls. Our stolen warship is parked a few hundred yards away, dwarfing the sparse trees nearby, its tank-sized exit ramp extended. I keep catching glimpses of the monstrous ship out of the corner of my eye, and every time, I have to resist the urge to run for cover. Hard to believe that's ours now.

Marina runs two hands through her hair. 'I talked to him about this, about controlling his anger . . .'

Nine chuckles. 'Was that before or after you tried to stab Five in the face with an icicle? *Again?*'

'After, actually,' Marina replies stiffly. 'I thought he was managing his grief, at least. But flying off alone to do battle with another warship. My God, Six, it's suicide.'

'I don't know,' I reply. 'You didn't see him up there. He was pretty much unstoppable.'

'He's not thinking,' Marina says, shaking her head emphatically.

'Part of him truly believes he can do this himself,' Ella puts in. 'And another part of him doesn't want to see anyone else get hurt. He's convinced it will be better for everyone if he does this alone.'

We all fall silent for a moment, considering Ella's words. It's pretty obvious to me at least that she plucked those feelings right out of John's brain. No way did he confide that in her.

'Aw, hell with that nobility shit,' Nine says. 'This is our war too. I'm going to beat his ass when he comes back.'

'You realize what he's left us with is a pretty big deal, too, right?' I ask, looking around at the others. I don't want to spend any more time talking about John. 'Delivering these cloaking devices is going to save a lot of lives potentially. It's the key to humanity being able to win the war.'

Nine scoffs and walks away. Marina sighs and folds her arms across her chest, half turning to gaze out over the river. Ella just stands there, still holding on to the satellite phone that John gave her. I glance down at my own phone, the one that Sam gave me that's hopefully emulating the cloaking device's frequency.

Seventeen per cent battery life. When that runs out, according to Sam, this crappy old cell phone will forget the instructions he gave it. We better hurry up with this test.

No sooner do I start to worry that we're running out of time than I hear the rumble of an engine. A jeep drives into view, bouncing over the rough terrain of the clearing, Lexa at the wheel.

Lexa pulls up in front of me and gets out, the engine idling.

'Good timing,' I tell her.

'The Canadians said they'd prefer if we didn't crash it,' Lexa says with a shrug. 'They were real polite about it.'

'All goes well, their car will be just fine,' I reply.

I notice Adam appear at the top of the warship's ramp. Rex stands behind him – more like hides behind him – looking as timid as a mouse. I take a few steps towards the warship and wave to them. Meanwhile, Nine jogs over to my side.

'Is it ready?' I yell, cupping my hands around my mouth.

'Yeah!' Adam shouts back. 'The force field is fully functional!'

I squint at the warship. I can't actually see the force field from this distance. Like before, when we were flying towards it, you can't really see the dull blue energy until you're nearly right on top of it. I edge closer to the ship. Nine puts a protective hand on my upper arm.

'The hell are you doing?' he asks.

I glance down at his hand. 'Same question.'

'You don't want to get too close to that shit,' Nine says. 'I had to nurse Johnny back to health after he took a header into one of those force fields.'

'I know what I'm doing,' I reply, and shrug Nine off.

I edge as close to the warship as I dare, right up until the force field becomes visible. Then, using my heel, I dig out a line in the grass.

'That's our target,' I say as I jog back to the others.

'If we push the jeep past that with Sam's cloaking device attached, we know it works.'

'Why bother with the car? Why not just float Sam's device through the field with our telekinesis?' Marina asks.

'We know the Mogs' cloaking devices cover an entire vehicle,' Lexa says. 'We don't know that Sam's has the same range.'

'Assuming it works at all,' Nine adds.

I take the flip phone and set it on the jeep's dashboard. Then I back up and look around.

'That's all you need to do?' Marina asks with a raised eyebrow.

'I guess,' I reply. 'Sam said it's just constantly sending out the cloaking frequency or the data packet or whatever the hell.'

'Data packet.' Nine groans. 'This is boring. You know, I'm actually hoping the jeep blows up so we can see some action.'

'Real nice, Nine,' Marina says.

I wave him off. 'Ready to push this thing?'

Lexa puts her hands on the back of the jeep, which continues to idle in neutral. 'Ready,' she says.

We all stare at her. Finally, Nine laughs.

'Aw, lady, we don't push like that,' he says.

Lexa stands back and the four of us – me, Nine, Marina and Ella – all concentrate on the jeep. We shove it forward with our telekinesis. It kicks up dirt and grass, the wheels spinning, moving fast.

'Easy,' I warn the others. 'We don't want it to explode if it hits the force field.'

'A real vote of confidence for your boyfriend's work,' Nine mutters.

I frown. It's going to work and – even if it doesn't – at least Sam is trying, not just complaining about not getting to kill things like Nine is. I open my mouth to respond sharply, but Marina gets there first.

'Do you think it is just coincidence, Nine, that one of our closest allies should manifest exactly the Legacy we need to fight off the Mogadorian invasion?' Marina shakes her head passionately. 'It is the will of Lorien itself that we received this gift.'

With that I feel Marina increase her telekinetic push on the jeep, speeding it along at a breakneck pace towards the force field. Nine shuts up and watches with the rest of us. Hidden from the others, I cross my fingers.

The jeep crosses the line I made in the dirt.

Its front end heaves upwards like it just hit a tremendous bump. The windshield and all its windows shatter inwards. There's a resounding magnetic hum from the force field that I can feel in my teeth.

But it goes through. Mostly intact.

Marina and Ella let out simultaneous cries of triumph. I turn to Nine and grin. He shrugs at me. 'Props to Sam,' he says.

Adam runs down the warship ramp to examine the jeep. From the other side of the still-active force field, he yells to us, 'It was a little rough, but it worked!'

Adam reaches into the jeep and pulls the cell phone off the dashboard. He tries to hold it between two fingers but ends up dropping it – even from here, I can tell that the thing is smoldering. A wisp of smoke rises up from where the phone burns the grass.

'I think it's a one-time deal, though,' Adam concludes.

'Better than nothing,' Nine says.

Excited, I take the satellite phone from Ella and dial the number for Sam's phone.

'Sam!' I exclaim as soon as I hear his voice.

'Hey!' he responds, sounding relieved. 'We just heard. Did you guys really steal a whole warship?'

'Never mind that,' I reply. 'But yes. Listen – your thing, the cell phone, it worked! It blew up right after and maybe wasn't the gentlest ride through the force field, but it *worked*.'

I hear a muffled cheer from Sam. He's probably covering the receiver with his hand. 'It worked! My Legacy worked!' I hear him yell to whoever else is in the room with him. There's an immediate clamor of voices.

'This is amazing,' Sam says, speaking to me now. 'I've made more since this morning, just in case it paid off. The other guys here think, now that we've got Earth-made technology aping the frequency, maybe it'll be easier to replicate. You know, without using a superpower.'

'You're a hero, Sam,' I say with a grin. Next to me, Nine rolls his eyes, but he's smiling too. 'We're going to start delivering cloaking devices soon. Get your stuff ready so we can pass it out.'

'I will,' he replies. 'I –'

A loud bang on his end of the phone cuts Sam off. In the background, I hear Malcolm say, 'What on Earth was that?'

'Sam?' I ask, my brow knitting with concern.

'Hey, sorry,' he says. 'Something just exploded. Probably the new kids training.'

Before I can respond, I hear an unmistakable popping sound from Sam's side. The noise sounds like fireworks going off in the distance, but I learned long ago what that sound really signifies.

That's gunfire.

And it isn't letting up.

Now, the voices around Sam are hushed. Everyone's listening. My grip tightens on the phone. I feel a clenching in the pit of my stomach.

'Sam, talk to me.'

Hearing the strain in my voice, the others around me stop what they're doing and draw closer. The smiles from our successful experiment with the warship all slowly fade.

'Six . . .' Sam's voice is pitched just above a whisper. 'Six, I think we're under attack.'

21

They leave just enough slack in the Voron noose so that it doesn't immediately cut my head off. Instead of executing me, they make Mark hold the rope like a leash. As I crawl forward across the floorboards of Patience Creek, towards the hidden elevator that it took the Mogs all of two minutes to find, I can feel the razor-sharp collar scraping against my throat whenever I fall even a little bit behind.

Worse than those cuts is the pain from the three oily tentacles connecting me to Phiri Dun-Ra. My entire side sizzles like something boiling and caustic is leaking under my skin and spreading through my body. Phiri Dun-Ra walks alongside me as I'm dragged after Mark. She toys with a small ember of purplish fire that floats up from her palm. I can sense that she's draining me. It feels like stitches being ripped up and pulled loose from somewhere deep inside me. She's taking my Legacies.

The worst pain, though, is knowing what's coming.

Death. Destruction. Failure.

'Mark . . .' I manage to choke out with a pained breath. 'Help me . . . stop them.'

He doesn't even turn his head. I can see veins of the black ooze pulsing in his neck, and I can sense the Thin Mog, the one who's got some kind of mind control working on Mark, standing nearby.

Phiri Dun-Ra laughs when she overhears my pleading.

'It is a great honor for Beloved Leader to visit one's dreams,' she says. She extinguishes the fire in her hand so that she can ruffle Mark's hair. 'This little human, he proved to have a very open mind. He wanted something — something that you were unwilling to give him. He wanted Beloved Leader to restore his little friend . . .'

Sarah.

Unwilling to give him. My God, I'd have brought Sarah back from the dead in a heartbeat if it was within my power. Did Mark think Setrákus Ra was capable of that? Did they convince him?

Did he bring them Sarah's body?

I manage to grasp the long part of the noose with one hand. I tug on it, trying to get Mark's attention.

'You didn't, Mark,' I growl. 'Tell me . . . tell me you didn't.'

Phiri Dun-Ra titters again. 'As if Beloved Leader would squander such a gift on a mere human. No, your friend had second thoughts. But by then, it was already too late. We knew where to find him. We were forced to interrupt his mourning.'

Paradise. They tracked Mark to Paradise. Setrákus Ra broke into his dreams and manipulated him, just like he tried to do to Marina and Five, then captured him when Mark came to his senses. I assumed that I had thought of everyone Setrákus Ra could've gotten to, but I'd completely forgotten about Mark. 'It wasn't hard for us to get your location from him,' Phiri continues. 'Our little human does whatever we ask.'

I watch Mark's hand shake on the noose. His knuckles are a vivid white. His muscles are rigid. He's struggling against their control, but to no avail.

'We'll make you like him soon,' Phiri tells me, and I notice the Thin Mog wet his lips in anticipation. 'But first I want you all to myself.'

One of Phiri's tentacles twists inside me, pain shoots through my core and I collapse over on to my side. They let me lie there for a moment, gasping for breath.

With bleary eyes, I try to take in how many of them there are.

The front room of Patience Creek is packed with blaster-toting vatborn. In one corner, they've piled the bodies of the soldiers who were guarding the surface level. From the looks of them, they died quickly and savagely.

Besides Phiri Dun-Ra, I make out three other augmented trueborn.

There's the Thin Mog. The one exerting control over Mark. He stands nearby, watching Mark closely, his spidery hands clasped behind his back. If I want to save Mark, I'm going to have to take him out.

Then there's the Shadow Mog. He's younger, maybe only a few years older than Adam. As I watch, he steps out of a shadow like it's a pool of water, rising straight up through the floor. He brings with him a couple more Mog warriors. He's how they teleported in without being seen.

'Join the team at their cave entrance. No one gets out alive,' Phiri orders, and the Shadow Mog disappears back into the floor. The fact that she's using English isn't lost on me. Phiri Dun-Ra wants me to know that there's another squadron positioned at Patience Creek's vehicle entrance. She wants me to know that everyone down below is trapped.

She wants me to know how hopeless this is.

Finally, standing right in front of the elevator is the Piken-Mog. The other three Augments I've noticed at least still mostly look like Mogadorians. This one is freakish, with a normal-sized lower body attached to a torso that is completely disproportioned. He stands about eight feet tall despite a hunched back, his skin is the leathery gray of a piken and he's got the steroidal muscles to match. His fingers are long, thick and tipped with razor-sharp claws. His head, buried as it is in a throbbing mass of neck mus-cles, is regular-sized except for his jaw, which has grown out from his face, creating a fanged under bite. Most disgusting of all is that it's possible to see the seams where his pale Mog skin stretched and ripped across this new body.

He looks like he's in pain, and he looks like he's furious about it. He grunts and shifts from foot to foot, waiting for an order.

I watch as Phiri makes note of one of the security cameras. She doesn't seem concerned. 'Surely they know we're here by now,' she says, then turns to the Piken-Mog. 'Go down there and say hello.'

The Piken-Mog replies with a moan, then pries open the elevator door and hops down the shaft.

Soon, through the floor, I hear gunfire and screaming.

With a smile, Phiri Dun-Ra looks at me.

'How many Garde are here, hmm?' she asks me. 'How many of your friends do I get to eradicate today?'

'I'm not . . . I'm not telling you shit.'

Phiri rolls her eyes and pulls a blaster off her hip. She points it at the back of Mark's head.

'Want to tell me now?' she asks me, jabbing the base of Mark's skull with her gun.

When he feels the muzzle against his head, Mark manages to jerk away. Something inside him, a survival instinct, lets him fight the Thin Mog's control. He drops the noose, fingers flexing like he's finally got feeling back in his hands, and turns on Phiri Dun-Ra. He takes a halting step towards the woman. That's all he can manage. Saliva flecks from his lips as he growls, the strain of battling against the Mogadorian mind control evident. Phiri doesn't even flinch.

She glances at the Thin Mog. 'He's fighting you.'

'He will give his fragile brain an aneurysm before he overcomes my will,' the Thin Mog replies simply.

The Thin Mog's eyes narrow, and Mark's every muscle goes rigid, like he's been electrocuted. He stands up on his tiptoes, unnaturally taut, joints popping and teeth clenched. He lets out a strangled cry.

'See?' the Thin Mog says.

Phiri Dun-Ra holsters her blaster and crouches over me. 'Truth is, it doesn't matter how many of your friends are down there. We're going to kill them regardless. I just enjoy watching you squirm.'

Up close, the mass of ooze that's replaced Phiri's arm smells like rotten meat. If she'd only move a little closer, get a little more in my face . . .

'You know, John, our paths intersected once before,' she continues. 'I was in charge of operations in West Virginia when you helped Number Nine escape. Did you know that? That . . . unfortunate incident got me sent down to Mexico as punishment. Forced to work on the impossible problem of the Sanctuary. Turns out, all I had to do was wait for you idiot Loric to show up.'

She stands back up and holds out her arms, the tentacles burrowed into me twisting and pulling. I'm glad for the pain; it makes it easy to hide my disappointment. I almost had a shot at her.

I've got one desperate play. One trick literally hidden up my sleeve. The Mogs were too confident in their control to check me for weapons. I've still got Five's blade sheathed against my forearm.

I just need an opportune time to strike.

'What is it the humans love to say? Everything happens for a reason.' Phiri chuckles, going on. 'Look at how far I've come, John. In a way, it's all thanks to you.'

I grit my teeth and meet her eyes. 'You won't . . . you won't win.'

'Mm-hmm, Mr Big Hero. You're going to find a way to save them all, right?' Phiri glances over at Mark, still frozen in that awkward position, still shaking lightly as he fights against the Thin Mog's control. 'Let's see.'

The tentacle buried in my armpit yanks loose. It's a momentary relief from the pain. I watch as Phiri's writhing limb snaps through the air, its end sharpened like a dagger.

There's nothing I can do. It happens too fast.

Phiri drives the tentacle into the underside of Mark's jaw and through the top of his head. He spasms once, his eyes wide but unseeing. She holds him up there for a moment, pierced by her tentacle, so that I can get a look at him. Then she pulls free and lets Mark's body drop to the floor next to me.

I scream. In rage, in pain, in terror.

'Oh-for-one,' Phiri says to me.

I clamp my mouth closed. I can't take my eyes off Mark's body, his dead eyes staring right at me. This is my fault.

Hell with this. If I'm going to die, it's going to be on my terms.

With a burst of motion, I pop Five's blade from its forearm sheath and slice it through the two tentacles still piercing me. She screams and recoils. The oozing appendages sizzle when they hit the floor. Already, barely seconds after I chop them off, the tentacles start to regenerate.

I had hoped that my Legacies would come flooding back to me. That's not the case. There's still remnants of Phiri Dun-Ra writhing inside me. I can feel my healing Legacy kick in, trying to fight them off. I scramble to my feet and attempt to generate a fireball or to turn on my stone-vision. Those powers don't respond. They put too much physical strain on my body, which is still too drained from the attack.

A vatborn clocks me in the head with his blaster. I'm falling right back to the floor. Time seems to slow down.

My telepathy. I can at least use that. Even though my body is weakened, my mind is sound.

As soon as I open my mind, I shudder. There's so much fear and pain radiating from the sublevels of Patience Creek that seep in when I use my telepathy. I steel myself, focus and reach towards a mind that I'm relieved is still out there.

Sam! I shout telepathically.

I can sense where he's at. Running down a hallway, Malcolm

next to him, a handful of scientists and soldiers on either side. Sam's got a heavy weight on his back – a pack filled with random electronics, mostly cell phones.

His experiment with his tech Legacy. It must have worked. And now it could be doomed . . .

John? Am I hallucinating this? Sam thinks back.

No, I'm upstairs.

Oh, thank God –

They've got me, I tell Sam. *Mark led them here. Not by choice. They've got Leg – augmentations.*

Holy shit – Mark – they're trapping us down here. Sam's thoughts come in a jumbled rush. I sense him skid to a stop, Malcolm grabbing him by the arm. *I'm coming to help you, John. I'm coming!*

No! I think back, weighing Sam's chances against the Mogs versus the value of what he's carrying, the importance of pre-serving his Legacy. It could be humanity's best hope. *You have to escape! There's a mass of them at the underground exit, but I think most of the ones that have powers are with me. Find a way to get through and –*

I don't get to finish that thought. A fresh jolt of pain stabs through me, Phiri's tentacles making three new holes in my back. Only seconds have passed. Once again, my Legacies feel out of reach. A group of vatborn pin me to the ground and rip away Five's blade.

'Nice try,' Phiri says with a gloating smile. She picks up the end of the noose dropped by Mark, and I brace myself for what comes next. Phiri seems to know exactly what I'm expecting because her smile only widens. 'Oh no, John. You don't get to die yet.'

She drags me forward. I scramble along after her since the alternative is a slashed throat.

The elevator is waiting and open. There's a pool of fresh blood on the floor and dents in its walls. Whoever was defending the elevator downstairs must have fallen prey to the Piken-Mog.

'Come on; let's go say hello to your friends,' Phiri says.

Phiri, Thin Mog and a squadron of vatborn surround me in the elevator. We descend a few floors. I try to get a look at where exactly we are but can't be sure. All the halls down here look alike. Where are Lawson and Walker? The human Garde? Sam and Malcolm?

I hope they're on a different floor. I hope they're finding a way out.

The vatborn take the lead, Phiri and the Thin Mog behind them, and me forced to crawl alongside Phiri. They don't meet any resistance outside the elevator. We pass by a few bodies – soldiers – that have been practically ripped limb from limb.

'I hope he left some for us,' the Thin Mog says dryly.

The first shots are fired as we round a corner. A handful of marines are hunkered down in a kitchenette and manage to gun down a few vatborn. The Mogs return fire, but the soldiers have dumped furniture across the hallway and take cover behind it.

'Get them,' Phiri Dun-Ra says.

The Thin Mog smiles. He cups his hands in front of his mouth and blows out. Tiny black spores rise up from his palms and float down the hallway. I try to yell out a warning, but Phiri twists her tentacles inside me. The soldiers are completely unprepared for this kind of fight. How could they be? I've never seen anything like it either. The spores head right for them, like they've got a mind of their own, slipping through gaps in the barricade. I can't see exactly what happens, but I can hear gagging noises. Then, silence.

The Thin Mog makes a lifting motion with his hands, and the marines stand up as one. Black veins have spread beneath the skin on their faces. They move the same way Mark did, like puppets, their eyes completely terrified as their bodies act out the Thin Mog's commands.

Now, the squadron of marines leads the way for the Mogadorians.

Soon, we encounter another group of soldiers trying to lock down a hallway. They hesitate, seeing their friends walking towards them.

'Kill them,' whispers the Thin Mog.

Without hesitation, the mind-controlled marines let loose on their comrades, shooting indiscriminately. The vatborn Mogs watch with glee. The hallway fills with smoke from all the shooting. Phiri Dun-Ra laughs as I look away.

'Isn't this fun?' she asks.

Suddenly, every mind-controlled marine's assault rifle is ripped from his hand by an unseen force. The vatborn raise their blasters and are summarily disarmed as well.

Telekinesis.

It's just like Nine taught them. Disarm your opponents.

'Bloody hell,' I hear Nigel's voice. 'Careful, Ran, those are friendlies!'

A moment later, when the hallway explodes, I know the Japanese girl didn't listen.

Ran must have thrown one of her charged projectiles, because bodies fly everywhere. Some of them are the mind-controlled soldiers and some of them are vatborn, many of the latter disintegrating from the force. I'm tossed backwards as well, and I can feel the noose gouging my neck as a result, warm blood pouring down my shoulder. I'm only alive because the impact caused Phiri Dun-Ra to let go of the leash.

My ears ring. The hallway is even smokier than before. I catch sight of the Thin Mog and some disarmed vatborn taking cover in an empty room off the hallway. I try to crawl away, but Phiri's tentacles are still piercing me. She's nowhere in sight and I'm still stuck to her somehow.

At least I can get rid of this noose. I reach up to pull it off.

Wait.

I've lost sight of myself. I can't see my hands, my arms, my . . .

We're invisible.

Phiri Dun-Ra is using my Legacy. She's making us invisible.

We flicker back to visibility for a moment. Phiri's control is shaky. But she spots me messing with the noose, and immediately her tentacles twist inside me. My hands drop away from my neck and clutch at my midsection.

Then we're invisible again.

As the smoke begins to clear, I see Ran and Nigel inching their way down the hallway. Fleur and Bertrand are with them too. All of them are armed with assault rifles except for Ran; she's got an old paperback novel clutched in her hands, the thing glowing, charged with her explosive Legacy. They've already got plenty of scrapes and cuts, and all of them look pretty shaky.

They're walking right towards me, which means they're walking right towards Phiri Dun-Ra.

'Look out!' I scream. 'Get back!'

As a group, they jump at the sound of my voice. But they can't see me.

And now it's too late.

Phiri Dun-Ra appears from thin air. So do I, and the sight of me – leashed, impaled, on all fours – is exactly the distraction the Mogs need. All four of the human Garde look at me in shock and terror. Even Ran lets the glow fade from her projectile.

'Jo– John?' Nigel stammers, wide-eyed.

'RUN!' I shout in response, even though I know it's too late.

Before the others can act, Phiri Dun-Ra unloads.

First, she extends her hand palm out towards Fleur. Six icicles, jagged and sharp, the frozen water not clear like when Marina or I use this Legacy but tinged an ugly rust color, rocket into Fleur's chest. The girl crumples with a gasp that's wet with blood.

'No! Fleur!' Bertrand shouts. The kid tries to do something heroic. He reaches down and grabs Fleur around the shoulders, attempts to drag her out of harm's way.

Phiri Dun-Ra engulfs them both in a fireball, the flames tinged purple and smelling like burned tires.

These are bastardized versions of my Legacies she's using to kill the human Garde I was stupid enough to invite here. The ones I swore to train and protect. I want to close my eyes and stop watching.

'You bitch!' Nigel screams, his eyes filled with tears. He manages to raise his gun, but Phiri Dun-Ra twists the barrel down with telekinesis. When he pulls the trigger, the weapon backfires in his hands. Nigel cries out. I'm not sure where he's hit or how bad — it won't matter in a moment.

Except there's Ran. Luckily, Nigel stumbles backwards into her. She grabs him by the scruff of the neck and slings him down an adjoining hallway. With a parting glance at me, Ran does what I told her. She runs, pushing the injured Nigel along as she goes, just ahead of another one of Phiri Dun-Ra's fireballs.

She starts after them, but I put my weight down. Her tentacles dig deeper into my body, and I can taste blood in my mouth. I slow her down, though, and knowing that she needs to stay connected to me to maintain my stolen Legacies, she doesn't give chase.

'You are only delaying the inevitable, John,' she says. Phiri looks down at the two bodies — Bertrand and Fleur, barely recognizable, their skin charred black — and a new tentacle juts out from her oily mass of an arm, probing around them. She sighs. 'The spark in these two had barely even started, hmm?'

'You picked them before they were ripe,' says the Thin Mog as he and the other vatborn emerge from the room where they'd taken cover. The vatborn scramble around, grabbing their blasters.

Phiri Dun-Ra picks up my leash — I never got it over my head — and shrugs at the Thin Mog. She looks down at me. 'I wonder, is this how you felt as you slaughtered your way through our warship?' She makes a sound that's close to purring. 'Did you enjoy that as much as I am enjoying this?'

She gives my noose a tug, and we're moving again. As she drags me past Bertrand and Fleur, I reach towards them. I know it's futile — I'm cut off from my Legacies as long as Phiri Dun-Ra has control of me — but I harbor a desperate hope that I'll somehow be able to push some of my healing Legacy into them. My fingers barely manage to graze Fleur's shoulder; nothing happens, and then I'm forced onwards.

We turn down the hallway where Nigel and Ran fled, the vatborn once again leading the way. At this point, the only thing I can do to help is slow the Mogs' pace. Ignoring the bite of the Voron collar, I follow Phiri's lead as slowly as I can.

It's not entirely a defensive strategy, I realize as my vision begins to swim. I'm losing a lot of blood. At one point, I fall down on my elbows and hear something in my shoulder crack. There's so much pain and I'm so disoriented, I'm not even sure where we are in Patience Creek anymore.

I can't believe this is how it ends.

The sound of fighting rings out from all around the base. Distantly, I'm aware of shooting and screaming. Echoes of losing battles nearby. We stick to the quiet halls, hunting stragglers.

'There!' the Thin Mog shouts.

I look up just in time, peering between Phiri Dun-Ra's legs, as a lone person skids into view. The vatborn immediately take aim and open fire.

'Shit!' Sam yelps as he dives for cover around a corner.

Oh no. Not Sam. Please not Sam. I don't want to see this.

He didn't run like I'd told him. He didn't escape. He's alone now. I don't know what happened to Malcolm and the other scientists, to the Chimærae that were with them, but I can't help but imagine the worst. Before he disappears from view, I notice that Sam's not wearing that heavy backpack anymore. Maybe he stashed it somewhere, or maybe it got lost during the fighting.

The vatborn charge after Sam. They have to jump back when he uses a blaster to blind-fire around the corner.

'John?' he yells. 'Is that you?'

'Sam . . .' I gasp weakly. 'Sam, get out of here.'

'I'm going to save you, John!' he shouts back.

Phiri Dun-Ra giggles. 'Oh, how touching. Get this one and bring him to me. I want to make it slow.'

As ordered, the warriors barrel heedlessly around the corner. Phiri, the Thin Mog, a handful of vatborn and I bring up the rear, safe from any stray blaster fire. I can hear Sam's footsteps pounding down the hallway, sprinting away from his attackers.

'Lights off!' he shouts breathlessly. 'Lights off!'

The overhead halogens click off at Sam's command. Now only Mogadorian blaster fire lights the way. Phiri growls impatiently.

I get the sense that Sam is leading us somewhere. I turn my head from side to side, trying to figure out where we are. It's difficult in the dark, and, in the flashes of light from the blaster fire, all I can make out are a series of identical closed doors.

Over gleeful Mog shouts and blaster discharges, I hear a loud metallic noise, like a heavy bolt being thrown open. Up ahead, a door creaks open. Did Sam just lock himself in somewhere? Did he make it to safety?

Suddenly, the dark hallway gets a lot quieter. The shooting stops. I hear a grunt of pain followed by a noise like a sharp breath being exhaled.

That's the sound a vatborn makes when it turns to ash.

Phiri Dun-Ra and the Thin Mog exchange a look. We halt as the group leading the way goes quiet.

From the darkness, I hear metal banging against metal. Rhythmic and echoing.

Clang. Clang. Clang. Clang. Clang.

It sounds like clapping.

With Phiri Dun-Ra distracted, I manage to get on to my knees.
I realize now where we are. Those identical rooms on either side
of me are cells. Sam wasn't locking a door.

He was unlocking a cell.

'You seem pretty good at killing, lady,' a familiar voice growls
from the darkness.

Phiri Dun-Ra holds her hand in front of her and creates a ball
of fire that illuminates the entire hallway. Then she takes an
involuntary step back.

Five stands in the middle of the hallway about twenty yards
away. He wears nothing but his cotton boxers and an open bathrobe. In one hand he holds a Mogadorian blaster, which he bangs
against the side of his head, creating the metallic ringing sound.
Every inch of his fleshy frame has taken on the same sheen as
the blaster's gunmetal-gray alloy. In his other hand he holds a
Mog warrior by the throat. With a squeeze, Five snaps his neck,
the Mog turning to dust in his hand, which Five then smears
across his bare chest. The flame from Phiri Dun-Ra's fireball
reflects in his remaining eye, wide and locked in. When he speaks,
it's through an insanely wide smile.

'Let's see which one of us is better.'

22

My hands grip the back of Lexa's seat as I lean over her shoulder. Through the ship's windshield, I see treetops flying by, the roads below a blur. Even in here, the rush of wind across the ship's hull is loud, a constant shriek.

'Can't this thing go any faster?' I ask her through my clenched teeth.

Lexa half turns from her controls to give me a look, like, *Are you really asking me that?*

There's a little red triangle flashing on Lexa's console. Her speed is too high. She's going to burn out the engine if she keeps this up.

It doesn't matter. We need to make it back to Patience Creek. We need to make it there *now*.

In the copilot seat, BK stands with his front paws on the dashboard. His furry body is pointed straight ahead, back straight, teeth bared. He's like an arrow aimed at Patience Creek. He knows our friends are in trouble; maybe he's got some kind of animal sense about the direness of the situation.

We lost our connection with Sam shortly after he told us Patience Creek was under attack. Before the connection was severed, I could hear shooting and screaming, all of it human.

Mogs don't really scream, I guess.

Once we lost our connection with Sam, we couldn't get him back on the phone. Worse still, we couldn't get any of the numbers for Patience Creek to work. Neither could the Canadians when we asked them for help.

And that brings us here. Flying in this goddamn ship towards yet another tragedy.

I glance behind me into the passenger compartment. Nine paces back and forth. He keeps raising his fists like he's going to punch something, then angrily thrusting them back to his sides. He hasn't stopped moving since we all climbed on board. I'd yell at him to keep still if I wasn't feeling the exact same way. Completely useless.

Marina and Ella sit opposite each other. Ella's eyes are closed, the girl trying to work some telepathic magic. There's strain on her face and a spot of blood under her nose. Marina catches my eye and gently shakes her head.

'She's not as strong as she was,' Marina says quietly.

I've noticed that the glow of Loric energy that surrounded Ella after she took her header into the Entity's energy fountain has been fading gradually over the last few days. It looked especially dim after she reactivated the Loralite stone at Niagara Falls. In that meeting with Lawson, she was able to spy on Setrákus Ra telepathically from miles away. Now, trying to reach Patience Creek with her mind looks like a strain.

'What perfect timing,' I say.

Marina reaches out and squeezes my hand. 'Sam is going to be fine,' she says.

I pinch the bridge of my nose. 'Yeah. You don't know that.'

'Destiny, Six. Lorien would not have given him those Legacies – him or any of the other humans who have joined our fight – if they were not meant to play an important role in the final battle.'

'You've got a lot more faith than me,' I say to Marina bitterly. 'It's all just random, if you ask me. I mean, if Legacies equal destiny, how do you explain a piece of shit like Five? Or Setrákus Ra?'

'I . . .' Marina shakes her head, not knowing how to respond.

Ella opens her eyes, takes a deep breath and snuffs away the blood in her nose. She looks up at me and shakes her head.

'We're still too far away,' she says. 'I can't reach anyone. I don't know what's going on.'

'What about John?' I ask. 'Could you track him down?'

'I tried,' she replies. 'He's out of range too.'

I bite my lip to keep from yelling out in frustration. What a terrible time for John to go running off on his own. Not like he could've known that the Mogs were somehow going to track us to Patience Creek, but damn it, we need him with us now.

'Can't you like' – I wave my hand at Ella – 'juice up your power? Pull him into a dream like you did before?'

'It doesn't . . .' Ella frowns and looks away from me. 'My brush with Legacy, the power I gained, I guess it was only temporary. I'm returning to normal, and the energy is going back where it belongs.'

I push my fingers through my hair and squeeze my scalp. 'So that's a no.'

A shrill beep from the cockpit gets my attention.

'That's our warship,' Lexa calls back to me. 'They're trying to open a communication channel.'

We left Adam, Dust and Rex back in Niagara Falls, manning the warship as best they can with a two-person crew. They're following after us, but in terms of speed, that mammoth ship isn't able to keep up with Lexa's little craft.

I hop back into the cockpit as Lexa hits a button that calls up a holographic projection of Adam in one corner of the windshield. He's standing on the elevated commander's platform of the warship, and, with nothing but emptiness behind him, he looks small and out of place. I expect him to ask if we've gotten any word from Patience Creek. However, as soon as Adam sees me, he starts pressing a button on a console in front of him.

'Guys, I'm going to patch a broadcast through to you,' Adam says gravely, in a rush. 'This is going out live right now.'

'What are you talking about?' I ask, confused. The idea that there could be something more urgent than what we're rushing towards just doesn't register with me.

'Every warship in the fleet is receiving this,' Adam says. 'And from what I can tell, he's hijacked every still-active satellite to broadcast to the remaining news channels as well.'

'Who –?'

Before I can finish my question, Adam goes to split screen. The new feed causes a hitch in my breathing, and I have to sit down on the arm of Lexa's chair.

It's Setrákus Ra. Alive and well.

'Have I not been patient?' he asks, his dark eyes staring directly into the camera.

The shot of Setrákus Ra is from the chest up. He sits in an ornate chair that's best described as a throne. Behind him, I can see the stone walls of a cavern. He wears a blood-red silk shirt with the buttons undone halfway down his sternum. It's a ridiculous look, but it's also a message. A message for me.

There's no scar on his chest. No mark. Nothing.

'My warships hold your world's most important cities. It should be clear by now that your planet is finished. And yet, you still resist . . .'

Setrákus Ra's tone is even and condescending. Marina, Ella and Nine crowd in behind me as he drones on.

'Did he get plastic surgery or something?' Nine asks. 'What's with his face?'

I take a closer look. Setrákus Ra's features are as sharp as ever, his head still shaved, the purple scar on his neck still puffy. He's pale, dark eyed, and yet . . . he looks less haggard than when I last saw him. He doesn't look so old or nearly so monstrous. He looks much closer to the young version of Setrákus Ra that we all saw in Ella's vision.

'He can shape shift, can't he?' Marina asks.

'No,' Ella says. 'The staff he used for that was destroyed in New York City. This . . . this is something else.'

'Lorien,' I say. 'It's got to be from the Loric energy he stole.'

'I gave humanity an ultimatum,' Setrákus Ra continues. 'Surrender unconditionally and turn over to me those humans infected with Legacies. Only the wise leaders of Russia saw the wisdom in my words. Only they understood that these Legacies now afflicting humanity are a disease, something passed on from an alien species driven extinct by their own hubris. They are a sickness that only I can cure.'

'I am not fucking extinct,' growls Nine.

Setrákus Ra puts a hand on his chest, like he's feeling an emotion. 'I understand how paradigm shifts can be difficult. I understand that acknowledging humanity's subservience is troubling for the unenlightened. I am not a monster. I do not wish to see your cities razed, to shed blood needlessly, and so I allowed the deadline I set to lapse. I gave humanity time to come to its senses. I showed mercy.'

Setrákus Ra leans towards the camera, and I instinctually lean away from the screen.

'No more,' he says, his tone suddenly icy. 'This transmission is being broadcast simultaneously to the captains of my fleet. My loyal followers, humanity has refused to embrace Mogadorian Progress. They must be shown the way. We will lead them towards enlightenment with fire and blood.'

Marina covers her mouth with her hand. Ella stares daggers at the screen. Lexa focuses on flying, pushing the ship's engine beyond its breaking point. Nine's fists clench, his knuckles cracking. I stare at the spot on Setrákus Ra's chest where I struck, where I almost killed him. Not good enough. None of it was good enough.

Setrákus Ra takes a deep breath and bellows.

'All warships! Open fire!'

23

Five flies forward at top speed. He holds his blaster by the barrel, not bothering to shoot it. Instead, he wields the weapon like a club. He hits the line of Mog warriors like a whirlwind, caving in their skulls with his weapon's handle. As he dusts one Mog, he grabs a second blaster from the Mog's disintegrating hand. When one of the warriors tries to leap on his back, Five throws a vicious elbow, his metal carapace causing a resounding crunch. He shoves one Mog back with telekinesis, lets him bounce off the wall, then headbutts him to the ground.

I've never been so happy to see Five.

'Traitor! Beloved Leader gave you everything!' Phiri Dun-Ra shrieks at Five. She unleashes a fireball in his direction. Five ducks to the side – his bathrobe catches on fire – but the heat doesn't harm his metal skin.

'He gave me nothing!' Five yells back, and flings one of his blasters end over end at Phiri. It hits her right between the eyes and knocks her off her feet. Dark blood coats her face, her nose broken.

If I was Phiri Dun-Ra, I would've caught that blaster with my telekinesis, no problem. I realize that just because Phiri is capable of stealing my Legacies, that doesn't mean she knows how to use them. She's lashing out with one Legacy at a time, trying to do the most damage while not playing any defense.

It gives me an opening.

With Phiri stunned, I wrap my hands around the Voron noose and yank it out of her grasp. I pull it over my head before any of her cronies can stop me. Most of them are too distracted with Five anyway.

Now I just need to get her piercing tentacles out of my back.

Phiri's pushed herself up on her elbows, shaking off Five's blow. I lunge forward from my knees and drive my forearm right into her throat, trying to cave in her windpipe.

She gurgles once and then reacts. I feel a tearing sensation in my back as Phiri's tentacles lift me off of her. They turn me over and send me straight up, face-first into the ceiling and then back down to the floor.

I'm dazed, the wind knocked out of me, a tooth loose in my mouth. I'm still hooked to Phiri Dun-Ra. I can hear her coughing, as well as the dull, bludgeoning sounds of Five working his way through the vatborn squadron.

When my eyes finally focus, I notice the Thin Mog has edged closer to the fray. He cups his hands in front of his mouth and exhales another cloud of those spores he used to mind control Mark and the soldiers. In the darkened hallway, the only light Five's smoldering robe, the spores look like a cloud of spiders.

'Five!' I manage to yell, tasting blood as I do. 'Watch out! Don't breathe those in!'

Five slams one of the last vatborn to the ground just as I finish my warning. He turns his head, confused, and sees the spores coming at him. His chest puffs out as he tries to hold his breath, but they're already all over his mouth and nose. They move with a mind of their own, forcing their way up his nostrils and through his lips.

No. If they mind control Five, all will be lost. No one will survive this place.

I try to shove myself towards the Thin Mog, but Phiri's tentacles are still digging into my back. I'm too weak.

The telltale black veins are already spreading across Five's face. His grip loosens on his blaster, and his skin goes back to normal. His back arches as the burning robe comes in contact with his normal flesh.

'Yes . . .' the Thin Mog commands. 'Don't fight it.'

Five glares murderously at the Thin Mog. He's frozen in place, though, his muscles twitching, out of his control.

'Hey.'

The Thin Mog manages to half turn at the voice. That's the last thing he does. Sam, having crept out from one of the nearby cells, pulls the trigger on a blaster at point-blank range. The shot takes the back of the Thin Mog's head clean off. The hallway is suddenly filled with those spores, like a piñata burst. It's like the Thin Mog's entire head was packed with the moldy growths, the things now floating harmlessly to the floor, where they wilt and turn to ash.

Rattled, Five sneezes and spits, shaking off the Thin Mog's grasp.

'John –' Sam starts to say, but then his eyes widen, and he dives back into the cell just ahead of a jagged piece of dark-colored ice.

Phiri Dun-Ra is back on her feet. She reels me towards her using her tentacles. With most of her backup dead, her eyes are suddenly wild and desperate.

'Extraction!' she shrieks into an earpiece. 'I need extraction!'

Five rams into her, grabbing her around the throat with two hands. His skin is the speckled white and black of the tile floor. Phiri lets a gout of fire loose in Five's face, but it only singes his carapace and makes him angrier. His hands tighten around her neck.

It's a relief when one of Phiri's tentacles slides out of my back. That feeling doesn't last long. Phiri lashes the oily appendage around Five's neck and lifts him off the ground so that his feet are no longer touching the tile floor. His skin loses its hardened coating – now it's back to normal – and Phiri is able to squeeze his throat closed with her tentacle.

Now's it's Five wheezing for breath.

'Let's see what you have for me, boy,' Phiri says. The sharpened end of her tentacle slaps across Five's face, seeking out his empty eye socket. She's going to attach herself to Five like she's attached herself to me.

That's when I see Five's blade lying abandoned on the floor. One of the Mogs he dusted must have been carrying it.

'Five!' I shout, trying to get his attention as he starts to turn blue. I stretch my leg out as far as I can and kick the blade towards him. I hope he can hear it skittering across the floor.

Before Phiri can plug into Five, he uses his telekinesis to yank his blade towards him and strap it to his arm. It's so smooth, I get the sense that's not the first time Five's practised that move. And what comes next . . . well, I know Five's got experience in this area.

With maniacal glee, Five stabs at Phiri Dun-Ra. He hacks away at the tentacle around his neck until it's nothing but pulp and he's able to drop to the floor. His skin takes on the hardened tile texture again, just in time to absorb a desperate burst of fire from Phiri. Undeterred, Five goes right for the mass of ooze attached to her shoulder, mutilating it until the tentacles attached to me drop loose and wither to ash. Phiri screams in frustration, even as her sick appendage keeps regrowing. Every time it does, Five seems almost glad to get another chance to slash it apart. I'd almost forgotten how sadistic he is.

'Just kill her, Five!' I yell, edging backwards across the floor and grimacing as I notice the size of the blood trail I leave behind.

'Don't rush me,' he snarls.

The Shadow Mog emerges from the darkness behind Phiri Dun-Ra. This must be the extraction she was screaming for a few seconds ago. He wraps his arms around Phiri's waist and yanks her backwards, the shadows like liquid around them, swallowing them up.

Except Five doesn't let go. He buries his blade in Phiri's shoulder and launches himself through the shadows after them. The teleportation is completely soundless. One second they're here and the next the hallway is completely still. Wherever the Shadow Mog brought Phiri to, he took Five with them.

'John!'

Sam falls to his knees on the floor next to me. I can tell by the look on his face that I'm a mess. There are puncture wounds on my side and my back, broken bones in my arm and deep gashes around my neck. Everything is sticky with my blood.

'I'm . . . I'm all right,' I tell him.

'Shit, no, you are definitely not,' he replies. 'Can you heal?'

'I am healing,' I say.

Sam looks down at me. 'No. You're bleeding.'

'It's . . . it's going to happen slow.'

Now that I'm separated from Phiri Dun-Ra, I feel my Legacies gradually returning. With some effort, I lift up my arm and examine the puncture wound underneath it. The black oil is slowly seeping out of me, pushed out by my Legacy as it struggles to knit my body together. Once all that's cleared from my system, I hope my powers will be fully charged. It'll just be a matter of me having the strength left to use them.

Sam rips off a piece of his T-shirt and clamps it to my neck.

'This cut isn't closing even a little,' he says.

'It won't,' I tell him. I weakly hold up the noose. 'They used that Voron noose on me. Like what Pittacus used on Setrákus Ra.'

'Oh man, you're going to have a scar,' Sam mumbles, shaking his head.

There's movement on the ceiling. I spot the Shadow Mog just in time. He falls feet-first out of the darkness, a blaster pointed at us. Back to finish us off.

I shove Sam off me and roll on to my back. The blast burns into the wall between us. Sam reacts swiftly, getting his blaster oriented to return fire. The Mog drops straight down, into another patch of shadows on the floor, and disappears through them.

'Keep your head on a swivel,' I warn as I sit up, clutching the noose.

The Shadow Mog walks out of one of the darkened cells behind me. I don't turn around in time, but Sam uses his telekinesis to knock the Mog's blaster aside. His latest shot sizzles into the floor next to me. With a frustrated grunt, our enemy again dives towards some darkness.

I fling the noose towards him.

It isn't my brightest idea. Without my telekinesis, there's no way I can make that throw. Luckily, Sam catches on quickly and uses his own telekinesis to guide my impromptu lasso. We get the noose around the Shadow Mog's head before he disappears, and I yank back on it with what little strength I have left.

I'm hoping to take his head clean off, but no such luck. The Shadow Mog stops mid-teleport, waist deep in shadow, and clutches the noose. It's a tug-of-war, and he's winning. The Voron rope, slick with blood, starts to slide through my hands.

'Behind you!' Sam yells.

I manage to flick a glance over my shoulder. The Shadow Mog's legs are ten yards down the hall, emerging from another pocket of shadows. He's just going to keep teleporting through the darkness until he wears us down. The Voron rope slips a little farther out of my hands.

'Lights on!' Sam shouts.

All at once, the lights in the hallway come back on brighter than ever. No more shadows.

The Mog lets out a gasp. His torso flops to the ground in front of us, and his legs drop behind us. He's been cut in a perfectly straight line through the waist. I yank the noose through his neck with little resistance – he's already beginning to disintegrate.

'Nicely done,' I tell Sam as he kneels down next to me.

'Guy was really pissing me off,' Sam grumbles, once again fussing over the cut on my neck. 'This is going to need stitches, man.'

I put my hand over his as he applies pressure. 'Sam, where's your dad . . . ?'

'He's fine! I mean, he was the last time I saw him. There was no way out, so he and the other scientists hid down in the old library. The Chimærae were keeping them safe. He's got my homemade cloaking devices. I ran off to, uh, to let out our secret-weapon psychopath there before Dad could stop me.' Sam takes a breath and looks around. 'Where's Mark?'

I compress my lips and shake my head. Sam looks away from me.

'Goddamn them,' he says quietly. 'Goddamn them for all this shit.'

We both go silent at the sound of gunfire from an adjoining hallway. The shooting is cut off by an animalistic roar, desperate screams soon following. That's got be the huge, deformed Aug-ment that I saw upstairs, the Piken-Mog. It's close.

Sam looks at me. 'Can you fight?'

I grimace and manage to create a weak ball of fire with my Lumen. As soon as I do, my healing Legacy stops working, and my torso is pure agony. I extinguish the flame and focus on heal-ing, shaking my head at Sam.

— 'Not yet,' I say.

'Then we better move,' he replies. 'Unless you want to try that lasso trick again.'

'No thanks,' I say. 'This one doesn't teleport. He knocks down walls.'

Sam gets his arms under me and gently helps me to my feet. I fling my good arm over his shoulders, the other clutched against my stomach, and we shuffle quickly down the hall. Sam's got one arm around my waist, and the other points a blaster straight ahead. Behind us, the heavy footsteps and grunting of the Piken-Mog echo, slowly becoming more distant.

'You know what I thought the first day I met you in school?' Sam asks me, his voice low, breathing heavily.

I raise an eyebrow at the question. 'Uh, no. What?'

'I thought, here's a guy who's going to make me carry him half-way across New York City and then later through a top secret underground military base while he bleeds all over the place. I hope we can be best friends.'

I actually laugh at that, even though it hurts my punctured ribs. 'You've gotten really good at it,' I say.

'Yeah, thanks,' Sam replies with a grim smile.

We edge around a corner, and a gunshot rings out. I feel the bullet whiz right past my cheek.

'Hold your fire!' yells Agent Walker. 'Goddamn it, they're ours!'

Agent Walker stands with an assault rifle at the ready, her face smeared with ash, a nasty-looking blaster burn on one of her legs. In front of her, one of them still aiming a pistol in our direction, are the twins, Caleb and Christian. It was the dead-eyed one, Christian, who took a shot at us. Caleb punches him in the arm to get him to finally lower his gun.

'Sorry,' Caleb says, nodding towards Sam's blaster. 'We saw the blaster coming around the corner and . . .'

'Don't sweat it,' Sam says. 'I've been getting shot at for a long time.'

'Good God, if *you're* here, how are we losing?'

That comment, directed at me, comes from General Lawson. He's sandwiched between Walker and the twins, like they're his bodyguards. The whole unflappable-grandfather act is out the window. Lawson looks like crap. His uniform is torn and blood-stained, he's got an open gash over his eyebrow and he looks about ten years older than I remember.

'They got the drop on me,' I say through gritted teeth. 'I'm out of the fight for now.'

'They got the drop on all of us,' Walker says with a glare in Lawson's direction. She walks over to my side and helps Sam support my weight. 'You . . . you're going to heal, right?'

'Mostly,' I reply. The punctures are only now beginning to close up, oily black residue leaking out of them.

'Is there anywhere safe?' Sam asks.

'We tried to break through their ranks at the garage,' Lawson says, his expression darkening. 'Took heavy losses while they kept bringing in reinforcements. They've got a teleporter.'

'Not anymore,' Sam says.

'Did you know about that?' Lawson asks, looking at me. 'That they have Legacies?'

'Those aren't Legacies. They're sick copies. Augmentations,' I say. 'But no, they're a new thing.'

'They stole that from you,' Lawson says, putting two and two together. 'That's what you were talking about at the meeting the other day.'

'We should keep moving,' Walker puts in.

Lawson shakes his head, still looking at me. 'I was not fully informed just how fubared we are.'

'We were doubling back towards the elevators,' Walker says, taking over. 'We hoped there would be less resistance.'

'Might be,' I say. 'Five just took out a squadron that came down with me. Not sure how many more, but . . .'

We all hear it at the same time. Heavy footfalls bounding down a hallway. Too close.

'There's a big one,' I tell them. 'It's hunting. It's —'

'Tearing people apart,' Lawson says. 'We saw the bodies.'

Sam glances at Christian. 'It probably heard your shot.'

'We need to go,' Walker says. 'Now.'

We push on, hustling through one hallway, then zagging down another. The Piken-Mog has our scent, though. I can hear it behind us, getting closer, wailing excitedly.

I realize that I'm the one slowing us down. I glance over my shoulder and see its mammoth shadow moving down the hallway we just left.

'Go,' I tell the others. 'Get to the elevator. I'll hold it off.'

I have no idea how I'm going to do that, but they don't need to know that.

'John, don't be stupid,' Sam says. He drags me along, and I'm powerless to stop him.

'You're a brave kid,' Lawson grumbles. 'But you're our biggest asset. If we get out of this, we're going to need you.'

The Piken-Mog comes into view about fifty yards down the hall. It roars, excited to finally have us in its sights. The thing, barely more than an animal, beats its thick fists against the scarred flesh of its bulging pectorals.

Lawson turns to Caleb and Christian. 'You're up.'

The twins nod in unison. Christian immediately turns around and starts walking right towards the Piken-Mog.

'Stop!' I yell at him, then turn on Lawson. 'Are you crazy? You can't just send him to die!'

At first, the Piken-Mog seems confused by this development, some remnant of its trueborn brain registering that this solitary human must be insane. But then, with a line of drool dangling from his under bite, the Piken-Mog charges, bearing down on Christian.

'It's okay,' Caleb interrupts. 'Watch.'

Of course I watch. I couldn't look away if I wanted to, even as we back down the hallway. Christian unloads his gun into the Piken-Mog, but the bullets are either absorbed or deflected by its thick hide.

Lawson grimaces. 'Was hoping bullets might do it.'

'*That's* your plan?' Sam shouts, wide-eyed.

The gorilla-sized Mog reaches Christian in seconds and claps his hand over the kid's head. He hoists him up like that and smashes him first against the wall, then against the floor. Christian doesn't make a sound. He even keeps on shooting.

And then, after a particularly sickening slam against the floor,

Christian evaporates in a burst of blue energy. The Piken-Mog looks stunned.

'What the –?' Sam exclaims.

Next to me, Caleb begins to glow. His whole body begins to vibrate, blurring, splitting apart.

A second later, there are two more of him. Two brand-new twin versions of Caleb. They blink their eyes, getting their bearings, then look at the original. Caleb nods towards the Piken-Mog, and they sprint into a hopeless battle.

He never had a twin brother. It's a Legacy. He can duplicate himself.

'Two at a time,' Lawson says. 'Getting better, son.'

'Thanks,' Caleb replies as we retreat. He looks a little wobbly. Behind us, I hear the Piken-Mog thrashing these newest twins. A glance over my shoulder reveals that they're playing it smarter than Christian did, using hit-and-run to distract the brute. They won't last long, but they should at least slow him down.

'I have questions for you,' I say to Caleb.

'I figured you would,' he says, not meeting my eyes.

'But all of them can wait, except one,' I continue. 'How many duplicates can you create?'

'Not enough,' he replies, swallowing hard. 'It's hard. I'm . . . I'm only learning.'

'That beast is shrugging off bullets like they're mosquitoes,' Sam adds. 'We need to lose this thing until one of us, uh, until one of us with *every* Legacy can take him down.'

I glance down at myself, looking at my wounds. Closer now. I can feel my power slowly returning. I also feel light-headed on account of all the blood lost.

Our group takes a few sharp turns through the twisty subterranean hallways. I think we've doubled back at this point. We pass bodies, places where battles took place, but no one is alive. There's a good chance we're the only ones left.

Soon, we hear the thumping footsteps again. The snarling, the knuckle dragging.

'Bastard doesn't give up,' Lawson says.

I try to fire up my Lumen as a test, but again my body clenches in agony. Every ounce of me needs to be dedicated to healing right now.

We turn another corner and –

'Shit!'

A line of vatborn Mogs with their blasters pointed in our direction block the entire hallway. Walker, still under one of my arms, shoves me hard to the side and brings up her rifle. As I fall towards the floor, knocking into Sam as I do, the agent sprays down the entire line of Mogs. Chunks of them ricochet through the hallway.

The Mogs are frozen in stone.

'What the hell?' Walker says.

'You really saved our lives there,' Sam says.

'Shut up, Goode.'

I look around. 'Daniela was here, if –'

A roar from behind us. The Piken-Mog again barrels into view.

'Through here!' Caleb yells, already helping Lawson squeeze between two stone Mogadorians. 'These should at least slow him down.'

I'm not so sure about that. The Piken-Mog is charging hard, its shoulders lowered. It'll plow right through us and those stone Mogs. It's now or never. Damn the pain. I start to build up a fireball in my hands, even though doing so makes my whole body clench up.

'Get down!' someone shouts.

I duck my head just as a silver beam of energy streaks from behind the Mog statues and hits the Piken-Mog. It spreads across his massive frame, slowly wrapping him in a stone covering. He's frozen about ten yards from us, fists raised in the air, mouth open in a bloodthirsty cry.

Done using her stone-gaze, Daniela rubs her temples like she's got a splitting headache. Seeing me and Sam, she cocks her hip and raises an eyebrow.

'Is this, like, my official role with you people? Monster stoner and saver-of-asses? Because . . .' Daniela trails off as she sees the kind of shape I'm in. 'Goddamn, man.'

'Yeah, thanks for the help,' I say, squeezing her shoulder as I climb through her wall of statues. Daniela is scuffed up like everyone but overall in pretty good shape. There are stone Mogs everywhere in this hallway. She's been wearing out her Legacy.

'Oy, you made it,' says Nigel. He and Ran are huddled in between some Mog statues, using them as a hiding spot. The British kid is pale, the wounds he suffered against Phiri Dun-Ra still bleeding heavily.

I nod, feeling guilty, like I let them down. Too much death here. Too much destruction.

'Come on,' I say. 'Let's get the hell out of here.'

Patience Creek has gone quiet. Without anything chasing or shooting at us, our ragtag group makes the elevator without a problem. It still works, although we have to spend some time clearing out a couple of bodies. There are a lot of those. And not enough survivors.

We head to the lowermost level first and find Malcolm, along with a few scientists, Agent Noto and the five Chimærae. All the animals made it through the fighting with nothing worse than some singed fur and, in Bandit's case, a mangled tail. Everyone, humans and Chimærae alike, look downright exhausted.

After that, we start to search the other floors. We don't encounter anything but death until we reach the uppermost level, the one where Lawson previously kept his control center. There, we're drawn to the sound of televisions tuned to what sound like a dozen terrified newscasts.

Five stands in Lawson's office, his back to the door, watching

247

the news on the wall of screens. He extends his blade when he hears us coming but quickly sheaths it once he realizes that we aren't Mogs.

'She got away,' Five says simply, sounding frustrated. 'They had a staging area a few miles south of here in the forest. Took off when they realized the tide was turning. I know how they operate. They'll be back soon with reinforcements.'

Sam and I enter the room cautiously while Five speaks, the rest of our group waiting outside. Five wears a set of fatigues that he either found lying around Patience Creek or stripped off a dead soldier. I guess the latter is more likely considering the blood splatters on the camouflage.

'You going to try locking me up again?' Five asks, looking at me over his shoulder.

'No,' I reply.

'Good.'

Sam and I come to stand alongside Five, the three of us staring at the monitors. The Mogadorian bombardment has begun. We're looking at footage from at least ten different cities, all of them being slowly erased by warship fire. My eyes bounce from catastrophe to catastrophe, eventually settling on the Arc de Triomphe as it crumbles down the middle, its two pillars breaking apart against each other.

'This planet is toast,' Five says.

Sam ignores him and looks at me. 'What now, John?'

'We throw everything we have at them,' I say immediately, glancing in Five's direction. 'Everything. And we either end this war, or we die trying.'

24

We don't have time to mourn our dead. Our friends, and the ones we barely got a chance to know. We don't have time to grapple with how many lives were lost, our responsibility for that.

It's probably for the best.

By the time we land Lexa's ship outside of Patience Creek, the massacre is over. We're just in time to help the survivors escape. We don't want to be here when the Mogs send in reinforcements. There are other battlefields that need our attention.

We fly into the night, leaving the quaint cabin and its secret tunnels behind.

News trickles in from around the world. Some cities have already fallen as a result of the warships opening fire. Others are holding strong, fighting a protracted cat-and-mouse game against the Mog ground troops, staying one step ahead of warship bombardment. Some armies have pulled back, waiting to launch a counterstrike.

They're waiting for our help.

'One coordinated assault using the cloaking technology you've provided,' Lawson says, once again going over the details. His satellite phone has been buzzing nonstop since we picked up him and the others. 'All our allies – England, China, Germany, India, every country with any military capability – we strike back simultaneously, before they realize we've cracked their shields. We throw everything we've got at them while we've still got the element of surprise.'

'And while that happens, we hit West Virginia,' John says. 'We take out Setrákus Ra and destroy what he's built there.'

John looks terrible. The wounds that he suffered at the hands of Phiri Dun-Ra have healed up with the exception of the cuts ringing his neck, but his pallor is still dramatic, the bags under his eyes now deep purple. With all of us crammed into this little ship, John is one of the few people who sits. He looks like he needs it. While he goes over the plan with Lawson, Marina stitches up the deepest of the gashes in his neck. He winces a few times. We didn't think to bring one of the surviving army medics on board with us. It's been a while since we couldn't just heal an injury.

'You know . . .' Lawson says thoughtfully, eyeing Sam. 'If this young man can talk to machines, he should be able to communicate with the enemy warships. We could use him to bring down their shields.'

Sam's eyes widen a fraction. 'I . . . I'd have to be really close,' he says, trying to be helpful. 'And I'm not sure how long it lasts exactly –'

'Like hell you're going to use him,' I say, interrupting. 'Sam's the only one who's been able to copy the signal, and you're talking about flying him into twenty different war zones so he can shout at their ships? Hasn't he done enough already?'

Lawson stares at me with a raised eyebrow. 'It was only a thought. Admittedly, the risk seems greater than the reward.'

'We stick with the plan,' John says. Sam gives me a relieved look. I keep glaring at Lawson.

'If this fails . . .' Lawson begins.

'It won't,' John insists.

'If it does, I can't speak for every country in the world, but it will be America's position that if the enemy is unbeatable, we focus on saving lives.'

'You're talking about surrender,' I say.

Lawson's lips form a tight line. 'Cutting our losses,' he replies. 'Living to fight another day. Preserving the maximum number of lives possible.'

John and I exchange a look. If our counterattack fails, we probably won't be alive to see what comes next anyway. What Lawson does in that bleak future doesn't much matter.

'Do what you have to do,' John says.

We drop Lawson in an open field outside of Pittsburgh. There's a military convoy waiting for him, replacements for the squads that died at Patience Creek. The headlights of their Humvees are the only illumination out here. A cool breeze blows across the field, swaying the overgrown grass. Our group – Loric, human Garde, friends, survivors – stand outside of Lexa's ship. Gradually, the humans begin to drift towards the convoy, the scientists and the handful of surviving soldiers limping that way. Wherever they end up next, it'll surely be safer than staying with us.

'I've got teams standing by at the coordinates you gave me, guarding those alien rocks of yours,' Lawson says. 'They're waiting on you. Once they're armed, we'll begin our attack.'

'We're on it,' John replies.

'How exactly are Earth's armies planning to take down the warships?' I ask, curiosity getting the better of me.

'Every country's a little different,' Lawson replies grimly. 'From what I've heard, China and some others are planning to go nuclear. Most of the EU doesn't want to risk the fallout, so they're going with missile bombardment. The hope is that these big hulks of theirs can't absorb much damage once you're through the force field.'

'And America?' John asks.

Lawson smiles. 'At my suggestion, we're taking a page out of your book, John. Flying the biggest personnel carriers we've got right down their throats, boarding those ships and gunning down every goddamn alien we see.'

'I like it,' I say.

Lawson nods. He hooks his thumbs through his belt loops and looks us over. Then he nods to himself, like he's satisfied we're his best chance. Or resigned to the fact. Hard to say.

'I suppose that's it,' the general says. 'See you all on the other side.'

With that he walks across the field towards the convoy. Caleb, whose twin brother apparently never really existed, moves to follow after him.

'Caleb, wait,' John says.

With a nervous glance at Lawson, Caleb stops midstride and turns back to face the rest of us. He stands next to Nigel and Ran. The Japanese girl is unreadable as usual. Nigel, on the other hand, looks shaken up. All the bluster from before is gone. His ragged Misfits T-shirt still bears the bloodstains from

Patience Creek. Even though Marina healed his wounds, this latest taste of combat left more than physical marks on the Brit. Daniela stands next to those two, watching over them. I'm not sure exactly what happened inside Patience Creek, but it seems like the hard city girl has developed some protective feelings for the two other human Garde.

'Our planet's Elders sent us to Earth to keep us safe, so that we'd one day be ready to fight back and avenge our planet,' John says, addressing the humans. 'Today is that day. Where we're going next, it isn't a battle that you're ready for. We've trained our whole lives for it. Your training is just beginning. Your day will come.'

Daniela opens her mouth to protest. I catch her eye and subtly shake my head, shooting a look towards Nigel and Ran. She gets the message and stays quiet.

'Win or lose, tomorrow, your world will be a changed place. It's going to need protectors. Eventually, you'll need to step up.' John glances at Sam, who stands nearby and manages a smile. 'For now, though, I think the future protectors need protecting. We all had charms burned into our ankles that would keep us safe, at least for a time. We can't do that for you guys, but we can give you something else . . .'

I'm not sure what John's talking about until Regal, our hawk-shaped Chimæra, lands on Caleb's shoulder. The boy jumps, settling down only when it's clear the bird's talons won't pierce him. Regal spreads out his wings and ruffles Caleb's hair.

Bandit, the raccoon, scratches at Nigel's leg with his black paws until the Brit is forced to pick him up.

Gamera, trundling across the grass in turtle form, ends up staring up at Ran. She bends down to run one finger over his scaly forehead, and, for the first time, I see her crack a smile.

'His name is Gamera,' Malcolm says to Ran. 'I named him after a favorite old monster of mine.'

Ran stares blankly at Malcolm.

'He fought Godzilla,' he explains further.

At the very least she must understand 'Godzilla', because Ran rolls her eyes and goes back to stroking the turtle.

The golden retriever Chimæra, Biscuit, the one that Sarah was especially fond of, ambles over to Daniela, happily wagging her tail when Daniela starts to scratch behind her ears. I notice a flicker of something on John's face; it's hard to say exactly what in the near darkness, but he seems pleased.

And finally, with impossible agility for a feline of his girth, Stanley leaps into Sam's arms. He laughs, and, at the sound, a tightness in my chest eases. I'd been so terrified that something horrible had befallen Sam at Patience Creek and that we were going to be apart when it happened – just like John and Sarah. Only now am I finally able to relax a bit.

'All right, Stanley, all right,' Sam says, holding the heavy, purring cat in his arms. 'We can make it official.'

Nine scowls. 'You need to rename that stupid cat.'

'These Chimærae will be your protectors until you've come to fully grasp your Legacies,' John continues, glancing at Bernie Kosar, who, in beagle-form, sits quietly at his feet. 'And then they will be your most valuable allies. One day, hopefully, we'll be able to help you more, train you like our Cêpans trained us . . .'

Five, standing off to the side of everyone, chuckles darkly at that. Everyone looks in his direction, Marina's glare particularly icy, and he edges farther away in response.

'But until that day . . .' John continues, and then trails off. He doesn't know what to say. Or maybe he doesn't think that day will ever come.

'Kick some ass and do Earth proud,' Nine finishes for him.

After that, Caleb, Nigel and Ran say their goodbyes and join Lawson's convoy. Daniela lingers a little longer. She gives me a big hug, then turns to John and Sam.

'You know, I'm definitely badass enough to help you guys out,' she says. She jerks her thumb over her shoulder at the other humans. 'But someone needs to watch out for them.'

John nods, smiling tiredly. 'Take care, Daniela.'

'Don't die,' she responds, then joins the others.

Sam strokes Stanley's head, an eyebrow raised at John. 'I know you're not expecting me to leave with them.'

'No,' John replies with a shake of his head. 'You're stuck with us.'

Malcolm crosses his arms, looking at Sam. 'I'm coming as well. Your mom would kill me if I let you face the end of the world without some form of supervision.'

I slip my arm around Sam's waist and rest my head on his shoulder. 'Seriously,' I say, scolding him. 'Call your mom.'

Agent Walker is the last one to join the convoy. She stands in front of our group awkwardly, looking from me to John to Nine. Finally, she sighs.

'I just want to say . . .' She hesitates. 'I want to say thank-you. For giving me a chance to fix some of the damage I caused. For . . .' She shakes her head and waves her hands. 'Thank you.'

'Don't mention it,' Nine says.

'Take care of those kids, Walker,' John replies. 'They need someone to watch out for them. Someone who doesn't want to just use them for their powers. That could be you.'

Walker nods, turns and heads towards the headlights of the convoy. Soon those headlights become taillights, and then we're alone in the dark field.

Me and Sam. Malcolm and Lexa. John and Bernie Kosar. Nine. Marina and Ella. Five. I'm the one to break the silence.

'Let's go win this war.'

Yet again Lexa flies us north to Niagara Falls. The ride is quiet and somber, everyone too tired, or too much in their own head, to say much. John falls asleep for what must be the first time in days, Marina next to him, her eyes drawn to the wound on his neck that defies her healing ability. Five chooses not to ride in the ship but rather fly alongside it, a decision I think everyone is grateful for.

Sam and Malcolm use the time to call Sam's mom. It's a tearful conversation, one that I try not to eavesdrop on. Across the aisle from me, Nine catches my eye.

'Must be nice to have people to say good-bye to, huh?' he says quietly.

I frown. 'Nobody's saying good-bye to anyone, Nine.'

'Come on, Six. You really think that's true?'

When we reach Niagara Falls, Adam and Rex have just finished preparing our deliveries. The two Mogs have packed heavy-duty backpacks – courtesy of the Canadians – with cloaking devices picked clean from our stolen warship's Skimmers. Into those packs we divide the cell phones and gadgets that Sam has talked into copying the cloaking devices signals.

Nine eyeballs Rex. 'If I double-check these bags, am I going to discover you, like, sabotaged some of the merchandise?'

Rex runs a hand through his short black hair, uncertain how to respond. Adam steps forward.

'Enough already, Nine,' he says. 'Rex is solid. We can trust him.'

'All this, it feels like throwing pebbles at a god,' Rex says quietly, surveying the backpacks. 'I only hope it's enough to make Beloved Leader fall. That . . . that would be something to see.'

'Well, at least he's optimistic,' Nine says dryly.

All told, each pack has roughly thirty cloaking devices. One pack per war zone.

'Will it be enough?' Marina asks.

'It has to be,' John replies.

Ella directs traffic. She knows the locations of the Loralite stones, the new outcroppings that have blossomed from the earth since we released the Entity. According to Lawson, there should be people waiting at each spot to take our deliveries. From there it's up to them how they use the cloaking devices. I hope they've got solid plans.

'You just need to picture the place you're going,' Ella explains as we stand in a semicircle around the Niagara Falls stone, the dull-blue glow it emits the only light. 'If you have trouble, I can help . . . put an image in your mind. When I was bonded with Legacy, I saw all the stones simultaneously, so I know what their surroundings look like.'

'That's good,' Sam says, glancing down at the list of locations. 'Lion's Head is a place and not a, uh, actual lion's head, right?'

Ella looks up at him. 'I'll help you, Sam. Don't worry.'

Nine raises his hand. 'If we do picture an actual lion's head . . .'

'No,' Ella finishes his thought. 'You will not teleport on to a lion.'

I allow myself a brittle smile. They're joking around; in the face of everything that's happened, they can still do that.

'Let's get this done,' John says briskly.

We break up into teams of two to make the deliveries. Nine and Marina. Me and Sam. Since no one wants to pair up with Five and no one wants to be left behind with him, John agrees to go with him. The rest of our group stays behind. Adam and Rex take Malcolm on to the warship to show him some of the controls, hoping that he can help pilot the massive thing when our attack on West Virginia comes.

'Ready?' Sam asks.

'Ready,' I reply, and, holding hands, the backpack of cloaking devices slung over Sam's shoulder, we touch the Loralite stone and focus on a mental image that Ella telepathically sends to us.

A warm glow of energy washes over us, and a second later we're both shielding our eyes. It's early morning in South Africa, and we're standing on the summit of Lion's Head mountain. There are man-made cobbles set up here that intersect with manicured gardens – a place for tourists to take pictures. The Loralite stone juts up from right beneath them, cracking the cobbles and displacing the plants. The view here is breathtaking and dizzying. We're level with the clouds. If I turn to my left, I see crystal-blue ocean, the sun streaking golden across the waves. If I turn to my right, I see the crowded white buildings of Cape Town.

The scene would be peaceful if not for the helicopter idling just a few yards away. Its rotors make a steady *whup-whup-whup*, trampling over the quiet morning. There's a group of camouflaged soldiers standing watch nearby. When we appear from thin air, a few of them jump, and a couple point their assault rifles in our direction. Most of them are completely unperturbed. I guess you get used to crazy things happening during an alien invasion.

Two of the soldiers jog over to us and grab the backpack from Sam. They don't say anything to us, and we don't say anything to them. Soon they've all piled into the helicopter and are off to bring down the nearest warship. Johannesburg, I think.

'I mean, a thank-you would've been nice,' Sam complains.

I shrug it off and turn to take in the view. It's beautiful enough to make me forget, for all of five seconds, just what we're doing here and the daunting odds we're up against.

'You know, I've always wanted to see the world,' I say.

'You mean in a context when you're not running for your life or fighting an alien warlord.'

'Yeah,' I say with a sly smile. 'I believe you earthlings refer to them as vacations.'

Sam sidles up next to me, and together we gaze out at the ocean.

'Maybe when . . .' He starts to say something, then trails off.

I look over at him. 'Maybe when . . . ?'

Sam's eyes search for his sneakers. 'I was going to say that maybe when this is over we could take one of those vacations. I shouldn't talk like that. Making plans. I mean, with everything that's happened. Eight, Sarah, Mark . . .' Sam shakes his head. 'I still can't believe it, you know? Can't even wrap my head around it. These people I grew up with, that I've known my entire life. Jeez, the entire world. It's all turned upside down. We're probably going to die in a few hours. And I'm thinking about vacations. It feels wrong.'

I run my hand up the back of Sam's neck, tangle my fingers in his hair and give it a yank. 'Nobody's dying, Sam.'

'Ow. Everybody's dying, Six. I mean . . . like, everywhere.'

'We're going to make it,' I say, pulling his face close. 'And if you think you're about to die, Sam, I want you to remember this moment. Remember that we're fighting for this, for the future. Our future.'

Sam breathes in deeply. 'Okay. Okay, you're right.' He glances over his shoulder at the glowing Loralite stone waiting to take us back to Niagara Falls and then on to our next delivery. 'We should get going.'

I tilt my head back and take a deep breath of air – crisp and cool at this height, with just a little tang of ocean.

'One minute,' I say, interlocking my fingers with his. 'One minute to look at the world.'

And so we stand there for one minute. Take it all in.

We do the same thing when we teleport into the rolling sands of the Sahara, the air dry and blistering, the outcropping of Loralite like a glowing oasis.

And again when we reach Mount Zao in Japan, the Loralite stone there next to a volcanic crater lake that glows brighter than even the stone. Snow blows across our faces, and we actually laugh. The Japanese soldiers pick up the equipment and look at us like we must be crazy, like we're wasting time.

We can spare a few minutes.

We stop in Portugal. We stop in the Australian outback. One extra minute spent in each place, one minute that serves no purpose other than to see. A five-minute vacation.

Soon enough it's over. The deliveries are done. We're back in Niagara Falls, it's the middle of the night and we've only got one final destination. West Virginia.

Sam and I share one last smile and then we take our positions. We get ready to do what needs to be done.

By dawn, one way or another, all this will be over.

25

Our warship soars towards west Virginia. The night slides by through the vast windows of the Mogadorian bridge. Stars wink overhead while down below, streetlights and houses are lit up, this part of the northeastern United States as yet untouched by the invasion. I wonder if anyone down there happens to look up and see our massive, scarab-shaped vessel. Or are we just another dark cloud passing across the night sky?

I light up my Lumen. It feels good to have my Legacies back in full after what Phiri Dun-Ra did to me. It's like my eyes are able to see color again. I still feel the dull ache of overuse inside me, like a thread that's slowly fraying in my chest, not to mention the burning sensation in my hands that won't go away. I ignore all that just like I ignore the sharper pain of the wound on my neck, still raw from Marina's mostly unpractised stitches.

I hold my hand out like a blade and make a small, concentrated fire jet out from my fingers. Push the temperature, get it white-hot, a blowtorch of my own making. Then I set to work.

I'm alone on the observation deck, a small balcony designed to be comfortable by Mogadorian standards, positioned over the bridge. Down below, most of the others are at work preparing for our attack. We've got our course set, and, luckily, maintaining altitude and flying in a straight line are things Rex can do on his own. Lexa watches over his shoulder, trying to pick up a few things in case she needs to help pilot later.

There are four weapons stations, one for each quadrant of the warship, and each features an array of buttons that command different guns along with holographic video feeds for aiming. There's also a fifth station that operates the ship's main energy cannon, a smaller version of the one on the *Anubis* that is capable of quickly erasing entire city blocks. According to Adam, there are supposed to be teams of engineers belowdecks to deal with loading power cells and making sure the weapons don't overheat.

I killed them all, so we're just going to have to hope nothing explodes or runs out of batteries.

Malcolm sits at one of the weapons stations, getting a crash course in how to operate the guns from Five. Surprisingly, Five is pretty patient with him. I remember back in Chicago when they both first joined us, Sam's dad was pretty decent to Five. He's been good to all of us, really. I direct my hearing in their direction as Five's explanation winds down.

'Do you mind if I ask how you know all this?' Malcolm asks Five.

Five runs a hand over the bristles of hair on his scalp. 'I was supposed to command one of these,' he says simply. 'At least, that's what he told me.'

'I see,' Malcolm says. There's an awkward silence. 'Could you show me again how to deploy the chaff?'

'Sure.'

Behind Malcolm and Five, Sam and Adam stand at the commander's station. Adam is drilling Sam on different functions of the warship. He outlines which consoles control the shields, engines and life support. He gives Sam an idea of which systems are absolutely necessary and which we could lose in a pinch. The hope is that Sam will be able to use his Legacy to communicate with the warship, verbally giving the ship commands to replace the roles of the dozens of crew members we simply don't have. Six sits nearby, watching them with a bemused smile. I listen in.

'You know,' Six says, 'the last time he communicated with a ship, he almost crashed it.'

'Hey,' Sam replies. 'That's not fair.'

263

Adam frowns at Sam. 'Maybe I should be writing some of this down.'

We know the *Anubis* waits for us in West Virginia. The flagship of the Mogadorian fleet stands between us and Setrákus Ra. We need to take it down with an untrained skeleton crew. Both warships are shielded, but the *Anubis* has bigger guns. According to Adam, our shields will degrade faster than the Mogs.

Good thing we're packing more than just their weapons.

I look away from the others at the sound of sizzling in my hands. My white-hot Lumen torch is starting to work.

I hold in my hands the Voron noose that once scarred Setrákus Ra and now has scarred me. On closer inspection since it's not tied around my throat, the noose's material looks like a vine you'd find hanging in a jungle, except it has the texture of hardened plastic. Each edge is razor sharp, and as I melt it down, I'm careful not to cut my fingers. The material, found only on Lorien, glows a deep purple as I heat it up and begins to take on a consistency like candle wax. I don't let the melting material drip to the floor. Instead, I catch it with my telekinesis and begin to reshape it.

When I'm done, I've turned the noose into something more like a dagger. It's about the length of my forearm, with a makeshift handle where I allowed the Voron to bell outward into a guard. The blade itself is diamond shaped, with four edges and a wicked point at the end. I turn it over in my hand, test the weight and slash it back and forth.

This is what I'll use if they manage to take my Legacies away again. I'll put this right through Setrákus Ra's heart.

'Badass,' Nine says from the entranceway.

I was so focused, I didn't even hear Nine approach. He grins at me, eyeing the blade. I float it over to him with my telekinesis, and he plucks it out of the air, taking a few overhand swings with it.

'Not bad,' he concludes, floating it back to me. 'I miss my staff, man. Can't believe that shit got broken.'

'Yeah, I miss my shield,' I reply, tilting my head in Nine's direction. 'So, what's up?'

'Eh . . .' Nine comes farther into the room and leans against the railing at the edge of the deck. He lowers his voice. 'I, uh . . . I wanted to say sorry for that time I beat you up in Chicago.'

I actually snort from surprise at that. 'Nine, what?'

'And also in New York when I blew our stealth approach by clapping my hands with those stupid thunder gloves. Sorry about that too.'

'Okay,' I say, holding up my hands. 'What are you doing?'

'Pretty much any time that I said something that pissed you off or almost got you killed. I'm sorry for all that.'

'Okay, look, if you're going through all this because you think we might die down there, it's not necessary.'

'Oh, there's no might for me,' Nine says, locking eyes with me. 'I'm definitely living through this shit. You, on the other hand, you've got this whole fly-off-on-your-own-don't-need-friends thing going, like you're just gonna rage until you burn out. Like you don't care what happens to you.' I start to protest, but Nine holds up a hand. 'No, it's cool. The rest of them might not get it, but I do. Leave it all on the field. You do what you need to do, man. But I don't want you dying while I've still got all this shit on my conscience.'

'Okay, Nine,' I reply, shaking my head. 'You're forgiven.'

'And also,' he continues, 'you should know that I'd prefer it if you made it out of this alive with me. You're my brother. And, uh . . . that would be ideal.'

Before I can stop him, Nine has me wrapped up in a bear hug. It doesn't last long, and it ends with him pounding on my back hard enough that I cough.

'You've always been the best sidekick a guy could ask for,' he says.

'Eat shit, Nine,' I reply.

He grins at me. 'See you out there, Johnny.'

Nine leaves me alone on the observation deck. I hook the Voron dagger through one of my belt loops. We're closing in on West Virginia now. I should make my way down and get ready. Instead, I linger up here, thinking about what he said. Is he right? Do I not want to make it through this? I try to imagine an after – a world where we've defeated Setrákus Ra and I'm still alive. Used to be daydreams like that were what I lived for.

Now, I can't picture it.

There's no fear in me. Fear, I guess, is rooted entirely in antici-pation. Worrying that things won't turn out the way you've planned, that something will hurt; dreading the sorrow to come – all that goes away when you simply accept finality.

It isn't so bad, knowing there's no future. It's freeing.

On my way down from the observation deck, I bump into Mar-ina. She stands on the stairs, arms crossed, looking out over our friends as they acquaint themselves with the warship. I know exactly where she's staring.

Five. His shoulders are hunched as he sits at one of the weap-ons consoles, running a diagnostic while Sam and Malcolm look on. He must feel her glaring at him, but he chooses to endure it rather than acknowledge it. When I get close, I notice that the air around Marina is a little cooler.

Marina looks over at me, and her lips quirk downward in a frown.

'I already know what you're going to say,' I tell her. 'We can't trust him. He's dangerous. All of which I agree with.'

'And I already know what you are going to say to me,' she replies, mimicking my tone. 'He is a necessary evil. The enemy of my enemy is my friend. Desperate times call for desperate measures.'

'Tell me I don't use that many clichés.' She frowns at me. I rub my hands together to warm them up. 'He saved lives at Patience Creek, Marina. He saved my life.'

'Yes, I heard about his . . . performance,' she replies, a note of distaste in her voice. 'Sam told me how he relished what he was doing, how he could've simply killed Phiri Dun-Ra but instead repeatedly chopped at her arm. If we let ourselves become that ruthless and that brutal, do we really win?'

I think about how many Mogs I killed during my attack on this warship. And then I remember how Five looked at me when I first spoke to him at Patience Creek. How he told me I was like him now.

A shadow must pass over my face, because Marina squeezes my arm.

'I'm sorry. I don't mean to lecture,' she says. 'I just want us to remember, where Five is concerned, killing a common enemy does not make him an ally. Using him as a weapon does not mean he's willingly saving lives.'

'Usually, I'd agree with you. But not tonight.'

Marina nods slowly, resigned to the fact she'll be fighting alongside Five. 'And what about after, John? Will he pay for what he did?'

There's that word again. 'After.' I look away from Marina.

'After will be up to you,' I tell her.

She starts to ask me another question, but I'm already hustling the rest of the way down the steps. Adam catches my eye as I stride on to the bridge.

'We're almost there,' he says. 'I don't want to get us too close, in case they've got scouts deployed.'

'All right,' I reply, and glance over at Ella. She sits at one of the abandoned stations massaging her temples. 'Were you able to create that map?'

She nods. 'I scanned it in. Malcolm helped with estimating the scale.' At that, Sam's dad tips an imaginary hat.

'Pulling it up now,' Adam says.

A wide section of the bridge's floor-to-ceiling window goes opaque, and, a second later, a three-dimensional map of the Mogadorian mountain base appears on screen. It isn't exactly blueprint quality considering Ella and Malcolm produced it by hand and from memory. But it's accurate. Those memories were drawn from me, from Nine, from Six and Sam and from Adam. We'd all been inside the mountain base before; we've all carried around visions of its interior, even though they're colored with panic or chaos or torture. Ella sat with each of us for a few minutes, plucked out those memories and turned them into something tangible.

'All right, once we've dealt with the *Anubis*, we're attacking here.' I indicate the mountain's cavernous entrance. While the entrance is at ground level, it's at about the midway point of the map. The Mogs have hollowed out the mountain both above and below the entrance. 'We've got one cloaking device still hooked up to Lexa's ship. She'll drop us through the base's force field and then pull back to a safe distance until we need extraction. It'll be me, Six, Marina, Nine, Adam and Five down there.'

Sam's brow furrows at that, like I expected it would. 'Wait. What are the rest of us doing?'

'At first, Ella will be coordinating the different groups telepath-ically. In the event that Setrákus Ra takes away our Legacies, I want a backup team to bring in Ella so she can use her Dreynen and even the odds.' Ella nods at that, although she looks uneasy at the prospect of facing her great-grandfather again. 'Until then, the rest of you will be flying this warship and destroying anything that comes out of that mountain that isn't one of us. With your Legacy, Sam, you'll do more good up here.'

Nine snaps his fingers at Rex and gets the wide-eyed Mog's attention. 'And don't try any bullshit. My man Sam Goode here will kill you.'

268

Sam sighs and looks apologetically at Rex. 'I'm not going to kill you,' Sam says, although he immediately reconsiders that statement. 'I mean, I will if you try something, but you seem like an okay guy so, yeah, don't do that. I'll mess you up.'

Adam pats Rex on the shoulder. The other Mog shakes his head and becomes real interested in the schematics in front of him.

'We're expecting to hit heavy resistance in the fifty yards between the force field and the entrance,' I continue. 'We're going to use blunt force to fight our way in.'

Five and Nine both smile at that.

'Except for Five,' I continue, and his face falls.

'What?' he asks.

I turn to him. 'You're going to fly Six and Adam through the entrance — while invisible.'

Six looks in Five's direction. 'You're sane at the moment, right?'

'Yes,' Five answers brusquely. He keeps his eye pinned to the map and takes a deep breath. 'It's a good strategy.'

'No one was asking you,' Marina says.

I press on before this can get any more heated.

'Once they're in, Six and Adam will attempt to disable the base's shields.' I point to an elevated section above the entrance. 'We're not exactly sure where those controls are, but Adam thinks they're around here. While they're doing that, Five will hit the Mogs from behind.'

Sam raises his hand. 'What are the rest of us doing up here?'

'Once the shields are down, hopefully you guys can give us some air support. You'll want to have the main energy cannon ready to go.'

'We've got a mountain to knock down,' Six adds.

'Exactly. We're going to bury Setrákus Ra in there. But first we've got to make sure whatever twisted experiments he's concocted are destroyed.' I point into the depths of the mountain, down twisting corridors and across narrow rock bridges. I remember the sounds that came from those depths from the last time I visited the mountain base – animal screams, tortured cries. 'We figure if Setrákus Ra is anywhere, he's down here. That's where the vats are. It's where he'll be working his experiments.'

'You assume he doesn't come up to say hello when we knock,' Nine says.

'You're right,' I agree. 'He might come out to fight us. Either way, he and everything he's touched gets destroyed. By the time the sun rises, he's dust in a fucking crater.'

'You make it all sound so easy,' Five mutters.

'Oh, it won't be easy,' I reply. 'But we can do this. We have to do this.'

'It's everything,' Six adds. 'This is for *everything*.'

I can sense some of my friends looking at me expectantly. I try to think of the kind of speech I would've given a few days ago, when Sarah was still alive.

'Look, there's nothing more I can say. We've come this far together, and we're going to get through this together. No more running, no more hiding, no more words. We fight until we win.'

Nods all around. I look at every face, meet every set of eyes or eye, and I'm amazed by how calm I feel. I look beyond the mountain map on the window, into the night. The stars are out.

It's time.

'I'm going to go scout the *Anubis*,' I say. 'I'll tell you when you're clear to approach.'

'Be safe,' Marina says, her words echoed by most of the others.

'Adam, help me work the airlock, would you?' I ask on my way out. The Mogadorian raises an eyebrow at me, surprised to be asked to help with a task that he knows I could do on my own. He doesn't make a thing about it, though. He simply nods and follows me into the hallway.

Together, we walk down the empty corridors of the warship. The signs of our earlier attack still linger, Mogadorian ash crunching beneath our feet. Adam doesn't say anything. He waits for me to speak.

'Listen,' I start, when I'm sure we're out of range of any enhanced listeners. 'Once you disable the force field, I need you to come back up to the warship.'

'Okay . . .' Adam says.

'There's a chance things might not go as planned down there,' I continue. 'If that's the case, I'll let you know telepathically. When I tell you, no matter what, no matter who on board might try to stop you, you've got to fire the warship's cannon. Destroy the mountain. Erase it. It doesn't matter if some of us are still inside. Setrákus Ra and his work can't be allowed to see the sunrise.'

Adam stops midstride and grabs my arm. 'You're serious?'

'You know I am.'

His hand tightens on my arm, then drops away. He keeps his tone measured. 'Why . . . why are you asking me to do this, John? Because I'm the Mogadorian that means I'm cold and heartless? That I don't care about what happens to you all?'

'No,' I say, taking him by the shoulders. 'I know you care, Adam I know it'll kill you to do it. But you also know that I'm right. That stopping Setrákus Ra is more important than . . . than anything. If worse comes to worst, you'll pull that trigger.'

Adam holds my gaze for a few seconds, then looks away. He steps back so that my hands fall off his shoulders.

'Okay, John,' he says simply.

'Okay.'

I don't actually need him to help me with the airlock.

Alone, I pass through the warship's ravaged docking bay, open up the exit and fly into the night. Wilderness passes by beneath me, peaceful and untouched. The wind plucks at my clothes, cool against the sweat on my back.

The mountain rises up before me. Dark purple in the night. Waiting for me.

I go invisible.

The *Anubis* hovers over the mountain, an insectoid guardian. Its metallic hull reflects the moonlight. Searchlights from the warship's underbelly comb the side of the mountain, the cleared space around the cavern entrance, the sparse woods beyond. They're expecting us. The *Anubis* does a slow circle around the mountain's peak, prowling just like it did in New York City.

This time, I'm not running away.

From my back pocket, I produce my satellite phone. I dial the number programmed in for Lawson. Two simple words.

'Open fire.'

I don't listen for a response. I know what happens next. Soon, all around the world, counterattacks will begin.

I drop the phone. Let it smash down in the woods a few miles down. I won't need it anymore. No more talking, no more politics.

I reach out to Six telepathically.

The Anubis *is over the mountain. Get ready.*

I glance back in the direction I came from. Our warship is too far off to see, but the storm clouds aren't. Thick and dark, they blot out the stars, ruining what was a perfectly clear night sky. Lightning shivers through them, the wind picks up and I can hear hailstones falling in the distance. They roll towards me, towards the *Anubis*.

It'll be a storm like the Mogadorians have never seen.

We're coming.

26

'Gain some altitude, Rex,' Adam says. 'I want to swoop down from above them. That good for you, Six?'

'Yeah,' I reply distractedly. 'Got it covered.'

I stand right in front of the enormous windows on our warship's bridge, my hands raised in the air, fingers twisting. I can see reflections of the others in the glass, but I'm more focused on what's outside. I pull at the indelible threads of atmosphere that only I can sense and caress the wind into doing my bidding. If it wasn't for the thick sheet of glass in front of me, I could reach out and touch the roiling clouds that I've created.

A storm. A bigger storm than I've ever managed. Over the years, I've mostly relied on lightning strikes, high winds, sudden surges of cloud cover – quick effects. Not much can stand against Mother Nature for long. I've never really needed to build and sustain a massive storm front before.

Well, Katarina used to say, *discovery is born of desperation.*

'Visibility is really bad,' Rex calls to Adam.

'It's okay,' Adam replies. Ella stands next to him, her eyes rolled back in her head, seeing everything that John sees. 'We know where we're going, and our target's hard to miss. Keep us climbing.'

I have surrounded our warship with storm clouds and fog. Lightning strikes sizzle right in front of us and sting my eyes with their brightness. Our ship is big, but my storm front is bigger. It stretches nearly a mile wide and up, up, like a tidal wave crawling through the sky. Adam has triggered a scrambling device for radar so, between that and the static from the lightning, we should be wreaking havoc on the *Anubis*'s sensors. They'll definitely know that we're coming, but they won't know where exactly in the storm we're hiding. Not until it's too late.

Marina stands at my side. She's ready to enhance my storm with chunks of ice when needed. For now, she wipes some sweat from my forehead.

'You're doing great, Six,' she says.

It isn't until I try to smile at her and hear my teeth chatter that I realize I'm shaking.

Press on. Grow the storm. Bigger and bigger.

The winds howl outside, audible even in here. Thunder rumbles.

'Imagine the looks on their faces,' Five comments from his spot at one of the weapons panels. 'They're probably shitting their pants.'

'Shut up,' Nine replies automatically.

The edge of my storm reaches the *Anubis*. At first, the clouds break across their force field, keeping the air within one hundred yards of their ship completely clear.

'Do we know if weather will breach their shields?' Sam asks.

'Let's find out,' Adam says. 'Pour it on, Six.'

In my mind, I take hold of a lightning bolt. Just a small one, a probe, and sling it against the *Anubis*'s force field. The streak of electricity bends, turned back by the Mogadorian technology.

'Doesn't seem like it penetrated,' Rex reports, sounding anxious.

'No, it doesn't matter,' I reply through gritted teeth. 'We're close enough now. I don't need to break their force field. I can go around.'

I let the dark clouds and swells of fog coalesce around the *Anubis*, hiding us, blinding them beyond the range of their force field. Then, maintaining that, I start over. My left hand twirls above me, spinning the wind, building it up, creating pressure. This time, the storm gathers within their shields.

'The air . . .' I say. 'The air belongs to me.'

The wind outside the *Anubis* screams, the pressure drops. The wind swirls into a vortex, its velocity as fast as I can make it, fast enough to uproot trees and tear off weapon arrays, so fast that I'm starting to get a little dizzy. The vortex splits, then splits again. Three small funnels on top of the dark metal hull of the warship, shearing away at its armor, knocking it out of its orderly hover. Three tornados to shove this bastard to the ground. I send in some rain as well, and, next to me, Marina presses her hands to the glass. She freezes the water as it lands on the *Anubis*, adding weight, hopefully jamming up important functions.

'It's retreating!' Rex yells. 'The *Anubis* is retreating!'

'That's not a good thing,' Adam replies. 'Six needs to be able to create weather inside their force field's perimeter to knock down their systems.'

'Keep me . . . unh. Keep me close,' I grunt.

The farther the *Anubis* edges away from our hiding spot in the clouds, the harder it is for me to maintain control of the weather around it. The strain is immense, each weather pattern pulling at a part of me, requiring my attention. To keep our camouflage up along with the attack on the *Anubis*, I need us to be within a few hundred yards of each other.

From the corner of my eye, something bright red explodes in the air outside our ship. A second later, it happens again. Like fireworks going off.

'They're shooting at us!' Sam yells.

'They're blind-firing,' Adam replies calmly. 'Steady, they can't see –'

Explosion. The entire floor bucks, our ship vibrating. We've been hit. For a moment, the entire world is colored red. It's our own warship's shield activating in response to being struck by the *Anubis*'s energy blast, the impact illuminating the force field outside. It effectively highlights our location for the Mogadorians.

'They see us!' yells Rex. 'Locking on . . .'

'Brace yourselves!' Adam screams.

The next impact is worse. It's a sustained torrent of energy that rocks our ship. I crash into Marina, and we both fall to the floor. Everyone else holds on to their station for dear life. A siren begins blaring inside the warship, the same one that went off before when we were the ones doing the attacking.

'Shields are down to forty-eight per cent!' Rex says.

'Forty-*what*?' Sam exclaims. 'I thought these force fields were impenetrable!'

'Impenetrable to *your* weapons,' Adam snaps as he begins hurriedly tapping buttons on the command console. 'They're recharging their main cannon. I don't know if we'll survive another hit.'

Nine scrambles over and helps Marina and me back to our feet. My head hurts, and I realize there's a small cut on my forehead. For a moment, my concentration was lost, and that's all it took. My storms have begun to dissipate. Worse yet, below us, the *Anubis* is moving out of range of my Legacies.

'Hurry up and hailstorm their asses!' Nine yells at me.

I press my hands to the glass. 'Get me close!'

'Help me, Rex,' Adam says. 'Divert all unnecessary systems to power the shields. Bring us around so we can get a clear shot at them with our cannon.'

Rex leaps up from his navigation console, and Lexa sits down where he was. Working the levers, she keeps us floating above the *Anubis*, brings us steadily closer.

'Here they come,' Five growls.

From my vantage point, I see the *Anubis* open up, and a swarm of flies explode forth from its side. Skimmers. The little ships pour from the *Anubis* and streak through the night sky towards us. With their cloaking devices still equipped, this armada will pass right through our force field and take easy potshots at our warship.

'Weapons ready!' Adam yells at Malcolm and Five, who immediately key in to their stations. 'Don't bother shooting until they've cleared the shield radius of the *Anubis*.'

'How will we know —?' Malcolm starts to ask, a sweat ring visible around his neck.

'Now!' Adam barks.

The warship rattles as Malcolm and Five begin

discharging the auxiliary guns. The effect is like a cluster of fifty Mog blasters going off at the same time. Five fires wildly, his breathing sharp and excited, while Malcolm takes his time and tracks his targets methodically. It only takes one shot to bring down a Skimmer, but there's a whole hell of a lot of them.

I notice that some of the Skimmers careening towards us drop out of the air without even being hit. Each time before it happens a silver glow illuminates the Skimmer and then it drops like a rock . . . because it is a rock. That's John out there, invisible, flying, using his stone-vision to play defense.

'Closer!' I shout over my shoulder, gathering the winds again.

'On it,' Adam replies. 'Rex, how are those shields?'

Rex hurriedly pounds away at a keyboard. When he answers, he sounds terrified. 'I . . . I'm sorry; I can't get the power to reroute. I'm a navigator; this isn't my area of expertise.'

'You sabotaging us, loser?' Nine snarls.

'No!' Rex replies. 'I swear, I need another minute or two –'

'Let me try!' Sam says, wiping sweat off his forehead. 'All power to shields!'

Our warship's siren stops blaring.

The guns stop firing.

And we start to fall out of the sky.

'Tell me you didn't just shut off another ship!' Lexa cries.

'Uh, I –' Sam starts to respond.

'All power to shields,' Rex repeats, then louder, like we're doomed. 'All power to shields means we can't fly!'

'I can fix it,' Sam says. He looks at Adam.

'Restore power to the engines,' Adam says with forced calm. 'Start there, Sam.'

'Power to the engines!' Sam yells.

Nothing changes. Sam repeats himself, but the ship either isn't listening or Sam's Legacy isn't working. Behind me, I can hear Rex hitting his console furiously.

We're falling.

My feet actually lift off the floor of the bridge. Marina grabs on to me, and Nine grabs on to her. Thanks to his antigravity Legacy, his feet never leave the floor. I keep the storm churning, even as we start to nose-dive towards the *Anubis*.

'Come on, you Mogadorian hunk of junk!' Sam yells. 'Engines on! Give me something!'

'Wait,' Adam says, looking out the window at what I'm seeing. 'It's okay. We're okay.'

A streak of vivid red energy shears towards us from the *Anubis*'s main cannon. Our shields flare to life, and this time I can feel some of the heat bleeding through. The window in front of me, thick as bricks, begins to crack.

'Shields held!' Rex reports. 'Barely.'

'I think you saved our asses, Sammy,' Nine says. 'For a few minutes anyway.'

'We're still falling, you fools,' adds Five.

'Good,' says Adam. 'We're going to ram them. Six?'

'Yeah?'

'I need everything you've got. Bring them *down*.'

We plummet towards the *Anubis*. I concentrate. A Skimmer collides with our hull, explodes, and a small fire bursts to life in one corner of the bridge. I can actually feel wind hissing in through the cracks in front of me as we pick up speed.

That's my wind out there.

Closer and closer we get. Falling.

I raise my hands anew, churning them into the empty air. One tornado, another. Freezing rain that Marina bolsters with gigantic chunks of ice. All this I shove down towards the *Anubis*, the entire weight of the sky, ripping off metal panels and breaking apart their blasters.

I see energy gathering in their main cannon. The red glow is like a bull's-eye. It's like threading a needle, but I command a bolt of lightning right through it. There's a flash, an electric shriek, and the cannon explodes in a halo of fire. When the main cannon blows, it takes a huge chunk of the ship with it. Small explosions burst to life all across the warship.

The *Anubis* teeters.

'Keep going!' Rex yells. 'You could knock out their systems!'

I send lightning through the cockpit, right through the windows where I'd be standing if I was on that deck instead of this one. Push my wind in there, tear it up, turn it inside out. I see Mog bodies sucked out into the night, swallowed up by my tornado.

We're going to crash. Force field to force field. I don't know what the hell happens then.

Nine has a hand around my waist, another around Marina. He keeps us steady, his own feet stuck to the floor.

'You know, if I'm going to die, there could be worse positions . . .'

I wish I had the energy to slap him. All my anger, years and years of suffering and fear, I pour it into this storm. The swirling vortex is strong enough that trees from the mountainside are ripped up and ignite against the *Anubis*'s force field.

Until one of them doesn't.

'Their shields are down!' Rex yells.

'You must have blown them out,' Adam yells to me. 'Keep going! Brace yourselves!'

We ram into the *Anubis*. Our own force field collapses part of their hull with an electric scream and grinding of metal that makes my bones vibrate. More fires start on the bridge, consoles sparking and exploding from the impact, and Marina breaks away from Nine to put them out with splashes of ice.

The *Anubis* flips, end over end.

It's going down.

A tower of orange fire explodes in the air as the *Anubis* smashes into the force field around the mountain base, bounces off and crashes to the ground. It pinwheels through the woods, shearing through, breaking apart, leaving a massive trench in the earth.

'Thrusters!' Adam yells. 'Sam, get me back thrusters.'

'Ship! Engage thrusters!' Nothing happens. 'Damn it!'

'Ella, I'm trying to imagine how these look . . .'

That's it. The same trick we used at Niagara Falls.

'Done,' Ella says immediately. 'Over to you, Sam.'

'Ah . . . thrusters! Ship, give me back thrusters!'

It works. The ship actually listens.

We level off. We don't crash. The seesawing in my stomach calms.

And the storm outside parts, revealing nothing but flaming wreckage below.

Everyone on the bridge cheers. Marina hugs me. So does Nine. I elbow him in the stomach.

It's not over yet.

I turn to look out through our cracked window. We're hovering over the mountain now, a few hundred yards from its force field. The entire area is illuminated by the trails of fire left by the *Anubis*. I see them down there, piling out of the cavernous entrance to the base. A horde of Mogadorians, their blasters pointed up at our ship.

Maybe it's my imagination, but I think those assholes look scared.

27

I try not to stare too long at the fiery swath of destruction created by the crashed *Anubis*. There's still work to be done, but the sight of the warship broken into pieces on the mountainside gives me an undeniable thrill.

Still invisible, I fly underneath one of the Skimmers that survived the titanic clash of the two warships. Quickly, I unleash a torrent of ice that freezes the engines. The small ship drops like a rock, right towards the steadily gathering crowd of Mog vatborn outside the base entrance.

For a moment, the sky is clear. I've taken care of all the Skimmers that weren't destroyed by our warship.

There's an explosion to my right. The Mogs down below aren't happy. They're taking potshots with their blasters, and others are letting loose with what look like bazookas. Nothing penetrates the shields of our warship.

They aren't prepared for this kind of attack. Why would they be? Their base's force field, not to mention their regular energy weapons, are enough to repulse anything the humans could throw at them.

Overconfidence gets you dead.

I fly behind the safety of our warship's force field and back on board the ship. The others are waiting for me in the docking bay.

I'm soaked from the rain and bleeding from my neck. The stitches pulled while I was out there using my stone-vision to knock down Skimmers, all while darting around lances of energy from the *Anubis* and getting thrown about by Six's wind gusts.

Six looks almost as rough as me. Her hair is a tangled mess, like she was in the windstorm, sweaty and matted to her face.

'So far so good,' she says.

'Most beautiful storm I've ever seen,' I tell her.

Lexa is already in the cockpit of her ship, with Marina riding shotgun. Adam sits in the back, a Mogadorian blaster across his lap. He avoids making eye contact with me. I notice a rustling in the front of his shirt and realize he's got Dust with him, the Chimæra shrunk down to a gray mouse until it's time to join the fight. Nine piles in across from Adam, and Bernie Kosar bounds in after him. Five follows after Nine but pauses in front of me and Six, his one eye lingering on the light show outside.

'You know, they're going to shoot us to pieces the minute we fly out of here,' he says.

'Not if we give them something else to shoot at,' I say.

Six and I usher Five on to the ship, follow behind him and close the door after us.

'Good to go?' I call out to Lexa.

'Say the word,' she replies.

Sam and Rex, now in charge of maneuvering our warship, have us positioned so that the docking bay doors are right above the horde of Mogs gathered below. They crowd the area in front of the mountain's entrance, shooting up through the force field that prevents us from returning fire. They haven't breached our warship's defenses yet, but that doesn't stop them from trying. I guess we made them mad when we took down their flagship.

'All right, everyone with telekinesis, grab hold of those Skimmers,' I say, indicating the dozens of Mog ships that we stripped for parts earlier. 'Let's dump them. Lexa —'

'Use the ships as cover,' she finishes my thought. 'I got it, John. The drop won't take more than ten seconds.'

Nine cracks his knuckles. 'We're ready.'

As a group, we exert our telekinesis to shove the dormant

Skimmers out the docking bay doors. To the Mogs down below, it must look like they're being dive-bombed by dozens of their own ships. Lexa eases our ship out with the others. If it wasn't night, if it wasn't chaos, maybe the Mogs would be able to pick our vessel out from the others. Instead, they shoot at everything; the darkness comes alive with streaking arcs of blaster fire.

It's oddly silent on board the ship.

For a moment, we're in free fall. All of us hold on to seatbacks or safety harnesses. We absorb a few hits from the blaster volley but nothing that knocks us off course or does any real damage.

The first of the Skimmers begin to hit the mountain's force field and explode above the Mogs. Nothing gets through, of course. That doesn't stop some of the stupider ones from scattering or ducking for cover. Little fireballs pockmark the force field, and it's through that heat that we pass.

'Here we go,' Lexa says.

At the last possible moment, she brings us out of free fall with a flourish, levels us off and drops us to ground level. She lands our ship right on top of a few dozen Mogs, crushing them into the ground. Now that we're the only ship that's gotten through the force field, they're focusing their fire on us. Nine kicks open the exit ramp, welcoming it.

'LET'S GO!' he bellows as the whistle and hiss of blaster fire fills the air.

Five leaps towards Six and Adam, scoops one up in each meaty arm, and flies them out the exit. They go invisible before they're outside the confines of the ship. Five's a skilled flier; I have to trust that he'll carry them unharmed over this mass of Mogs and get them in the entrance.

That leaves me, Nine, Marina and BK to lead the assault.

None of us says anything as we stride into the chaos, right towards hundreds of Mogs ready to kill us. We don't need to discuss strategy. We've done this before.

As soon as we're clear of the ramp, Lexa gets her ship out of harm's way. She doesn't fly straight up, though. Instead, she takes off with a corkscrew, cleaving through the first wave of Mogadorians. I'm grateful for that.

Blaster fire burns the air around us. With the chaos created by Lexa's departure, the explosions overhead and the fact that they're all crammed together in front of the cavern entrance, the Mogs are just as likely to hit each other as they are to hit us. Even so, Nine and Marina don't waste any time telekinetically ripping their guns away from them. Soon, it's raining hardware as they bring the blasters down on the Mogs' heads.

I unleash my stone-vision, painting it across the nearest row of Mogs. As soon as I've done that, Marina jackhammers those Mogadorian statues with a barrage of icicles. Their bodies break apart into shards that Nine catches with his telekinesis and sets to spinning around us. It's like we're surrounded by a meteor shower of broken Mogadorian body parts. All the debris serves to act as cover, deflecting most of the Mog blaster shots.

There are a few piken scattered in the crowd of Mogs. The big beasts are fired up from all the mayhem and end up trampling through the vatborn to charge us. Hideous as always with their muscular bodies that look like someone crossbred an ox and a gorilla, then added fangs, claws and spiky gray skin, I briefly remember how one of these things used to terrify me. Back in Paradise, just one piken rampaging around our school almost killed our whole group.

Now, I stand my ground.

The piken closest to me gets met with a jet of fire from both of my extended palms. It screams and cooks, its thick body engulfed in flame. I pick it up with my telekinesis and sling it back into the crowd, hoping to crush some Mogs before the thing fully disintegrates.

Bernie Kosar latches on to a second piken. My old friend has taken on one of his favorite battle shapes: powerful wings, a lion's body, an eagle's head — essentially a griffin. With a flap of his wings, he gets over the piken, then smashes his beak through its spine.

Another piken bears down on Marina. Nine flashes in between them and punches clear through the piken's snout. He grabs the underside of the beast's jaw and lifts, snapping its head apart before tossing it aside. Nine's arm is all carved up from shoving into the piken's mouth, but Marina quickly heals him.

I sling fireballs into the Mogs. Whenever the blaster fire gets too heavy, I create some new cover with my stone-vision. We press forward, gaining ground. The Mogs are beginning to back-pedal towards the cavern entrance.

That doesn't last long. Five appears behind them, his body completely steel, holding a blaster in one hand and brandishing his blade in the other. He lights up a bunch of Mogs from behind before taking to the air. With methodical glee, Five repeatedly cannonballs into the crowd, crushing Mogs beneath his heavy metal frame, standing up, stabbing any around him then taking flight again to repeat the process.

John, a calm voice in my mind, a reprieve from the madness around me. It's Ella. *Six says the shields are down.*

I look around. We've halved the number of Mogs out here, but there's still a lot of fighting to be done. I've got blaster burns on my arms and chest that I quickly heal. Nine and Marina are con-stantly needing to heal between assaults too. Five's the only one who looks like he'd be happy mopping up vatborn for the rest of the night. Time to finish this up.

Marina, I reach out telepathically. *Give me an igloo.*

Marina reacts immediately. She creates a dome of ice over her and Nine, thick and sturdy. As soon as it's created, I hit the structure with my stone-vision, turning it from ice to solid gran-ite. Then I run forward, joining them underneath it. BK charges in, too. Five sees what we're doing and snorts. Instead of diving in with us, he simply flies clear of the battle. Mogs run towards us, but Marina and I quickly seal the entrance.

'Sweet bunker,' Nine comments in the dark.

Open fire, I tell Ella.

The four of us huddle underneath the stone igloo as our warship bombards the Mogs surrounding it. The ground shakes, and the air gets hot enough that Marina has to start generating a field of cold to keep us from boiling. Cracks form in our makeshift structure, and chunks rain down on our hair; but I quickly seal them up with my stone vision.

It only takes about thirty seconds.

When the shooting stops, Nine slams through the stone cover with his telekinesis. Outside, the ground is completely scorched. Thick dust hangs in the air, and twisted chunks of melted blasters litter the ground.

The entrance to the mountain base is clear.

Five floats down from above. 'There weren't many left inside,' he says with a crazed smile. 'They panicked when you brought down the *Anubis* and rushed out here to honor their Beloved Leader.'

'Did you see him?' I ask. 'Any sign of Setrákus Ra?'

He shakes his head. 'Probably cowering down in the vats.'

We take a moment to catch our breath, then move forward into the cavernous complex. The place is just like I remember it. The gray stone walls are polished smooth, accented every twenty feet or so by a power conduit or a halogen lamp. The air is cool in here, the ventilation system on full blast. On our left, there's a staircase carved out of the rock that leads up to where we think the control rooms are. On our right, a tunnel slants downward, deeper into the mountain, down to the vats.

He's waiting for us there. I know it.

A handful of vatborn come charging out from the tunnel.

Stragglers who missed the real fight. I dispatch them with a fire-ball, almost like an afterthought.

There's no sign of Six and Adam yet.

'What are we waiting for?' Five grumbles. He and Nine press ahead, towards the down-sloping tunnel, like they're in a competition to get there first. Marina and BK stay on either side of me.

Six says to give her a minute, Ella's voice enters my mind.

Is there a problem? I think back at her. I'm about to cast about with my own telepathy for Six, find out what is delaying her, when a pained shout draws my attention up ahead.

'That was Nine,' Marina says, alarmed.

We run forward and down, BK on our heels, into the narrowing tunnel. Nine and Five, so eager for more combat and looking to show each other up, got way too far ahead of us. As we run, the air gets humid and stifling, laden with a smell like rotten meat covered with gasoline.

After a quick sprint through the bottleneck, Marina and I emerge in the mountain base's cavernous central chamber. Here, a rocky ledge spirals downward along the walls, passing dozens of tunnels, crisscrossed here and there by arched stone bridges. Two huge columns run from the floor to the ceiling overhead. Last time, I remember how busy with Mogadorians this place was, how the structure reminded me of a beehive and the Mogs drones. Now, the place is all but empty.

The ledge terminates a half mile down at a vast lake of the black Mogadorian sludge. I remember that being green the last time I was here and reeking of chemicals, but that was before Setrákus Ra arrived on Earth and really put his experiments to work. There are machines down there now, jutting up from the lake of ooze like oil derricks. Even from this height, I can see the occasional blue spark of Loric energy bubble up from that goo and then, just as quickly, dissolve.

'There!' Marina shouts, grabbing my arm.

Nine stands on the ledge just underneath ours, clutching his face. I grab Marina and fly us over to him.

'Thing came out of nowhere,' he growls. The side of his face is burned and cracked, like it was splashed with chemicals, patches of hair on that side of his head now bleached white. Quickly, Marina presses her hand against Nine's cheek and begins to heal him.

'Where —?'

I don't need to finish my question. I see them, swooping through the air below our current perch. Five flies in a loop, dodging away from a Mogadorian trueborn, definitely an Augment, one that can fly also. It reminds me of a ghost, its form raggedy, wisps of shadows trailing out from its lower body.

I jump off the ledge and fly down to help Five. BK follows me, back in his griffin form. I quickly glance over my shoulder and see Nine, healed, sprinting down, too, using his antigravity Legacy to stick to the walls. Marina clings to him in a piggyback position.

As I get closer, I get a better look at this latest Augment. His entire lower body is missing. From the waist down, he's nothing but semisolid shadows. These shadow limbs wave back and forth like fishtails and propel him through the air. Worse yet, his jaw and a good part of his upper chest are missing. It looks like he's stuck in a perpetual scream, an acidic green spray frothing from his mouth. That's what burned Nine, and it's what is currently tormenting Five, the spray melting through even his metal-encased skin.

The Augment doesn't see me coming. He's about to take another pass at Five when I hit him full speed with both feet between the shoulder blades. I pin him like that and ride him two hundred feet down, on to the ledge, where he smashes with a sickeningly wet sound and stops moving.

Five lands next to me and, with no fanfare, shoves his blade through the back of the already-dead Augment's head. Making sure, I guess. He looks up at me, and, for the first time, I see something like horror in Five's eye.

'Did you see that thing?' he asks me.

'I saw it.'

'Why . . . ?' He shakes his head. 'He promised the Mogs, *he promised me*, new Legacies. Who would want something like *that*?'

I shake my head and approach Five, touching the eroded sections of his arms and shoulders so I can heal them. He flinches away for a moment, then calms down and lets it happen.

'He's a madman, Five,' I say. 'You were taken in by a madman.'

'He has to die.'

'Finally, we agree on something,' Nine says, jumping down from the ledge above ours. Marina climbs off his back and studies the dead Augment.

'This is an abomination,' she says. 'He has twisted the work of Lorien into something . . . something . . .' Marina covers her mouth with the back of her hand and walks away. Her path takes her across the entrance to the nearest tunnel, where she immediately freezes. 'Oh . . . oh my God.'

We all rush to her side.

It's the smell that hits me first. The rotten odor, the stench of decay, made all the more inescapable by the oppressive heat, down here, close as we now are to the vat of black ooze.

Bodies are piled high in this tunnel. Some of them have the dark hair and pale skin of Mogadorians. Those are half-disintegrated, warped, their limbs turned into fragile, dusty husks. Others are unmistakably human. They look like they've been drained, their flesh gray and puckered, dried black veins visible beneath their skin. It looks like he's sucked the vitality right out of them. A closer look reveals that, despite their shriveled appearances, the human bodies are exclusively teenagers.

I remember Lawson telling me about how the Russians were

turning over suspected Garde to the Mogadorians, and it dawns on me. These are ours. The human Garde from the countries that surrendered and the other ones his people tracked down. He pulled the Loric spark right out of them.

Staring at this, unconsciously, I've drawn my Voron dagger. It glows with a dull red energy now. Seeing it in my hand, Nine takes a step back.

'Careful with that thing, Johnny,' he says weakly. His eyes are actually filled with tears from the sight of the bodies. Marina covers her face. Five simply stares.

I've charged the dagger with Dreynen without even realizing it. When I talked to Ella, I was worried that I wouldn't be able to use my Ximic to copy this power because of how unnatural it feels. But no, I've never wanted to cut someone off from Lorien so badly as I do Setrákus Ra.

I spin away from this latest atrocity, stand at the edge of the ledge and scream.

'SETRÁKUS RA!'

There's a rumble overhead. Rock dust drifts down from the ceiling. It feels like the earth itself moved. I'm not sure if that was caused by my yelling or something else.

And I don't care. Because I see movement down below. In the center of the lake of Mogadorian ooze.

Setrákus Ra emerges from the oily muck, rising up from the depths. The worms of ooze don't drip off him, rather they slither under his skin like they're seeking shelter. He wears the red-and-black Mogadorian armor that I've seen before, ornate and showy, with a flowing black cape attached to his studded shoulders. His bulbous, pale head is coated with thick bristles of dark hair. That's new. Similarly, his features aren't so sunken anymore, not so old. Even the purple scar around his neck has begun to fade. He's younger, healthier than I've ever seen him. He floats with his hands spread out at his sides like some twisted savior.

He cranes his neck to look up at us and smiles. 'Welcome,' he says. Noticing the tunnel we're standing in front of, he lowers his eyes and frowns, mockingly demure. 'Please, do not be offended by the sight of my failures. They were not fit to carry my gifts. Like you all, they were not ready for prog—'

No more goddamn words.

I pitch a fireball at him. I don't expect it to hit; it's just meant to cover my approach. I fly forward, reckless, as fast as I can. Behind me, I can feel the others moving forward too. This is it.

Kill or be killed.

Setrákus Ra raises his hand, and a plume of ooze shaped like a shield extends from his palm. My fireball is absorbed. Doesn't matter.

With him distracted, I fling my dagger at him. I use my telekinesis to boost its speed.

The blade buries itself in his shoulder, punching right through his armor. A wound that he won't be able to heal thanks to the Voron and no more Legacies thanks to my Dreynen.

Except, it seems too easy. Almost like he wanted me to hit him.

'Very good, John,' Setrákus Ra says smugly. 'You've mastered Dreynen.'

Nothing happens. He still floats. He still smiles.

'You've cut me off from that piece of Lorien still living within me. I won't be able to take your Legacies,' Setrákus Ra continues conversationally. 'It won't matter.'

Setrákus Ra pulls the dagger out of his shoulder and whips it back at me. I fly aside and, behind me, Nine catches the weapon with his telekinesis.

'I am beyond that now. Beyond Legacies. Your powers derive from a primitive being with no rhyme or reason. My Augmentations are of my own choosing, limited not by an outside Entity, but only by my own genius. Which, I might add, is staggering.'

The wound on his shoulder doesn't heal. Instead, it fills with the black ooze.

I barely have time to process this information as I propel myself forward, enraged. If Dreynen won't work, there are other ways.

Brute force.

I slam into Setrákus Ra with my shoulder. He barely budges. Quickly, I light my Lumen, my fists spouting white-hot flames, and throw one punch, two punches, three punches. He moves his head just enough to the side each time, his speed impossible.

The next punch he catches. I smell burning flesh as his hand covers mine. He doesn't seem to notice.

'After all these years,' Setrákus Ra says, the two of us face-to-face, 'do you still not understand?'

Five crashes into Setrákus Ra's back and starts to stab him. He jams his blade through Setrákus Ra's throat, into his back, through his cheek.

Each wound is quickly sealed over by black ooze.

Setrákus Ra's free arm rotates around in the socket 180 degrees. His hand turns over like he's double-jointed, and, without turning away from me, he grasps Five by the throat. Now he's holding on to both of us.

'You could never win,' Setrákus Ra finishes his thought. 'You were only sent here to die.'

Then he crushes my hand. I feel every finger break, every knuckle get compacted. The pain is excruciating. He flings me away from him with such force that I lose control of my flight. Luckily, Nine leaps up in the air and catches me around the waist. Marina, positioned on the ledge, creates an ice floe on the lake of ooze where Nine and I can safely land.

Nine stares at me, wild-eyed. 'John, what . . . what the hell are those powers?'

I swallow hard, trying to quickly heal my hand, grimacing as the compacted bones pop back into place. 'I don't know.'

Meanwhile, Setrákus Ra swings his arm around to its normal position, still holding Five by the neck. Five has given up on stabbing the Mogadorian and is instead desperately prying at Setrákus Ra's fingers.

'You,' Setrákus Ra says. 'One of my greatest disappointments. The power I could have given you, boy . . .'

Setrákus Ra holds up his hand. His fingertips shimmer, each of them tipped with a razor-sharp claw. He wants us to see this. He's toying with us.

I pull at Five with my telekinesis. I sense that Nine and Marina do the same. We aren't strong enough to drag him from Setrákus Ra's grip.

There's a piercing screech of metal, and then Five starts to scream. Setrákus Ra drags his clawed fingers over Five's face, slicing through his steel skin like it was butter. Then he peels it away, like taking off a mask, and tosses the metal chunk of face aside.

Five's not screaming anymore. I'm not sure if he's conscious or even alive.

'Let me show you what you missed out on, traitor,' Setrákus Ra says.

Setrákus Ra's arm stretches out as if it was made of rubber, and he dunks Five into the Mogadorian slime. Now, Five thrashes; and, briefly, his skin changes consistency, taking on the oily quality of the ooze. As I watch, bits of light-blue energy are sucked out of Five and drawn into the muck.

It only takes a few seconds until Five stops moving. Setrákus Ra lets his body sink beneath the surface of the muck. I grasp at my ankle, but there's no new scar. Either Five's somehow still alive, or Setrákus Ra and his muck have stripped away the energy that granted his Legacies so that the charm no longer recognizes him.

A single bubble rises up to the surface of the ooze, pops, and then the dark lake is still. There's no way anyone could survive that.

Setrákus Ra turns to us. Smiles.

'You children were never meant to live this long,' he says. 'A discrepancy I shall soon remedy.'

28

When we make it up to the mountain base control room, there are only six Mogs left in a space that could accommodate five times that. They're all glued to a bank of monitors attached to the cave wall, fixating on the screens that show the base's exterior. On those screens, the rest of our group are destroying the many vatborn protecting the entrance to the mountain.

Adam and I are invisible. These six don't hear us come in. I give his arm a squeeze, asking if he's ready to take this group down. He pats my hand slowly twice. A signal to wait.

Looking closer, I realize all these Mogs are trueborn. They cradle blasters, but they don't look all that eager to rush out and join the fray.

A male trueborn with a stupid Mohawk says something in Mogadorian to a female trueborn with long braids. She snaps back at him. They're arguing. The others join in.

Suddenly, Mohawk aims his blaster at Braids's face. She follows suit. In a matter of seconds, they're all pointing guns at each other, still yelling harsh words in Mogadorian.

It's a tense situation that I'm happy to help along.

With my telekinesis, I depress one of the blaster triggers, then another. The trueborn do the rest, screaming with rage and firing into each other. In a matter of seconds, they're all down. A few of them begin to disintegrate in sections.

I let go of Adam's arm, and we turn visible. He puffs out his cheeks with a sigh, looking down at these dead trueborn with disappointment, and then begins searching the control panels for the one that operates the mountain's force field.

'What were they fighting about?' I ask him. Like the Mogs before, my eyes are drawn to the battle playing out on screen.

'The one with the Mohawk wanted to know how this could happen. He wanted to know why Beloved Leader would allow the *Anubis* to fall, why he'd let the Garde get this far,' Adam explains morosely. 'The woman, she said that Setrákus Ra has gone mad, that the Augmentations are disturbing. The others called this blasphemy and . . .' He waves his hand in the air, indicating that I know the rest.

'Huh,' I reply, glancing down at the female Mog. Unlike the others, she hasn't disintegrated at all. I nudge her with my toe, and her head lolls to the side. It's weird to me when they leave bodies. Makes me feel something I'd almost call guilt. 'Maybe we should've helped her.'

Adam shakes his head. 'She would've tried to kill us,' he replies.

'Rex didn't.'

'If there are other sympathetic Mogadorians like Rex, we will not find them in the heat of battle,' he responds.

Adam finds the right interface and begins to hit a few buttons. A flashing symbol pops up on his screen – a warning in any language. He makes an annoyed noise and keys in another sequence.

'I've got to bypass a security protocol,' he says. 'See if there's a key card on one of those bodies.'

Quickly, I pat down the Mogadorian uniforms. I find a plastic chip in the front pocket of the first trueborn I check, blow some dust off it and hand it over to Adam.

'Great,' he says. He inserts the key card, throws a lever, and seconds later there's a loud electric sigh. Adam turns to me. 'Shields are down.'

'Awesome,' I reply. I feel a tickle in my mind, like for a moment there's someone else taking up space in my brain. That's Ella checking in. She's probably already reported our progress to John. I clap my hands. 'Let's hit it.'

'Wait,' Adam says hesitantly. 'There's something I need to tell you before – before it's too late.'

I cock my head. 'Right now?'

Adam nods, his lips in a tight line. 'John has asked me to go back to our warship and destroy this mountain. If you don't kill Setrákus Ra – he wants me to bring it down even if you're still in here.'

I think this over for a moment. 'Okay. So?'

'So?' he replies, incredulous.

'Yeah, so what? If we don't kill Setrákus Ra, then we're probably dead anyway, right?' I shrug. 'Do what he told you.'

'What about living to fight another day?'

'I think we're about out of more days, don't you? Time to end this, one way or the other.'

If Adam has any more protests to make, they're

cut off by a flash of light on the monitors. Both of us turn to watch as our warship opens fire on the Mogs outside, John and the others safely ensconced under what looks like a stone turtle shell.

'They'll be in soon,' I say. 'Let's get down to meet the –'

My sentence finishes in a wet cough. I look down at myself, puzzled by a sudden pain in my chest.

There's a sharpened tentacle of oily Mogadorian ooze protruding from under my left breast. It went in my back, between the shoulder blades. I can feel it, itchy and burning inside me. Nicked a lung, probably. My breath wheezes out of me, blood on my lips.

'Oh' is all I think to say.

'Six!' Adam shouts.

'Oh, how I hoped it would be you two,' says a familiar voice behind me.

I turn my head because I'm unable to move the rest of my body, impaled as I am by a tentacle. Phiri Dun-Ra stands in the control room doorway. Her Augmentation is just like John described: a sickening mass of writhing black ooze that's attached to her shoulder where her arm should be.

She's killed me. I can't believe it.

Dust acts the quickest. He lunges away from Adam's side, his wolf form growing huge, gray fur bristling over his muscular back, teeth gnashing. He hits Phiri Dun-Ra with his massive front paws and knocks her off her feet. His teeth snap in front of her face, but she manages to lean her head back just enough to avoid getting bitten. One of her tentacles wraps around Dust's snout, muzzling him. The others begin to stab at his body. Still, the Chimæra struggles, clawing at her and pressing his weight down.

As a result of Dust's attack, Phiri's tentacle snaps out of me. I would probably fall over if Adam wasn't there to catch me. He presses a hand to my wound, helping me to lean against the wall. My blood bubbles over his hand, and I can tell by the panic in his eyes that it doesn't look good.

'Six, we need to get you to Marina or John –'

Adam's cut off by a yelp, and then a heavy weight smashes into both of us. It's Dust, thrown by Phiri Dun-Ra's sick appendage. His fur is soaked with blood, piercings from Phiri's tentacles all over his rapidly shrinking form. He tries to stagger to his feet and almost makes it before his legs buckle. Dust's dark eyes settle on Adam as he lies down on his side, whimpers once and then is still.

Adam screams.

Phiri Dun-Ra has only now gotten back to her feet, her face and chest covered in Dust's claw marks. Adam takes up his blaster and fires. He gets her once in the chest, but the next two shots are absorbed by her tentacles. She ducks back out the doorway, running for cover.

Six! It's Ella's voice in my mind. *I'm sending the others up to help you!*

No! I think back, forcing myself to stand. *We've got this. Tell them to focus on Setrákus Ra.*

But –

I imagine Phiri Dun-Ra taking control of my or Adam's Legacies, using them to get behind the rest of our friends, then wiping them out. I call to mind John's secret orders to Adam, how he's supposed to destroy the mountain base if anything goes wrong. And I think about the time Ella herself leaped into a torrent of Loric energy because she knew it meant defeating Setrákus Ra.

Priorities. Sacrifices.

We stop Phiri Dun-Ra here. We make sure the others don't have any surprises creeping up behind them.

I stagger to my feet even though it isn't easy. When I try to take a deep breath, my body's response is to fill my chest with a shooting pain. It feels like I've got a stitch in my entire left side. I can still fight, though.

I have to.

I cover my wound with one hand as best I can and limp after Adam. He's already barreled his way into the hallway, enraged, chasing after Phiri Dun-Ra. He squeezes off a couple more blaster shots. She leaps up, her tentacle wraps around a stalactite and she yanks herself over Adam's attack. Then she slings herself back at Adam.

Phiri Dun-Ra kicks the blaster out of Adam's hand. Before she can slice into Adam with her tentacles, I shove her with my telekinesis and slam her into the wall. I keep her pinned there, a telekinetic weight against her chest. The muscles in her neck strain as she tries to jerk forward and can't.

'Six, you –' Adam looks surprised to see me standing, like he's going to admonish me for getting back in the fight. I try to gulp down a breath while maintaining my telekinetic hold on Phiri and feel like I'm about to throw up. I lean against the doorway of the control room.

'I'm fine,' I wheeze. 'Finish her.'

Adam turns to Phiri, and, of course, she starts talking.

'Doesn't it bother you to be on the losing side of history, Sutekh?' Phiri asks, high-pitched desperation in her voice.

'This is what winning looks like to you, Phiri?' Adam replies dryly, picking up his blaster.

Phiri rambles on, screeching. 'When these battles are added to the Great Book, you will be a cautionary tale, a traitorous footnote, a —'

'Shut up already,' I say.

She strains against my telekinesis to no avail, even her Augmented appendage futilely squirming, only capable of writhing against the wall. Unlike in Mexico, Marina's not around to keep us from killing this bitch. After what she did to John, to Dust, to everyone at Patience Creek, I don't think Marina would raise any objections even if she was.

The sound of a blaster ends Phiri Dun-Ra's pleas.

My back burns.

Phiri Dun-Ra cackles.

Adam spins around, wide-eyed.

I glance behind me. See the trueborn woman with the braids, the one we thought was dead, half sitting up.

She just shot me in my back.

Adam fires on her, takes her head clean off.

But the startling fresh pain was enough. For the briefest of moments, I lose my grip on Phiri Dun-Ra.

Her tentacles lash out. Two of them plunge right into Adam's abdomen, and he immediately doubles over. The other gropes for me, but I throw myself backwards, into the control room, avoiding it. Through all the pain I'm feeling, I try to grab Phiri Dun-Ra with my telekinesis.

She stomps down on the ground, and a seismic tremor knocks me backwards, slamming me hard against one of the metal computer cases. There's a groan beneath us, like old stones shifting and scraping together. I cough blood on to the shaky floor.

Phiri Dun-Ra laughs cheerfully. 'Amazing! I wasn't sure if you'd have a Loric spark to feed on, Adamus. I thought you were simply an early Augmentation, a failed experiment.' Phiri smacks her lips, like she's trying to figure out what she's tasting. 'But you really are like them! Will it make you happy to die knowing you were special? The worst of both worlds?'

Adam hangs limp from Phiri's tentacles. I can see motes of Loric energy winking through the oily mass of her deadly limb, pulled from Adam and into her. I try to push myself up, but my arms give out.

Slowly, Adam raises his head, tossing dark hair out of his eyes. He stares at Phiri Dun-Ra.

'I *am* like them,' he says through gritted teeth. 'But I am also like *you*.'

Adam plunges his hands into the black oil of her tentacles. They both gasp – her in shock, him in pain – as the ooze coalesces over his hands. He pulls backwards, and the ooze begins to tear itself away from the stump of Phiri's shoulder and bond with Adam. It must recognize his Mogadorian genetics. The sick substance is tangled between the two of them. The flow of Loric energy from Adam to Phiri stops.

'What –?' she starts to say, wild-eyed.

Adam stomps on the ground. A powerful tremor spreads out from him.

The resulting rumble is deafening. The cavern floor breaks open. Stalactites snap loose from above. A chasm opens up beneath the two Mogadorians. Phiri Dun-Ra tries to recoil, tries to grope for the ledge with her arms, her tentacles. But Adam holds on to her tightly.

They fall into the darkness.

'ADAM!' I scream. Despite the jagged, blinding pain throughout my chest, I dive towards the edge of the newly created pit. I reach out with my telekinesis.

Too late. Nothing but shadows down there.

He's gone.

'Adam . . .' I say, my hands hanging limply into the chasm, blood pooling on the rocks beneath me.

29

Everything.

Everything I've got, I throw at him.

First, my Lumen. My oldest, most trustworthy Legacy. I fly off the ice floe that Marina made, leave Nine behind and blast Setrákus Ra with two twin torrents of fire. His stupid cape ignites, his armor heats to red-hot. I watch as his pale skin bubbles and chars, peels back and, in the blink of an eye, is smoothed over by the arteries of ooze that circulate through his body.

He doesn't even seem bothered by my attack. It's like he doesn't feel any pain. He just floats above his lake of black muck, staring me down, an infuriating hint of a smile on his face.

'Is that the best you can do?' he asks.

Setrákus Ra flies towards me at a speed I couldn't duplicate and punches me square in the sternum. There are spikes growing out of his knuckles that weren't there a second ago, and I hear my ribs crunch. I'm tossed backwards on to a rocky outcropping at the edge of the vat, skidding to a stop on my elbows. Immediately, I start to heal my broken ribs.

I'm going to need to keep healing as fast as he can hurt me and hope that I can figure out a way to outlast him.

With a roar, Bernie Kosar flies towards Setrákus Ra. In his griffin form, he's a formidable opponent, even if Setrákus Ra is moving at super-speed. Maybe one good bite could make the difference.

BK never makes it there.

Setrákus Ra raises a hand, and the ooze from the lake springs up around BK. It forms a cage over him, like something out of a zoo, the bars thick sections of oil. Slashing and biting, BK can't break free. Slowly, the cage begins to contract around him, forcing him to shape shift into smaller and smaller forms or be crushed.

'I never did finish my work with the Chimærae,' Setrákus Ra muses, watching as the muck swallows BK. 'Thank you for bringing me one.'

The cage stops compressing when BK is squished down to beagle form. BK tries to go smaller and sneak between the bars, but the whole thing instantly seals up like a cocoon. I can't see him anymore. BK floats in a solid bubble of ooze just above the lake's surface.

At least, from the sound of it, Setrákus Ra doesn't plan to kill him right away.

Can't say the same about the rest of us.

As I scramble to my feet, Setrákus Ra lands a few yards away. He holds out his hands like a saint in a stained glass window. My lips curl in disgust.

'Like insects before a giant,' he says. 'So do you children quail before a god.'

'You're no god,' I reply, tossing a fireball at him that he simply absorbs.

He snorts. 'You Loric, so pious even at the end. The thing you worship, the Entity that now hides beneath the earth, it is nothing more than a resource. Like ore, like water. You pray to a river while I create dams. You rely on the whims of nature while my intellect shapes galaxies. Do you not see now what my work, my progress, has the power to create?'

'I see a lonely old asshole living in a fucking cave!' shouts Nine as he launches in from the side.

Nine throws a haymaker that Setrákus Ra easily ducks under. As Nine stumbles and tries to regain his balance, Setrákus Ra grabs him by the hair and yanks him backwards. Setrákus Ra's hand is flat, the edge gleaming like the blade of a sword. He swings in a chopping motion for Nine's neck.

I yank Nine to me with my telekinesis before Setrákus Ra can cut off his head. He's left with a handful of Nine's hair, ripped right out of his head.

The speed. The invulnerability. Twisting his body into whatever sick shapes he can imagine. It's crazy to think I was once intimidated by Setrákus Ra when all he could do was change sizes and cancel out our Legacies.

This monster before me is so much worse.

'Ideas?' Nine says to me.

'Flank him,' I reply, and we spread out.

Nine holds up my dagger. 'May I?'

'Be my guest.'

We're trying to put on a show of confidence, but I can tell Nine's shaken by Setrákus Ra's display of power. We're in trouble.

With a wolfish smile, Setrákus Ra starts to advance on us. Before he gets too close, he's peppered by a volley of icicles from the ledge above. He's a pincushion, the ice shards stabbing up and down his back.

'All you've made is pain and suffering!' Marina yells down at him. 'All those bodies up there! For what? So you could craft these hideous powers?'

Setrákus Ra chuckles. 'Oh no, my dear. Lorien is stingy with its gifts. The pitiful sparks that hide within all of you are mere drops in the bucket. I needed to tap directly into the source to create what you see down here.' He runs a hand vainly across his own cheek. 'Draining those others was merely a trial run of one of my new Augmentations. They died in service to glorious progress.'

'You're mad!' Marina counters. 'For all your supposed genius, you've never created anything as beautiful as Lorien did!'

A sudden wave of heat radiates from Setrákus Ra, and the icicles melt right out of him. Then he spins around to face

Marina, his appearance changing. His skin darkens to a caramel color, and his head sprouts a mop of curly dark hair.

'Haven't I?' he asks. His face, his voice — he's taken on the shape of Eight.

Marina recoils in horror as he starts to float up to her.

'Didn't I promise to reunite you with your love?' Setrákus Ra asks, his eyes filled with malice Eight's never held in life. 'That could still be yours, dear Marina . . .'

Using my stone-vision, I turn his lower half into solid granite and connect that to the cavern floor so Setrákus Ra is now a stalagmite rising up from the rocks. He looks down at himself — Eight's appearance abandoned, his own younger self returned — and makes a face.

'Primitive,' he growls.

Primitive or not, it slows him down. Nine charges in, runs up my rock formation and takes a swipe at Setrákus Ra with my Voron dagger. Stuck in place, Setrákus Ra can't dodge, and Nine cleaves off a huge chunk of his face. For a moment, I think I see blood. But then the Mogadorian sludge fills in the wound, smooths it over, and his face is back to normal.

Still, he was hurt. We can find ways to hurt him.

As Nine comes around for another pass, I push out with my telekinesis. I put pressure on the armor that Setrákus Ra wears, crushing it, compacting it, hoping to tighten it around his guts. I sense Marina add her strength to mine, and soon we're squeezing the armor like a tin can.

Bellowing, Setrákus Ra rips the armor loose and tosses it aside. He's bare-chested now. Right over his heart, in the spot where Six impaled him, there's a throbbing mass of the black ooze, like a spider at the center of its web.

The stuff isn't concentrated like that on any other part of his body. That has to be where he's deriving all this power from.

Nine! Instead of speaking, this time I use my telepathy. I don't want Setrákus Ra to know we've figured him out. *Go for the heart!*

Duh, he thinks back.

Setrákus Ra kicks free of the rocks I built around his legs like they were nothing more than pebbles. As soon as he's free, I activate my stone-vision and trip him up again. At the same time, Marina assails him with another vicious barrage of ice. He swats the frozen daggers away, growling, distracted.

'This grows tiresome,' he says.

And then Nine is on him, leading with the Voron dagger, powering out of a crouch, thrusting forwards with all he's worth.

Stabbing Setrákus Ra right through the heart.

Nine buries the blade to the hilt. Its tip pokes out through Setrákus Ra's back.

Setrákus Ra looks down at the weapon.

He smiles.

'Is this a children's story?' he asks, sounding amused. 'I have spent centuries perfecting my work. And you think . . . what? That there is a weak point?'

He takes a deep breath, and the blade, along with Nine's hand still on the hilt, is sucked fully into the black mass on his chest. Setrákus Ra looks towards Marina.

'Behold, a demonstration.'

Nine screams. His arm first turns blue, like the circulation's been cut off, then gray and withered and finally as black as the ooze. The muscles melt, his skin sags off his bones. It's like watching time-lapse photography of his arm decomposing.

Setrákus Ra again stomps free of the stone I placed around his legs and kicks Nine in the chest. Nine flies backwards.

His arm stays with Setrákus Ra. It hangs from his chest for a moment, and then it's like the ooze begins to digest the limb, breaking it down, drawing it into Setrákus Ra. When the process is over, the arm is fully absorbed. Nine lies on the ground, clutching the empty space where his arm used to be. Marina leaps down, wide-eyed.

'Oh God, oh God,' she mumbles, groping at the spot on Nine's shoulder. There's no blood; the flesh is dried and dead. Still, she activates her healing Legacy and tries . . . tries something.

Setrákus Ra advances on them, wetting his lips.

I fly forward — stone-vision, a bombardment of ice, a blast of fire — try to slow him down.

I'm not strong enough.

He grabs my head, palms my face and slams me down to the stone floor.

'You will be last, Pittacus,' he says.

Blood streams into my eyes. Woozy, dazed, I struggle to my knees as Setrákus Ra stalks towards my friends.

We can't win this.

Marina throws up her hands, and a wall of solid ice separates her and Nine from Setrákus Ra. The Mogadorian sighs, annoyed, and punches straight through it.

While this happens, I reach out with my telepathy. Search for Adam's mind. In the heat of battle, it didn't occur to me until now that Six never showed up. Maybe she went back to the warship with Adam for some reason, I allow myself to briefly hope.

Nothing. I can't find Adam's mind.

Or Six.

Split seconds pass telepathically, but it feels like an eternity of searching. Finally, I manage to make contact with Ella, still floating above the mountain in our warship. The anxiety radiating from her mind is palpable as soon as we connect. She anticipates my questions.

Adam . . . Adam fell into a chasm with Phiri Dun-Ra, Ella tells me. *And Six, she's hurt bad. I think she's unconscious.*

Damn it.

I switch from Ella's mind to Sam's. I can sense him up there, pacing back and forth, watching the darkened entrance of the Mogadorian base through the warship windows.

Sam. I make an effort to keep my thoughts calm and collected. Like my friends aren't dying. Like I'm not losing this war.

I need you to do something for me.

John? His mind practically leaps towards mine. Our entire conversation takes place in the space of one of his nervous strides, his foot hovering above the floor of the bridge. *What's happening? Ella won't say.*

I need you to do something for me.

Anything!

Use your Legacy. Command the ship to destroy the mountain.

. . . What?

Images flash to the forefront of Sam's mind. He and I walking through the halls of Paradise High School. Nine grabbing him in a loose headlock. Most prominently, he and Six standing on a breathtaking mountaintop somewhere, gazing out at a crystal clear ocean.

It's the only way to stop him, Sam. He's strong, but we can trap him down here!

No! I won't! Not while you're all still in there!

All this telepathy happens at the speed of thought as I get to my feet, as Setrákus Ra crosses towards Marina and Nine. I'm out of time, though — he's there; I need to act.

'Get up, Nine, come on,' Marina pleads, still trying to heal the dead flesh on his shoulder.

Holding Sam in my mind, letting him see what I see, I fly towards Setrákus Ra, hoping to buy Marina some more time.

He anticipates me. Backhands me with a force that cracks my jaw and sends me crashing to the cave floor, skittering through the broken shards of Marina's ice wall.

Nine is still on the ground, moaning and shaking, probably

going into shock. Marina presses both her hands to his stump. Our healing Legacies don't regrow limbs, though. There's nothing we can do.

Setrákus Ra grabs Marina by the hair and yanks her off her feet. She thrashes, raking her hand across his face. She hits the exact spot that Nine sliced with the Voron blade just a minute ago.

Setrákus Ra drops her, recoils and clutches at his cheek.

That part of his face slips off, the black oil holding it together receding into his body.

Marina and I make eye contact.

What did you do? My thought hits her mind with urgency.

Healing! she replies. *I was still using my healing!*

I remember New York City, right before the invasion. Secretary of Defense Sanderson and the black ooze running through his veins. It took minutes and it was exhausting, but I was able to burn that gunk out from inside his body by using my healing.

We can kill Setrákus Ra. We just have to make him Loric again. We have to expel these Augmentations and destroy what's left of the man.

Marina's already got the idea. As Setrákus Ra recovers, she flashes forward, hand extended in his direction.

Setrákus Ra sidesteps. He catches her by the elbow and twists, wrenching Marina's arm behind her back and dislocating her shoulder. Then he slashes her face with his claws, opening up four deep scratches diagonally across her face. Meanwhile, his own sick visage has already been restored by the ooze.

I fly into Setrákus Ra before he can finish off Marina. I wrap my legs around his chest and grab him on either side of his head, pumping as much of my healing energy into him as I can. At the same time, I muster as much force as I can and fly us across the cavern, hoping that keeping him away from his vat will weaken him further. I can feel the Augmentations inside him, the oil writhing in every part of his body. There's more of that inside him than there is man. It's like I'm trying to beat back a tidal wave.

Still, I have to try. This is the only way it ends.

Setrákus Ra screams as I force healing into him. But quickly, he fights back. He bites down on my shoulder, his mouth hideously huge, teeth sharpened, and tears off a chunk of flesh.

'John!' Marina shouts. Her one arm hanging limp at her side, blood streaming down her face, she races forwards to help.

Spikes of hardened ooze thrust forth from Setrákus Ra's body. One goes through my leg, another my side, another my shoulder. I'm not even sure if he's controlling this or if it's a reaction brought on by my healing, like the ooze is trying to escape. Either way, now we're pinned together. Another spike nearly makes it to Marina's eye before she skids to a stop a few feet away.

I redirect some of my healing to my own wounds. Try to close them as fast as Setrákus Ra can make them while still beating back the vileness that's spread throughout him.

As my healing Legacy drives it from Setrákus Ra's body, the ooze coalesces around us in battering tendrils. Marina can't even get close anymore.

'Go!' I yell at her. 'Take Nine and get out of here!'

'I'm not leaving you!'

'Six is in the caverns up there; she needs healing,' I tell her, gritting my teeth against the pain. 'Please – *gah* – please, Marina – GO!'

Marina looks at me, tears in her eyes. I can barely see her anymore through the mess of ooze thrashing around me. I see her look up doubtfully at the spiraling pathway that leads back to the surface, then down at Nine.

With a groan, Nine touches Marina's leg. He shudders.

'Just . . . just like we practised,' he says deliriously, transferring his Legacies to her.

I remember that. Capture the Flag in Chicago. Nine's team won because he gifted Marina his antigravity Legacy.

Marina scoops Nine up with her working arm. She's got his strength too. With one last look at me, she runs straight up the wall, leaping over the ledges as she sprints for the surface.

Via my telepathy, Sam has witnessed this whole thing. He feels what I'm feeling. The ebb and flow of pain, the tearing throughout my body.

Sam. The others are coming out. Will you do it now, Sam?

John . . . His sadness flows into me, worse than all the pain.

He'll do it. I know he will.

I turn off my telepathy. Focus only on healing. I let all the Loric energy stored inside of me cascade forth.

I pray it's enough.

I am face-to-face with Setrákus Ra. The two of us locked together. My healing continues to pour into him, and, with every second, his young face melts away, the oil driven back. His pale skin returns, his bulbous bald head, the sunken cheeks, the vivid purple scar. He snarls at me. He spits in my face. Headbutts me.

In his black eyes, for the first time, I see doubt.

'I'm going to kill you,' he snarls, his breath hot and wretched against my face.

I know this is true. I'm going to die down here. Tangled together with my worst enemy. Healing him, even as he tears me apart.

'You . . .' A bubble of blood pops when I try to speak. 'You'll die first.'

A tendril of his ooze, razor sharp and ice-cold, slashes across my abdomen. Opens me up.

I push warm, healing energy into him. Watch as his face turns gray and wrinkled. A centuries-old man.

The ooze coalesces around my legs. Crushes them like a vice, my bones snapping like twigs.

More healing. A little bit for my body – just enough to keep me going – the rest for him.

A chunk of hardened ooze falls away from him and turns to dust on the cavern floor. Setrákus Ra bellows.

He rips into my rib cage. His claws dig through my flesh, saw through bone. He's trying to dig out my heart.

Hold on, John.

I let him shred me. Focus on the warm glow. I could melt away in that glow . . .

'Do you . . . do you really think you can outlast me?' he sneers. A black vein bursts on his forehead.

'I've done it all these years, what's a few more minutes?'

'You were always a fool, Pittacus.'

'I'm not Pittacus Lore,' I say through gritted teeth. 'I am Number Four. I'm the one who kills you.'

A tremor. The entire cavern complex shakes. Out of the corner of my eye, I see a vivid flash of red light.

The bombardment has begun.

Thank you, Sam.

Just keep him here. Bury him down here, with all his horrible experiments.

The withered, hideous face before me laughs maniacally.

I close my eyes.

Picture Sarah. She holds up a camera, snaps a photo and smiles at me.

I let my Legacies pour out of me. All of them.

Until there's nothing left.

30

Consciousness comes back slowly. The cavern floor vibrates under my face, a rumble louder than thunder shaking the entire complex. I come dangerously close to the edge of the chasm that Adam and Phiri fell down. With a groan, I roll away from the gap, on to my back, and try to sit up.

'Ugh . . .'

My mouth tastes of blood. Every breath feels like I'm rolling around on broken glass. The mountain shakes again, and rock-dust falls from the ceiling. I close my eyes to avoid the stinging debris. *Maybe,* I think, *I'll keep them closed a little longer.*

Six! You stay awake! You get up!

Ella, her voice coming through a megaphone directly into my brain, so loud that it makes my head ache.

'I'm up, I'm up,' I reply out loud as I struggle into a sitting position. It hurts to bend like that, and I have to stifle a cry. 'What's happening?'

We're going to bring down the mountain, Ella replies. *Sam's chipping away at it, but we're not unleashing the main cannon until you're out.*

'Guess I better get up then,' I grunt, and struggle to my feet.

So Sam's been forced to play the role Adam was meant for – if everything goes wrong, blow the whole thing up. Adam . . . I just couldn't get to him in time.

I peek over the edge of the chasm but see nothing but jagged rocks and shadows. Something along the edge catches my eye, though. A thick blood trail that wasn't there before that stretches from the control room to the chasm.

Dust's body isn't where it fell. Was the Chimæra still alive? Did it go down after Adam?

I cup my hands around my mouth and shout into the gulf. 'DUST? ADAM?'

No response. The yelling causes a fresh lance of pain in my lungs. I hold both my hands over the hole in my chest and stagger backwards, supporting myself against the nearest wall.

Marina and Nine are on their way up to you, Ella guides me. *They'll meet you in the main entrance.*

I can make it that far . . . I think.

Slowly, I begin to navigate the twisting cavern corridors. I have to pause to catch my breath a few times, and each time I have to choke back a little blood. I glance over my shoulder and notice that I'm leaving a blood trail of my own. Looking back makes me feel a little woozy, my eyes getting hooded.

Keep going. Straight ahead now. Almost there.

'Six!'

I stumble into the main entrance at the same time that Marina emerges from the narrow passageway that leads deeper into the complex. Nine is flung over her shoulder like a sack of potatoes. Never knew Marina to be the body-building type – Nine must have transferred his Legacies before he went down. I cringe when I see Nine's condition – unconscious, face ashen, missing an arm. Marina makes as if to reach out to me with her free arm, but the shoulder is dislocated, so she ends up awkwardly jerking her shoulder in my direction.

'Where's John and Five?' I ask her.

'Five . . . no one deserved to die like that, Six, not even him.' Marina shakes her head disgustedly as she delivers this news, avoiding my eyes. 'John is still down there, holding Setrákus Ra until we can drop this place on top of him.'

As if to punctuate Marina's words, another tremor passes through the mountain base. That would be Sam, very slowly demolishing the Mogadorian lair.

Marina takes a look at the hole in my chest, and her mouth opens like she's surprised I'm still standing. 'Can you make it a little farther? I'll heal you once we're clear.'

'No,' I tell her. 'Heal me now.'

She glances up at the ceiling. 'But . . .'

'Ella, if you're listening, you tell Sam to cut that shit out!'

'You didn't see Setrákus Ra, what he's become,' Marina says, her eyes wide. 'Six, this might be the only way to stop him.'

When Adam told me about collapsing this mountain, I supported it. But that was when it was a last resort, when none of us were left standing to fight against Setrákus Ra.

Well, I'm still standing.

'Fuck that,' I respond to Marina. 'I'm not letting John martyr himself. I'm going down there. When I've got him, you can go right ahead and drop this mountain on whatever's left of Setrákus Ra.'

I add that last part more for Ella, who I'm sure is listening in telepathically, than for Marina. I want Ella to relay that to Sam.

Keep this place standing. Let me have a chance.

Marina looks in my eyes, and I can tell she's trying to decide whether I've lost it or not. Then she carefully sets Nine down, the big guy groaning deliriously, and presses her good hand against my chest. As her cool healing energy flows into me, I greedily suck in the first deep breath I've been able to take since my fight with Phiri Dun-Ra.

'I should go with you . . .' Marina says. Her gaze drifts towards Nine.

'No, he doesn't look good,' I reply. 'Stay with Nine; make sure he doesn't die. Nobody else dies today, okay?'

Marina finishes healing me. She grabs my hand.

'Be careful, Six,' she says.

Feeling rejuvenated, I sprint in the direction that Marina just came from. I remember this place well – it wasn't too long ago that I escaped from these caverns. Never thought I'd see the day when I'd be running back into its depths, especially not when blowing it up is a viable alternative.

I won't let John die down here. He thinks he can win this without the rest of us, thinks he needs to shoulder all this to make up for what happened with Sarah.

He doesn't need to carry it alone.

So I run. My feet slap hard against the uneven terrain. Soon, I'm sprinting down the spiral ledge, deeper and deeper. I can see the disgusting reservoir of black ooze below. I know that's where they'll be. I hurdle a fallen chunk of rock, duck under a sagging stalactite and leap from the ledge on to one of the narrow stone bridges to save time. The descent is dizzying, and my heart is pounding.

At the bottom, I slow down and turn invisible. As soon as I reach the edge of the ooze lake, I stop in my tracks.

A mess of the black oil is spread across the stone floor here, almost as if a balloon filled with the stuff exploded. Some of the tendrils flop back and forth on the ground like fish out of water. Most of the stuff is dry and hardened, though.

John lies at the epicenter of it all. He looks like he's been put through a meat grinder. There's not an inch of his body that isn't soaked with blood. His skin is shredded, mutilated, bones poking through in places. I think his legs and arms are broken. I watch his chest for a few seconds, hoping to see it rise and fall.

He doesn't move.

I remember the way he was when I first tracked him down in Paradise. Handsome and brave, so naïve. Ready to put his life on the line. I remember holding that hand – the fingers now shattered, cut to ribbons – and I remember the warmth, the comfort that he gave to me when I needed it.

He died down here alone.

I should scream. But after all these years, all these deaths, I don't feel rage and sorrow like that anymore. I feel cold determination.

Finish this.

I swallow back bile and turn my attention to the other form on the cavern floor. Frail and withered, an old man, his skin splotchy gray in some spots and, in others, a hardened black like the ooze spread across the floor. Even as I watch, those dark sections of his body slowly disintegrate, blowing away like ash off the end of a cigarette. The old man leaves a trail of the sooty substance as he drags himself across the rocks, inching towards the lake of ooze, his gnarled hand outstretched.

The purple scar around his neck is unmistakable. Setrákus Ra. Still alive. Barely.

Inch by inch, he drags himself towards the muck.

I start forward. With my eyes locked on Setrákus Ra, I don't notice the Voron dagger that John made until my foot bumps up against it. The blade makes a skittering sound as I kick it a few feet across the stones.

I pick up the dagger. When I look back at him, Setrákus Ra has turned over on his side. His dark eyes cast about, searching for the source of the noise. His nose is completely missing, just a skeletal hole in the front of his face, and his mouth is completely empty of teeth.

He's afraid.

I turn visible and meet his eyes.

'Hello, old man.'

He lets out a low moan, turns back on to his belly and increases the pace of his crawl towards the oil.

I overtake him with ease, kick him in the side and roll him over. My foot actually punches a hole in his body, like kicking into a beehive. His chest is skeletal, concave, with a darkened space where his heart should be. He makes a sloppy swipe at me with a hand tipped with disintegrating claws. I swat his hand away and drop down on top of him, digging my knee into his belly.

'In a few minutes, this place is going to come down on top of what's left of you,' I tell Setrákus Ra, keeping my voice cold and steady. 'I want you to know, after that, I'm going to track down every copy of your stupid fucking book and burn it. All your work, everything you made – it's getting unmade.'

He tries to say something but can't. I twist my knee lower.

'Look at me,' I say. 'This is what progress looks like, bitch.'

I hack the Voron dagger into the side of his neck, right at the scar. Setrákus Ra gurgles. I slice again.

I drop the dagger and stand up.

I hold Setrákus Ra's head in my hands.

It only takes a few seconds before it starts to disintegrate. I wait until it's all gone, the pieces of the Mogadorian warlord, the destroyer of my world, killer of my people, of my friends, fluttering through my fingertips like dark confetti.

I dust off my hands.

There's a wet bursting noise behind me. I spin around to see a bubble of the black ooze that had been hovering over the lake pop. Bernie Kosar springs free, shaking off his coat, and immediately loops to the floor. BK looks at me and lets go a low, plaintive whine.

We both go to John's side. He's a mess, almost unrecognizable. BK lies down on his belly next to him and nuzzles his hand. I touch John's forehead, smoothing back an errant piece of blond hair that's sticky with blood.

'You stupid idiot,' I whisper. 'It's over, and you don't even know, you goddamn moron.'

John gasps.

I jump back, startled at first, tears stinging my eyes. It's a sharp noise, and his entire body arches. He spasms, coughs, trembles in my arms. I cling tighter to him. When I look down, I see that his injuries are beginning to mend. It's slow, almost imperceptible compared to how fast we normally heal, but it's happening.

His eyes are swollen shut. One of his hands grasps my upper arm weakly.

'Sarah . . . ?' he whispers.

I kiss him. Just a quick one on the lips, tears streaming down my face. I'm sure Sam won't care. Considering the circumstances, I bet he'd kiss John too.

John smiles a little, then falls unconscious again, breathing ragged but steady.

BK turns into his griffin shape, and, very carefully, I settle John on to his back. I climb up behind him. We fly upwards, towards the exit to the cave, leaving the dark stench of the Mogadorian world behind.

'Ella, guys,' I say to the air, hoping someone is telepathically listening in. 'We're coming.'

Outside, dawn is just beginning to break.

ONE YEAR LATER

'Coming up on *the invasion: a look back*, we interview – *zzt* – the courageous members of Australia's Royal Eleventh Brigade – *zzt* – who staged a daring raid on a Mogadorian warship on VH Day. But first – *zzt* – the Loric? Gods? Heroes? Illegal immigrants? Our – *zzt* – panel discusses –'

I turn off the television. It gets terrible reception way up here anyway. With the background noise gone, I can focus totally on my scrubbing. My hand's a little sore from gripping the brush, pushing it back and forth across the stone wall. It'd be easier just to use my telekinesis, but I like the work. It feels good to use my hands, to worry at these ancient paint stains until they flake away, or until my forearms are too tired to continue.

Used to be there was a painting on this wall of Eight getting run through by a sword. Now that's completely gone. I scrubbed that one away first. The only prophecy left here is the painting of the Earth split in half, one part alive and the other dead, with two ships approaching the planet from opposite sides. The one I'm rubbing away now.

I actually kind of like this one, which is why I saved it for last. My reading is that the painter didn't know who would win the war for Earth. That's why they left it so vague. It still has to go. I'm trying not to dwell on the past so much anymore.

I want this place to be about the future.

So I keep scrubbing.

'I think it's clean, John.'

Ella's voice breaks me out of my trance. I'm not sure how long I've been scouring the wall. Hours, maybe. The muscles in my arm are numb. I've probably been buffing stone for a while, the painting completely erased.

'Spaced out for a bit,' I say sheepishly.

'Yeah, I've been sitting here for about ten minutes,' she replies.

Ella tracked me down a few months ago and has been hanging around ever since. I'm still not exactly sure how she did it. I guess being a telepath probably helped.

In the Himalayas, I thought I'd found a pretty good place to hide out for a while, to get my head straight. I heard about this cavern from Marina and Six. Back when they were on the run in India, this chamber of prophecies suffered a cave-in during a Mog attack. I'd arrived intending to excavate and see if anything could be salvaged, but those Vishnu Nationalist Eight guys had beaten me to it. Apparently, the cave is a revered place for them. They'd already started digging it out and let me join their efforts with no questions asked. These days, they secure the area, keep random hikers away and generally stay out of my hair. I guess one of them could have leaked my location to Ella, but I kind of doubt it.

Looking at her, I think there's still something a little other-worldly about Ella. The crazy spark that used to be in her eyes has faded, although right now, bathed in the cobalt-blue light of this cavern, I see some of Lorien lingering in her pupils. Maybe she saw me and my project in one of her visions and decided to come help.

I don't mind the company.

Ella's grown up a lot over the past twelve months, entered those real gawky teenage years that I don't miss one bit. Her face is suntanned from being outside, her hair braided like one of the locals. She goes to school in the little village down the mountain, and the seven other kids in her class pretend like she's not different at all.

She sits cross-legged on the massive table I've installed in the center of this cavern — my project — picking at a thread on the tarp I've got covering it.

'So, the walls are clean,' Ella says.

'Yeah.'

'Now you've got no reason left to procrastinate.'

I look away from her. She's been needling me on an almost daily basis to go out and find the others. I always intended to — the work I'm doing up here, it's not just for me. However, I think a part of me came to enjoy the solitude and the rooted feeling of the Himalayas. When was the last time I got to stay in one place without constantly looking over my shoulder?

Plus, I'm a little nervous about tracking everyone down. A lot can change in a year.

From behind her back, Ella pulls out the wooden cigar box where I've been storing the other pieces of my project. She holds it out to me.

'I took the liberty of getting this for you,' she says. 'You can leave right away.'

I narrow my eyes at her. 'I wish you wouldn't go through my stuff.'

'Come on, John. We're telepaths. You know boundaries are hard.'

I take the box from her. 'You just want to see Nine again.'

Ella's eyes widen. 'Hey! Now who's snooping?'

She's right, though. It's time. No more putting this off.

Outside the cave, there's a little snow on the mountain. I jog down the rocky path, into the sunny day, feeling the weather warm up as I get lower. The air is crisp and clean, and I take a deep breath, wanting to savor it, or maybe wanting to stall. I stop just before I reach the small encampment that's home to a rotating group of Vishnu Nationalist Eight soldiers. One of them spots me and waves. I wave back.

I take a deep breath. I'm going to miss my solitude.

Then I leap up in the air.

It's been a while since I've flown. Even though I'm a little rusty, I'm still better at it now than I was a year ago. As I soar through clouds, feeling their chill moisture on my skin, I have to resist the urge to let out a cheer. It feels good to be out here; it feels good to be stretching my Legacies in a way that I haven't in a while.

It feels good to be flying towards a situation that won't be deadly.

Well, hopefully not anyway.

Of course, as soon as I have that thought, two giant paws strike me right between the shoulder blades and send me tumbling towards the earth.

I shout as I manage to right myself. As soon as I'm safely floating, the griffin makes another pass. I dodge through the clouds, avoiding its beak, its claws – laughing all the while.

'I'm sorry I didn't say bye to you!' I yell at BK. 'You were off sunning yourself somewhere, you lazy mutt!'

The Chimæra seems to accept my apology, because instead of coming in for another attack, he flies alongside me. I hook on to one of my old friend's massive feathered wings and let him pull me forwards for a while, laughing and stroking his fur. Before we leave India's airspace, BK shakes loose, gives me a friendly roar and turns back.

'I'll be home soon, BK!' I shout into the wind.

I put my arms to my sides, keep my legs close together, chin pressed to my chest. It's my most aerodynamic posture. I turn myself invisible and settle in, my mind emptying out just like when I was scrubbing those cavern walls. I guess I've become the kind of guy who meditates.

It's going to be a long flight.

They're building the Academy in a secluded patch of forest just across the bay from San Francisco. As I descend, I can see the

330

Golden Gate Bridge and the city beyond. Below me, newly constructed dormitories and lecture halls rise up from the greenery, cranes and cement trucks parked nearby where the work isn't yet finished. It's like a quaint private school, if you ignore what hides beyond the forested perimeter: an electrified fence, barbed wire, heavily armed soldiers patrolling the Academy's only exit road.

Ostensibly, all that is to keep the human Garde safe. I wonder, though, what would happen if one of the human Garde decided they had enough schooling and wanted to wander off campus. Would the soldiers manning the gate allow that?

I don't ponder that question for long. That's not why I'm here.

For all their security, the Academy isn't prepared for invisible flying men. I land on the campus without being detected.

This place was built as part of the Declaration of Garde Governance, a set of laws adopted by the United Nations after Victory Humanity Day. Teenagers from around the world will be sent here to learn how to control their powers and, eventually, to work towards the betterment of humanity. There are other laws, too — stuff about the Loric and the Mogs, rules about when Legacies can be used, that kind of thing.

To be honest, I haven't really read them.

The campus is largely deserted right now. From what I've heard, the only students currently training here are the ones with no place else to go. The ones who lost their families during the invasion. The rest won't be showing up for a few months when the place opens for real.

In the entryway, there's a blown-up poster of an image that circulated everywhere during the cleanup effort that followed the invasion. In it, the president's daughter stands astride a pile of rubble in New York City, using her super-strength to lift a stack of debris so that a mother clutching her two young children can safely escape from underneath. In the background, a glamorously tattered American flag waves. The news reports claimed that family was stuck down there for a week, but I always thought the whole thing looked staged. Inspiring, yeah. But staged.

Across the bottom of the poster, the slogan reads: earth garde peacekeepers – you are the brave new world.

Still invisible, I walk through the halls of the Academy. It doesn't take long until I hear the sounds of training. I head in that direction, knowing that's where he'll be.

In an outsize gymnasium, a handful of kids practise their telekinesis with each other. Pairs of them toss footballs back and forth without using their hands, and, every time a whistle blows, they add another ball to the mix. When a group lets one of their balls drop, they heave a collective groan and start running laps.

Nine observes all this from a catwalk high above. He's dressed like a football coach – sweatpants and hoodie. One of his sleeves is pinned up on account of his missing arm. His dark hair is tied back in a ponytail. I thought maybe the government would make him cut it, but no such luck.

'Professor Nine, how long do we have to keep doing this?' one of the kids complains, and I have to stifle my laughter.

'Until I get tired of watching you screw up, McCarthy,' Nine barks back.

I float up to the catwalk and land gently next to Nine. He senses the movement and turns his head just as I become visible.

'Look at this sellout, working for the gov – *Oof!*'

Nine nearly clotheslines me off the catwalk with his one-armed hug. When he's done squeezing the life out of me, he holds me out at arm's length, studying me like I was just secretly studying him.

'Johnny Hero, holy shit.' Nine shakes his head. 'You're here.'

'I'm here.'

Detecting a lack of movement from the kids below, Nine looks down. His group of orphaned Garde have all stopped practising to stare up at us. To stare at me in particular.

'What the hell?' he shouts. 'Back to work, you maggots!'

Reluctantly, the kids do as they're told. I can't help but grin at Nine's control over them. He turns back to me and pinches my cheek, where I realize I've got a patchy beard growing. It's probably been a few months since I shaved.

'This peach fuzz supposed to make you incognito?' Nine asks. 'It ain't working.'

'Professor Nine, huh?' I respond, smirking.

'That's right,' he says, puffing out his chest.

'You never even finished high school, man.'

'It's an honorary title,' he replies with a devilish smile. 'Look at you, all reclusive mountain man and shit. Where you been? You know, it wasn't cool you skipping out on us after my crippled ass spent a week nursing you back to health.'

I snort at that. 'You weren't nursing me. You were laid up in the next bed.'

'Yeah, providing important emotional support.'

I know Nine's joking, but there's a bit of truth to what he says. After West Virginia, as soon as I was feeling well enough, I did bail on the others. I rub the back of my neck. 'I feel bad about that. I needed to get my head right after . . .'

'Ah, shut up about it,' Nine says, patting me on the shoulder. 'You're back now.' He nods his head at the kids below, many of whom are still furtively glancing at us, screwing up their telekinetic tosses, and thus running a lot of laps. 'You want to say a few words to the next generation? They'd eat that shit up. These are my favorites. The messed-up ones. They remind me of us.'

I take a step back from the catwalk's railing and shake my head. 'I'm not ready for anything like that,' I tell him. From behind my back, I pull out the small box I've been carrying with me since the Himalayas. 'I actually came here to give you something. Lexa, too, if she's around . . .'

Nine raises an eyebrow at me. 'Yeah, let's go say hi. I've got something I want to show you.'

Nine dismisses his class and leads me to an office on the building's third floor. It looks out over the sprawling campus, or it will once the windows are put in – right now, there are a bunch of blue tarps covering the opens spaces in the wall. Lexa sits behind a desk, staring at a multiscreen computer rig. Like Nine, she's dressed casually and seems at ease here. Her smile is wide when she recognizes me, and she immediately leaves her screens behind to give me a hug.

'So, are you a professor too?' I ask her.

Lexa scoffs. 'No, Nine outpaced me there. I'm back to my favorite role: benevolent hacker.' She waves me around the desk for a look. 'Check it out.'

At a glance, it's hard to take in all the information that flows across Lexa's screens. There are world maps with little blue dots, multiple search-bots trawling the internet, dark net forums and boxes of encrypted data speeding through processes I don't understand.

'So, what am I looking at?'

'I'm keeping tabs on the Garde,' she explains. 'Scrubbing their information if it gets made public. Keeping their families confidential. Even once they're under the protection of the Academy, you can't be too careful. Not to mention, some governments still aren't super-enthusiastic about this whole initiative.'

'Is this necessary?'

'Better safe than sorry,' she responds. 'Lawson and the other Earth Garde people have been good to us, but . . .'

'But then there's shit like this that makes you wonder,' Nine interjects, handing me a piece of official-looking government stationery. I give it a quick read.

I, the undersigned, affirm that I am a naturally born human of Earth and a law-abiding citizen of an Earth Garde nation. With my signature I pledge an oath to Earth Garde, a fully sanctioned peacekeeping division created by the United Nations and administered by the United States. I do solemnly swear that I will defend the planet and the best interests of my nation and its allies against all enemies, earthly and extraterrestrial; that I will bear true faith and allegiance to the Earth Garde; that I will only use my Legacies in service to my planet; and that I will obey the orders of the jointly appointed Earth Garde High Command according to regulations and the Uniform Code of Military Justice.

I look up at Nine, feeling a little bewildered. 'Is this legal?'

'I don't know, John, I'm a professor, not a lawyer.'

'Lawson assures us that it's just a formality,' Lexa interjects. 'But we're keeping our eyes open, just in case.'

'Well, if it ever looks like they're not on the level . . .' I start to say, then show the two of them what I've brought with me.

In New York City, the rebuilding is still in progress. A year later and they're still hauling away the debris from the Mogadorian bombardment. In places they've finished clearing out, construction crews are getting ready to put the city's skyline back together. A similar process is happening in major cities all around the world. VH Day wasn't without damage or casualties.

I float above a construction site, smiling at a familiar flash of silver energy. In a pit that will one day become a skyscraper, Daniela uses her stone-vision to shore up a cracked section of foundation.

'Shit,' grouses a guy in a hardhat. 'You keep that up, I'm gonna be out of a job, honey.'

335

'I ain't your honey, old man,' Daniela replies, and elbows her way through a crowd of construction workers. By the way they watch her strut away, grinning and exchanging glances, I think this might be a pretty common scene.

Daniela climbs out of the construction site and heads to the sidewalk, where she's approached by a middle-aged woman who walks with a cane. The lady stops to hug Daniela, and Daniela stoops to pet the golden retriever the woman has on a leash. The woman looks familiar, and it takes me a minute to figure out why.

'You forgot your lunch, baby,' the woman says.

'Thanks, Mom,' replies Daniela.

Not every scene that I encounter during my trip around the world is a sweet one. Some endings aren't so happy.

It's night in Montreal when I find Karen Walker. She walks across an almost-deserted airport parking lot, a trench coat drawn up to protect her from the cold evening air, a newspaper tucked under her arm, her heels clicking.

There's only one other person in the long-term parking lot – a pale, middle-aged man with a terrible comb-over who drags an overstuffed rolling suitcase behind him.

One of the parking lot's light poles is out, leaving a small row of cars bathed in shadows. When the man reaches that section, Walker yells to him.

'Excuse me!' she calls, waving the newspaper. '*Excusez-moi*! You dropped your paper!'

The man turns around, puzzled. 'Huh? That's not –'

Fft-fft.

Two silenced rounds from the gun hidden inside her news-paper, one in the chest and one in the head. The man never saw it coming. He drops, and Walker goes to him immediately. She starts dragging his body into the shadowy space between two cars.

336

I help her out with my telekinesis, appearing a few feet away. She jumps, points her gun at me, then quickly lowers it and pretends she wasn't startled in the first place.

'John.'

'Karen,' I reply. 'I hope you've got a good reason for this.'

'I do,' she replies.

Walker unzips the dead man's suitcase and tosses aside a pile of his clothes. She digs around until she discover a dog-eared copy of the Bible. She opens the book, revealing that it's hollowed out.

Inside are three vials of black oil. My skin crawls at the sight of it.

'How much of that is out in the world?' I ask her.

'I don't know,' Walker says. 'Any amount over none is too much for me.'

Walker produces a vial of her own from within her trench coat. By the rotten-egg smell, I think hers is sulfuric acid. Carefully, she pours some into each of the Mogadorian vials, destroying the contents.

'Who was this man?' I ask her.

'Just a name on a list,' she replies, looking me in the eyes. 'A really long list. You know, I could use some help working through it.'

I take out my cigar box and open it up. 'We can talk about that soon.'

Seeing that sludge brings me back to our last battle with Setrákus Ra. Everything after I looked up with Setrákus Ra is like a dream. I remember how broken my body was, how destroyed, and I remember a vision of Sarah, a hallucination leaning down to kiss me, to make me keep going.

I remember flying. Up, out, leaving that heat behind, escaping the stench of death. I remember Bernie Kosar's coat soft against my caved-in face.

I remember the sound of someone crying, and I remember us stopping short, still inside the mountain. I remember being able to open my eyes just enough to see a gray-furred creature — part wolf but with legs like a spider, covered in dried blood, motionless. A Chimæra frozen in its last form.

And I remember Adam cradling that Chimæra, Dust, and crying into the fur of his neck.

'He pulled me out . . . He saved me . . .' I remember Adam saying to Six, delirious, near death himself.

I closed my eyes for good after that. I couldn't stand to see any more.

I'd learn what happened later. How Dust dove down after Adam, took on a shape that would let him climb out of the chasm and dragged Adam as far as he could away from the caverns. He had to bite Adam to carry him to safety, and, after he died, one of Dust's fangs was still embedded in Adam's shoulder.

Adam wears that fang around his neck now, attached to a plain leather strap. It's one of the few comforts he's allowed here in Alaska.

When I find him, Adam is standing in front of a small bonfire, his hands shoved into a threadbare winter coat. It's freezing out here. Adam's dark hair, grown longer than before, pokes out from beneath a wool hat. Even bundled up, he shivers. Snow blows in sideways. It's the midafternoon, and there's no sunlight. This part of Alaska — fifty miles north of the nearest town — doesn't get a lot of light this time of year.

This specially constructed prison camp is where the UN put the Mogadorians that surrendered. The ones that were captured. The vatborn fought to the last; they didn't know any better. The trueborns, however, self-preservation kicked in for some of them, especially once Setrákus Ra was killed.

A dozen longhouses with spotty heating, food air-dropped in and nothing else. A village of Mogadorians in the middle of nowhere — one with a perimeter of UN soldiers who outnumber the surviving Mogs twenty-to-one at all times. There are missiles aimed here perpetually. Drones designed to withstand the elements fly overhead.

There was talk about executing them all. There still is. For now, the captured Mogs stay here and wait.

'I renounce the teachings of the Great Liar!' shouts a Mog with scars across his bald head from where he carved off his tattoos. He throws a copy of the Great Book into the bonfire, and a small huddle of Mogs, Adam and Rex among them, come forward to hug and congratulate him.

Maybe there's hope for rehabilitation.

Another, larger contingent of Mogs watch the book burners. There's nothing but malice in their eyes. One of them in particular stands out to me. She's a dark-haired girl a few years younger than Adam with his same sharp features. This girl and her group seem like they want nothing more than to murder Adam's followers, and, judging by the scrapes and bruises on the faces of some of Adam's trueborn friends, there have been attempts.

Adam stares back at the trueborn malcontents watching him, his chin raised in defiance.

A siren blares overhead. A warning that the Mogs need to disperse. One of the rules here is that they aren't supposed to gather in large numbers.

As the chastened Mogs head back to their destitute bunks, I float down alongside Adam.

'Probably wouldn't be a good idea for me to be seen here, huh?' I whisper to him without turning visible. The siren is loud enough to mask my voice.

Adam's whole body tenses, his fists ball, and for a moment I think he's about to swing at me. He's on edge and afraid of getting snuck up on.

'Easy now,' I say. 'It's me.'

Adam quickly regains his composure. He kneels down in the snow and pretends to tie his boot. The other Mogs from his group drift sullenly towards the longhouse, giving us room.

'John,' Adam says quietly, the ghost of a smile on his face. 'It's good to see . . . ah, it's good to hear your voice.'

I put my hand on Adam's shoulder without turning him invisible too. I let my Lumen trigger a bit, radiating some heat.

'You're going to spoil me,' he says with a sigh.

'I could get you out of here right now,' I say. 'No one would know.'

'My people would notice when there was no one here to defend them from the others,' he replies sadly. 'And besides, technically, I can leave at any time.'

This is true. Owing to his role in fighting off the Mogadorian invasion, Adam received a pardon pushed through by General Lawson himself. He elected not to use it. When the captured trueborn started getting shipped in to Alaska, Adam was here waiting for them.

'I saw a girl in the crowd who looked like you,' I say tentatively, not sure how nosy I should be.

'My sister,' Adam replies gloomily. 'She loved our father. I think she hates me now, but maybe one day . . .'

'What about your mother?' I ask.

Adam shakes his head. 'She disappeared. Maybe she died fighting in the invasion, maybe she's in hiding. A part of me hopes she'll show up here one day, and a part of me hopes that she doesn't.'

'You don't want her to have to live here,' I say.

'More like I'm worried whose side she would be on,' Adam says. 'It's bleak, John, but this is my duty now. I'm doing more good here than I could do anywhere else.'

I let that sink in. I hate to see my friend up here, lumped in with the rest of them, so I don't want to come out and agree. But he could be right.

I take Adam's hand and press an object from my wooden box into it. He looks down, startled at the cobalt-blue glow that radiates from his palm. Quickly, he hides what I gave him underneath his shirt.

'For when you're ready.'

I've already gone out of my way by visiting Alaska before my next destination. It's my last stop to make in North America. I've put it off long enough.

I haven't been back to Paradise since Sam and I snuck back into town to seek out his dad's hidden bunker. I almost got myself killed that night, but I just had to try seeing Sarah.

I break out in a cold sweat as soon as the small town comes into view. My eyes are drawn to the Jameses' house. The roof is caved in, the sides still black and charred. They never rebuilt after the fire that happened there during Mark's party, the one where I got caught jumping out his window.

I never got along with Mark. We never liked each other. He did his best to help us, though. He did good, and he died in a horrible way that he didn't deserve. In all the retrospectives they've been playing on television, no one mentions Mark James.

Someday, I think maybe I'd like to track down his father. I did some quick internet sleuthing but could only find out that he quit his sheriff's job and left Paradise. I'd like to tell him what happened to Mark and what he did for us before he died, even if he might not want to hear that.

There are some things I'm not ready for. That's one of them. The other is here too.

I land in the Goode family's backyard, happy to find Malcolm working in the garden. It takes me a minute of watching him to realize why the patch of earth he's tending looks so strange — it's where his bunker used to be hidden. Looks like Malcolm and Mrs Goode decided to level the old well that used to lead down

341

to Malcolm's secret chamber. In the fresh soil, they've planted flowers of every conceivable color. I assume Pittacus Lore's body is still buried underneath there, and, if so, I imagine he'd be pleased with this resting place.

Malcolm hugs me for a long time when I surprise him. My eyes well up when he does. It's the place. I can't help thinking about everything that happened here. I can't help imagining, for just a second, that Malcolm is Henri.

After I give him the same gift that I've given all the others, Malcolm tries to get me to stay for dinner.

'I can't,' I tell him. 'Too much left to do.'

He shakes his head ruefully. 'Still off saving the world, huh?'

'Nothing quite so serious,' I reply. 'I'm going to visit Sam next.'

'Tell him to call his mother!' Malcolm says with a shake of his head. 'And tell him he needs to come home eventually and finish high school or he'll never get into a good college. There's a limit to how much vacation a young man should be allowed to take, no matter how many planets he's helped saved.'

Laughing, I promise to tell Sam all that. Then I fly out of Malcolm's backyard, turn invisible again and land a few houses over.

Sarah Hart's house.

I stand on the front walk, not turning visible, not moving. It's just like I remember it. I imagine jogging up the sidewalk and ringing the doorbell, how excited I would be to see her, my heart racing. She'd invite me in, and her house would smell amazing like it always would, and we'd —

There's no movement in the windows. The house is dark. There's a FOR SALE sign driven into the front yard.

I've imagined this a hundred times over the last year. How I would come here and ring the doorbell like old times. How I would see Sarah's parents and tell them how much I loved their daughter, how much she meant to me, how much she meant to the world even if not many people know it and how sorry I am that I dragged her into everything that happened. I would tell them that I miss her every day. And then I would throw myself on their mercy.

I've imagined it so many times, but I can't do it. I can't take that walk up those steps.

I'm too scared. I don't want to see the look in their eyes. I don't want to grapple with the pain I've caused them.

Maybe someday I'll be ready.

Not today.

In their tour of Europe, Six and Sam have made it to Montenegro by the time I catch up with them. They're camping on a secluded part of Jaz Beach. Even at night, the water shines like crystal, the purple swells of the nearby hills a stunning contrast. I'm happy for them — the way they've traveled, how much they've seen in a year — and at the same time, my heart aches because it isn't me.

On the beach, I find their campfire and their tent, but I don't find Six or Sam. No, for that I need to follow the trail of clothes towards the water's edge. I see them out there, silhouettes in the moonlight, tangled together in the water.

I laugh quietly and look away.

I'm not going to be a third wheel here, even if I do miss them both badly. I also haven't talked to Six since — well, since she saved my life. A life that I was more than ready to throw away. Like Sarah's family, I'm not sure what I'll say to her. For now, better to let it go unsaid.

From inside my wooden box, I withdraw two pendants. They're carved from Loralite stone that I chipped off the main rock back in the Himalayas. Chiseled into both of them is the Loric symbol for Unity. I drape these across their sleeping bags and find a scrap of paper to write them a short note. I let them know how the pendants work, that they just need to visualize the

Himalayas and it should bring them to the chamber I've set up, the one I've scrubbed clean of the past and made ready for the future.

I write that I hope I'll see them soon, and I mean it.

Marina is the hardest to find. If it wasn't for her sporadic phone calls to Ella over the last few months, it might have taken me weeks to track her down. When I would ask her about Marina, Ella would always get quiet. She said Marina didn't seem like herself. That she seemed paranoid. Angry.

I find her navigating a speedboat between deserted islands in the South Pacific. Her face is sunburned, her wavy hair crisped straight from salt water, and there are deep bags under her eyes. I get the feeling that she's been alone for a while – I recognize the signs; I've seen them in myself. Her lips move when she's not talking, her hands shake, her eyes don't always stay focused.

We were raised in a war, and now – now we're free. Everyone is handling it differently.

When I first appear to her, she doesn't startle as much as the others.

'Are you really there, or have I truly gone crazy?' she asks me.

'I'm here, Marina.'

She smiles that gentle, patient smile. I'm glad to see it.

'Thank God,' she says. 'You showed up at a good time.'

I don't ask her where we're going. She drives the boat purposefully, like she'd made this trip before. I lean back and let the spray tickle my cheeks, feel the sun beat down on my neck and shoulders.

Eventually, Marina hands me a cell phone. Our fingers brush, and I notice that she's ice-cold.

'I saw this on the internet, and I – I couldn't let it go,' she says.

She plays a video that she downloaded off YouTube. Of course I recognize the scene. It's the mountain in West Virginia, or what's left of it. Really, it's a crater filled with scorched rubble, the end result of our bombardment of that hellish place. The video was shot a week after our last battle there, when various government agencies had begun picking over the remains.

As a crew clears away some rocks, something knocks them backwards. A shape streaks upwards from the debris like a missile and disappears into the sky. The camera tries to follow it but isn't nearly quick enough.

'We never got that fourth scar, John,' Marina says, her voice a little shaky.

'Maybe the charm was broken,' I say.

'I thought that for a while. Tried to convince myself . . .' She shakes her head. 'I know the kinds of places he likes. I remember from . . . from when he told us about himself. Warm and tropical. Secluded.'

'And?'

'I found him last week,' Marina says.

Marina cuts the boat's engine as we approach a small island. It would probably take you less than an hour to walk its entire perimeter. Just white sand and a small copse of palm trees. We drift closer, the waves tugging us in.

The guy standing on the beach with a wooden fishing pole in his hands looks frighteningly skinny. From where we are, I can see the outline of his ribs and spine. There are loose flaps of skin on his arms and belly from where the weight came off too quick. More disconcerting are the dark patches of skin, like tumors, like hardened obsidian, that make a patchwork of his skin. Maybe that's a result of being drowned in Setrákus Ra's lake of ooze. Another permanent disfigurement to go with the missing eye.

That is most definitely Five standing there. There's no chance he doesn't see us. There aren't any other boats for as far as the eye can see. He probably heard us coming miles off.

'When I saw him die, John, all I could think was how horrible it was. To be killed in that way . . .' Marina begins hesitantly, staring across the shallows at Five. 'But I also felt — I am not proud to admit this — I also felt there was justice there. That he had at last gotten what was coming to him.'

Marina hugs herself. Even in the sun, a light frost forms on her skin.

'I've prayed, John. I've — I've tried to get over it, like so many of the others have done. But the deaths haunt me. Not just Eight, but Sarah and Mark, Adelina and Crayton, all those people we saw in the mountain, the millions killed in the bombardment. And I think — how can anyone just move on? How? When there are still people like him in the world? When there is no *justice*?'

I swallow hard. 'I don't know, Marina.'

'I've been coming here for a week. Sitting out here. Watching him. He knows we're here, obviously, even if he doesn't say anything. It's like — it's like he's daring me. Or he's asking for it. He wants me to put him out of his misery.'

Looking across the water, Five does look to be in rough shape. Left to his own devices, I'm not sure how much longer he'll last out here.

'You told me, John, that it would be up to me what happens to him. *After*, you said. But I do not want that responsibility. I don't want to keep carrying this around — him, the war, all of it. It is too much to bear alone.'

I put my arms around Marina. She's cold to the touch, so I turn on my Lumen, counteracting her chill. She cries, one hard sob, and then claps a hand over her mouth. She steels herself, knowing that Five will probably hear.

'Let's get out of here,' I say, producing the last of my pendants. 'Let me take you someplace where we can figure out what's next. Together.'

Marina hesitates, staring at Five. 'What about him?'

'He's a ghost,' I reply. 'We aren't.'

*

Marina comes back to the Himalayas with me. When she sees what I've done with the cave, with Eight's cave, she runs her hands across the places where the prophecies used to be etched, feeling the smoothness of new stone, the possibility of a blank canvas. She lets herself cry at last.

After that, Marina stands right in front of me. She reaches out and takes my face in her hands. 'Thank you, John,' she says quietly. The tears haven't dried on her cheeks. I brush a streak away.

She kisses me. I don't know what it means.

Maybe nothing.

Marina blushes, smiles at me and slowly pulls away. I smile back. This Himalayan cave is suddenly a lot warmer.

Maybe something.

In the center of the cavern, I pull back the tarp to show Marina what I've spent the last year working on. Carved from trees I cut down off the mountainside, it's a table that uses the Loralite stone as a base. It is huge and circular and modeled off my memories of the table in the center of the Elders' Chamber on Lorien. Like the pendants, I've used my Lumen to burn the Loric symbol for Unity into the wood.

Eventually, the others will come. Some of them only for a visit, some of them for a longer stay. One day, I hope, this will become a place where great ideas are exchanged. A place kept safe from the corruption and pettiness of governments. Where the safety of Earth and the happiness of its people are assured.

There are threats still facing this planet – ones that need a united front of Loric, humans and even Mogs. We will gather here to solve those problems – us, the Garde, our old allies and ones we haven't even met yet.

In the meantime, we have more than enough things to figure out, together and apart. Finding our places in this new world, making amends with those we've hurt, living up to our potential – these are the truly scary things.

347

There is one difference between the table I built here and the table used by the Elders. I didn't carve nine specific spaces in the wood. There's no spot for Loridas, or Setrákus or Pittacus. There aren't even nine chairs. There's as many as we need there to be, more than enough room. And if it gets too crowded, we can squeeze.

I'm done with numbers.